Hart's Landing

ALSO BY MELANIE HARLOW

CHERRY TREE HARBOR SERIES

Runaway Love
Hideaway Heart
Make-Believe Match
Small Town Swoon
Slap Shot Surprise

Hart's Landing

USA TODAY BESTSELLING AUTHOR

MELANIE HARLOW

Entangled Publishing, LLC
644 Shrewsbury Commons Ave., STE 181
Shrewsbury, PA 17361
rights@entangledpublishing.com

Amara is an imprint of Entangled Publishing, LLC.
Visit our website at www.entangledpublishing.com.

Edited by Liz Pelletier and Rebecca Heyman
Cover design by Elizabeth Turner Stokes
Cover images by Honyojima/Shutterstock
Edge design by Elizabeth Turner Stokes
Edge images by AlexGreenArt/Shutterstock
Interior design by Britt Marczak

Paperback ISBN 978-1-68281-666-0
Walmart Signed Edition ISBN 978-1-68281-729-2
Ebook ISBN 978-1-68281-676-9

Manufactured in the United States of America

First Edition May 2026

10 9 8 7 6 5 4 3 2 1

For my mom, who is kind, funny, generous, and loving. I wish everyone could have a mother like her.

Hart's Landing is a heartfelt, steamy, swoony romance with mystery, family drama, strong female friendship, and an HEA. However, the story includes elements that might not be suitable for all readers, including the on-page portrayal of a narcissistic parent, and references to parental abandonment, alcoholism, divorce, and domestic abuse. *Hart's Landing* also portrays explicit, enthusiastically consensual sex. Readers who may be sensitive to these elements, please take note.

Prologue

Lydia

AUGUST 10, 2015

I would have been eighteen today.

Dying young put a serious wrinkle in my plans.

But it also put an important plan in motion for my four best friends. They're getting together at the old foundry site—our secret meeting spot on the edge of town. It's where we shared a million secrets, confessed crushes, told stories, talked shit, dreamed dreams, and occasionally passed around a bottle of cheap strawberry wine.

Today, they're here to keep a promise.

Mila is the last to arrive.

"Sorry," she calls, hurrying through the break in the fence. She moves with the agile, graceful steps of a dancer. "Class ran over."

"That's okay." Gabi scoots over to make room for her in the circle, then hands her a bag of homemade cookies.

"Thanks." Dropping to the ground, Mila tucks the sweets into her bag.

"I thought you were quitting ballet," Rachel says.

"I am, but I haven't exactly told my mom yet." Mila yanks the hairpins from her bun and pulls the elastic from her ponytail, red hair spilling over her shoulders and highlighting the freckles sprinkled across her nose. "She's still not over my rejection from Juilliard, so I'm trying to space out the disappointments."

Yasmine shakes her head. "I still can't believe she didn't speak to you for two weeks over that."

"You got a scholarship to NYU," adds Rachel. "That's

practically an Ivy League school."

"Yeah, but Juilliard was her big dream for me. And since she trained me, she took the rejection personally." It's instinctive for Mila, making excuses for her mother. She shouldn't. "So what did I miss?"

"Nothing yet," says Gabi. "Hey, can I use your ponytail holder? Mine snapped on the way here."

Gabi grins when Mila hands it over. "Ooh, it's one of the good ones. Thanks." Gabi lifts her thick blond hair off the back of her neck and puts it up. The light glints off the ladybug charm resting just above her collarbone.

Mila looks around the circle and smiles, a little sad, a little hopeful. She plays with the ladybug charm she wears around her neck, too. "It feels good to have all four of us here together, doesn't it?"

I can hear it in her voice—the fear that they're all growing apart. That nothing will ever be the same. They're all feeling it. To be honest, I'm worried too. Because if my friends lose each other, they'll lose me.

That's another thing they don't tell you until your heart stops keeping time: when the people you love stop loving each other, their memories of you fade. *You* fade. I might have been able to accept dying young from leukemia, but I'm not ready to be forgotten.

"It's weird without her, though." Yasmine glances at the empty space beside her, where I used to sit. "Even though she's been gone for six months, it's like I keep expecting her to text me. Or call. Or just show up. I can't believe I'll never see her again."

"Same," Rachel says softly. She wears her ladybug charm on a bracelet, which she cradles now in her other hand. "I have the letter for Alice."

Alice. My little sister. If my heart could still beat, it would beat for her.

"What should we do with it?" Mila wonders.

"Rach, why don't you keep it?" Gabi suggests. "There's a reason

Ladybug gave it to you, don't you think?"

"Maybe." Rachel sniffs. "God, I miss her."

I miss them too, but I gotta say, death would have been way less scary if I'd known how often I'd get to see my besties from the other side.

But what I've seen lately is them pulling away from each other instead of coming together. Rachel clinging to a shitty relationship. Yasmine's anxiety keeping her awake all night. Gabi's constant stress-baking. Mila exhausting herself trying to please people.

Tonight, I want them to remember who they really are.

I want them to remember me.

"So, let's focus on what we came here to do," Gabi says in her captain-of-the-volleyball-team voice. "What we *promised* her we'd do—live tonight like there's no tomorrow, because tomorrow is never guaranteed."

Fun, right?

A lot more fun than sitting around crying over me. I've seen enough of that.

On my birthday, I wanted them to push each other to be brave, have an adventure, take a risk. My one condition was that each girl let the group choose her adventure, rather than deciding for herself. They know each other well enough to pick the perfect—and perfectly scary—thing.

"Did everyone bring their ideas?" Yasmine asks, pulling a leather-bound planner from her bag. She's the self-appointed secretary for this meeting, preparing to write down everything they decide.

"Okay," Gabi says. "Who wants to be first?"

No one volunteers.

"We could start with the easy one," suggests Yasmine.

"Who's the easy one?" Mila asks.

"You are," the other three say at the same time.

"You need to let a certain person know how you feel about him," Yasmine says.

Immediately, Mila starts shaking her head.

"A person whose family owns the bakery where you work," says Rachel.

They're talking about Gabi's brother, Everett McKean.

"I can't," Mila blurts.

Yasmine leans forward. "Why not?"

"For one thing, he's twenty. *Twenty.* He's been at college for two years already. I'm just his kid sister's friend back home. He still calls me 'Freckles!'"

"Because he *likes* you," Rachel points out. "If he didn't, he'd just ignore you."

"Exactly." Gabi looks at Mila. "Look, Everett's my brother, and I personally think he's a disgusting cretin, but you've had a crush on him forever. Wouldn't it feel good to just put it out there?"

Mila chews her bottom lip. "Put it how there how?"

"Kiss him," says Yasmine, probably thinking of her latest romance novel.

"Kiss him!" Mila shrieks. "Out of nowhere? That's terrifying!"

"More terrifying than always wondering what might have happened if you'd been less afraid?" Rachel asks.

"Um, one hundred percent yes."

"What's the worst that could happen?" Yasmine asks.

"Let's see, he rejects me and I die of humiliation?" Mila slaps her hands over her face. "Please don't make me do this."

"I happen to know he's making a fruit delivery to the bakery tonight." Gabi's eyes gleam with mischief. "You're on the closing shift, right?"

"Yes, but—"

Yasmine raises a hand. "All in favor of Mila making a move on Everett, say aye."

"Aye," echo the other two.

"All opposed?"

Silence.

"Great." Yasmine clicks the pen and narrates as she writes.

"Mila will kiss the cretin. Sign here, please."

Mila reluctantly takes the pen and signs her name.

"Why does it feel like my life is jumping the rails right now?"

They all laugh and move on to assigning the next task.

Mila doesn't know it yet, but she's right. After tonight, her life will never be the same.

She rides her bike to work that night.

When she reaches the fancy, wrought-iron truss bridge that separates the two halves of Hart's Landing, she hops off her bike and leans it against one of the stone structures connecting the bridge to the embankment of the White Pine River.

I know what she's doing.

Local legend holds that, during the 1800s, a girl was forbidden to marry the poor sailor she loved because her family had arranged her marriage to a wealthy man. Every night, she tossed a stone into the river, whispering her longing beneath the stars. On the night before she was to be the rich man's bride, she went to the river and never returned. Some say she sailed off with her love in the moonlight; others say she drowned. Either way, lore has it that if you toss a stone with your beloved's name off the century-old bridge, you might see her ghost at the water's edge. But she's not a malevolent spirit—if your love is true, she'll see it returned to you.

I haven't met her yet, but I'm on the lookout.

Near the riverbank, Mila picks up an oblong rock, gray and smooth, about the size of a bar of soap. She takes a Sharpie from her small backpack, double-checks no one is watching, and prints *Everett McKean* across the surface in neat letters.

Scrambling back up the bank, she grabs her bike and walks it to the middle of the bridge. She looks at the stone in her hand, at the name printed on it. Then she draws back her arm and sends it sailing out through the latticework.

She doesn't say anything out loud, but I know she's making a wish as she watches it hit the water and sink below the surface, which glitters beneath the bright afternoon sun. For a moment, she thinks she sees someone at the river's edge. Dark hair. A pale dress. She blinks, and the figure is gone.

A trick of the light.

Just after seven, Mila's about to flip the OPEN sign in the window to CLOSED when the bell above the door jingles.

Twelve-year-old Stevie MacDougal stands in the doorway. "Hi, Stevie."

"Hi," he says adoringly, pushing his thick glasses up his nose. They make his eyes look huge. Or maybe that's just what happens when he's staring at Mila. "Is it too late to get a cherry lemonade?"

Mila smiles. "I can make you one."

"Thanks." He follows her to the counter and watches her pour him a cold drink like she's a movie star and he's her biggest fan. (He is.) A skinny, ginger-haired seventh grader, he's been in love with her since she first started babysitting him, when he was just nine years old. He figures they're destined to be together since they've got matching hair, and he comes into the bakery at least once every time she works a shift.

"Here you go." She hands him his lemonade.

"Thank you." When he digs in his pockets for money, she waves him off.

"On the house tonight," she tells him.

"Wow, thanks." His eyes go impossibly wider as he sips from the straw. "Want help cleaning up or anything?"

"No, that's okay. But you better go so I can close up."

Once Stevie leaves and she locks the front door behind him,

Mila moves through her closing tasks on autopilot. When the bakery is sparkling clean, but Everett still hasn't arrived, she brings her bag to the kitchen, digs past the detritus that always seems to accumulate at the bottom, and closes her hand around the letter.

The one with the Juilliard return address.

The one that would have changed her life.

She takes it out and stares at it. Then, calm as can be, she crosses to the stove and lights a burner. When the flame clicks to life, she tentatively touches it with the corner of the paper. She switches off the burner and moves carefully to the sink, where she watches it burn.

When the flames threaten her fingers, she drops the remains of the letter into the sink and runs the water.

The back door opens. Everett stands in the doorway, backlit by the gloaming laying the day to rest.

"Hey," she says casually, even though her pulse is thrumming like a train coming down the tracks. Because of what she just did, or because he's finally here, I'm not certain.

"Hey." Everett gives her a lopsided grin and runs a hand through his shaggy brown hair. "You're still here. My deliveries took longer than usual tonight, so I thought maybe I missed you."

"I'm still here."

His mouth hooks up again. "I'm glad."

Mila sways, and for a second I wonder if she's about to faint. "Want something to drink?" she asks.

"Sure. I'll just unload and move the truck so it's not blocking the alley. Meet you up front?"

She nods and heads into the shop. He watches her go, admiring her long legs and the gentle curve of her hips. Her cute butt in those denim shorts. That red hair falling down her back.

He's into her. Even from here, I can tell.

Everett turns out all the lights in the kitchen before making his way up front. It's dark there, too, where Mila waits with two glasses of cold lemonade and a pounding heart. The only light comes from the street lamps shining through the windows.

I move a little closer. I always did love a front-row seat.

Mila hands Everett a glass and hoists herself up onto the back counter.

He takes a sip from his drink. "So what's new, Freckles?"

"Are you ever going to stop calling me that?"

"Are you ever going to stop having freckles?"

She sighs. "Probably not."

He grins. "You're heading to New York, I hear."

"Next week." She hopes a sip of ice-cold lemonade will slow her racing pulse. "Going back to MSU soon?"

"Couple weeks." He pauses. Then he moves closer, leaning one hip against the counter. Right next to her leg. He takes another drink and sets his glass down. "It's hot tonight."

Now we're getting somewhere.

"It is." Mila is barely breathing.

"We should go swimming or something."

"Swimming? Where?"

"The beach."

"Like…right now?"

He laughs. "That's kind of what I was thinking."

Mila's expression is panicked. On a night like tonight, the beach will be full of kids hanging out. She'll lose her nerve. She knows she has to do this here and now.

Like there's no tomorrow.

She slides off the counter and faces him. Her next breath shudders a little when she exhales, her terror palpable enough for an incorporeal spirit to detect. Everett tilts his head and gives her a funny look. "You okay?"

With *zero* finesse whatsoever, Mila clutches him by the front of his shirt and pulls his mouth to hers. I'm cringing over here. But no sooner do their lips crash together than Everett puts his hands on her shoulders and lifts his head.

"Oh God." Mila lets go of his shirt and takes a step back. "I'm so sorry."

"Hang on. Do you smell something—"

BOOM!

Out of nowhere, a deafening crack shakes the ground beneath their feet, and a blast of heat and pressure rockets through the room. Mila covers her ears. Smoke pours into the front of the bakery from the kitchen.

Glancing toward the back, Everett curses and grabs Mila by the arm. He races toward the door, where he fumbles with the lock. Once he gets it open, he shoves Mila outside and follows right behind her.

"Go!" he commands, pushing her onto the sidewalk. "Run fast! Get away from the building!"

They barely make it across the street when the front windows of the bakery shatter.

Within a minute, sirens are screaming in the dark.

Chapter One

Mila

TEN YEARS LATER

"I scheduled the surgery," my mother announces right after I pick up her call and say hello. Her voice is heavy with foreboding, as if she's having a heart transplant instead of a hip replacement.

"Hi, Mom." I set my watercolor pencil down and lean back in my chair. "Good, I'm glad to hear it."

"I'm doing both hips at once. Dr. Rodriguez said I'd need to have the second one done soon anyway, and one recovery period is better than two."

"Okay." Moving my sketchpad out of the way, I reach for my planner and open it up. "What's the date?"

"September eighth."

I blink. "As in one week from today?"

"Yes. I was lucky to get in so quick, and insurance has already approved it. You'll have to come home immediately and stay for six weeks."

The familiar headache begins to build, like someone is tightening screws at my temples. "Mom, that's— That's going to be hard for me."

"You knew this was coming, Mila," she says, her tone clipped. "I told you months ago."

"I know, but you said you didn't want to do it until after the holidays."

"I changed my mind. What, you're so busy doodling flowers,

you can't come home to take care of your mother?"

I let her usual dig at my job as a botanical illustrator go by without comment. "Of course I can. It's just that a little more notice would have been nice."

"I've put this off for a year already. And the pain I'm in is excruciating. I can hardly teach advanced ballet anymore." A carefully weighted pause. "But I suppose if you're too busy for me, I could hire one of those home health aides. Let a complete stranger come into the house..."

The headache intensifies behind one eye. I switch off the gooseneck lamp on my drawing table in an effort to stave off the inevitable pain that accompanies most conversations with my mother. "That won't be necessary."

"Or I could ask your cousin Lauren," she says with an air of martyrdom. "She was so good to your Aunt Jackie when she had her knee surgery. Although Lauren will have her hands full running the studio while I'm recuperating."

My left hand curls into a fist, nails digging into my palm. "You don't need to ask Lauren, Mom."

"Well, I don't want to be a *burden*." Her voice lingers dramatically on the word, one of her favorites in any performance. I imagine her at the height of her career, leaning into a perfect penché arabesque.

"You're not a burden." With the phone sandwiched between my ear and shoulder, I pencil in the surgery date for Monday the 8th and circle it. "When would you like me there?"

She sighs. "I suppose I can handle this week's pre-op appointments on my own, but I'll certainly need help preparing the house over the weekend. I have a whole list from the doctor's office—rearrange the furniture, remove all trip hazards, and a dozen other things I can't possibly manage alone. Can you be here by Thursday?"

Thursday. Today is Monday.

Flipping calendar pages for the next six weeks, I look at deadlines I'll need to meet, appointments I'll have to reschedule, events I'll have to miss. Not to mention the classes I'll have to teach virtually instead of in person—*if* the college where I'm an adjunct professor agrees.

"Mila, did you hear me?"

"Yes. I heard you. Thursday." I rub my temples with one hand.

"You'll be here?"

"I'll be there."

"Thank you, darling." Only she can wield an endearment like a knife. "I don't know why you have to make things so difficult. I'm going to lie down now. I'm getting one of my dizzy spells."

I end the call and set my phone on the table.

Hart's Landing. Immediately. For six weeks.

My mother.

My hands ball up reflexively, and my breathing quickens. I do an exercise my therapist taught me called box breathing, where you inhale for four counts, hold for four, exhale for four, hold for four.

As if she senses I need a calm presence, my glossy black Bombay, Beatrix, sidles up and winds her way around my ankles. Unclenching my fists, I reach down to pet her. "Looks like we're taking a trip to Hart's Landing, Bea." She gazes up at me and meows in protest. "I know what I always say. But I don't think I can get out of it this time."

Normally, I avoid returning to my hometown by suggesting my mother meet me in Manhattan for a girls' weekend. There's nothing she loves more than shopping on Fifth Avenue, sipping cocktails on rooftop bars, and pointing out all the places she used to go when she lived in the city that never sleeps. Before I ruined her life.

My head is still pounding, so I get up from my work table and shuffle into the bathroom, where I tip two ibuprofen into my palm. My cat follows me, watching with her absinthe eyes as I lean over, cup water from the faucet, and swallow the pills.

"She didn't give me any choice." I backhand my mouth as I face my accuser. "Don't look at me like that."

Beatrix looks at me like that.

"What was I supposed to do, say no?"

A vehement meow.

"Even if she wasn't the best mother in the world, she raised me all by herself, didn't she?" I run through the list of excuses I always make for Mom. "She gave up her ballet career when she got pregnant with me. She moved back to her hometown so we'd have support. She put food on the table and clothes on my back, and I can't think of anything I lacked growing up."

Beatrix tilts her head.

"Okay, maybe one thing." I flip off the bathroom light. "But I don't want to talk about it."

That evening, I'm in my bedroom packing when my roommate Jess appears in the doorway. She's an attorney at the Securities and Exchange Commission, wears a suit and heels every day, and always remains in complete control of her emotions. We're total opposites, but somehow, living together just works.

"I got your text," she says. "Yes, I can water your plants. But you're going *where* for six weeks?"

"Hart's Landing, Michigan. Where I grew up." I glance at Beatrix's carrier, which I've placed on the floor to allow her to explore it. She's been keeping her distance, eyeing it suspiciously from her perch on the windowsill.

Jess's eyebrows shoot up. "I thought you never went back there."

"I don't." I pull some nicer things off hangers in my closet—a couple of blouses, a skirt, a stretchy black dress. "But my mom is having a double hip replacement next week and needs my help."

"Next *week*? She didn't give you much notice, did she?"

"Giving me notice isn't really her style."

Jess shakes her head. "You know, you really need better boundaries."

"Boundaries?" I tilt my head like a dog who just heard a strange noise. "What are those?"

"Those are things you set so that people like your mom and your asshole ex-husband don't constantly take advantage of you."

I give her a wry smile. "I'm working on it."

"How? Your no-dating rule?" She shoots me a pointed look. "That's not *working on it*. That's avoiding it."

"You sound like my therapist."

"I'm serious, Mila." She folds her arms as she cross-examines me. "How are you going to teach your classes? What about the design project for Ivy & Stone? You've been waiting years for an opportunity like that."

"I spoke with the college. Both of the courses I'm teaching—color theory and botanical art history—can be taught remotely until I'm back. As for the design work, I'll figure it out." I toss a pair of heels into my bag. Some sneakers. My flip-flops. "It's not like I'll have anything else to do while I'm there. I plan to just lie low and get through it."

Jess wanders into my room and sits on the end of my bed. Leans back on her hands. "So what's it like? Hart's Landing?"

"Same as any small town. Everyone knows everyone's business. Gossip moves faster than traffic. Nothing ever changes."

"Why do you hate going back so much?"

In my head, the sirens are still screaming. "It's complicated."

"Do you still have friends there?"

The hidden ache in my heart swells. "Not anymore. I used to have the best friends ever in Hart's Landing—there were five of us who grew up together. We were inseparable."

"What happened?"

The ache sharpens into knife-edged pain. "One of them—her name was Lydia, but we called her Ladybug—had leukemia. She died February of our senior year. Things fell apart with the rest of us that summer." I pause. "Or maybe I should say they blew up. The last time I saw any of them was ten years ago. August tenth."

"Wow. You remember the exact date?"

"Yes." Exhaling, I cringe. "It was the night I set fire to the bakery."

Jess bolts upright. "The night you did *what*?"

"Not on purpose," I explain quickly. "It was an accident—a flour dust explosion after my shift."

Don't think about the letter. Just don't.

"Wait a minute. Back up." She holds up her palms. "Flour dust is explosive?"

"Yes. And it's Bakery Safety 101 not to kick up too much of it when you sweep, but I was so nervous that night, I forgot. All it needs is the right amount of heat to ignite—could be static electricity, faulty wiring, an oven left on." *A burner not switched all the way off.* "The official investigation was inconclusive. But since I was the closing employee, everyone in town blamed me for being negligent. Or at least distracted."

"Distracted by what?"

Wrong question, I think. It's whom I was distracted by, not what.

I knot my fingers together and stare down at them. Remember the way I clutched Everett's shirt in my fists. "I wasn't exactly alone when the fire started."

"Who was with you?"

I proceed to tell her everything: about Lydia, the grief we felt after her death, the promise we made to honor her birthday by living the night like there was no tomorrow. I remember our meeting at the foundry like it was yesterday, so I tell her about that too—about the task my friends chose for me. I don't tell her about throwing the stone in the river, because I've *never* told anyone about that.

That stone was just for me.

"Holy shit. So you locked lips with this guy, and the place exploded?" Leave it to a lawyer to summarize the whole saga in a sentence.

"Pretty much." I close my eyes, remembering all the repercussions of that night. "Insurance didn't cover the damage, so the McKeans had to sell the property. I felt awful."

"Jesus. I can't believe you never told me about this."

"By the time I met you at freshman orientation, all I wanted was to leave Hart's Landing and what happened there behind me." Kneeling down, I refold some items to make more room in my suitcase. "I got a new phone. Switched my major from dance to art. Chopped off my hair."

"It *was* shorter when I met you," she recalls, thinking back.

"I missed my friends so much it physically hurt. Even with a new number and shorter hair, living in a new place and meeting new people… I thought about them every day and felt horrible about the way things ended. I still do. But I learned an important lesson."

"What was that?"

"You can't live your life like there's no tomorrow." I close my suitcase and zip it. "Because tomorrow has a way of always showing up."

Chapter Two

WELCOME TO THE LANDING PAD

Community Updates From The Hart's Landing Gazette (Online Edition)

PSA: The Hart's Landing Curb Appeal Society wants you to know: brown patches on your lawn are not an appropriate aesthetic choice for fall! 'Tis the season for aerating and over-seeding.

Community question (submitted by GrannyB43): Does anyone know the location of this month's Coffee with the Mayor? I'm going to bring my granddaughter with me. My hairdresser told me Mayor McKean's mother mentioned he likes chicken fricassee, and nobody fricassees a chicken like my Gracie!

EVENTS: Entry forms for the Best Pie Contest at the Founder's Day Festival must be submitted by the end of the week. The Festival would once again like to remind residents that anyone caught submitting multiple entries will be disqualified.

EVENTS: The Diner Detectives True Crime Fanatics Club will meet at their regularly scheduled time, 10 a.m. on Tuesdays, at Ernie's Diner. This month, get "fired up" to revisit the details of the 2015 Tart and Soul blaze. What actually happened that night? Join us to turn up the heat on a cold case!

Chapter Three

Mila

My mother greets me at the front door with, "There you are! I thought you said you'd get here by lunchtime. It got so late, I finally ate without you."

"Sorry, Mom." The words come easily, accustomed as I am to leading with an apology. "My flight was delayed. Didn't you get my text?"

She frowns. "I must have missed it. Next time, call. I'm not looking at my cell phone constantly like your generation."

Willing myself to have patience, I open my arms. "Hi. It's good to see you."

She lets me hug her, enclosing me in her long, slender arms without actually making me feel like I'm being embraced. The familiar scent of her Chanel perfume triggers the hollow feeling in my belly I experienced as a kid when I looked for affection from her.

"How are you feeling?" I ask.

"The same," she says with a sigh. "The pain is just terrible. I—" Her eyes widen as she spies Beatrix's carrier, which is resting on the cement stoop behind me. She points at it. "What is that?"

"It's a travel carrier for my cat."

"You brought a cat?"

"Yes. *My* cat, Beatrix. I'm going to be here for six weeks, Mom. I couldn't leave her behind."

Given her horrified expression, you'd think I was trying to enter her house with a rabid skunk I found on the side of the road. "You know I don't like animals in my house, Mila."

And you know how badly I wanted a pet all my life, I feel like saying. Instead, I take a breath. "I know, Mom. But she's really sweet. She won't bother you at all, I promise."

She flattens herself against the door while I bring Beatrix inside, as if my cat might spring from the carrier and attack her. Then comes the first sneeze, which is entirely artificial, just like the dozens that follow. "Oh, dear. I must be allergic."

"I'll take her right to my room and come back down for the rest of my stuff," I say, heading straight up the stairs.

Our house is a bungalow with a converted half-story loft that serves as my bedroom. The ceiling up here is low, and two of the walls are steeply pitched about four feet up. The only windows are on the two pentagon-shaped flat walls at each end. When we moved in, my mother said the space was too suffocating for her and took one of the two small bedrooms downstairs. I was eight at the time and couldn't believe my luck—an entire *floor* all to myself!

Of course, there was no door at the top of the stairs, which left much to be desired as I got older and wanted more privacy. But by that time, my mother was so busy with the dance studio that she wasn't around all that much to intrude. When she was, I got used to her knocking on the wall at the bottom of the stairs and yelling my name. She rarely came all the way up, so it felt like my own little world.

I switch on the light and smile. My room, always a refuge for me, looks pretty much the same as when I left it ten summers ago. Same floral quilt on my twin-size bed. Same soft-blue paint on the walls, although my old Twilight posters have been taken down (Team Edward forever). Same dresser my mom and I found at an antique store downtown and painted white in the garage. I can still picture my mother in old clothes, a scarf holding back her hair, a spot of paint on her forehead. She seemed like a mom from a TV show that day—warm and fun, beautiful but messy.

It's one of my best memories of her.

Setting Beatrix's carrier down on the floor, I let her out, and she immediately scurries beneath the bed. "I don't blame you," I say softly, glancing over my shoulder at the stairs. "I might join you under there if it gets bad."

My dresser is tucked against the slanted wall opposite my bed. I wander over and sweep my hand across the surface, dusty from neglect. On a whim, I open the top drawer. Expecting it to be empty, I'm surprised to find a framed photo. I take it out and study it, my throat growing tight.

The five of us at the beach—Lydia, Yasmine, Gabi, Rachel, and me. We're dressed in bathing suits, our wet hair clinging to our shoulders, and our joy leaps out at me from behind the glass. Lydia is making a peace sign. Gabi blows a kiss. Rachel's dimples pop. Yasmine is making bunny ears above my head, and I look like I'm laughing at something, my mouth open wide, my eyes closed.

I remember that day like it was yesterday.

It was the summer before senior year. Before Lydia was diagnosed. Before any kind of separation loomed. Back then, we couldn't imagine a world in which we weren't always this close.

"Mila? What's taking you so long? I need you!"

"Coming!" I start to tuck the photo back into the drawer, but at the last second, I prop it up on top of the dresser instead.

When I go back downstairs, my mother is lying on the living room couch with a wet cloth over her eyes. "Could you please look in the bathroom for an antihistamine? My eyes are very itchy."

"Sure," I reply, biting back the suggestion that we immediately inform her surgeon—and maybe the Pentagon—that we are dealing with an outbreak of severe, sudden-onset cat allergy.

The bathroom is across from her bedroom. Kneeling down, I open the cabinet beneath the sink to find it a complete mess of hair tools, beauty products, skincare, first aid, medicines. It surprises me, since it isn't like my mother to be so disorganized. Maybe the pain in her hips prevents her from bending down enough to keep things tidy? A twinge of sympathy pinches my stomach. Tomorrow I'll reorganize this cabinet and ensure the items she might need more regularly are in easy reach.

I dig around without success. "I think you're out of allergy medicine," I call. "Want me to run to the store real quick?"

"Well, I don't want to be a burden..."

Rolling my eyes, I get to my feet. "It's no trouble. I'll be right back."

Someone calls my name as I walk from the house to the garage.

"Mila? Is that you?"

Our longtime next-door neighbor and notorious Hart's Landing busybody, Vera Pratt, approaches the old chain-link fence between our yards. Pasting a smile onto my face, I offer a wave. "Hello, Mrs. Pratt. Yes, it's me."

"Well, Lord love a duck! I was wondering whose car had pulled into your mother's driveway. I always keep an eye out for strange vehicles in our neighborhood—I'm the President of the Concerned Citizens Brigade and run the Suspicious Activity Group for The Landing Pad. Have you been reading the Pad?"

"The what?"

"The Landing Pad. It's the community news board on the *Gazette*'s website. I subscribe to text updates—never miss a thing." She raises a knowing eyebrow, and I get the impression that what she really means is that she'll make sure everyone in town knows I'm back in the time it takes me to get to the pharmacy.

"I can't say I've seen The Landing Pad, no."

"Make sure you do. Especially if you're back for good."

I shake my head vehemently. "I'm not back for good. Just six weeks to help my mother after—"

"I heard about your D-I-V-O-R-C-E." She stage-whispers the letters behind the back of her hand.

I jingle the keys, unable to scrounge up any more W-O-R-D-S.

But Mrs. Pratt seems eager to move on anyway. "You know, you're still famous around here." She laughs with delight. "Or should I say infamous? Everyone remembers the fire."

"It was pretty memorable."

"The *Gazette* just printed a ten-year anniversary article, so even people who weren't living here at the time know all about it. Your picture made the front page!"

My stomach plummets. "There was an anniversary article? With a photo of me?"

"Your graduation photo, if the caption was correct. Article ran just last week. I kept a copy if you'd like to see it."

"No, thanks."

Mrs. Pratt leans in closer, her rheumy gaze sharpening like a hawk spotting prey. "What *I've* always wanted to know is what the two of you were doing in that bakery all alone at night. They say the lights were already out and the place was completely dark."

"I have to go, Mrs. Pratt." I resume my walk toward the garage. If I were a betting woman, I'd say Mrs. Pratt fills her days listening to true crime podcasts and watching old episodes of *Law and Order*. No doubt she finds intrigue wherever she looks, even if there's nothing to see.

"Nice chatting with you!" she calls. A glance back confirms she's already typing furiously on her phone. The Landing Pad will have a new post in no time.

"No, it wasn't," I mutter, opening the driver's side door to my mother's Buick.

Just what I need. An anniversary article. With a photo.

So much for lying low.

I back out of the driveway and head downtown, all the while trying to forget I'm in a car with a license plate that reads PRIMA1.

Chapter Four

Everett

"You see, Mr. Mayor, I just think it sends the wrong message about what kind of town Hart's Landing is."

I smile at widowed Mrs. Biddle, lifelong resident of Hart's Landing, fervent defender of its history and traditions, and my former second-grade teacher. She never misses Coffee with the Mayor and always has some new, urgent issue to bring to my attention.

Today, it's the new stoplight.

"Hart's Landing needs to preserve its provincial feel," she continues, two hands clasped over the top of her purse. "That's the charm of a small town. People come here to get away from the chaos and noise and pollution of the big city."

"I understand your concern, Mrs. Biddle. I just don't think one stoplight on Main Street is going to ruin our small-town charm."

"One stoplight today, ten slick high-rise office towers tomorrow!" She furrows her penciled-in eyebrows. "They already turned the old shipping dock into *condominiums*," she says, as if a nuclear power plant had gone in on the riverfront instead of senior housing. "And I'm sure you've heard the rumors about the old Hart Iron Works building being purchased by some foreign billionaire and turned into a—a—" She leans forward and lowers her voice to a scandalized whisper. "A sex club!"

I choke back the laugh threatening to erupt from my throat. "I haven't heard that one, but I assure you, such a thing would never be approved by the town council. The Hart family would like to donate the old foundry site and office building for a community center."

"Oh." Her expression is slightly crestfallen. The billionaire's sex club is definitely a better story. "Well, mark my words, it's a slippery slope. We must remain vigilant in the face of modernization."

I pick up my mug and sip my coffee. I didn't anticipate these kinds of conversations when my jackass friends bet me I wouldn't run for mayor.

Another thing I didn't anticipate? Winning.

After all, I was a thirty-year-old farmer, a college dropout with zero political experience. What did I know about executive planning or local government? But it turned out that the citizens of Hart's Landing didn't really care. When the *Gazette* interviewed people after the election, they said they voted for me because I seemed real and down-to-earth. I had a firm handshake. I looked them in the eye. No one minded that I was young—they liked my youthful enthusiasm for problem-solving. They liked that I was a fourth-generation cherry grower whose family had lived in Hart's Landing for over a century. They liked that I wore flannel and denim, not a suit and tie. It showed that I was willing to pitch in, work hard, and get things done.

So here I am—Mayor Everett McKean.

And actually, I'm pretty fucking good at it.

"Tell you what, Mrs. Biddle." I set my cup down and lean on the table with both elbows, like I have a secret for her. "Lately, I've been thinking more about the old train depot. It's been empty for years now, and there are plenty of people who want to see it torn down."

Mrs. Biddle's spine snaps ramrod straight, as if I suggested she commit murder. "No! That building is over a hundred years old! I used to board the train there all by myself to visit my grandparents with a little note pinned to my dress. The conductor always had a lollipop for me."

I smile. "I think the old depot would make a perfect location for a new Hart's Landing Historical Society and Museum."

Her wrinkled face seems to smooth out for a moment. "That's

a wonderful idea!"

"I'm glad you think so. I'd like to form a committee to explore potential ideas. I could really use someone on it with extensive knowledge of Hart's Landing's history, as well as a strong commitment to preserving it." I've built up an arsenal of persuasive expressions as mayor, and here I deploy one of my best weapons—the Prince Charming grin. "I was wondering if maybe you'd like to be the founding member?"

Her eyes mist over, and she places a blue-veined hand on her heart. "I'd be honored. Truly honored."

"Perfect." I stand up and hold out my hand. "Good seeing you, Mrs. Biddle. I'll be in touch."

"Always a pleasure. You certainly did grow up nicely."

"Thank you."

"I had my doubts, I don't mind telling you." After shaking my hand, she points a knobby finger at me. "You had the handwriting of a moral degenerate, and you never stayed in your seat. But look at you now!"

I trot out an aw-shucks chortle, lowering my head to surreptitiously check my watch. Coffee with the Mayor officially ended an hour ago, but I stayed late to make sure everyone who came got my ear for at least a few minutes. But I have to get out of here, or I'll be late for my meeting with the environmental consultant I hired to conduct an assessment on the old foundry site. Test results are in.

"All you're missing is a wife," Mrs. Biddle tuts. "You know, my granddaughter Charity is about your age, and she's single, too. Why don't I have you both over for dinner sometime?"

"Thanks, but I'm not looking for a wife."

She purses her lips. "Why not? It's not good for a man to be without the influence of a woman to soften his rough edges."

I laugh. "I like my rough edges."

"But you must be so lonely."

"I've got a dog."

Mrs. Biddle's Stern Teacher face hasn't lost its edge. She wags a finger at me. "That's not what I meant, young man, and you know it."

"I don't have time to be lonely, Mrs. Biddle." That much is true. Between keeping the family farm afloat, serving as mayor, and ensuring my name stays at the top of the axe-throwing leaderboard at The Axe & Barrel pub—my top three priorities in life, in that order—I don't have a single minute to spare. "But thanks for coming today. Have a good afternoon."

She totters off with a frown, muttering what sounds like "moral degenerate, mark my words." I'm used to disappointing the matchmaking mavens of this town, who are always trying to fix me up with a daughter, granddaughter, niece, neighbor, hair stylist, dental hygienist…basically, any human female they can find within a twenty-mile radius. It's practically a competitive sport, and Coffee with the Mayor is their favorite playing field.

When I originally had the idea, I imagined informal conversations once a month where I could get to know my constituents, hear about matters important to them, and learn more about what I could do as mayor to make Hart's Landing a great place to live, run a business, raise a family, or take a vacation. In reality, I usually get about ten percent of that and ninety percent complaints about the condition of people's lawns, the need to change the high school team name to something more ferocious than the Mighty Muskrats, and elevator pitches from grannies who have "just the girl" for me.

And now that it's September, there are the pies.

"Hello there, Mr. Mayor." Beaming, Judy Gillis sets down a stunning example—lattice crust golden and flaky, luscious red fruit peeking out between the lines. A dusting of sugar crystals sparkles on top.

"Hi, Mrs. Gillis." My stomach growls audibly. I skipped lunch, and it's nearly half past three.

"Hungry, dear?" Her eyes take on a mischievous gleam, and she bats her lashes. The eye shadow covering her lids is sky-blue, and her lips are painted bubble-gum pink. “Have a slice of my strawberry-rhubarb pie. It’s fresh from the oven.”

The tart, buttery smell reaches my nostrils, and my stomach moans with hunger. “It looks delicious.”

“I’m so glad you think so. I made it just for you. I thought you might like to try it before the contest.”

Best Pie is the most coveted prize at the Founder’s Day Festival, and despite *many* efforts to get out of it, I’m the judge.

“There’s not a pie in this town that can touch mine.” She winks flirtatiously. “Just one taste will tell you.”

Slightly revolted, I clear my throat. “Thanks, but I never eat on the job. If you’d like, you can put it over there with the others.” I gesture toward a table on the far side of the community room within Town Hall, where several other pies have been left and a few people stand chatting near the coffee urn.

Judy’s jaw drops like the blade of a guillotine. “Is that Vera Pratt? Did she bring her blueberry crumble? The nerve! I told her I was bringing my strawberry-rhubarb for you. She stole my idea!” Without another word, she picks up her pie and marches across the room to have it out with Vera.

Recognizing my chance to escape, I say goodbye to the Town Hall manager and hurry outside. On the sidewalk, I pull out my phone to dash off a quick text to the consultant, apologizing for running late. But as I began typing, something catches my eye on the far side of the street. A woman with long, coppery hair is hurrying down the block. When she crosses in front of the wine bar, she slows for a moment, then speeds up again and disappears inside the pharmacy two doors down.

My pulse quickens.

I’ve only ever known one girl with penny-colored hair like that, but I haven’t seen her since the night of the fire.

Many times since, I’ve thought of her. Wished that that night had gone down differently. Wondered what if.

I'm tempted to wait around a couple of minutes and see if I can catch a glimpse of the woman's face when she emerges. But I'm already behind schedule, and this wouldn't be the first time I mistook a random redhead for the girl I once knew.

It's always wishful thinking. Never her.

So I finish my text to the consultant, hit send, and continue down the block toward my truck. Besides, if Mila Ferguson really is back in Hart's Landing, I'll hear about it soon enough.

I'm the mayor, after all.

Chapter Five

Mila

The cashier at the pharmacy, a tall, thin, twenty-something white guy with a reddish-brown ponytail, gives me a strange look before ringing me up. He looks slightly familiar, but I can't place him. The register is slow, and he continues to stare at me while I wait for my total to appear. I lower my chin.

"You don't remember me," he says.

"Sorry. I moved away ten years ago and haven't really been back since."

"I looked different back then. I wore glasses, and my voice was a lot higher." His expression gets a little sheepish. "But you used to make the best cherry lemonade in town."

Now I see it. "Stevie?"

His cheeks turn red. "It's just Steve now."

The total pops up on the reader, and I tap my card. "Wow, it's been a while. How are you?"

"Fine. I graduated from college last year, but I'm still trying to figure out what I want to do."

I give him a sympathetic smile. "That can take time."

"You haven't changed a bit," he says adoringly.

"Thanks." The purchase goes through, but he just keeps staring at me. "Um, am I done?"

"Oh, sorry." He staples my receipt to the bag and hands it to me. "Maybe I'll see you around."

"Maybe." Flashing him a quick wave, I hurry out the front door and turn left. When I pass Novel Vine, the wine bar I noticed earlier, I stop again. The striped awning and elegant gold lettering on the window remind me of Paris. Moving closer, I peer through the glass.

It isn't open yet, but I see someone behind the bar—a woman I recognize instantly.

Yasmine.

My heart trips faster. Is this her business?

Knock on the door, urges a voice in my head. *Say hello. Say you're sorry it's been so long. Say you've missed her.*

But after so many years, it feels daunting to make the first move. What if she isn't the same Yasmine anymore? What if she's angry we lost touch? After the catastrophic events of That Night, she tried her best to keep us together, but the damage had been done.

I should have been better. I could have reached out. I didn't need to shut her out so completely.

With a decade of time—and a good amount of therapy—between then and now, I can see things differently. Admit that I played a role in things falling apart the way they did. But I can't carry the fault alone.

My phone buzzes with a text from my mother.

Mom: *Where are you? My eyes are getting worse.*

I reply with an apology, saying I'll be there in five minutes.

When I look up, Yasmine is gone.

I pull up at home, but I don't get out of the car right away. Instead, I open Instagram on my phone and find the account for Novel Vine. It's Yasmine's place for sure, and as I scroll through posts about the renovation and grand opening, the sight of her smiling face makes my throat catch. She looks so happy.

I'm dying to know what the last ten years of her life have been like. Where she's been. How she's changed, and how she's stayed the same. I'd like to laugh about old times, rehash crazy stories, revisit inside jokes. I want to know if her grandmother is still alive, the one we all called Sitty, who draped paper-thin bread dough over pillows to stretch it out and made us all try the raw meat with spices she called kibbeh nayyeh. I remember how scared I was to try something so different from the rabbit food I was used to at home. I wondered if anyone would notice if I put the Lebanese delicacy in my purse instead of my mouth.

But of course, it was delicious. Maybe Yasmine makes it herself now.

My finger hovers over the blue follow button. I got rid of personal social media several years ago, so the only account I have is for Lavender Ladybug, my freelance botanical design studio. She won't recognize the name, but one look at the profile and she'll know it's me.

I tap the screen.

And maybe it's a stupid small thing, especially after so many years, but it feels big.

Like I'm setting something in motion.

Inside, I bring my mom the pill with a glass of water. "Need anything else before I unpack?"

"Not right now," she says. "I'll just rest for a bit then fix us some supper."

"Don't worry about it, Mom. I can take care of supper. Did I tell you I took a gourmet cooking class recently?"

"No, but there's a lot you don't tell me."

My body goes rigid. She's referring to the fact that I didn't tell her about my divorce until a couple months after my ex filed. A year ago, I might have swung at that pitch, but my therapist has encouraged me to let those go by. Without another word, I head upstairs to unpack.

When I come down an hour later, my mother's bedroom door is still closed, so I use the opportunity to set up a workspace in the small spare bedroom at the back of the house. My mother converted it to a dance room when we moved in, so it has smooth wood floors and a wall full of mirrors. There are two windows, which will provide some natural light, but I also packed my gooseneck lamp.

I lug a folding table up from the basement and set it up near one window before unpacking all my supplies. Tomorrow morning, I'll teach my virtual classes, then spend the rest of the day preparing the house so it's safe for my mother post-surgery.

I'm just checking my email when her bedroom door opens and she wanders out. She stops short when she sees what I've done. "You've taken over my studio," she says, appearing slightly miffed.

"Sorry. I need a space to work and teach classes while I'm here. I didn't think you'd be using this room much while you recover."

She presses her lips together. "I'm getting hungry."

"Okay." I close my laptop. "Are there any tomatoes left in your garden? I can make us a caramelized onion, tomato, and goat cheese tart. It was one of the recipes from my cooking class."

"I don't eat goat cheese," she sniffs. "But there are plenty of tomatoes in the garden. I haven't been able to work out there much this summer because of my hips."

"I'll go pick some right now." From the kitchen, I grab a bowl and head out the side door.

Her garden is at the back of the yard. At the sight of it, my shoulders droop. It's more overgrown than I've ever seen it, another indication of my mother's pain level. Normally, she keeps her yard as meticulously neat as her home. As I fill the bowl with ripe cherry tomatoes, I vow once more to have patience with her.

Inside, I put the tomatoes in a colander and give them a rinse. When I come out of the kitchen, my mother is watching *The Bachelor* on TV. "Can you wet this again?" she asks, handing me the cloth she had on her eyes. "Very cold water, please. It was too warm earlier."

I do as she asks, running the tap for a minute to make sure it's icy. After wringing out the cloth, I return to the living room and hand it to her.

"I saw you chatting with Vera Pratt in the driveway," she remarks, placing the cloth over her eyes. "What did she have to say?"

"Not much. She saw me arrive and came out to say hello." I drop into a chair opposite the couch. "She mentioned there was an anniversary article about the fire in the newspaper."

"Yes. It gave me a migraine."

Annoyed, I fold my arms. "Why is a ten-year-old fire front-page news?"

"This is a small town, Mila. Drama never gets old."

"Well, I don't want to be small-town drama."

"Then you shouldn't have set the bakery on fire."

"For God's sake, Mom, I didn't—" I stop myself from diving headfirst into this rabbit hole. Deep breath in, long exhale. "Never mind," I say, working hard to keep my tone breezy. I push myself out of the chair and head into the kitchen to make supper.

When I see a bottle of Pinot Grigio in the fridge, I unscrew the cap and take a swig straight from the bottle.

It reminds me of old times.

Chapter Six

Everett

After my meeting with the consultant, I make the fifteen-minute drive back to the farm with a dull ache at the base of my skull. I've got a huge problem on my hands and no clue how to solve it.

But I find my thoughts drifting.

Even though I've got way more pressing questions to answer, it's Mila Ferguson on my mind as I turn into the driveway of McKean Cherries. Was it her I saw in town?

I take the long dirt road that winds through the farm, past barns and outbuildings, past the farmhouse where I grew up, past the sycamore tree where I caught Mila before she hit the ground. The memory makes me smile. How old would she have been? Ten? Twelve? I picture her back then, a skinny kid with knobby knees, long red hair, and all those freckles. Just another one of the girls my kid sister ran around with in those days. I barely paid her any attention.

Until the summer I came home from my sophomore year at MSU. Suddenly she was eighteen and hot as fuck. She was still hanging around with my sister a lot, but I'd see her alone at Tart and Soul. Back then, the bakery was a McKean family business, locally famous for the miniature cherry pies bursting with fruit from our orchards. Tart and Soul wasn't always on my delivery route, but that summer, I started checking the schedule to look for Mila's shifts. And if I happened to take care of the bakery's deliveries those days… Well, I'm sure it was just a coincidence.

Her cheeks would turn *so red* when I called her "Freckles" or asked who she was dating or teased her about falling out of that tree.

Not once did she ever flirt back.

Which was why I was so shocked that night.

I pull up next to the cabin at the back of the McKean property, a small rectangular building with just one bedroom and bathroom, a tiny kitchen, and a living room. It's small and sparsely furnished, but it's plenty of space for me and Merlin. He greets me with classic yellow-lab energy when I come through the door, overjoyed and eager to play. I'm starving, but I grab the leash and take him outside.

When I can't ignore my empty stomach any longer, I drag Merlin back inside, feed him, then open my fridge, hoping for a miracle. Like maybe my dog's namesake has been here while I was gone and magically stocked the shelves with delicious, nutritious foods that can be assembled with minimal culinary skills. Merlin trots over, also hoping for some wizardly intervention.

Alas, it looks the same as it did yesterday. Condiments, a takeout container of petrified lo mein, and some shredded cheese that has probably expired. Merlin pokes his nose around and gives me a disappointed look. Exhaling heavily, I give his ears a scratch and shut the fridge. "Come on, boy. Let's go see what's cooking at the house." Mom can always be counted on to feed me.

I know, I know. At thirty, I should be feeding myself. But I hate grocery shopping and I can't cook, and in exchange for letting me mooch meals in her kitchen, my mother expects me to take care of the house, which I do.

We leave the cabin, Merlin in the lead. Occasionally, he's distracted by a squirrel or bird or rabbit scurrying across the road, but only because he wants to make friends. He weighs nearly a hundred pounds, but it's all heart.

I study the house I grew up in from the back as we approach it. Built by my great-grandfather, it's a two-story structure with white clapboard siding that's been painted so many times the corners aren't even sharp anymore. A deep wraparound porch hugs three sides, its pine floorboards worn and grooved in the high-traffic areas.

It isn't a showplace by any means—the upstairs hallway tilts, bedroom doors have to be jammed shut in the summer, windows rattle noisily during storms—but it's withstood over a hundred Michigan winters, and I appreciate that kind of resilience. As I step onto the back porch, I recall all the summer days I went running out the screen door, its squeak and slam behind me like a fond farewell. All the winter mornings I trudged out to shovel a path. The ball games on the lawn. The snowball fights. The mud pies. Good times.

Of course, there were bad times too. Dark times that made me want to leave this place and never come back.

But I try not to linger on those. You play the hand life deals you.

The tantalizing aroma of meat and potatoes greets me as we enter the kitchen, and my stomach growls. My mom is pulling something from the oven.

"Hey," I say as the door bangs shut behind us.

"Hey." She sets a large, steaming dish on the stovetop. "Did you smell my cowboy casserole from clear across the yard?"

"Must have. Got extra?"

"Don't I always?" She pulls the oven mitts off her hands. "Make yourself useful and set the table while I put a salad together."

"Yes, ma'am." I grab two mismatched plates from a cupboard with a door that hangs slightly crooked off the hinges and make a mental note to add it to the endless list of things that need to be fixed around here.

"How was your meeting with the science guy?" she asks.

"Not great." I open the silverware drawer and grab two forks. All the cutlery in this house is mismatched, too.

"What was the news?"

"What I expected. Soil sampling showed contaminants at levels exceeding state standards."

"But they tore down the old foundry decades ago."

"Doesn't matter. It was there for eighty years, and it left a mark."

"How's the Hart family gonna feel about that?"

"Pissed. They were expecting this to be a straightforward

donation of the property for a community center. Lots of warm and fuzzy press to combat the perception that they profited at the expense of community health for a hundred years." Reaching over her shoulder, I steal a crouton from the salad. "But you can't build a community center on a contaminated site."

"No, I guess you can't. So what are you going to do?"

"I don't know yet."

We fill our plates and take them to the table. Mom is moving with a pronounced limp. When she sits, she lowers herself gingerly into the chair, her expression tight with pain from her fibromyalgia.

"Are you okay?" I ask.

She shrugs. "Going up and down the stairs is getting a little rough."

"The new medications aren't helping?"

"I don't like how they make me feel." She shifts uncomfortably in her chair.

"How's that, pain-free? Mom, Doc prescribed them for a reason."

"Gabi says I should try water therapy," she says stubbornly. "They do it at the place where she works."

"Mom." I set down my fork and look at her. "You have to take the meds. I'm worried you're going to fall."

She tuts as she places her napkin on her lap. "The one messes with my stomach, and the other makes me feel dizzy and confused. It's like you gotta choose between your body and your mind. If one works, the other doesn't."

"So we'll go back to Doc. There are all kinds of drugs you can try."

She clenches her jaw and looks away from me. "I don't want to take anything that can be habit-forming."

Guilt slips into the cracks of my frustration. In addition to abusing alcohol, my father got hooked on opioids after back surgery.

Which he needed because of me.

"I know," I say, softening my tone. "But let's talk to Doc about some other options, okay? You can't live like this. How are you going to pick up the grandchildren you're always bugging me to give you?"

She points a finger at me. "You give me the grandkids, I'll take the meds."

"Is that blackmail?"

"I'm not above it." A look around the kitchen has her sighing. She spreads her arms. "All this space and just me to take it up. Three empty bedrooms upstairs! Three!"

"It's a crime," I say as I shovel in a mouthful of cheesy meat and potatoes.

Narrowing her eyes at me, she takes a bite of salad. "So how many pies were you offered today?"

"Four, plus a berry crumble." While we eat, I give her the rundown of Coffee with the Mayor.

"Those two have always been so competitive," she snickers. "It goes clear back to high school when Judy was named cheer captain and Vera spread a bunch of rumors about her and the quarterback."

I shake my head as I take our dishes over to the sink. "Do people forget anything in this town?"

"Sure, just not grudges or gossip."

I rinse my plate and fork and load them into the dishwasher. "Hey Mom, you remember Mila Ferguson?"

"Of course I do."

"Is Gabi still in touch with her?"

"I don't know." She's silent for a moment. "Things were so hard after…that night."

"Yeah." For a moment, I hear voices from the past.

Yelling at the top of the stairs. Rage. Threats. Tears.

Shaking off the memory, I close the dishwasher and turn around to find my mom eyeing me curiously. "What made you ask about Mila?"

"I saw someone in town today who looked like her."

"Oh." A pause. "You know, I did hear that Eliza Ferguson is having hip replacement surgery. I wonder if Mila is home to help her."

A spark shoots up my spine. Maybe it wasn't wishful thinking for once. But I try to sound casual. "Could be."

My mother sighs. "I always felt sorry for Mila after what happened. It wasn't fair, the way everybody made it sound like the fire was her fault. It certainly wasn't her fault your father let the insurance policy lapse. But things that seem perfectly clear now didn't feel that way back then, did they?"

"No. They didn't." I don't like thinking about that night or what came after—the upheaval, the loss, and selling the bakery that had been in our family for sixty years.

Dropping out of college.

Taking over the farm full-time.

Watching the new owners of Tart and Soul rebuild a beloved Hart's Landing institution—one that the McKeans were no longer a part of.

Trying to fix the problems my father had created, protect his reputation, and keep McKean Cherries—and the McKean family—from going under. Pretty sure I didn't sleep for at least five years.

But I did what I had to do, and I'd do it again.

My mother tries to get up and winces. "Oof. Could you bring me a couple ibuprofen, honey?"

I reach into the cupboard where she keeps over-the-counter meds, shake out two Advil, and bring them to her.

"Thank you." She swallows them with some water. "Did you ever call that nice girl I told you about from the yarn shop?"

"I must have forgotten," I lie.

She watches me clip the leash to Merlin's collar. "I hear Bella's engaged."

"I heard that, too."

"It doesn't bother you?"

"Not a bit," I say, and it's the truth. "Bye, Mom. Thanks for dinner." As I walk back to the cabin, five words keep circling around my brain.

It could have been her.

Later, I drop into one of the Adirondack chairs on my porch and pull my phone from my back pocket.

My sister's face appears on the screen. "Hello?"

"Hey."

"How's Mom?"

"Not great and not taking her meds."

My sister sighs and sets the phone on her kitchen counter. I hear the hollow *tap*, *tap*, *tap*, of an egg against the countertop, watch her crack it against the side of a mixing bowl. "I was afraid of that. Because of Dad?"

"I think that's a big part of it. It's hard to be firm with her when that's the issue."

"I know. I told her we can explore non-pharmaceutical options." Gabi blows her hair out of her eyes. Another egg gets cracked. "There's some new research that says green light therapy is effective for fibromyalgia."

I frown. "What the fuck is green light therapy?"

"You're exposed to green light for an hour a day. Studies have shown it reduces pain and increases quality of life."

"Sounds like weird hippie shit to me."

"It works. And it's in better alignment with Mom's beliefs."

My sister is big on *alignment*.

"I'll come up sometime this month and see what options there are nearby," she says.

"She mentioned the stairs are getting tough—I'm worried about her falling."

"Maybe you should move in with her."

"Maybe *you* should move in with her."

Gabi sighs. "She needs to do some strength training. While I'm home, I'll try to find a fitness place where she feels comfortable."

"Sounds good." She moves out of the frame, and I hear the sound of an oven door closing. "So what else is new with you?"

"Not much."

"I heard Bella is engaged."

I roll my eyes. "Yes. I'm happy for her."

She's quiet for a moment. Wipes her forehead with the back of a hand. "Do you think you'll ever get married?"

"I don't know," I say honestly. "Mom and Dad didn't make it look like much fun. At least not after a while. I guess I'm just waiting for the person who makes me forget all that."

"Yeah," she says. "That's how I feel, too."

Chapter Seven

Mila

Friday morning, my mother enters the spare room twice while I'm teaching classes, despite the fact that I reminded her about them multiple times over breakfast.

"I'm sorry, I forgot," she says when I come out of the room just before noon. She's looking at an old photo album on the couch. "I'm used to being able to come and go in my house as I please. I didn't realize my studio would be off-limits while you're here."

"It's only off-limits while I'm teaching, Mom."

"Well, how often is that going to be?"

"Monday, Wednesday, and Friday mornings from ten to twelve."

"What about this Monday? That's my surgery," she says pointedly, like I might have forgotten.

"I canceled classes that day."

"Oh." She turns a page in the album. "I guess that's fine."

"What are you looking at?" I ask, moving closer.

"Photos of your ballet career. I put the album together after you left for school. It helped me deal with the loneliness." She flips another page. "And then when you quit, it helped me cope."

Swallowing the reply I want to make, I sit down next to her. "Can I look?"

"Sure." She shifts the album so I can see too. Many of them are from the Youth America Grand Prix competition. "Remember this variation? From *Sleeping Beauty*?"

I smile at the pink platter tutu and sparkling tiara. "I do. That tiara weighed a ton."

"I still have it."

"You do?"

"Sure. It's right there above the fireplace."

I glance at the mantel, and sure enough, there's the tiara, sitting between multiple photos of me from my ballet days.

"Ooh, look at this one from Swan Lake," she says, pointing at a picture of me mid-fouetté, wearing black and gold. "Simply stunning."

Turning the page, I point out a photo where I'm barefoot, wearing a simple emerald-green leotard, executing an attitude turn. "I *loved* that piece."

My mother scoffs, but it's gentle. "You always did like the contemporary. I preferred the classical."

"I liked both, Mom."

She sighs heavily. "It still breaks my heart, you know. I think about it all the time, how different it would have been if you'd gotten into Juilliard."

"It wouldn't have been any different," I say gently. "I was burned out."

"You would have found new inspiration there." She shakes her head, like she won't hear differently. "I'm sure of it."

I close the album. "How about some lunch?"

That afternoon, I shop for items on the list the surgeon's office provided: a raised toilet seat with handles, a shower chair, some grab bars. I bring everything into the house.

From her spot on the couch, my mother frowns at the growing collection of items on the living room floor. "I don't want any of those things, Mila. They're for old people."

"They're on the list."

"Well, I won't use them. And I don't want to look at them." With some difficulty, she rises from the couch, walks into her bedroom, and shuts the door.

I stand there for a moment, fighting the urge to hop on the first flight back to JFK.

I will not let her get to me, I tell myself as I do a few rounds of box breathing. *I will remember that she is in pain. I will be understanding and empathetic. She is my mother. She gave me life.*

But goddamn, she's difficult.

After tucking the equipment I purchased into the hall closet, I clean out the bathroom drawers and cabinet. I check expiration dates, throw away old pills and products, and move a few things to a shelf so she won't have to bend down to reach them.

Next, I focus on eliminating trip hazards. I move all the first-floor furniture aside, roll up the area rugs, and drag them into the basement. While I'm down there, I poke around in some of the storage boxes labeled with my name—things I packed up before moving out but didn't take to New York.

That's where I see them: the three framed drawings of orchids I gave to my mother last Christmas.

I lift one out and study it, my throat growing tight. Orchids are her favorite flowers, and I worked on these for months, desperately hoping she'd fall in love with them. Display them where she'd see them every day. Show them off.

Instead, that infernal tiara sits on the mantel, and these drawings are gathering dust in a cardboard box in the basement.

My gaze wanders over the painstakingly drawn blossoms and stems and leaves, down to the bottom corner where I signed my name. The lump in my throat thickens.

Swallowing it down, I replace the drawing in the box and tell myself it isn't a big deal. Maybe she forgot they were down here. Maybe she doesn't like them—art is subjective. Maybe it isn't personal.

But it feels personal.

When I turn around, I spy a walker shoved into a corner next to the ironing board. Guessing the doctor or maybe even a neighbor provided it to practice with, I yank it free and haul it upstairs. I put it right where she'll see it.

Boundaries are hard.

I'm better at small acts of rebellion.

Around six o'clock, my stomach begins to growl, so I start dinner. While the rice simmers, I sauté chicken breasts with more tomatoes from the garden and some garlic. My mother finally comes out of her room, entering the kitchen as she inhales deeply.

"Mmm. That smells good," she says.

I smile. "Thank you."

"It's nice to have you home again. I appreciate you taking care of me."

"Of course, Mom." My heart warms with pleasure, and I feel a little guilty about the walker.

But the evening goes downhill from there.

She's mad I removed all the area rugs. "Why did you get rid of the one under the coffee table? It makes that room work. Put it back."

She claims she can't find anything in the bathroom since I reorganized the cabinet. "Did you throw away my Vitamin C serum? I know there was some left, and it's very pricey!"

And when she sees the walker, she pitches a fit. "What's that doing up here? I put it out of sight for a reason, Mila. I don't want to be reminded that I won't even be able to walk on my own. It's very insensitive of you to put that contraption right under my nose."

By eight o'clock, the dishes are done, the kitchen is clean, and my empathy gauge is on E. Originally, I'd planned to spend the evening working on sketches for Ivy & Stone—a homewares giant that tapped me to design textiles for a new collection—but if I have to spend another hour in this house, I'll scream.

"Mom?" I call, coming down the stairs from my room. "I'm

heading out for a bit. Okay to take your car?"

"Where are you going?" She looks over at me from the couch, where she's watching a dating show for people over forty and making critical remarks about all the female contestants.

"Just into town."

"Dressed like that?"

I look down at my white tee, denim cutoffs, and comfy sneakers. On my head sits a plain black baseball cap, my ponytail trailing through the opening in the back. "Yes. I'm comfortable."

"Comfort is well and good, but you're not doing your figure any favors with your wardrobe choices. Do you want to be single forever?"

"I won't be late," I say, moving through the living room before I lose my mind.

"But what if I need something?"

"Call me."

"What if I have an emergency?"

"Call 911." I snatch her car keys off the kitchen counter and leave through the back door, yanking it shut behind me.

Outside, I pause for breath.

One night down.

Forty-one to go.

Chapter Eight

WELCOME TO THE LANDING PAD

Community Updates From The Hart's Landing Gazette (Online Edition)

POLICE BLOTTER: A resident reported a strange vehicle parked on Merriweather Lane. Officers responded to find a rideshare service dropping off a passenger at a local resident's home.

EVENTS: Formation of the Hart's Landing Historical Society: Upstanding community members concerned about the preservation of town history are invited to gather at the library next Tuesday at 1 p.m. Contact Betsy Biddle for details.

Community question (submitted by KnittingBiddy): A certain pediatric nurse was seen trying on wedding gowns at From the Hart yesterday! Remember when we thought her romance with the new veterinarian was a rebound fling after her relationship with the mayor ended?

🪓 AXE GODS 🪓

Hunter Gannon: *Axe tonight?*

Ben Hart: *Yeah but I'll be late. At the clinic until seven and then taking Viv to dinner before I drop her at her mom's.*

The Fucking Mayor: *I'll be late too.*

Hunter Gannon: *Doc has a kid. What's your excuse?*

The Fucking Mayor: *I have a contamination problem.*

Ripley Wilder: *Try showering.*

Chapter Nine

Everett

The job of mayor isn't glamorous, nor does it pay much, but it does come with one nice perk—a prime parking spot right on Main Street.

It's right in front of Town Hall, which is just up the street from The Axe & Barrel pub. After the week I've had, I'm more than ready for a cold beer and some hot wings, so having a guaranteed place to park my truck will come in handy.

Except that when I pull up, someone else's car is in my spot.

The Buick's brake lights are on, so I circle the block, expecting the driver to leave. When the car is still there after my third time around, I find a spot in the public lot two streets over and walk back toward the pub. The Buick's engine is off now, but the driver is still in the car.

As I get closer, I see a woman in a baseball cap at the wheel. Curious, I stand on the sidewalk for a moment, waiting to see if she'll get out of the car, but she just sits there, gripping the steering wheel with both hands and talking to herself. In fact, she appears so distressed that I wonder if she's okay.

I walk over to the driver's side and knock on the window. "Excuse me, ma'am. Do you need help?"

The woman jumps, emitting a little shriek I hear through the glass. When she looks at me, I realize who it is.

"Mila?"

Her eyes close, and all the life seems to go out of her body. She tips her head back and moans something that might be "Why me?"

I open the driver's side door, but for a moment she stays right where she is—hands on the wheel, face toward the sky, eyes closed—as if she's hoping I might just go away. But eventually, she swings her feet to the ground and stands up.

"Hi," I say, shutting the door behind her.

"Hi." Her gaze meets mine for a fraction of a moment before flitting away, hummingbird-quick.

"It's been a while."

"I know." She peeks at me for the space of two whole breaths. *Progress.* "That was kind of on purpose."

I smile. "What are you doing out here?"

"Having a meltdown."

"Why?"

"Because I'm a terrible person."

"Well, I'd argue with you, but you parked in the mayor's personal parking spot, and that *is* pretty terrible." I point at the sign that reads RESERVED FOR MAYOR.

She looks at it and sighs, closing her eyes. She's making it hard to decide if they're as blue as I remember. "Figures. I should have known this spot was too good to be true."

Even in the dark, her skin is luminous. She's still got freckles smattered across her nose and cheeks, and I'm ridiculously glad to see them. "It *is* a pretty good spot."

"You know what?" Her eyes open, and she stands up taller. "I really need a drink, so I'm parking right here while I go get one. If the mayor wants to have me arrested, he can find me at The Axe & Barrel and take me out in handcuffs. I'll chance it." She moves past me and marches toward the pub.

"Well, I'm not going to have you arrested," I call after her, "but that bit about the handcuffs sounds interesting."

She stops moving. After a beat, she turns around. "*You're* the mayor?"

Stepping onto the sidewalk, I doff my cap and replace it. "At your service."

"Since when?"

"Since I was duly elected by the citizens of Hart's Landing last November."

"My mother never mentioned it." She frowns, looking at her feet. "Then again, my mother's favorite person to talk about is herself, so maybe it's not all that surprising."

"Do you want to see my credentials?"

"No. I believe you." She starts toward the car. "I'll move it."

"No, wait." I stop her with a brief touch on her arm. "I was actually hoping to run into you. I heard you were home."

"Home is Brooklyn. You couldn't *pay me* to move back to Hart's Landing."

I put a hand on my chest. "As mayor, I'm deeply offended. First you steal my parking spot. Then you insult my town."

Her eyes widen. "That came out wrong. I didn't mean—"

"There's only one way to fix this. You have to let me buy you that drink."

She looks at me like I've lost my mind. "Why do you want to buy me a drink?"

"Because I'm a nice guy. And because I haven't seen you in ten years, and I've always wondered."

"Wondered what?"

"Just...wondered."

She knots her hands together at her waist, fiddling with her keys. "You don't think it's weird?"

"What's weird about it?"

"That you'll be seen having a drink with the girl everyone thinks burned your family's bakery to the ground?"

"No one thinks that."

She gives me a dubious look. "I beg to differ."

"Well, *I* don't think that. And if I recall, the last time I saw you, we were right in the middle of a conversation when we got interrupted."

"A conversation?" She blinks.

"Yes. So come on." I take her by the shoulders, turn her a

hundred eighty degrees, and nudge her gently in the direction of the pub. "I'll ignore my friends, and we can grab a beer and hide out on the back patio. We don't have to talk about the fire at all. You can catch me up on the last ten years—college, your job, all the hearts you've broken."

She shakes her head. "I have not broken any hearts."

"I find that hard to believe." When we reach the door, I pull it open for her. "By the way, are those handcuffs still an option?"

She wants to laugh, I can tell. But she gives me a firm "No."

"Can't blame a guy for trying." I follow her into the bar, surprised by how fast my heart is beating.

Laughter, deep voices, and rock music bounce off the brick walls and cement floor of the pub as we make our way toward the copper-topped bar. A vintage B-movie—Ripley loves them—is being soundlessly projected onto one wall, and an old jukebox stands in one corner. Every few feet, someone recognizes me and wants to say hello, shake my hand, inquire about the upcoming Founder's Day Festival, or ask me if there's anything I can do about their parking tickets.

Usually, I stop and chat with people, but I try not to make eye contact tonight. I'm aware of the stares, though. I'm not sure if it's because they're curious to know the identity of the woman with the famously single mayor, or if Mila was right—they know who she is and they're shocked.

She walks ahead of me, the taut lines of her neck and shoulders radiating tension. Anxiety pours off her so thickly that I'm like a rowboat trying to cut through the wake of a battleship. When we reach the bar, I touch her shoulder and lean close enough for her to hear me over the Red Hot Chili Peppers song blaring from the speakers. "What would you like to drink?"

She turns her head, the bill of her cap bumping my chin. Whatever perfume she's wearing smells like orange blossom. "Vodka and soda with a lime?"

"You got it." I make eye contact with Ripley Wilder, the owner of The Axe & Barrel and one of my closest friends. Ripley is tall and broad, his jaw thick with dark brown facial hair and his arms heavily inked. He played college football until an injury took him off the field, but he still looks like he'd have no problem tackling anyone who gave him a problem.

"Mr. Mayor," he greets me, leaning on the bar with the heels of both hands. "What can I do for you?"

"I'll take an old-fashioned and a vodka soda with lime." I pull out my wallet and hand him my credit card. "You can start a tab for me."

"Sounds good." His eyes linger on Mila for a second before recognition dawns on his face. "Mila! I heard you were back."

She shakes her head in disbelief. "How does everyone know I'm back? It's been *one day*."

He shrugs. "I saw it on The Landing Pad."

"You two know each other?" I ask.

"Sure." Ripley nods. "We graduated high school together. You were good friends with Yasmine Khoury, right?"

"Yes."

Ripley grins as he muddles a sugar cube in the bottom of a glass. "She's already been over here twice tonight telling me to turn down the music. Apparently, she's having a poetry reading next door."

"Did you turn it down?" I ask.

"No!" He laughs. "Who has a fucking poetry reading on a Friday night? She knows how loud it gets over here on weekends. She might be running a library over there, but I'm running a bar over here, and bars are noisy. It means people are having fun."

I shake my head. Ripley is always torturing poor Yasmine. I don't know how she puts up with it. "Doc and Hunter around here somewhere?"

"Yeah. Back by the lanes, I think." He sticks a lime and a straw in Mila's drink and hands it to her. "Here you go. You guys gonna put your names in to throw?"

"Not tonight," I say. "I think we're just gonna sit out back for a while."

Ripley nods. "Beer garden is open. Good seeing you, Mila."

"You too."

"Go straight out the back door," I tell her. "Past the neon sign that says Kick Some Axe. I'm right behind you."

We snake through the crowd, dodging servers carrying trays of drinks and appetizers, and head down the center of the throwing lanes. When she looks back at me, as if to make sure I'm still there, I put a hand on her shoulder blade to reassure her. It might be wishful thinking, but the tension in her muscles seems to melt a little under my hand. I hear my name a few times and call a hello, but I don't stop moving.

As we pass the lane where my friends are hanging out, I catch Hunter's attention. His eyes widen at the sight of me following a woman so closely, my hand on her back. He elbows Doc like a middle schooler and nods in my direction, and Doc's hand pauses with his beer halfway to his mouth.

True to my word, I ignore them and keep walking until we're outside on the patio. Gravel crunches under my boots as I head for a table fashioned from an old apple barrel. String lights and greenery twine around the rafters over our heads, and the music is much fainter. "This okay?"

"Yes." She sits down on a wooden folding chair, relief easing her hunched shoulders. "This is perfect. Thank you." She ditches the baseball hat and sets it on the table, dragging the elastic from her ponytail. After tugging it onto her wrist, she gathers her hair over one shoulder.

I take the opposite chair and watch as she sips her cocktail. She has a heart-shaped face and a wide, full-lipped mouth. One of her legs is crossed over the other, and her ankle wriggles restlessly.

I glance pointedly at it. "Nervous?"

"Kind of." Two lines appear between her eyebrows, which are a shade darker than her hair. "I mean, the last time I saw you, we were running out of a burning building."

"We survived."

"The bakery didn't."

I shrug. "It was rebuilt."

"But your family sold it."

"Yes."

She takes a breath. "I'm sorry. I'm really, really—"

"Hey." I meet her eyes. "It wasn't your fault."

She takes another sip. That ankle won't stop jittering.

"Let's talk about something else," I say. "What brings you to Hart's Landing, home of the Mighty Muskrats?"

"My mom. I'm in town for six weeks to take care of her while she recovers from a double hip replacement. The surgery is Monday."

"Wow, taking care of someone for six weeks. Doesn't sound like something a terrible person would do."

"Maybe not, but I said something shitty to her before leaving the house tonight."

"Told her to fuck off? She's dead to you?"

A flicker of a smile graces her lips. "It wasn't anything like that. I was just sort of rude. But she makes me feel guilty about doing *anything* for myself, and she twists things around so that I end up apologizing. Then she'll be like, 'I don't know why you have to make things so difficult.'"

I nod, swirling the ice around in my glass. "Mothers are good at pushing buttons."

"Tell me about it. She's always critical of me, but today was ten out of ten unbearable."

Curious, I tip my chair back onto its rear legs. "Critical about what?"

"You name it—my clothes, my cooking, my cat, my wedding."

The front legs of my chair hit the gravel. "You're *married*?"

"Not anymore." She sucks up more of her drink. "I was, for about a year."

"I'm sorry it didn't work out," I lie.

"Don't be. I'm better off without him."

I tip up my glass. "So, Brooklyn, huh? What do you do?"

"I'm a freelance botanical illustrator. Or as my mother likes to say, I doodle flowers." She laughs after she says it, but I can tell the insult bothers her.

"I'm sure there's a lot more to it than that. Show me something you drew."

"Right now?"

"Yes. I want to see what you do."

After another slow sip of her vodka soda, she sets the glass down and picks up her phone. "I have some things on my Instagram." She swipes and taps at the screen, then hands it to me. "Here."

"Wait a minute." I look up at her, incredulous. "You drew that?"

Color creeps into her cheeks. "Yes."

"Holy shit." I look again at the detailed rendering of two apples hanging on a tiny cut branch. It's as real and textured as a photograph, but as beautiful as a painting. You can see delicate veins on the leaves, the reflection of light on the fruit's pink-and-green skin, the rough surface of the branch. At the bottom is an apple sliced in half horizontally, showing the star at the center, seeds spilling out. Gazing at this illustration, I can practically taste the fruit on my tongue. "Unreal. Can I see more?"

She shrugs, but her expression tells me she's pleased. "Sure."

I scroll through more drawings—a watermelon radish, a pair of daffodils, a few vanilla pods, a bright hibiscus blossom. Each one is exquisitely detailed and unbelievably lifelike. "Jesus, Mila, these are amazing. Like, fuck Van Gogh, that guy's a hack. You're the real deal."

She laughs. "Thank you."

A different sort of post catches my eye, a photo of her in a long black dress holding up some kind of certificate. "What's this?"

"It's an award I won last year for excellence in botanical design from the American Botanical Art Society."

"Congratulations."

"Thank you." Another self-conscious chuckle. "No one has ever heard of those awards, but it was a big deal for me."

Hungry to know more about her, I ask, "How'd you get into this field?"

"As a kid, I liked books illustrated by Beatrix Potter. I used to try to draw like her, but it was really just doodling. I'd cover my notebooks and folders with designs, but I never took it seriously. I was really focused on my dance training back then." She pauses to sip her drink. "My senior year of high school, I had a hole in my schedule, and my counselor suggested an art class. She'd noticed my notebook covers. The art teacher, Mrs. Frye, was really encouraging, and I fell in love with drawing."

"Mrs. Frye is still around," I tell her.

"Is she? Maybe I'll get in touch. I'm an adjunct professor now at a small art school in Brooklyn, and I often think about how she made a difference for me."

"You're dangerously close to unlocking my competency kink, Professor Ferguson."

Her blush practically radiates heat, sending a shock of satisfaction straight to my crotch. Ducking her head to hide a smile, she takes her phone from my hand and sets it down. "Okay, enough about me. Catch me up on you."

"Hmm, let's see. Last time I saw you, I was working on my family's farm, and now I work on my family's farm, but I'm also the mayor, and I have a dog." I grin. "That's about it."

She smiles. "What kind of dog?"

"A yellow lab. His name is Merlin. I got him from the rescue after he failed therapy dog school."

She bursts out laughing. "What?"

"Apparently he was too enthusiastic about comforting people to make the cut. He likes to give full-body hugs that aren't always gentle. But he's friendly. He loves playing with all the kids who visit the farm."

"How's everything at McKean Cherries?"

I lock my hands behind my head. "The usual. We had a late frost this year that made things difficult. And there are always issues with pests, root rot, labor availability, market timing… Are you turned on yet?"

"Didn't you hear my panties hit the floor?" she says, with so much wide-eyed earnestness that my brain momentarily short-circuits.

I clear my throat. "Then there's the pressure from land developers to just take their money and walk away."

"Have you ever been tempted?"

"All the fucking time, believe me. I nearly put a sign out when I got the property tax assessment this spring. But then I stood on the back porch and looked at the land three previous generations of McKeans have given their blood, sweat, and tears for, and thought, *I'll be damned if I'm the McKean to watch it become a fucking golf course.*"

She smiles. "And what made you run for mayor?"

"My friends bet me I wouldn't. I needed the money."

"Are you serious?"

"Yes. A hundred bucks is a hundred bucks." The sound of her laugh warms me right down to my boots. "Plus, I like a challenge."

"And you hate free time?"

"Apparently."

She pokes at the ice in her glass with the straw. "Are you good at being mayor?"

"I'm good at a lot of things, Freckles."

Her eyes meet mine, and a familiar blush creeps into her cheeks.

When I look at her, it's like no time has passed at all.

Chapter Ten

Mila

In what feels like an unfair move by the universe, Everett McKean is even hotter than he was ten years ago.

He's bulkier through the shoulders and chest, and his brown eyes crinkle at the corners when he laughs. His jaw is covered with scruff rather than the smooth skin of a teenager, and his face and neck are burnished from the time he spends working in the sun. He still wears his thick, wavy hair a little long, and I like the way it curls around the edges.

My fingers itch to touch it.

At the bottom of my drink, I find the courage to ask about his sister. "How's Gabi?"

"She's great. She lives in Detroit, but she comes up here quite a bit. Our mom has some health problems, and a lot of that has fallen on Gabi since I'm so busy. Our dad's been gone about three years now."

"I'm sorry."

"Don't be." He frowns. "Sorry, that sounded harsh. My feelings about my father are complicated."

"I get it," I say quietly. My memories of Mr. McKean are hazy. He wasn't around much when I was at the house, but Gabi told us about the drinking. I certainly understand what it's like to have conflicting feelings about a parent. "So, do you live in your old house?"

"No. I live in a cabin at the back of the property, a safe distance away from my meddling mother."

"Smart."

"I'm sure Gabi would love to hear from you," he says.

I set my empty glass down. "I don't know about that."

"Why not? You guys were so close—that whole group of girls

was always running around the farm, getting in my way."

The memory brings a sad smile to my lips. "Yeah. We were close."

"So reach out."

"It's been so long," I say hesitantly.

"So what? There's no statute of limitations on reconnecting with old friends, is there?"

"I guess not. But..."

"But what?"

I search for an excuse. "I don't even have her number anymore."

"Give me your phone."

I unlock the screen and hand it to him. "Are you putting her number in there? Don't you want to ask her first if it's okay?"

"I'm putting *my* number in here," he says. "Text me if you want Gabi's contact info. Or if you have any questions about the date."

"What date?"

"The date we're going on tomorrow night." He places the phone on the table between us again.

I glance at it, then at him. "We're going on a date tomorrow night?"

"Shit. Did I forget to ask you? Sorry. According to the town biddies, I'm a little rough around the edges." He shrugs. "Anyway, I'll pick you up at seven."

"You still haven't asked me," I point out with a laugh.

"Is that really necessary? I mean, I've saved your life twice now. Remember? The tree and then the fire?"

My laughter turns into a groan. "I remember."

"So I feel like one date is the least you can do to repay me."

From across the table, I take in the lopsided grin, the cocky set of his shoulders, and I know I don't have it in me to resist.

"Okay." I hold up a finger. "One dinner. But it's not a date."

"Why not?"

"I'm not dating right now."

"Fine, we'll just call it dinner." He leans back in his chair again, a twinkle in his eye. "I don't know why you have to make things so difficult."

Everett insists on walking me to my car, even though I tell him he doesn't have to.

"Listen, I have a reputation as a gentleman around here," he says as we stroll down the sidewalk, a little slower than when we walked the other way. "I can't have you ruining that for me."

"I wouldn't dream of it."

We reach my mother's car, and I take my keys out of my pocket. "Thanks for the drink. I had fun catching up."

"Me too." He tucks his hands in the pockets of his jeans. "I hope you're feeling better than you were earlier."

"I am." The eye contact is doing swirly things to my insides, so I look down at our feet. His leather boots are dark-brown and well-worn, creased with age and hard work. They shouldn't turn me on, but they do.

"What are you doing the rest of the weekend?"

"Helping my mom prepare for Monday. Mostly moving furniture around and trying to convince her to let me install the bathroom grab bar and the other safety equipment the doctors recommended—not that I'm very handy."

"Do you need help? I can come a little early tomorrow and lend you some muscle." He flexes one bicep. "Look, I have plenty."

My insides swoosh at the sight of his bulging arm. "That's nice of you, but I'm sure you're busy solving more important problems. Root rot and all."

"I don't mind. And that way, when I ask you for help with the Founder's Day celebration, you have to say yes."

I laugh. "What kind of help?"

"Well, the thing I *really* don't want to do is judge the Best Pie Contest."

I'm shaking my head before he even finishes the sentence. "No way. That competition is cutthroat, and those bakers are ruthless. I already have a bad reputation in this town. I don't want to make it worse."

"Hmm, true." He rubs a hand over his jaw. "What about something that shows off your artistic talent?"

"Like a poster or something?" I offer, wondering what that scruff would feel like against my face.

"Yes!" He snaps his fingers. "That's perfect. The person in charge of promotional materials is a nice lady, but she's not exactly a creative genius. She reuses the same flyer year after year, and I'm pretty sure it was created some time in the last century. It has this tragic font."

"Oh, dear. Comic sans?"

"Worse. Papyrus."

I hold out a hand. "Stop. Can you get me all the information that needs to go on it?"

"Yes." His brow creases, and he touches my shoulder. "But I just added something to your plate, and it's pretty full already."

At the moment, I'm not worried about my plate. I'm worried about the way my heart is racing. The way my palms are sweating. The way Everett McKean has things flowing in me that have been frozen solid for a year.

But being able to do something for him will feel really good. Nothing will ever make up for what happened, but even a small gesture might ease some of the guilt I've carried for ten years. "What you're talking about really won't take me long, and I already have an idea," I tell him. "Just give me a few days."

"Perfect. It's good to see you, Mila." Damn, that grin hits hard. "I'm glad you're back."

"I'm not back." I get behind the wheel and smile up at him, because it's impossible not to. "But it's good to see you too."

My mother has gone to bed by the time I get home. I try to be as quiet as possible as I wash my face and brush my teeth, but the moment I snap off the bathroom light and open the door, she calls out from her bedroom.

"Mila? Is that you?"

"Yes. I'm sorry if I woke you."

"Where were you?"

I hesitate, reluctant to tell her anything about my night, because I enjoyed myself and she'll find a way to chisel away at it. "The Axe & Barrel."

"*Alone*?"

"I ran into people I knew."

"Like who?"

"Everett McKean. Gabi's older brother."

"He's the mayor now, you know."

"I heard. I accidentally parked in his spot." I figure I might as well cough up the rest. "We're having dinner tomorrow night. And he might come over a little early to help me with a few things."

"He's coming *here*?"

"Yes. Is that okay?"

"Of course, darling. What time is he coming?" The excitement in her voice sets off alarm bells in my head. When I was younger, she often put on a sort of show when I had friends over. The kind of performance that made my friends think she was the coolest, prettiest, nicest mom around. The kind that made me feel like my perception of her must be warped.

"I'm not sure."

"Just make sure the rugs are back in place, please. And put the furniture back where it was. We'll also need to go to the store to make sure we have refreshments to offer."

"Mom, none of that is necessary."

"Of course it is. You want to make a good impression, don't you? Tomorrow, we can talk about what you'll wear."

I clench my teeth. "Good night, Mom."

"Good night, darling."

Upstairs, I strip off my clothes and put on my pajamas. After slipping between the sheets, I reach for my phone.

I gasp. Novel Vine has followed me back and hearted a bunch of my posts. Not only that, but I have a message from the account.

> Mila!!! Hearing from you made my day! How are you? There's a rumor going around that you're in town. I moved back to HL to open Novel Vine last year and I would love to see you.
>
> Also, your ART! It's incredible!

Relief overwhelms me, and my eyes fill with tears. She's not angry, even though she has every right to be. I was the one who cut her off—cut them all off. I was the one who tried to bury the guilt by shutting out my friends. Who let shame convince me that I didn't deserve kindness.

Everett's words come back to me. *There's no statute of limitations on reconnecting with old friends, is there?*

I decide he's right, and I message her back.

> OMG Yasmine, I'm so happy you reached out to me. I'm in HL now, and I walked by Novel Vine yesterday. Saw you through the window. I wanted to go in so badly, but I was too scared. I feel so bad that we lost touch. Can you ever forgive me? I'm here until mid-October taking care of my mom. I would love to get together.

I plug my phone into the charger and switch off my lamp, hopeful that I'll hear from her tomorrow.

Maybe not everything burned That Night, and something can be salvaged from the ashes.

The next morning, I wake up early—it's barely seven. I check my phone and find a new message from Yasmine.

> I can't believe you're here! I wish you would have come into the bar!! I would have given you the biggest hug. Of course I forgive you. Looking back, I can understand how it happened... That last year was just so hard on all of us. And everything that happened

That Night... It felt like the friendship apocalypse.

Anyway, let's get together as soon as you can! I'm working all weekend, but you're welcome to come into the bar any time!

PS. My dad still owns the Gazette, and I'm temporarily moderating the online forum while the regular mod is on maternity leave. I just saw the thing about you and Everett McKean on The Landing Pad. How unbelievable is it that he's the mayor now???

The thing about me and Everett on The Landing Pad?

I shoot Yasmine a quick note saying that I'm pretty busy with my mom this weekend since her surgery is Monday, but I'll come into the bar as soon as I can. I give her my phone number and tell her to reach out any time.

With a weird sense of impending doom, I create an account on the *Hart's Landing Gazette* site. Scared to reveal my actual name, I use Beatrix_Potter323 as my profile.

After I opt-in to receive updates via email—so at least I'll have some warning next time I'm a blind item—the page loads. A deceptively friendly banner welcomes me to The Landing Pad. Below that, the first item is decidedly less friendly.

Community question (submitted by TeaLover55): Spotted the mayor with Mila Ferguson last night at The Axe & Barrel. Weird that he'd cozy up to the person who burned down his family's bakery, isn't it?

Community question (submitted by ANONYMOUS AXE GOD): Nothing weird about two people enjoying a drink at the best pub in town.

GazetteMod: Please ensure Community questions represent legitimate inquiries. Thank you!

Community question (submitted by ANONYMOUS AXE GOD): Nothing weird about two people enjoying a drink at the best pub in town, amirite? Take that, @GazetteMod.

GazetteMod: Violations of our community guidelines may result in restricted access to The Landing Pad. To review our guidelines, click here.

In the photo accompanying the question at the top of the thread, Everett is relaxed and grinning, leaning back in his chair with his hands behind his head. I'm pitched slightly forward, smiling at something he said, my hair gathered over one shoulder. It's amazing to me that we didn't notice someone taking it, but then again, we were pretty consumed by each other, as the picture shows.

It has dozens of likes.

I groan softly, then spend a few minutes poking around The Landing Pad, marveling at all the gossipmongering, rumor-spreading, finger-wagging, and general nosiness disguised as legitimate community concern. Mayoral matchmaking seems to be the town's favorite sport, while there's apparently a thriving interest in true crime courtesy of the Diner Detectives, who want to look into the fire at Tart and Soul.

That's the last thing I need.

Too restless to go back to sleep, I get dressed, throw a sketchbook and pencil case into my backpack, and slip out of the house without waking my mother. The morning air has a chill that hints at the coming autumn, but the sun is out, and the sky is a glorious shade of blue. By the time I walk the half mile between my mother's house and the White Pine River, I'm sweating. I stop for a moment to tie my hoodie around my waist and then turn right, following the path along the water's edge toward the wrought-iron bridge.

The wishing bridge.

Lore aside, the structure is beautiful and iconic and enduring, a historic symbol of the town. I want to incorporate it into the poster

I'm designing for the Founder's Day celebration.

Leaving the paved path, I carefully make my way down the grassy embankment and choose a spot with a good view. After spreading my hoodie on the damp ground, I drop onto my butt, pull my sketchbook and pencil case from my backpack, and get to work. As the sun climbs higher, I do my best to capture the bridge's elaborate Victorian scrollwork, the graceful arch of its main truss, the aged-green patina of the metal, the sand-colored stone blocks anchoring each end of the bridge to the riverbank. The minutes fly by—there's nothing I like more than drawing outside. All my senses come alive.

When I'm done, I tuck my pad and pencils back into my bag and sit cross-legged for a moment, watching the water flow west toward the lake. I imagine all the stones that have been tossed over the side of the bridge and now lie at the river bottom, the names written so hopefully washed away by time. Somewhere down there is a stone with Everett's name in my careful printing. Despite the warmth, the thought gives me a shiver.

Squinting into the sun, I can practically see the girl I was standing up there in the afternoon light, the stone tucked tightly into her fist. Hope tucked tightly into her heart.

My cell phone buzzes from inside my bag, pulling me from the memory.

"Hello?"

"Where are you? I was calling and calling up the stairs for you."

"Mom!" I jump to my feet. "Are you okay?"

"I'm fine, but what if I wasn't?"

I close my eyes and take a breath. "Sorry. I walked down to the river at seven this morning to get a little exercise."

"It doesn't take two hours to walk to the river."

"I've been drawing. I'll head home now."

"Good. I need you to take me into town. I made a last-minute appointment at the salon. I could drive myself, but I'm worried I won't find a close enough parking spot."

"That's no problem. I'll drop you off."

After hanging up, I retie my sweatshirt around my waist, sling my backpack over my shoulders, and climb up the embankment. When I reach the path, I decide to send Everett a text telling him not to come early tonight. Something about the way my mother is acting—last night's excitement, this morning's salon appointment—has me on edge.

But I can't find his number in my phone.

"That's weird," I mutter. He said last night he added himself, but he isn't under Everett or McKean. Maybe it didn't save?

I scroll through all my contacts from A to Z, and when I get to H, I find him.

Chuckling, I tap out a message.

Mila: *Hot Mayor?*

To my surprise, he answers right away.

Hot Mayor: *Did it make you laugh?*

Mila: *At most a sensible chuckle, but yes.*

Hot Mayor: *Good.*

Hot Mayor: *Sorry about the thing on The Landing Pad.*

Mila: *I TOLD you people still think I caused that fire.*

Hot Mayor: *Now they all think it was our insane chemistry.*

I can't help smiling a little.

Mila: *Just wanted to let you know you don't have to come early tonight. Seven is good.*

Hot Mayor: *Okay. See you tonight, Freckles.*

I change his name to Everett McKean in my phone before hurrying home.

My pulse races the whole way.

Chapter Eleven

🪓 AXE GODS 🪓

Hunter Gannon: *Nice picture.*

Ben Hart: *I particularly like the pose with the arms up.*

Ripley Wilder: *It's giving deodorant ad.*

Hunter Gannon: *Speed Stick.*

Ben Hart: *Old Spice.*

Ripley Wilder: *If anyone knows about old spice, it's Doc.*

Ben Hart: *Asshole. I can't wait for one of you fuckers to hit 40.*

Ripley Wilder: *I'm just glad they didn't burn down the pub.*

Ben Hart: *Everett has obviously lost his touch.*

The Fucking Mayor: 🖕

Chapter Twelve

Everett

Around nine Saturday morning, I put Merlin on the leash and walk over to my mom's to beg for breakfast. The smell of bacon and eggs makes my mouth water as I enter the kitchen, where Mom is at the stove.

"Morning," I say. As soon as he's off the leash, Merlin hurries to my mother's side, hoping for handouts.

"Morning." My mom clacks her spatula twice on the rim of an ancient frying pan and sets it on the spoon rest before giving Merlin a piece of bacon. "I saw the photo."

"What photo?" I grab a mug from the cupboard and pour myself a cup of coffee from the pot.

"Everett McKean, don't play dumb with me."

Turning around, I lean back against the counter and sip my coffee. Remain silent.

She faces me, fists parked on her hips. "Well? What does it mean?"

"It means I ran into someone I used to know. We sat down and had a drink." My tone gives nothing away.

"Looked pretty friendly."

"I'm a friendly guy, what can I say?" Setting my coffee cup on the large wooden table, I take a plate from the cupboard and mosey over to the stove. "Any of this up for grabs?"

"Eat what you want. It's not like I have grandkids to cook for."

"But you have a grand-dog." I fill my plate and set it on the table. Then I grab a banana from the bowl of fruit on the counter. "Can Merlin have this?"

"Sure."

After peeling it, I break it into thirds and put them in the food bowl my mom keeps for Merlin near the back door. "Here, boy."

"You want some toast?" my mom asks.

"Yes, please." I watch with dismay as she limps to the toaster. "How are you feeling today?"

"Meh."

"Did you take your meds this morning?"

"I took some ibuprofen." She sticks two slices of bread in the toaster and pushes down the lever. "So what's Mila been doing with herself?"

"She's a botanical illustrator and college professor. Lives in Brooklyn." I pull a fork from a drawer that doesn't shut right and sit down at the table.

"Botanical…like plants?"

"Yes. You should see her drawings. They're incredible."

"How'd you see her drawings?" My mom is immediately suspicious.

"She showed me her Instagram account." I debate mentioning our dinner tonight and decide against it. Mom isn't as bad as some of the aspiring matchmakers in this town, but she isn't shy about letting me know she wants me to settle down and start a family. I could see her making more of it than the situation warrants.

"She still has that gorgeous red hair, huh?"

I picture that hair spilling over her shoulder last night and remember the way she smelled like orange blossoms.

"Yep." Realizing I'm staring into space, I refocus on my breakfast. Start chewing again.

"Well, if you see her again, tell her I said hello." The toast pops up. A moment later, my mother brings a cup of coffee and the toast to the table, taking the seat across from me. "What are you up to today?"

"Irrigation maintenance and then a meeting with the fertilizer guy. What about you?"

"I'll be at the store. I'm doing a soapmaking class this afternoon."

I nod. Summer is our busy season, but weekends in autumn still bring lots of tourists and local families. We have wagon rides, cider tastings, apple picking, preserve- and jam-making classes. My mother demonstrates how to make soaps and other skincare products from our goats' milk, and my cousin teaches goat yoga, which is the weirdest fucking thing I've ever heard of, but it brings people in.

"Going out tonight?" my mother inquires as I carry my dishes to the sink.

"Maybe."

"Don't tell me—you're going to the pub with the guys." Her aggravated tone tells me how she feels about my typical Saturday night. "How are you going to give me those grandchildren if you spend all your spare time throwing axes with Hunter and Doc?"

"Good question. Thanks for the grub." I grab the leash and whistle softly. "Come on, Merlin. Let's go."

Chapter Thirteen

Mila

My mother is in a suspiciously good mood when I pick her up from the salon. We eat lunch at a new farm-to-table vegan cafe called Heirloom Root, where the owner hugs my mom and tells me how loyal she is. "She got so many people to come in here and try us," the woman says.

Mom shrugs, but her smile tells me she's pleased. "It's so delicious, and it's healthy. Everyone *should* eat here."

As always, I'm amazed at the gap between my mother's public and private personalities.

After lunch, we go to the grocery store, where she hums along to the music as she fills the cart with cheese and crackers, dried fruit, and wine. In the frozen food aisle, I'm reaching for a carton of ice cream when I hear my mom greet someone.

"Catriona, hello! It's been ages!"

Catriona? As in Catriona Hart?

I turn around and see my mom air-kissing Rachel's mother on each cheek. The freezer door thumps shut behind me.

"Hello, Eliza. You look well."

"Thank you." My mother glances at me. "Mila is home for a couple months to help me recover from hip replacement surgery."

Catriona looks at me and smiles politely. "How nice."

She looks the same. Dark hair coiled into a bun. Tawny golden skin. Matching Chanel handbag and flats. I don't know whether it was her regal bearing or her strict parenting, but I was always intimidated by her. "Hello," I say, adjusting my hoodie to cover a spot of mustard I got on my shirt at lunch.

"Are you heading back to Florida soon?" my mother asks.

"Yes," Catriona says. "Monday."

"The day of my surgery. I'd much rather be going to Florida!" My mother's laugh tinkles like a bell—like her upcoming surgery hasn't filled her with even more spit and vinegar than usual. Catriona places a sympathetic hand on her arm.

"Poor dear. Thank you again for the free dance classes you provided in the Hart pediatric wing," says Catriona. "The children just loved them."

"Anytime. Once I'm all healed up, I'd be glad to do it again."

Catriona checks her wristwatch. "Well, I'd better get going. Good luck on Monday, Eliza." A short glance at me. "Nice seeing you, Mila."

"You too." I fidget with the zipper on my hoodie. I'm still a little afraid of her, but I can't resist asking about my old friend. "How's Rachel?"

Already walking away from me, Catriona speaks over her shoulder. "She's well. Living down in Florida and working for the company."

"Please say hello for me."

If she replies, I can't hear it.

"I haven't seen Catriona Hart in a long time," my mother says on the ride home.

"Me neither. Is she living in Florida now?"

"Mostly, yes. I think she comes up here for a month or so during the summer. She's never been a particularly outgoing person, but I think she became even more withdrawn after her husband died."

I nod. Mr. Hart had a massive coronary when we were in middle school. Rachel had been devastated.

"Of course, you can't blame her for being embarrassed," my mother remarks.

"About what?"

"You were probably too young at the time to pick up on the gossip, but he had the heart attack in bed...with another woman."

I gasp, realizing a moment too late that this is precisely the reaction my mother was trying to elicit. “He did?”

“Oh, Philip Hart was a ladies’ man, and everyone knew it. But no one talked about it because he was such a pillar of the community.” My mother sounds slightly gleeful that that particular pillar was knocked down.

“I never heard any of that. I wonder if Rachel knew.”

“I’m sure her mother tried to protect her. If there’s anything the Hart family is good at, it’s burying things they don’t want coming to light.”

When we get home, my mother asks me again to move the furniture in the living room back to where it was. “Just for this evening,” she pleads. “So it looks nice for your guest.”

I don’t feel like arguing, so I drag everything back into place, arranging it the way she wants. Afterward, I retreat to my little art studio and spend a couple of happy hours in my creative zone.

Until my mother opens the door, knocking after the fact. “Can I come in?”

“Sure.”

“What are you working on?”

I show her preliminary sketches I’ve made for Ivy & Stone.

“Mmm,” she says. “What’s this for again?”

I try not to be hurt that she doesn’t remember. “Their fall collection next year. The designs will be on wallpaper, bedding, and bath wares for sure, and maybe tabletop or kitchen, too.”

“Seems like things are going well for you.”

“Yes. This collaboration is a huge deal.”

She places the drawing on the table. “You get this from him.”

“Him?”

“Your father.”

My heartbeat slams on the brakes. "What? What do I get from him?"

"Talent, I suppose. He was an artist, too."

I force myself to speak calmly, as if she hasn't just dropped a bomb in the room. "You never told me that."

"He's not someone I enjoy talking about." With a quick pivot, she gives my clothing a once-over. "Have you decided what you're wearing tonight?"

"Not yet." I'm still trying to wrap my head around what I've just learned about my father. In twenty-eight years, she's only mentioned him a handful of times, never revealing anything more than a stray detail.

He was young.

He had no money.

He spoke two languages.

He was a beautiful liar.

As a kid, I hoarded those morsels like a squirrel hiding acorns for the winter. I formed an image in my head of a dark-haired man in his twenties with an accent, and turned "beautiful liar" into something more palatable, even glamorous—a handsome actor.

I concocted a completely fictional account of their love story.

He was a graduate student working as an usher at the theater where she danced. Every night, he watched her from the back of the house and fell more deeply in love. They had a whirlwind affair and she got pregnant, but his semester ended and he went back to his native country before she could tell him about the baby. But someday, somehow, *he would find me.*

I clung to this delusion well into my teens, until I overheard my mom telling my aunt that he'd abandoned her twelve weeks into her pregnancy. Just up and disappeared one day. Left a note saying it was too much, too soon.

At that point, I stopped fantasizing about him. It's been years since I felt even a glimmer of desire to meet the man who behaved so cruelly.

But it's hard not to be curious.

"So what kind of artist was he?"

"If you didn't pack anything appropriate for dinner out, you can always borrow something of mine."

"Thanks, but I have things I can wear." I try again. "Did he paint? Draw?"

Instead of answering, she turns toward the mirrors, smoothing her blowout and checking her neck for tautness. She leans closer to inspect her forehead. "Catriona's skin is incredible, don't you think? I wonder who she sees. Probably someone I can't afford."

"Did you ever see any of my father's work?" My tone is tight with desperation.

Facing me again, she starts fussing with my curtain bangs. "How will you do your hair tonight?"

"I haven't decided," I reply. My shoulders sag with defeat. If I keep asking questions, she'll only accuse me of trying to upset her. And, all things considered, we're having a good day.

"It's still so nice and thick." She gathers my hair in her hands. "Mine thinned out so much after I had you. It's never grown back the way it was before."

"It looks beautiful, Mom."

"Thank you." She smiles at me. "Have I told you I'm glad you're here?"

Guilt gnaws at my belly. I should be more generous toward her. She did her best as a mom, didn't she? All alone, abandoned by the man who'd gotten her pregnant. The beautiful liar who betrayed her trust. Maybe he took advantage of her. Maybe she loved him truly. Maybe her broken heart has never really healed.

Maybe her unhappiness isn't all my fault.

"I'm glad to be here too," I say, feeling shitty that it's only half true.

She yawns. "You know, I'm feeling a bit fatigued. I might just lie down for a bit and rest my eyes."

"Good idea."

I try to go back to drawing, but I'm too distracted to work.

My father was an artist.

It doesn't change what he did to her, to us, but somehow, it affects me. No, it *explains* something about me. It's like a window has opened up onto my soul, and light is pouring in. I don't have to admire him to appreciate what he gave me. I wish I'd known sooner. Why did she hide it all this time?

She had her reasons, says a voice in my head. *She thought she was protecting you. Maybe she didn't know how much it would matter.*

How could she not know?

My concentration is clearly shot, so I give up working and take a shower. Upstairs in my bedroom, I audition ten different outfits before settling on the long, clingy black dress. I do my makeup and hair just like I used to as a teenager, listening to music and sitting in front of the mirror on the inside of my closet door. At one point, my friends and I wrote all over it with dry-erase markers. I can still see the ghostly lettering of graffiti I didn't wipe off right away.

McKean #15

Rachel + Chad

Yasmine 4 Pres

Ladybug was here

I run my fingers over the glass. Maybe it's this room, maybe it's this town, maybe it's just nostalgia, but I miss my old friends more than I have in years.

I'm spraying on perfume when I hear Everett's knock.

My mother answers the door before I can get to the top of the stairs. "Well, good evening, Mr. Mayor!" she says brightly.

"Hello, Ms. Ferguson. How are you?"

"I'm just fine. And please, call me Eliza. Mila is still getting ready. Would you like to come in and sit down?"

"Sure."

I hurry over to my dresser and choose earrings, a few bracelets, and some rings. I wish I still had my ladybug charm necklace, but I lost it the night of the fire.

A final look in the mirror, just like old times.

My hair is bouncy and shiny. My eyeliner is miraculously even. I smile—no lipstick on my teeth. Turning around, I take a gander at my backside. My butt is the only part of me you'd call curvy, and this dress amplifies the effect. "Not bad," I tell my reflection.

I'm slipping on my denim jacket when Beatrix appears at my feet, and I crouch down to give her a little attention. She meows, and somehow it sounds like a scolding.

"What? It's not a date."

A distinctly judgy feline look.

"We're just friends."

She tilts her head.

"It's *dinner.* I have to eat, don't I?" I tickle her beneath her chin. "At the end of the night, I'll be home to snuggle with you."

But I stop halfway down the stairs and take off my jacket so Everett will get the full effect of the dress. At the bottom, I turn into the living room and smile. "Hey."

The smile fades fast. My mother is sitting on the couch next to Everett, her legs crossed toward his, one hand holding a wineglass, the other on his arm.

He's holding a framed photo in his hands, and he stands up when he sees me. "Hey. You look nice."

"Thanks." He looks nice, too. The jeans he has on hug the thick muscles of his thighs, and the white dress shirt he wears shows off his tan. But I can't shape the thought into a compliment because I'm too distracted by my mother, who has on black pants and a low-cut, silky black blouse. Her hair still looks like she just stepped out of the salon. Her gold kitten heels peek out from beneath her hems, and her signature Cherries in the Snow lipstick is freshly applied.

On the coffee table in front of them is a cheese board she evidently put together while I was upstairs. A bottle of white wine has been opened and three glasses poured.

"Darling, come join us for a glass of Riesling." My mother

gestures to the chair across from the couch.

Join them? Like this is their date and I'm a third wheel?

My legs feel shaky as I cross the room and perch tentatively on the edge of the chair. I meet Everett's eyes. "Do we have time?"

"Our reservation is at eight," he says. He's observing me carefully, trying to read my body language. He knows something is off.

"I was just showing Everett this gorgeous photo of you from the last time you competed at the Youth America Grand Prix." She gestures toward the picture in the frame. "Stunning, isn't she? Just *look* at that extension."

I cringe. The photo in Everett's hands is of me performing the Kitri Variation from *Don Quixote*. I'm balanced on the toe of my right pointe shoe, my left leg extended in a développé à la seconde, my right hand holding a fan. I'm wearing a fussy white-and-gold platter tutu, that stupid tiara, and a ruby-lipped smile that masks the pain in my right ankle.

"Mom, stop." I cross to them, take the frame out of Everett's hands, and set it back on the mantel.

"Sneakers, Mila? Really?" My mother clucks her tongue. "Did you forget to pack nice shoes?"

I look at my feet as my fingers curl into my palms. "I like sneakers. They're comfortable."

"My daughter has a thing about comfort," my mother remarks to Everett with a laugh. "She clearly prefers it to style."

"I like being comfortable too," says Everett, smiling at me.

I could kiss him.

My mom tugs his sleeve so he'll sit down again. "Stay for a minute. Mila's always running off somewhere. She's been here two days already, and I've hardly seen her."

He meets my eyes, asking a silent question. Duty gets the better of me, so I shrug and take my seat on the chair again. He lowers himself to the couch.

My mom smiles, happy she got her way. "How's your mom

doing, Everett? I haven't seen Patricia in ages."

"She's fine. She's got fibromyalgia, which gives her some pain, but she's busy at the farm." He sits stiffly, his back rigid, his hands on his knees.

"The poor dear. Don't get older, you two. Everything starts to go wrong with your body, even when you've spent your entire life taking good care of it." She sips her wine. "Did Mila tell you I'm having surgery?"

"Yes. It's nice that she was able to come home and help out."

"Oh, believe me, I had to practically *drag* her here," my mother says. "She's always so busy with her work or her friends or her activities. She just informed me she took a gourmet cooking class recently."

Everett looks at me. "You cook too?"

I open my mouth to answer, but my mother gets there first.

"She never used to. Now she claims she's able to make some kind of fancy caramelized onion, tomato, and goat cheese tart—doesn't that sound delicious? But I haven't seen any evidence of it yet."

"Because you told me you don't like goat cheese," I remind her.

"I never said that, darling." She sets her wineglass on the table and pops a dried fig into her mouth. "You must have misheard. I'd love to try your gourmet cooking. I think it's wonderful you're learning a useful skill."

Unlike doodling flowers.

I take another swallow of Riesling.

"Speaking of useful skills, Everett, you look like you're good with your hands." She pats his forearm. "Mila and I could use some help with a few things around here. Do you think you might be able to install a grab bar on a shower wall?"

My jaw drops. *Now* she wants the grab bar installed?

"Sure," Everett replies. "I did that for my mom, too."

"What a good son."

My head feels like someone is pummeling it with a hammer.

"That would probably take me about an hour, so I'll have to come back another time. Mila and I have plans tonight."

"On that note, let's get going." I set my wine down and stand up. "I'm really hungry."

"Mila!" my mother chides, as if I've said something to be ashamed of.

Everett rises too. "Why don't I come back tomorrow and get that grab bar in? Would that be okay?"

"Of course, dear."

He takes a step toward me. "Ready to go?"

"Yes." I make a beeline for the front door, grabbing my purse from a hook at the bottom of the stairs. "Good night, Mom."

Everett follows me out, pulling the door shut behind him. I walk on numb legs down the front walk toward his truck, which is parked at the curb. He opens the passenger door for me before going around to the driver's side.

After sliding behind the wheel, he looks over at me. "You okay?"

"Yes." I stare out the windshield, my hands clenched in tight balls on my thighs. The truck's cab is dusky and warm. I breathe in and hold it—the air smells like leather and coffee and whatever cologne Everett is wearing. It's woodsy and masculine, and it loosens some of the tension in my muscles.

Everett rubs the back of his neck. "The vibe in there was weird."

"I'm sorry."

"It wasn't your fault. She's kind of intense."

"That's one word for her."

"I thought you said she didn't want the grab bar."

"She didn't. She doesn't. I think she just wants the attention from you." I exhale. "But she *is* going to need it, and I'd be grateful for your help."

"Then I'll do it."

"Thanks." My throat tightens, and I swallow hard. "You know what sucks? Today was kind of a nice day with her. We had lunch together, we ran some errands, she even asked to see some of my drawings. When I showed her, she said she liked them."

I shake my head, still in disbelief. "And then she told me my father was an artist."

"You never knew that?"

"No! She never says anything about him! Not that I blame her—he abandoned her when she was pregnant with me. Rationally, I know he was not a good guy. I don't want to *find* him or anything. But it feels like she withheld a monumental piece of information from me."

He covers my nearest balled-up fist with his hand. The tightness in my chest loosens just a little, and I consciously relax my fingers under his palm.

"I don't even know his name. I've never felt any kind of connection to him—but one existed. And she *knew* about it." The injustice of it feels like sandpaper on a wound. "It makes me so mad."

Everett's thumb moves slowly over my knuckles. "I would be mad too."

When I look over at him, his dark eyes hold no judgment. "Are you sorry you asked me to dinner?"

"I didn't ask."

Laughter cuts through my murky mood. "That's right. You didn't. But you also didn't ask to hear about my drama. Why do I keep embarrassing myself in front of you? It's like a curse."

"I don't know. But as long as you're not going to set my truck on fire, I'm cool with it."

"Make another joke like that, and I might."

He grins and switches the engine on. "Come on, Freckles. Let's go eat."

Chapter Fourteen

Everett

"Wow, this is beautiful," Mila says after we've been seated at an intimate table for two in an elegant, high-ceilinged dining room.

I called in a favor and got us a reservation at Wardwell House, one of the big, old Victorians along Cottage Row, where millionaire lumber barons, railroad tycoons, and business magnates from Chicago and Detroit built summer homes over a century ago. Most of them have been converted to bed-and-breakfasts by now, and a few, like Wardwell House, have excellent farm-to-table restaurants. There's always a waitlist on weekends, but I know the chef pretty well since he buys fruit from us.

"Am I dressed okay?" Mila glances at her sneakers.

"Better than okay," I assure her. "You look perfect."

After listening to the server go over the specials, we order drinks and peruse the menu. At least, I *try* to look at the menu. But my eyes keep drifting to Mila across the table. Nothing on this menu could possibly taste as good as she looks.

Odds are she'd taste better than anything on this menu, too.

Her chin has a little dimple in it—I never noticed that before—and her hair cascades down her back in loose, shimmery waves. That notch at the base of her throat? It's killing me. I bet if I put my nose right there, I'd smell orange blossom, which is now the sexiest scent in existence. My gaze travels over the curve of her shoulder and skims across the tops of her breasts, barely visible above the scooped neckline of her dress.

Jesus.

I drop my eyes to my menu again, trying to redirect my thoughts to a more appropriate track. The last thing I want is for Mila to catch me staring at her chest.

The server returns with our drinks and takes our orders. When we're alone again, I take a sip of my old-fashioned and lean back in my chair. "So you were a dancer."

"I was."

"And obviously a good one."

She shrugs modestly. "Not as good as my mom."

"She was a ballerina too?"

"She was a principal with New York City Ballet before I was born," Mila says with reverence. "She gave it up when she got pregnant with me."

She smiles ruefully. "I remember discovering an article on the internet when I was twelve that lamented how 'her career had been cut tragically short by unfortunate life circumstances.'"

"The writer actually said that?" I frown. "What a dick."

She blinks. "Those were *her* words. A direct quote."

I'm not sure what to say. I try to imagine being a kid and seeing proof that my mom hadn't wanted me. It seems less a matter of *if* that would mess you up, and more a matter of how much.

The server appears with a bread basket, and Mila reaches for a slice of fresh-baked sourdough. I watch her butter one side and take a bite. I want to lick the butter off her lips, which is not an impulse I've ever had at dinner with someone before.

Quit acting like your dog at the table. Be cool.

To distract myself, I pluck a roll from the basket, tear a piece off, and toss it into my mouth. "So tell me about living in New York. What are your favorite places?"

Her face lights up as she talks about the Botanical Gardens, Hallett Nature Sanctuary in Central Park, a museum called The Cloisters in upper Manhattan. "Have you ever been there?"

"I've never been to New York City at all."

"Really?"

"I'm more of a country boy," I say, giving the words some

added drawl.

She laughs. "I can see that. But I still think you'd like New York. We have beautiful green spaces hidden like secrets among the skyscrapers. You should come visit sometime. I can show them to you."

I take a sip of my drink, letting the bitters and smoke roll over my tongue. I think about what it would be like to walk down a crowded Manhattan street with my hand on Mila's low back, keeping her close. What would it be like to take her somewhere no one knows us? Where no one expects her to be the girl who burned down the bakery, or me to be the mayor? Where she might take my hand and show me secret, beautiful places that matter to her? "Maybe I will."

Our salads arrive, and we talk more about Hart's Landing, things that have changed, things that will never change. She laughs when I tell her about the ongoing feud between Yasmine and Ripley.

"He drives her crazy," I say, tipping back the last of my old-fashioned.

"He always has." She gestures to the cherry in my glass. "You gonna eat that?"

I slide the glass toward her. "It's all yours." Watching it disappear between her lips is so hot, my cock jumps.

"Okay. Let's see if I can still do this," she says with what I can only call a mischievous twinkle in her eye. She places the stem in her mouth and sits up straight. Her jaw works as she manipulates the stem with her tongue, and her eyes slide to the side as she concentrates. Finally, she takes the knot from her lips and smiles. "Ta-da!"

I laugh and give her a few slow claps. "Very impressive." And hot as fuck, but I will not tell her that my brain is wondering what other talents her tongue might possess.

Guiltily, she hides the knotted stem under her bread plate. "I probably shouldn't do that in a nice place like this."

"I'm glad you did," I say. "Perfect manners are boring. Want another glass of wine?"

She thinks for a moment and shrugs. "Sure. Why not?"

"So, can I ask you a personal question?" I swirl the remains of my second cocktail around in my glass.

"Uh-oh. Should I be scared?"

"You don't have to answer if you don't want to."

"Okay. Shoot."

"Why aren't you dating right now?"

She pokes at a green bean with her fork. "I need to work on myself before I get back out there again."

"After your divorce, you mean?"

"Yes."

"What happened?" I ask, then immediately worry I've gone too far. "Sorry—you don't have to talk about this if you don't want to."

"It's okay." She sets her fork down and pats her mouth with her napkin. "So, Connor, my ex, is the perfect example of the kind of guy I fall for. Charming, successful, good-looking, but runs hot and cold. He could be incredibly attentive to me one moment, saying and doing all the right things, and completely disconnected the next."

I know the type. My father subjected my mother—and all of us—to his unpredictable moods. For years, every bender or beer-fueled outburst would be followed by flowers and flattery, until he just didn't care anymore. "Go on."

"He worked in finance, which meant a lot of late nights. There were trust issues."

Of course he worked in finance. I picture a suit-and-tie guy with a trust fund and a frat-boy grin. I bet he was a Yankees fan, too. Fucker.

"And I have this...*thing* I do, when it comes to relationships."

She picks up her fork again and rolls the green bean around on her plate. "I like to please people. So when someone I like shows me affection, I become very invested in trying to be exactly what he wants. I prioritize his needs. I diminish my own. I ignore all red flags. Whatever keeps the validation coming."

"You put up with his bullshit because you liked his attention?"

She nods slowly. "*A lot* of bullshit. So much that he felt guilty enough to propose. And I actually thought the rings and vows would mean a higher level of commitment. I convinced myself that marriage would bring emotional security. Things would get better."

"But they didn't."

"Nope. He worked even more than before. When he was home, he was distant. The harder I tried, the more he pulled away." She stabs at the green bean a few times, but not hard enough to pierce the skin. "And then I saw the texts from a female colleague at his firm that were definitely not work-related."

Beneath the table, I crack the knuckles of my left hand. "Did you confront him?"

"No." She stares at her plate.

"Why not?"

"I don't like to pull on loose threads. I'm always afraid everything will unravel."

As she speaks, something happens inside my chest. A sensation of breaking open. All my protective instincts are exposed. "I want to fucking lay this guy out, you know."

A tiny smile. She peeks up at me. "Thanks."

"So how did it finally end?"

"A few weeks after I saw the texts, he said he'd made a mistake and didn't want to be married. That I made him feel trapped, and he couldn't live like that." This time she spears that green bean with enough force to impale it on the tines. "We were three days away from our one-year anniversary."

"And when was that?"

"Six months ago."

"I'm sorry."

She shrugs it off. "We weren't meant to be. He hated my cat."

"You deserve a lot better. You *and* your cat."

"She hissed every time he entered the room."

"I like her already."

Smiling, Mila sets her fork down and lifts her wineglass to her lips. "Anyway, that's pretty much it. Connor said the divorce would be easy—his family lawyers would take care of it. All I had to do was sign some papers saying he didn't owe me anything. Which was fine with me."

Sawing off a piece of my steak, I stick it in my mouth and chew hard, angry with her ex for a thousand different things. Toying with her feelings. Taking her for granted. Cheating on her. Leaving her. Making her feel like any of it was her fault.

A man who mistreats the people who love him always sets me off.

"Want to hear the end of the story?" she asks, sounding surprisingly upbeat.

"Sure."

"As I was packing up to move out of his apartment, he told me in this stupid magnanimous tone that I could keep the ring."

"Did you throw it at him?"

She shakes her head, a gleam in her eyes. "I sold it and donated the money to a cat rescue."

Her resilience makes me smile, but I still hope that someday, somehow, I'll have the opportunity to punch her dipshit ex in the mouth.

"I started on a poster design for you," she says, licking vanilla ice cream with bourbon caramel sauce off her spoon while I try to keep my thoughts clean. "Don't forget to send me the information that should go on it. I'll scan my drawing and get you the digital file for printing."

"Thank you. I can't wait to see it."

"Everett, hello," murmurs a smooth female voice to my right.

I turned my head to find Tiffany and Tad Hart at the side of our table. Tad is a direct descendant of the town's founding family, and Tiffany is his Boston-born, my-family-was-on-the-Mayflower wife. Pushing my chair back, I stand and offer my hand. "Mr. Hart. Mrs. Hart."

Tad shakes my hand heartily. "Mr. Mayor. Good to see you." He's built like a refrigerator and still carries himself like the linebacker he was fifty years ago. He has considerably more paunch these days, but he maintains an air of intimidation—as much to do with his massive wealth as his size. "Where are we on the donation of the old foundry site?"

"Still doing some environmental assessment." The testing is already done, of course, but I don't want to get into the results tonight.

Tiffany Hart clasps my hand with cool, elegant fingers. As slender as her husband is thick, she wears a diamond the size of a doorknob on her left hand and gold bracelets on her right arm. She has to be close to seventy, but her golden-blond hair shows no sign of gray, and the skin on her face and neck is tight. "Is the assessment really necessary?" she asks. "The old office building is so beautiful. It will make a perfect community center. And there's plenty of space for a playground beside it. So many children live in the surrounding neighborhoods."

And those children are going to suffer from the neurological and respiratory effects of heavy metal toxicity, not to mention the increased risk of cancer, if we don't clean up the soil.

But I hold that back for now.

"It is beautiful," I agree, "but first we have to make sure it's safe to repurpose. I'm consulting with an expert."

"What's that involve?" Tad's bushy eyebrows furrow.

"Some soil sampling and groundwater testing. Plans for

remediation depending on the level of contamination."

Tiffany appears perturbed. "But we've scheduled a press release regarding the donation of the building for a community center. I'm already planning the grand opening for spring."

I offer her a polite smile. "We're working as quickly as we can."

"Hart Iron Works has always complied with all environmental regulations," Tad says, his hand slicing through the air horizontally.

"Of course. But regulations change, and the contamination could be from historical practices."

"What happens if they find it?" Tiffany asks.

"I'll tell you what happens—lawsuits," Tad grumbles. "And bad publicity."

Tiffany seems upset, yet her forehead still doesn't move. "Oh, dear. We don't want that."

"Who's conducting these tests?" Tad demands.

"A firm out of Lansing called Impact Environmental Solutions."

"Uh-huh." He scrubs a hand over his slab of a jaw. "And who's paying for them?"

"We had to find room for it in the budget, since the testing is required by law, and several concerned citizens have spoken up about the potential long-term health hazards of contamination."

"Tell you what, sport." Tad claps me on the back. "Why don't we make a donation that will cover the testing? You send me the total, and I'll cut you a check."

I know what his game is, and I'm not playing it. "That's a generous offer, but I can't accept it."

The old linebacker studies me with shrewd eyes. "Well, I'm sure you'll keep me informed. We're anxious to see that community center happen. For the children."

"Yes," Tiffany adds. "The children are the *most* important thing. We're making that very clear in the press release."

Tad refocuses his attention on Mila. "Sorry to interrupt your dinner, young lady."

She smiles. "That's okay."

"Mr. and Mrs. Hart, this is Mila Ferguson."

"You must be Eliza's daughter," says Tiffany.

"Yes." Mila tugs at a strand of her red hair. "I can't imagine what gave it away."

Tiffany lets out a peal of laughter. "You were a friend of our niece's, I believe. George's daughter, Rachel? George was Tad's brother."

"I *was* a friend of Rachel's," Mila says, her eyes widening. "You have a good memory. I just saw her mother at the grocery store this morning. She hasn't changed a bit."

"I know. It must be that royal blood."

"Royal blood?" Mila questions.

"Catriona is supposedly the second cousin once removed of a Spanish prince." Tiffany's tone holds a touch of awe.

"I thought she was from the Philippines," Tad says.

His wife sighs. "She is. Never mind, dear."

"Have you seen Rachel lately?" Mila's voice rises hopefully.

"Not in ages." Tiffany sighs and shakes her head. "The younger generation doesn't seem to come back much."

"It was nice seeing you, Mr. and Mrs. Hart," I say, eager to avoid a *kids these days* conversation.

"You too, Everett. Nice meeting you, Mila."

When they're gone, I take my seat. "Sorry about that business stuff."

"That's okay." She twirls her spoon in the melted ice cream and caramel sauce again. "It's not like the mayor can ignore the town's founding family. Though… It sounds like they aren't thrilled about the testing."

"Doesn't matter. It had to be done." I tip back the last of my old-fashioned. I make sure to leave the cherry where Mila can see it, just in case she wants to show me her little trick again.

"Why not let them pay for it? It must be expensive."

"It is, but if the Harts pay for it, they'll expect me to bury any results not in their favor."

She nods with understanding. "Do you think the results will show contamination in the soil?"

"I already know they do."

She sits back. "Oh, shit. What kind?"

"Chromium. Lead. Arsenic."

"So no community center?"

"It could still be done eventually, if I can find the funds for the clean-up."

She looks out the window into the dark. "It's funny about that place. My friends and I used to hang out there all the time. It was our secret meeting spot."

"You guys probably have lead poisoning."

Her lips twitch. "What does clean-up look like?"

"The consultant told me the standard approach is excavation and removal—basically, dig up the contaminated soil, haul it to a hazardous waste landfill somewhere, and backfill with clean soil."

"How long does that take?"

"Six to twelve months. But the bigger problem will be the cost. The consultant estimated three to five million dollars, which is more than the town can afford."

"Ouch." She sucks some caramel sauce off her finger in the most alluring way imaginable. "Will the Harts offer to help?"

"I doubt it." I try to casually adjust the crotch of my pants. "That would mean claiming responsibility, and they're clearly fearful of litigation. They just want this done quickly and simply so they can rid themselves of a tax liability while benefiting from a write-off through a charitable donation."

"So charitable of them to donate their contaminated land."

"Exactly."

"So what will you do now?"

"I have to figure out an agreeable solution for all parties. The town can't afford to make enemies of the Hart family. Their name isn't just on the biggest employer in this area, it's also on the health clinic, the lakefront park, the animal rescue—the town itself. So it's not just a straightforward question of ethics. I have to find the balance between keeping the Hart family happy and doing what's best for the residents of Hart's Landing, all within the constraints of a small town budget."

After one final lick, she sets her spoon down. "I take back what I said about the mayor not deserving a parking spot."

"Thank you." I smile. "How was your dessert?"

"Delicious." She puts both hands on her stomach. "But I'm officially full."

"Too full for another cherry?" I slide my empty cocktail glass toward her.

She laughs. "Are you asking me to perform my little trick again?"

"I think you should. Maybe you just got lucky the first time."

Her eyelids lower slightly as she reaches for the cherry. Within seconds, she's got the stem tied in a knot. "There," she says, holding it up with a victorious grin.

God, I want to kiss those lips.

I signal to the server that we're ready for the check. When it arrives, Mila suggests splitting it. "No way," I argue, tucking my credit card inside the leather holder before she can grab it. "I've got this."

"But—"

"I asked you to dinner tonight. It's my treat."

"You didn't ask," she reminds me. "But thank you."

Ten minutes later, we walk out of Wardwell House into the September night. A cool breeze ruffles Mila's hair, and she shivers. "Shoot. I forgot my jacket. I must have left it on the chair in the living room. I just wanted to get out of there."

"Here." I shrug out of my blazer and hold it up.

After slipping her arms into the sleeves, she frees her hair from the collar, and I want to gather it in my hands and bury my face in it. Inhale its scent. She turns to face me, and I notice that her hands have disappeared.

I cuff up the sleeves for her. "That's better."

She gives me a smile that quickens my pulse. "Thank you."

"What do you feel like doing? Would you like me to take you home, or do you want to hang out for a little bit, go get a drink or something?"

"Hmm." She thinks for a moment. "I'm afraid if we go to a bar, I'll see my face on the Landing Pad again tomorrow. Maybe a walk along the river?"

"Sure, we can do that. Let's grab the truck and drive downtown. We can take advantage of my hard-earned parking spot."

She laughs and sways in my direction, giving me a full-body side nudge. "Perfect."

As we walk toward the truck, I wonder what, exactly, is prohibited by a no-dating rule. Does it mean she's *completely* off-limits? Are there allowances for out-of-town flings? Am I the asshole if I make a move?

I don't want to be the asshole.

But I can't remember the last time I wanted to lock my fingers with someone else's. Drape my arm possessively around someone's shoulders. Kiss someone on a street corner in the dark.

I know just what she'd taste like. Vanilla ice cream. Bourbon caramel sauce. Cherry on top.

Our pinky fingers brush against each other's. Once. Twice. Then they're linked together, the small point of contact blooming with heat.

I slip my hand into hers, and she lets me hold it.

Chapter Fifteen

Mila

It shouldn't feel so easy.

Being with Everett, talking to him, wearing his coat. Even just walking hand in hand with him in silence. I don't feel the need to fill it up with anything. I don't need to *try*. I don't need to worry.

I can just breathe.

He's so comfortable in his skin. So at ease. So kind and curious about me. Not like guys I've dated in the past who don't shut up about themselves. And God, he's hot. All throughout dinner, I kept noticing different things about him that made breathing normally seem like an unreasonable ask of my lungs.

The muscular forearms below the cuffed sleeves of his dress shirt. The strong, thick wrists. The way those dark curls on his head resist the product he's put in his hair, springing rebelliously loose. The slow, sensual grin that hooked up one side of his mouth before the other when I said something that amused him.

It made my stomach tumble every time.

And he was sweet, too. Offering me his coat was nice enough. But standing there and rolling up the sleeves for me? I nearly melted right there on the sidewalk. I don't even know how we ended up holding hands, but it feels right. As we stroll down the path that follows the curve of the White Pine River, the contact between our palms sends an electric current zipping along my veins.

"So what do you do with your Saturday nights when you're not tricking women into having dinner with you?"

"Mostly, I hang out with my buddies at The Axe & Barrel. We play in a league every Monday night." He laughs. "Our group chat is called Axe Gods."

"Of course it is." I shake my head. "So who are the Axe Gods?"

"Ripley, Ben Hart, and Hunter Gannon."

"So you're pretty good friends with Ripley?"

"Yeah. For all that he's a menace, he's active in the chamber of commerce and always willing to host an event or pitch in when the local business community needs a hand. And he's a lot of fun, although he works his ass off at the pub. Most nights, he's managing *and* bartending. Does the books, too."

"How long has he owned it?"

Everett thinks for a moment. "About five years? He's made some good improvements, including axe throwing."

"And Ben Hart is one of *the* Harts, I assume."

"Yes, but he'll tell you he's on the poor branch of that family tree. His dad was the original Doc Hart—I think a second cousin or something to Tad? Ben took over his practice when he retired a few years back. So he's the new Doc Hart."

"Love it. Old Doc Hart was the best. So kind and gentle. I don't remember his son. Is he older?"

"Yeah. He turned forty this year, and we give him so much shit about it. But he's a great guy. He's got a daughter, Vivian, from his first marriage. I think she's in middle school."

"Is he remarried?"

"No. The Axe Gods are all single."

I laugh. "Who was the other god again?"

"Hunter Gannon. I think he might have been in your graduating class, but I'm not sure."

"He was. But I didn't know him well."

Broody and quiet, Hunter didn't really fit in with any of the cliques at school. He didn't play a sport, wasn't involved in clubs, and seemed to work a lot of hours at the service station. Rumor had it that his home life wasn't good, and also that he'd been arrested for something at one point, so we were all a little scared of him. But he was beautiful in a lean, angular kind of way. I recall how Rachel was assigned to tutor him senior year and freaked out about it.

"Didn't he join the military after high school?"

Everett nods. "He was in the Army. But he moved back to Hart's Landing a couple years ago, and now he's a firefighter. Really good guy." When we come to the bridge, we stop. "Want to walk across?"

"Sure." Side by side, we amble along until we reach the middle, where I turn and look out over the river, placing my hands on the iron rail. The moon's reflection glimmers on the water. In the distance, music drifts from the bars along Main Street. "So do people still do the thing with the stone?"

"I don't know." He glances at me. "Did you ever do it?"

"Maybe," I murmur, my tone mysterious.

"So is the legend true? Does it work?"

"I regret to say, it did not work for me."

"Maybe you should try it again."

"I don't think so."

He hesitates. "You know, not all guys are like your ex."

"It's not just because of Connor. I've got a long history of twisting myself into a pretzel trying to earn someone's love. I pretend to be something—sometimes many things—I'm not, just to keep someone else happy."

"Because you're afraid of being alone?"

Because I'm afraid that deep down, I'm unlovable. "My therapist and I are trying to unpack that."

"Have you ever tried being with someone who likes the actual you and not the pretzel you?"

I smile. "That sounds *very* healthy."

"So why not try it? I know someone who's kind of into you."

"Oh yeah? He likes emotionally cluttered women who may or may not have accidentally committed arson?"

He nudges me. "That's actually his favorite type."

"Mmm." God, he's tempting. But I've been here before. I get on this ride because it looks like fun, and then I can't get off. I end up either falling off, getting pushed off, or riding it alone. Gathering my strength, I exhale before facing him. "Everett, I can't. I made myself a promise. I need to figure out who I am when I'm not trying to please someone. And I need to learn how to put myself first."

"Or maybe try being with someone who puts you first," he suggests. "Let him show you how to do it."

"I wish I could." My eyes travel over his face, his shoulders, his chest. I even risk a glance at his crotch. "Seriously, I really, really wish I could."

Everett exhales. "Well, my friend is going to be very disappointed."

"Tell him I'm doing him a favor."

"He really wants to kiss you."

My breath hitches. "He does?"

"He had the chance once before, but things went wrong." He brushes my hair back behind my shoulders. "He thinks he deserves another shot. With your permission, of course."

"Look at you, asking for permission. What happened to your rough edges?"

"I'm on my best behavior. For my friend's sake."

My defenses are melting. One kiss would be okay, right? Just two pairs of lips meeting in the dark, nothing more. No one to see. No meaning attached. Just a tidal wave of validation for my teenage self. "All right, Mayor McKean. You've got my permission. One kiss. For your friend's sake."

He brings one hand to the side of my face, first touching my cheek with his fingers, then cradling my jaw, his thumb brushing my bottom lip. "Then I better get this right."

A moment later, his mouth is on mine. Softly at first, his lips warm and gentle, teasing mine open in a way that makes me yearn for more. A drizzle when I want a downpour. Then it deepens, his head tilting, his hand sliding into my hair. He wraps his other arm around my waist, pulling me closer.

I reach for the back of his head, my fingers slipping through those thick brown curls. He opens his mouth a little wider, stroking my tongue with his own.

Holy smoke.

This kiss is hitting me in all kinds of places. The backs of my knees. The hollow of my stomach. Deep in my chest. Gooseflesh blankets my skin. Whiskey, vanilla, and coffee swirl together to create a flavor better than any dessert I've ever had. His mouth moves across my jaw and down my throat. His tongue creates a hot spot on my neck that I feel between my legs. I moan softly. Helplessly.

"I should stop," he says, his breath tantalizing on my skin. "My rough edges will start to show."

God, I want to experience those rough edges. I want to get my hands on them. Wrap my legs around them. Swallow them whole.

He pulls back slightly, his eyes searching mine. "You sure we can't see where this goes? Because I feel like we could have a lot of fun together, Freckles. No strings attached."

"I'm even more sure than I was before. That kiss made this entire bridge tremble. I'll never trust myself around you again."

Laughing, he releases me from his arms. "Well, if you change your mind, you know where to find me."

Damn, he's good. Sweet and funny and so fucking *hot.* And as we started walking back toward the embankment, I have to wonder—how the hell is he still single? "Can I ask *you* a question now?"

"Sure."

"Why aren't the women in this town falling all over you?"

"Who says they aren't?"

I laugh. "Okay, so maybe that was the wrong question. How come you're unattached?"

"One, I'm too busy, and two, I don't want to date my constituents."

"That's fair." I glance at him. "Have you ever had a serious relationship?"

"I had a girlfriend around the time my father died, but we ended up going our separate ways shortly after."

"Can I ask why?"

"She wanted to get married, or at least talk about it. I didn't."

I nod. "Where is she now?"

"She's still around—a pediatric nurse at the clinic, actually. She also volunteers at the animal rescue."

I imagine a gorgeous blonde in nursing scrubs with puppies and kittens on them. She has perfect skin, an adorable giggle, and voluptuous breasts.

I am unreasonably annoyed.

"What's her name?"

"Bella."

Because of course it is.

We walk in silence for a few minutes, during which I continue to obsess over his ex.

"What are you thinking about?" he asks.

"Bella. *Duh*."

He laughs. "What about her?"

"She's obviously perfect."

"She is?"

"Yes. She drinks seventy-two ounces of water every day, wears sunscreen even in the winter, and when she gives shots to the kids, it doesn't even hurt. After your relationship ended, she probably jumped right back into the dating pool. She never thought it was her fault—she understood it was just bad timing. See, Bella doesn't fall in love with assholes, and she never doubts her self-worth. When she realized her life goals didn't align with yours, she didn't pretend they did just for the sake of hanging on to what was familiar. She didn't wait around for you to maybe change your mind. She loved and respected herself enough to say goodbye and move on."

Everett stops walking. "Jesus," he deadpans. "She *was* perfect. Maybe I should try to get her back."

"You should. I'll come to your wedding."

That makes him laugh. "Bella is now engaged to the local veterinarian. And I have no regrets."

"None?"

"Well, maybe one," he allows, tossing an arm around my neck. "But it has nothing to do with her."

When we pull up in front of my house, I notice the living room light still on.

"Is she waiting up for you?" Everett asks, putting the truck in park.

"I'm not sure. Maybe." I check the time on my phone. "It's late for her, but I'm sure she'll want to ask me a thousand questions."

"Moms do that." He switches off the engine and unbuckles his seat belt, but I put a hand on his leg.

"Don't get out. It's okay."

"Are you sure?"

"Yes. I feel like she's watching, and it'll just make things more awkward."

"Okay." We look at each other for a moment, my hand still resting on his thigh. The truck's cab is dark and cozy, and part of me wants nothing more than for him to lean forward and kiss me again. Put his hand in my hair and his tongue in my mouth. Make me feel beautiful, worthy, wanted.

But I've drawn a line, and Everett McKean isn't the kind of guy to cross it.

"Thanks again for dinner," I say. "I had a great time."

"You're welcome. I did too."

"What are you going to tell your friend?"

"Oh, man." He exhales in defeat. Ruffles his hair. "I guess I have to tell him that he's out of luck. But I don't think I'll tell him about the kiss."

"No?"

"Nah. He'd be jealous if he knew the truth about it."

"What's the truth?"

He gives me a sexy, side-eyed smirk. "I'm not sure I should tell you."

"Come on." I poke his shoulder. "Tell me."

"The truth is that I would burn this whole town to the ground just to do it again."

I laugh. "You would not."

"No?" He reaches for my jaw again, cupping it like he did on the bridge. Runs his thumb over my bottom lip. "Test me."

My smile fades. In the silence, my pulse is like cannon fire in my head.

Then he drops his arm. "You should go inside."

I unbuckle my seat belt and slip out of his blazer, leaving it on the seat when I get out. "Good night, Everett."

"Good night."

Breathless, I hurry up the front walk and dig around in my purse for my house key. Within seconds, the porch light comes on over my head, and the door opens. My mother appears in her robe, her hair and makeup still flawless.

"There you are! I've been waiting up." She looks past me toward Everett's truck. "Is he coming in?"

"No." I give Everett a wave over my shoulder, and he waves back before pulling away.

"Didn't you have a good time?" my mother asks, reluctantly stepping aside so I can enter the house.

"I had a great time."

"Then why didn't you invite him in?" She shuts the door while I hang up my jacket. "Don't you like him? He's very attractive."

"I'm really tired, Mom. I'm going to bed." Scooting past her, I start up the stairs.

"Well, wait a minute! I want to hear how it went. You've been gone for hours—you don't have two minutes for me?"

Halfway up, I stop and turn around. "Sorry. It was very nice. We went to an inn called Wardwell House."

"Oooh, fancy. What did you order?"

"I had chicken, he had steak. For dessert, I had vanilla ice cream with caramel sauce. Everything was delicious."

She wrinkles her nose a little when I mention dessert, like the indulgence is something unsavory. "What did you talk about?"

"A little of everything."

"Does he know about your divorce?"

I stiffen. "Yes."

"That's good. At least you know it didn't scare him off. Although I suppose if burning down that bakery didn't do it, nothing would."

Don't swing at that pitch. Don't swing at that pitch.

"So will you see him again?"

"I don't think so."

She sticks her hands on her hips. "He didn't ask for another date?"

"It's not that."

"Did you say something wrong?"

"No," I say tersely, my jaw tight. "I'm just not interested in dating while I'm here. I'm focused on your health and recovery."

She touches her chest. "Don't blame this on *me*, Mila."

"I'm not, I just—" I stop and take a breath. "Look, I'm just not interested in dating right now, period. It's got nothing to do with being here or not liking Everett enough to see him again. It's about me making space to create healthier boundaries for myself."

"Oh." Oddly, she seems to accept this. "Yes, maybe that's best. Men can be cagey, especially the handsome ones. You just never know what move they're going to make next. Better to protect yourself, or before you know it, your life is over and you're a single mom in a small town without a decent sushi restaurant for miles."

My hands curl into fists. "Your life wasn't over when you had me, Mom."

"I'm just trying to support your choice to be single and give you some advice," she says crisply, tightening the belt on her robe. "But if you don't want it, that's fine. Good night." She sweeps into the living room, trailing the scent of her perfume behind her.

Nothing she loves more than a dramatic exit.

Upstairs, I change out of my dress and into my pajamas. After some internal debate, I decide to ignore all of Beatrix's pointed looks and text Everett. A friendly note. Nothing suggestive.

Mila: *Hey. Thanks for listening tonight. It meant a lot.*

After a few minutes, I hear the bathroom door open and my mother's bedroom door shut. I go downstairs, scrub off my makeup and brush my teeth, and by the time I get back up to my room, Everett has replied. I flop onto my belly across the foot of my bed and open it.

Everett: *Anytime.*

Everett: *So texting is allowed? We're not breaking your rules?*

Mila: *I don't think so. We're friends, right?*

Everett: *Sure.*

Mila: *So, texting is allowed. As long as it stays clean.*

Everett: *Ma'am, the mayor does not sext. Screenshots are forever.*

Mila: *True.*

Everett: *Do you still want me to come by tomorrow and hang that grab bar?*

Mila: *Only if it isn't inconvenient for you.*

Everett: *How's 3:00?*

Mila: *Great.*

Everett: *See you then.*

Mila: *Good night.*

Everett: *Night, Freckles.*

I roll onto my back and hold my phone to my chest, a smile on my face.

See? It's fine. We'll be pals. Maybe hang out once in a while. A few texts here and there.

I won't think about the fact that he gave me the best kiss of my life. The kind of kiss you read about in books or see in the movies or hear about in love songs. The kind of kiss you recall on your deathbed as your life flashes in front of your eyes and think, *Well, I didn't win an Oscar, cure cancer, or broker world peace, or but I had that kiss.*

I bring my fingertips to my lips.

I had that kiss.

Chapter Sixteen

Everett

Owning a farm means I'm used to rising with the sun, but I wake up even earlier than usual on Sunday. A quick glance at the time tells me I don't have to get out of bed right away, so I roll over and try to fall back asleep.

But as soon as I close my eyes again, I see her. Appearing at the bottom of the stairs in a black dress that clings to her curves. Sitting across from me at dinner, laughing at something I said. Standing on the bridge, looking scared but curious, giving me permission to kiss her.

Last night, after she texted me, I sat on the porch for a while, questioning my motives. Trying to put my finger on what it is about her that has me so worked up.

It isn't just her looks. She's smoking hot, and I feel a strong physical attraction to her, but this feels like more than that. Maybe it's the unfinished business aspect—I always wondered what might have happened between us if there had been no fire.

My life was so chaotic after that night. Everything was in ruins—my family, our finances, the future. I was terrified of losing the farm, furious with my father, worried about my mother and sister.

And guilty. So fucking guilty.

By the time I picked up my head to look around and take a breath, Mila was gone. It felt too late to reach out—and anyway, at the time, I couldn't have been much to anyone romantically. I was too busy keeping my head above water.

Then there's her no-dating rule. I can't deny I'm a little fired up by the challenge of it, by the thought of being so irresistible she *has* to break it for me. Am I the biggest prick on the planet? Is it just a case of wanting what I can't have? If my sister had this rule and some dude was pressuring her to break it, wouldn't I kick his ass for being a disrespectful piece of shit?

The idea makes me uncomfortable.

No more teasing her about it, I decide. No more trying to charm her into messing around with me. No testing her limits. From now on, I will just be the good friend she needs—for all I know, that's what I would have been to her these past ten years if the fire had never happened. Given everything she's dealing with, what she needs is a safe place where she can learn to put herself first.

What she *doesn't* need is some guy trying to put his tongue in her mouth.

Or his hands on her skin.

Or his cock in her—

I throw off the covers and get out of bed. If I stay here thinking about her one minute longer, I'm going to end up with my dick in my hand, working off this tension while fantasizing about her in a way that is *not* in alignment with my new plan to be her safe place.

Pulling on some sweats, I take Merlin outside. The morning air is cool and damp, the sun just starting to rise. I decide I'll run into town and grab some donuts for my Sunday crew. The orchard, barn, and store will be busy all day, and the staff always appreciates it when I bring breakfast in. The gesture will make me feel like a good man—the kind of man who keeps his hands in his pockets and his tongue in his mouth.

Unless she changes her mind.

Then I'll put my tongue anywhere she wants it.

When I drive past my mom's house, I see lights on in the kitchen, so I park the truck and knock on her back door. She pulls it open, her expression surprised. "You're up early."

"I'm running into town to get some donuts for everyone. Want to come along?"

"Sure. Let me get my sweater."

I frown as I watch her hobble over to a kitchen chair and grab a cardigan hanging from the back of it. "How's the pain this morning?"

"Oh, you know." She slips her arms into the sleeves. "It's those steps. I wish we had a first-floor bedroom. My friend Theresa just moved into that new condo complex on the river. She said it's so nice having everything on one floor."

"Do you want me to have someone give us an estimate on adding a first-floor bedroom onto the house?" Not that I know where the money would come from, but I'd find it somehow.

"No, no. We can't afford that. I'll make do."

Outside, I help her into the truck. She greets Merlin, who's in the back seat, his tail wagging with excitement about the early-morning errand. The minute I start the engine, his head is out the window.

As I back out of her driveway, my mother sniffs. "What's that smell?"

"Dog?"

"No. It's floral. Orange blossom, maybe." She looks at me askance, with a mother's suspicious eye. "Either you're wearing some nice perfume or there was a woman in here recently."

I wait until I've turned onto the highway before answering. "I took a friend out for dinner last night."

"Mila Ferguson?"

"Is the gossip flying that fast these days? I just dropped her off like eight hours ago."

"I didn't hear it from anybody. It was just a guess."

"Heck of a guess."

"Not really."

"What's that mean?"

"It means there was something about the way you were talking about her yesterday morning."

I snort. "For all of two minutes?"

"It wasn't the length of time you talked about her. It was the *way*. There was definitely a *way*."

My laugh sounds unconvincing, even to me. "That's ridiculous. And don't get all worked up about it. It wasn't a big deal."

"I'm not worked up about it." She observes me shrewdly from the passenger seat. "*You* seem a little worked up about it, though."

"I'm not." I keep my eyes focused on the road. Clear my throat. Without even looking at her, I sense her smile.

"Did you have a good time with her?"

"Yes."

"Will you see her again?"

"No." I frown. "I mean, yes, I'll see her at three this afternoon because I'm helping her install a grab bar in the bathroom for her mom, but that's it. We're not going out again."

"Okay," she says, but what I hear is *I don't believe you one bit.*

"I'm serious. She's not dating right now."

"Why not?"

"She just got divorced from a husband who cheated on her, and she feels like she needs some time on her own."

My mother sighs. "I suppose you have to respect that. But it would have been cute. It was so obvious she had a big crush on you when you were kids."

"That's ancient history, Mom." Even if it didn't feel all that ancient last night.

"Well, you know what they say about history repeating itself."

"She doesn't want to repeat history. She just wants to help her mom and get back home to New York."

"If you say so, dear."

I set my jaw, trying not to recall the sweet taste of vanilla and bourbon on her lips. "I do."

A few minutes before three, I knock on the Fergusons' front door. Mila answers it in her bare feet, wearing jeans and an NYU T-shirt with a hole in one shoulder. Her hair is in a sloppy ponytail, strands straggling around her face. She isn't wearing makeup, which makes her freckles stand out even more.

My heartbeat skids to a halt. I could get used to that face.

"Hi." She gives me a tight-lipped smile.

My protective hackles shoot up. "Hi. You okay?"

"It's been a day."

"Is that Everett?" Behind Mila, her mother appears.

"Hi, Eliza. How are you?"

"Wonderful. I'm so glad you're here. Goodness, Mila, invite him in already. Where are your manners?"

As I enter the house, I try to catch Mila's eye to let her know I'm in her corner, but her gaze is locked on the floor.

It's more of the same over the next hour. While I install the grab bar in the shower, Mila sits in the bathroom doorway to keep me company. Her mother finds plenty of reasons to hover, and somehow, no matter what she asks me or what the topic of conversation is, she finds a way to take a shot at Mila. The only time she says something nice is when she reminisces about her daughter's dance training.

"She was so good, Everett. Just incredible. I named her for Mila Petrova, one of my ballet idols. I knew she would be gifted. Did you ever see her dance?"

"No," I say, snapping the cover plates into place.

"She had everything—technique, athleticism, musicality. The most beautiful lines I've ever seen. And her feet were exquisite."

"That's enough, Mom." Mila curls her hands over her bare toes.

"She won scholarships three years in a row at the YAGP! I should find some old videos so you can see how talented she was."

"She's still talented." I slip my drill back into the case. "I've seen her artwork."

"But dance is different," Eliza argues. "Dance is the actual physical embodiment of the art form, not just a representation of it.

It's artistry at a deeper level. Martha Graham called it the hidden language of the soul."

I have no idea how to argue with that. I can talk all day about long-range weather forecasts, irrigation lines, and the market price of Montmorency cherries, but the merits of one art form over another are beyond my scope of knowledge. And what the fuck is a hidden language? How is that even useful?

"I'm sure she was great," I say, disliking the way Mila seems to be shrinking into herself on the floor.

Eliza sniffs and folds her arms over her chest. "She should have gotten into Juilliard. Such a disappointment."

Mila's head snaps up. "Mom, it's been ten years. When will you get over it?"

"I'm not sure I'll ever be over it, Mila." Eliza throws her hands in the air repeatedly. "All that training. All that time and focus. All the expectations. For nothing!"

"It wasn't for nothing." Mila's voice finally has some punch to it. "I learned a lot from dance that I still use every day—discipline, dedication, resilience. Finding beauty in different forms. Making someone feel something with artistic expression."

My chest fills with pride. I nearly start applauding.

Standing over her daughter, Eliza purses her lips. "For God's sake, I was giving you a *compliment*, Mila. But I guess I can't do anything right."

Mila's head drops again.

Eliza looks at me, her gaze cool. "What do I owe you for the work, Everett?"

"Nothing." I hold up my hands. "Consider it a favor."

"That's very generous. Thank you." She executes a theatrical pivot and disappears into a bedroom, swinging the door shut behind her.

Mila looks up at me. "I'm sorry," she says quietly.

"Don't apologize. You did nothing wrong." I offer her a hand, helping her to her feet. "And I won't accept it, so you can just take it back."

The smile she gives me makes my heart feel like putty. "Thanks for doing this. I won't keep you any longer—I'm sure you have things to do."

I do, but I can't leave her like this. It feels like leaving a bunny alone with a hawk. "I have some time. Want to get out of the house for a minute? Take a walk or something?"

She glances over her shoulder at her mother's closed door. "I don't know if I should. I have to get dinner going soon. We have to be at the hospital really early tomorrow morning."

"Come on," I coax. She needs some distance between herself and her mom. "Fifteen minutes—a walk around the block. It's gorgeous outside."

Her bottom lip disappears between her teeth while she considers it. "Okay. Let me just put some shoes on."

While she's upstairs, I take the drill out to my truck. When I come back inside, I spot a black cat at the bottom of the steps. "Hey, there. You must be Beatrix." I crouch down and hold out my hand, pleased when she moves closer to sniff me. Her ears twitch forward.

"Wow." Mila pauses at the top of the stairs. "She likes you. It usually takes her a while to warm up to people."

"I'm good with kids, old ladies, and animals."

"Clearly." She comes down the stairs, unlaced sneakers on her feet. Sitting on one of the lower steps, she ties her shoes while I pet Beatrix. When the shoes are tied, Mila stands. "Okay, Bea, go back upstairs. You know the rules."

The cat scampers upstairs, and I rise to my feet. Since Mila is still on the step, we're chest to chest, her face level with mine.

It would be so easy to kiss her.

Her eyes drop to my mouth, making me wonder if she's thinking the same thing, especially when she runs her tongue over her lips. One step forward, and it's done.

Remembering this morning's vow to respect her space, I back up and hold the door open for her instead.

"Just a minute," she says, rounding the corner into the living room. "I should leave a note for my mom so I don't get a bunch of texts accusing me of ghosting her."

In my opinion, her mother deserves to be ghosted, but I keep my mouth shut. A moment later, she reappears and we head outside.

We wander slowly down her street. It's warm and sunny, with just a few wispy, white clouds in a sky the color of her eyes. At the corner, two neighborhood girls have a lemonade stand set up.

"How much?" I ask.

"Fifty cents," says the shorter one, who wears a unicorn headband.

"We'll take two." I put a five-dollar bill in the red solo cup serving as their bank. "Keep the change."

She and her business partner exchange a thrilled look. "Thanks!"

Carefully, they pour two lemonades for us, one holding the cup steady on the stand, the other grasping the pitcher with both hands.

"So how has business been today?" I inquire.

"Pretty good," replies the taller one, who wears glasses.

"Lots of customers?"

"Not lots, just some," says the unicorn.

"We'll send anyone we see your way," I tell them. "Are you guys friends or sisters?"

"Sisters," they answer at the same time.

"I'm older," adds the one with glasses. "I'm seven, and she's six."

"But the lemonade stand was my idea." Six wears a serious expression, eyeballing her sister like she expects her to argue.

"That's true," Seven concedes. "But we both made the lemonade. We used real lemons."

Six beams, revealing a gap in her front teeth. "I added the sugar."

I nod. "Teamwork. I like it."

When the cups are full, the sisters hand them over. As I give the first one to Mila, a woman comes out of the house with a toddler on her hip.

"Excuse me! Mayor McKean?"

I look up, surprised. "Yes."

The woman smiles and holds up her phone. "Could I take your picture with the girls?"

"Sure."

"Would you mind holding the baby so she can be in the picture too?"

"Not at all." I reach for the little tyke, another girl with a ponytail sprouting from the top of her head and the chubbiest cheeks I've ever seen. I wonder if she'll protest being held by a stranger, but she gives me a gummy smile and kicks her feet when I lift her up to the sky. Setting her on one arm, I move around to the older kids' side of the stand and position myself between their chairs.

Mila observes it all with an amused expression as their mother snaps a few photos. "Thanks," the woman says. "My name is Sydney Carr, and I do social media for the Hart's Landing Parents' Club. Would it be okay to put the picture online?"

"Fine with me."

"And I wanted to thank you for approving funds for the new splash pad at Riverfront Park. It was so wonderful all summer!"

"I'm glad." I hand the baby back to her.

"We'd been asking the council for years," Sydney says, bouncing the toddler on her hip. "They always claimed they couldn't find the money."

"Well, sometimes it's just a matter of looking in new places." I pick up the second lemonade and give the family a wave. "Good luck, girls."

"Thank you," they call back.

Mila and I resume our walk. "Well, that was adorable," she murmurs. "You *are* good with kids."

"Oh, I staged that whole thing to impress you. Did it work?"

She laughs. "Yes."

"Good, because those child actors are *expensive*." We reach the corner, and I look both ways. "Which way would you like to go? Toward Main Street? Or toward the park?"

"Park," she says, taking a left. I fall into step beside her.

A couple of minutes later, we enter the park and follow the jogging trail around the perimeter. When we come to a bench next to the pond, I turn to her. "Want to sit for a minute?"

"Sure." We take our seats, and for a little while, we just watch the ducks on the pond and sip lemonade, the sun warm on our faces. Every time the breeze kicks up, it carries the scent of orange blossoms in my direction.

"I don't mean to sound patronizing, but I was proud of you for defending your art career to your mom," I tell her. "You weren't lying when you said she's hard on you. I can't believe she said you were a disappointment."

"She doesn't mean it like it sounds." Unbelievably, it seems like Mila is actually defending her mother. "She just really wanted me to go to Juilliard."

I say nothing. Toss back the rest of my lemonade.

"She sacrificed a lot for dance. She didn't have a regular childhood. She left home at twelve to go study at a ballet school in New York. She lived with a family and was homeschooled with other dancers like her. No social life, no school events, no normal high school experiences. Dance was all she ever knew, all she'd ever worked for." Mila stares into her cup. "And then she had to give it all up for me."

"Do you feel guilty about that?"

"Wouldn't you?"

I shrug. "It wasn't *your* fault she got pregnant."

"Somehow, that's not the part that got stuck on a loop in my brain." She's silent for a moment. "When I was a kid, I used to try to make up for it."

"How?"

"By being perfect. Especially in dance."

"That's a lot of pressure on a kid."

"Didn't your parents put pressure on you?"

I think for a moment, squinting into the sun. "It was different. We just had to avoid setting my dad off. He had some predictable triggers, but sometimes you had no idea what would do it. So I learned to be hypervigilant, more to protect my mom and sister than anything else."

She turns her face toward me. In the afternoon light, her blue eyes glimmer with flecks of gold. "You like protecting people."

"It's the right thing to do when people can't protect themselves." Those eyes are killing me. And that mouth. If I kiss her right now, she'll taste like lemons and sugar and sunshine.

I lower my head. She lifts her chin. Our lips are barely an inch apart.

Then I slide to the far end of the bench, making her laugh.

"What's the matter?" she asks.

"Nothing. I'm just being a good friend."

"Ah."

"You're being a bad friend, by the way."

"I am?"

"Yes. If we're going to hang out, you shouldn't dress so cute."

She looks down. "Everett, I'm wearing ripped jeans and dirty sneakers. I slept in this shirt."

"Hmm, maybe it's not your clothes. Maybe it's your hair and makeup."

"I'm not wearing any makeup. And I haven't even showered yet today, let alone washed my hair. My mother kept me too busy."

I frown. "Then it's your perfume. I'm going to have to request that you don't put it on before you see me."

She shakes her head. "I'm not wearing any perfume, either."

"You mean to tell me that all this—" I make a circular gesture with my hand, framing her in. "All this is just...the real you?"

"Yes." Her cheeks grow pink.

"Jesus, that's even worse." I get up, walk down to the next bench, and drop onto it. "I better sit over here," I call out.

She laughs so hard her feet come off the ground. "You're ridiculous."

"Oh, and could you stop laughing so much, too?" Getting to my feet again, I walk slowly back to her. "Because I really like the way it sounds."

Her laughter fades as she looked up at me. Making a visor with one hand, she shields her eyes from the sun. "Everett?"

"Yes?"

"I need you to tell me some bad things about you. The worst things you can think of. Disgusting habits, horrible personality flaws, giant red flags."

"Hmm." I toy with the plastic cup in my hands and prop a boot on the bench. "I'm bossy. I'm competitive as fuck. And I always think I can solve other people's problems better than they can."

She ponders that and shakes her head. "Do better."

"I don't make my bed. I don't own wineglasses. When I do laundry, I don't separate colors, I just shove everything that's dirty in the washing machine together."

That makes her wince. "Keep going."

"I listen to yacht rock. I constantly scavenge for food at my mom's house because I can't cook a thing, and I hate grocery shopping. And here's one that will really get you—I don't own a single piece of artwork or have any framed photographs in my house."

She blinks at me. "What's on your walls?"

"Paint."

She nods slowly. "This is good."

"Have I sufficiently turned you off?"

"No," she says, rising to her feet. "But it's a start."

Chapter Seventeen

WELCOME TO THE LANDING PAD

Community Updates From The Hart's Landing Gazette (Online Edition)

PSA: The Curb Appeal Society reminds residents that the approved list of front-door paint colors can be found by clicking here. Non-compliant doors are subject to fines.

Community question (submitted by KnittingBiddy): Is the mayor really dating Mila Ferguson? Dinner at Wardwell House Saturday night, followed by a stroll along the river. I also have it on good authority that he was at her house the following day, after which they were seen walking in the neighborhood.

Comment by ANONYMOUS AXE GOD: People have too much free time on their hands. Go knit something.

Gazette Mod: Violations of our Code of Comment Conduct may result in restricted access to The Landing Pad. To review our guidelines, click here.

Community photo: [Alt text: Mayor McKean poses with the Carr children at their lemonade stand.] Caption: Looks like Mayor McKean will make a great dad someday!

EVENT: After record-breaking attendance at this week's meeting of The Diner Detectives True Crime Fanatics Club, President Daniel Bartok is pleased to announce that NEW evidence in the Tart and Soul fire will be revealed at next week's meeting.

Chapter Eighteen

Mila

I'm trying to keep from dozing off in the waiting room when I hear my name.

"Ms. Ferguson? I'm Dr. Rodriguez, your mother's orthopedic surgeon."

I look up from my third cup of weak hospital coffee to see an older man in scrubs removing his surgical mask. Salt-and-pepper hair, light brown skin, and a tired smile. I rise to my feet. "How did everything go?"

"Great. She's in the recovery room. Her vital signs are stable, and she's starting to wake up from the anesthesia."

I smile with relief. "Wonderful. Thank you."

"The recovery room nurse will come get you once she's more alert, likely in half an hour or so. She'll stay in the hospital for three days. Today and tonight are focused on pain management. Tomorrow morning, she'll see the physical therapist. They'll help her sit up at the edge of the bed and possibly take a few steps with a walker."

I say a quick prayer for that physical therapist.

"Because this was a double replacement," Dr. Rodriguez goes on, "it's necessary to be more cautious with her initial mobility, but getting her moving is important for recovery. She mentioned you'd be staying with her for a while?"

"Yes. For six weeks." I try not to sound like it's a punishment.

"Good. For the first week at home, she'll need assistance with almost everything—getting in and out of bed, using the bathroom, putting clothes on, making meals. And she'll need to use the walker for at least two weeks."

I attempt a smile. "Can *you* tell her that?"

He laughs ruefully. "I know Eliza can be stubborn. But she's in good health and should be able to handle basic activities within three or four weeks. By six to eight, she'll be more independent, though still using a cane."

A *cane*? She's going to throw a tantrum about that, too. "Thank you so much, Dr. Rodriguez."

"You're welcome. Tell Eliza I'll see her tomorrow." He gives me one final smile before heading beyond the big automatic doors.

I sit down again to wait for the nurse and see that a text from Everett has come in.

Everett: *How's it going?*

Mila: *She's in recovery, and the doctor said everything went well.*

Everett: *Good. How are you feeling?*

Mila: *A little tired. It was an early morning, and I didn't sleep very well.*

Everett: *Why not?*

Mila: *Just worried about the surgery.*

It's a lie. I lay awake half the night thinking about him. Doubting myself and my rule. Looking for a way to make an end run around my boundaries without actually knocking them down.

Everett: *Do me a favor. Don't forget to eat. Whenever my dad was in the hospital, my mother would have starved to death if someone hadn't fed her.*

Mila: *Right now, all I want is more caffeine. But I'll get some lunch in a little bit. Did you get the poster design I emailed you last night?*

Everett: *Yes, and it's amazing. Going to the printer this afternoon, and then your art will be in windows up and down Main Street. I can't thank you enough.*

Mila: *Happy to help.*

Everett: *Let me know if you need anything.*

Mila: *I will. Thanks for checking on me.*

Jess has also reached out to ask how the surgery went and cheekily let me know she's been enjoying having our apartment to herself. While I'm replying to her message, a text from an unknown number comes in.

Unknown Number: *Hey Mila, it's Yasmine. I hope your mom's surgery goes well today! I'm sure you're crazy busy taking care of her, but if you need a break this week, I would love to pour you a glass of wine and catch up. I'm working Wednesday through Friday!* ♥

Mila: *Thank you so much! The surgery went well. I'm not sure when I'll be able to get out, but as soon as I can, I'll definitely take you up on the offer.*

After hitting send, I scroll social media and do a little hunting for my old friends. Gabi used to post occasionally on Instagram while she was in college, but she deleted her accounts a couple years back. Yasmine is only active as Novel Vine on Instagram. She's posted photos from Friday night's poetry reading, so I like the post and comment that I hope I can make the next one. Once again, I search for Rachel without any results.

Recalling what Catriona Hart said about Rachel working for the family company, I open my browser and type "Rachel Hart Iron Works Florida" into the search bar. The top result is the company's website. There's a manufacturing facility and sales branch of Hart Iron Works outside Orlando, but I can't find Rachel's name listed anywhere.

So weird.

What happened to her?

A few minutes later, a nurse in maroon scrubs approaches. "Mila?" She beckons to me with a friendly, gap-toothed smile. "You can come see your mom now."

"Okay." I stand up and follow her, tucking my phone into my purse.

"I'm Jenny," the nurse says, leading the way through the big doors, past a central nurses' station, and down a wide corridor to the left. "I'll be your mom's nurse today."

"Nice to meet you." The light is bright, the smell antiseptic with a base note of chicken broth. A few patients in hospital gowns move cautiously behind walkers, physical therapists at their sides. At room 311, Jenny pushes open the door.

It's a private room. My mother is resting on a bed with side rails and what looks like a trapeze bar above her. Her eyes are closed. She looks wan and unfamiliar without her makeup, the lines on her face more pronounced. Her lips appear razor-thin, her auburn hair dull and lank on the white pillowcase. Above the blankets, her slender, graceful arms lie slack. I've never seen her look so weak or vulnerable.

She'd hate this, I think. I set my purse on a reclining chair by the window.

While Jenny checks her vital signs and IV, I glance around the room. Wall-mounted television. Bedside table on wheels. Whiteboard listing nurses' names, a pain management schedule, and my mom's information.

"Mila?" My mother's voice is raspy.

"Yes." I move to her bedside. "I'm here, Mom. Do you need anything?"

No response.

"She'll be in and out for a while," Jenny says apologetically.

"Okay."

The nurse leaves the room, and I tentatively pick up my mother's hand. Stroke the blue-veined back of it. If she was awake, she'd probably snatch it away from me. But since she's out cold, I hold her hand for a few minutes.

I had a terrible virus when I was eight, my fever so high that I had to be hospitalized for dehydration. I stayed two nights, and my mother never left my side. She slept on the chair beside my bed, encouraged me to sip water, asked my aunt to bring me my favorite stuffed animal from home—a penguin I called Mr. Cool.

When they released me, she set up a bed for me on the couch

in the living room and we watched all her favorite movies. That's when I fell in love with nineties rom-coms and knew I wanted to live in New York City someday. It strikes me as sad that we only have these tender moments when one of us is sick or incapacitated. As if emotional closeness requires some kind of physical vulnerability.

After I gently place my mother's hand back on the blanket, I sink into the recliner. Pull my phone from my purse and open up The Landing Pad.

Two posts immediately catch my eye.

The first is by the mom of the lemonade-stand sisters. I look at the photo of Everett with the three little girls, and my insides feel warm and slippery. Sydney Carr is right. He *would* make a good dad. I wonder if he wants children.

The second post is by the Diner Detectives, and it makes my jaw drop.

New evidence.

What the hell?

I shake my head, wondering what evidence there could possibly be that wasn't incinerated by the fire.

"Mila?"

Startled, I jump up, my phone clattering to the floor. "Mom?"

"Who else would it be?" Her voice is still raspy, but a little stronger.

"How are you feeling?"

"Like a train wreck. Can you get me out of here?"

I smile sympathetically. "No. Sorry. Dr. Rodriguez said three days."

She scowls. "They can't keep me here against my will."

"Are you thirsty? How about we get you something to drink?" I hit the call button, and Jenny arrives to check Mom's vitals. She promises to return with ice water.

My mother snaps her fingers and points toward the corner of the room. "Mila, can you bring me my bag? The small one with my toiletries."

Dutifully, I bring her the bag, and she digs out a mirror and hairbrush. "Good grief. I look frightful."

"Give yourself a break, you've been through a lot. But Dr. Rodriguez says everything went great. You'll feel like yourself again in no time." I decide that now isn't the time to talk about walkers or canes.

"Can I at least wear my own clothes?" My mother looks at the hospital gown with disgust. "I packed nice pajamas."

"Mom, you're not going to be able to change clothes yet."

"Why not? The pain isn't even that bad."

"That's the meds talking," says Jenny, entering the room with a tall white Styrofoam cup. She sets it on the bedside table and swings it over the bed. "They're numbing you pretty good right now. But no changing pajamas until tomorrow."

My mother harrumphs, sticking her brush and the hand mirror back in the bag and fishing out a lipstick. Jenny looks on with amusement as my mother paints her lips with Cherries in the Snow.

"I love it," the nurse says. "Whatever makes us feel good, right? Mila, the lobby desk called. There was a delivery for you."

I blink. "For me?"

"Yes. Did you order food, maybe?"

"No."

"Oh." She shrugs. "I'm not sure what it is, then."

I turn to my mom. "Are you okay if I run down there for a minute?"

"Go ahead."

"I won't be long." Grabbing my purse, I leave the room and hurry down the hall. After taking the elevator to the ground level, I approach the lobby desk. "Hi," I greet the woman seated there. Her name tag says Carmen. "My name is Mila Ferguson, and—"

"Oh, yes!" Carmen reaches for a white paper bag. "This is for you. And the coffee is yours, too." She slides a white to-go cup toward me.

"Thank you." Curious, I open the bag and discover two

individually wrapped sandwiches and a handwritten note. The savory smell of bacon and fresh bread makes my stomach growl as I unfold the paper.

Two of my favorite brioche sandwiches from
Tart and Soul for one of my favorite people.
Feel free to share, but EAT.

Everett

P.S. I noticed you drank your coffee black
after dinner the other night, so there's no
cream or sugar in this. Sorry if I got it wrong.

My entire body warms, and my brain regresses to middle school.

He likes me! He likes me!

He notices things about me, like how I take my coffee. He wants to do nice things for me, like making sure I eat on long days. He went out of his way to drop everything off, even though I'm sure he's busy.

I feel like twirling in circles. Jumping up and down. Kicking my feet.

I settle for a smile and tuck the note into my purse. I reach for the coffee and inhale the bittersweet aroma emanating from the lid.

"Lucky girl," Carmen says with a smile. "Is the mayor your sweetie?"

"No. Just a friend."

Her eyebrows peak. "A friend, huh?"

"Yes." I take a sip of coffee. It's hot and delicious. "But he's making it very hard to keep it that way."

Back in my mother's room, I offer her a sandwich. "Everett brought these from Tart and Soul. Would you like one?" I ask, pulling them out of the bag. "Looks like both have egg, one has bacon, and one has sausage."

"No, thank you. My stomach isn't up for that sort of thing." She sips her water through a straw, leaving a red lip mark on it. "Very thoughtful of him."

"Yes. I need to call him and say thanks." I sit down in the chair and take a bite of the bacon-and-egg sandwich.

"Of course. Just be careful, darling."

I swallow before inquiring, "Careful of what?"

She takes another sip of water. "I shouldn't say anything."

"But you did," I point out. "So what is it you're thinking?"

"I just know how you can come on."

"How I can *come on*?" The words feel hot enough to scald my tongue. So much for convalescence softening my mother's edges. "And how's that?"

"Well, too aggressively, if I'm being honest." One bony shoulder rises. "You seem to fall in love very quickly. I just think it would be wise to be more measured in your approach."

"More measured," I repeat.

"Yes. You don't want to risk turning him off by being too overzealous."

"And a phone call to say thanks for bringing me food is overzealous?" My voice rises like hot air.

"You don't have to get angry, darling. You know I'm only telling you these things because I love you."

I don't believe you.

"I'm only trying to protect you," she continues.

The few bites of sandwich I've eaten turn to lead in my stomach. "Protect me from what?"

"From making a mistake. Men don't like it when women are too easily won. It's better to be a little stingy with your affection."

Well, Mom, you're the expert on being stingy with your affection. How'd that work out for you?

The words are in my throat, but I manage to swallow them down.

Because this is all my fault. I never should have told her

about Everett. Maybe I shouldn't have gotten involved with him in the first place.

"I appreciate the advice, Mom." My voice is even and calm. "But it's not necessary. Everett and I are just friends."

"Good. You know I only want what's best for you, darling. And jumping into a relationship so soon after your divorce seems ill-advised. It would only be a rebound thing."

I put the rest of my sandwich back in the bag, my appetite gone.

Jenny arrives with soup and crackers for my mother, and she picks at the meal. A doctor comes in and checks on her, we watch some television, and she falls asleep by late afternoon.

Desperate to escape the room, I grab my phone and slip into the hallway. I take the elevator down to the first floor and go outside, inhaling deep gulps of fresh air, holding it in, counting to four, then exhaling slowly.

After a minute, I call Everett. His voicemail picks up.

"Hey Everett, it's Mila. Thank you so much for bringing the food and coffee today. That was very kind of you, although not necessary. I ate one of the sandwiches earlier, and I saved one for later. My mom seems to be doing well." I pause, hating that some part of my brain is questioning whether my tone seems measured enough. "Anyway, thanks again. It was good seeing you. Take care."

Cringing, I end the call, feeling like an idiot.

It was good seeing you? Take care?

In my quest not to sound overzealous about the fucking sandwiches, I sound wooden and disinterested.

Immediately, I start to text him.

Hey, sorry if I sounded weird on the VM I just left you. It's been a crazy day, and I was just trying to

I stop. Trying to what? Be more stingy with my affection?

I hate myself. What am I even doing? Why did I think I could handle this?

Maybe it's for the best if I sound disinterested. Maybe my mother is right about me falling in love too quickly, coming on too strong, being too easily won. I've been here before, haven't I? I've mistaken the fiery intensity at the start of a relationship for something that would last. I've substituted sex for connection. I've told men I loved them because I wanted to hear them say it back.

Beyond that, I've laughed at jokes that weren't funny, faked dozens of orgasms, and played down my intelligence to make a man feel smarter.

I've even pretended it doesn't bother me when someone squeezes the toothpaste tube from the middle—a vile offense in my estimation.

Mom is right. I'm not good at this. And if I'm not careful, I'm going to keep making the same mistakes over and over again.

After deleting what I typed, I go back inside.

Chapter Nineteen

Everett

Sitting in my truck Monday night, I listen to Mila's voice message again. Maybe I was wrong about the tone the first few times I heard it.

But it sounds just as off as it had earlier in the day. It doesn't even sound like *her.* It's polite and all, but distant. Like we're not even friends. Like I imagined the good vibes between us yesterday.

It was good seeing you? Take care?

I frown at my phone. That is definitely her building up a wall. And since I don't want to be an asshole, there isn't much I can do but give her some time on her side of it.

I grab my axe case off the passenger seat, get out, and shut the door. Shoving my phone into my back pocket, I head for the pub. I can't afford any distractions tonight. This is the first week of my axe-throwing league, and I need to come out strong. Pushing open the door to the pub, I evict Mila Ferguson from my head.

At least, I try.

"What's with you tonight?" Hunter takes a swallow from his beer and assesses me with dark, wary eyes. "It's not like you to let Doc get ahead of you on the scoreboard."

"My shoulder is bothering me a little," I say, going so far as to rub it.

Hunter laughs. "Maybe you need a massage. Where's your girlfriend tonight?"

I roll my eyes and grab my beer off our table. "She's not my girlfriend."

"So she dumped you already?"

"Fuck off."

"Listen." Ripley throws an arm around my shoulders. "If you need some advice, just ask. I'm an expert at romance."

I snort. "I don't think so."

"Bro, I go on *way* more dates than you."

"Everyone goes on more dates than him," Hunter points out. "Even Doc, and he's an old man with a dad bod."

"Fuck you, Gannon. I do not have a dad bod."

"You gotta show her that you're sensitive," Ripley goes on. "When I take my godson out in the stroller, the ladies swoon. You want to borrow him?"

"No. I'm not using your godson as a prop."

Ripley strokes his beard and thinks some more. "How about you invite her to the farm and let her see you playing with those baby goats?"

"Yeah." Hunter nods. "Baby goats would be good. And when she talks, really make it seem like you're listening."

"I *am* listening when she talks."

"What does she do?" Ben asks.

"She's an artist."

"Like a painter?"

"A botanical illustrator."

Ripley squints at me like it's smoky in here. "What the fuck is that?"

"She draws flowers, but they're scientifically accurate and really detailed. Fruits and vegetables too."

"Oh. Okay, great. So if she was talking to me about sketching plants and whatnot, I'd look at her like this, with some smolder—" Ripley gazes at me, eyelids half-lowered. "And be like, 'Tell me more about your creative process. What do you wear when you draw?'"

I put up a hand. "Stop."

"That's pretty good." Ben points the neck of his beer bottle at Ripley. "But maybe use some bigger words. Women like a good vocabulary."

"Yeah." Ripley nods enthusiastically. "But make it a little sexy, too. Like tell her you can totally feel the emotional resonance of her melons." He mimes hefting two melons in his cupped palms.

Ben rolls his eyes. "Jesus Christ. Do *not* do that."

"Say you appreciate the textural dimension of her tulips," says Hunter, cracking up. "Get it? *Two lips*?"

"Hey. Hey." Ripley pokes my shoulder a few times. "Ask her what's the biggest eggplant she's ever doodled."

"And does she want to get her hands on your banana?" Hunter proceeds to give his beer bottle a hand job.

The three of them bust up laughing.

"You guys are assholes." I pick up my axe. "And even if I needed romance advice—which I *don't*—I wouldn't ask any of you." I manage to throw better after that, but I still end up second on the leaderboard for the week.

I'm *not* happy about it.

After the league matches are done, Ripley goes behind the bar, and Ben and Hunter take off, since they both have to work early. I don't feel like going home yet, so I find a seat at the bar and take out my phone, hoping to see a new text from Mila.

Nope.

Ripley comes over and brandishes a tall glass. "One more?"

"Yeah, I'll do one more."

He fills the glass with my favorite IPA and sets it in front of me. "Everything okay? You seem a little off tonight."

"Just a lot going on right now."

"Farm stuff? Town stuff? Personal stuff?"

"There's always farm stuff," I grumble. "And yeah, I'm dealing with a tricky situation as mayor that I'm not sure how to handle."

"What's it involve?"

"The Hart family."

"Ah. The founding fathers. That always complicates things." Then he catches sight of someone over my shoulder, and his face breaks into a grin. "Veep! To what do I owe this pleasure?"

"Don't pretend you don't know!"

I turn on the stool and see Yasmine Khoury standing there, hands on her hips, mad as hell.

"You sent me a singing beer-gram," she accuses.

"How do you know it was me?" Ripley picks up a towel and starts drying a glass. The motion might look casual to someone who doesn't know him as well as I do, but as usual, he's putting on a show for Yasmine.

"Because only you would do that on Mindfulness Monday."

"Look, I wanted a Saturday, but Mondays were cheaper."

"So it *was* you."

Ripley guffaws. "Yeah, it was me."

"You are despicable. He showed up right in the middle of Meditation and Merlot!"

That only makes Ripley laugh harder. Yasmine spins on her heel and charges for the front door. She swings it open, turns around long just enough to give Ripley the finger, and sails through it.

"God, I love messing with her," he says. "And it's criminal how easy she makes it."

"Why do you have it in for her so badly?"

"Goes a long way back." He chuckles as he wipes down the bar.

"Did you guys date in high school or something?"

"Nah," he says with a glance at the door. "I wasn't her type. And she wasn't mine."

Something about his expression leads me to believe that isn't exactly true, but he turns the tables on me before I can press him.

"So what's going on with you and Mila Ferguson? I heard you

had dinner with her Saturday night."

I pick up my beer again. "From who?"

"My cousin is the hostess at Wardwell House. She texted my sister last night. My sister called me today. Also, I saw it on The Landing Pad."

I raise a brow. "Say what you will about the older women in this town, you're the worst gossip of the bunch. Nothing's going on, if you must know. She's in town helping her mom."

"And yet she's spent at least two evenings with you."

After a long swallow, I shake my head. "Not gonna happen."

"You're telling me there's a woman in this town who wouldn't drop her panties if you asked her to?"

"No, I'm saying it's complicated," I clarify, unwilling to concede *that* particular point. "She's just coming off a divorce, and I'm respecting her boundaries."

"What a nice guy." He trades out the polished glass for another one and resumes his busy work. "Did you see the Landing Pad post from that true crime group about doing a deep dive into the Tart and Soul fire?"

"No." Confused, I adjust my hat on my head. "Why would they do that?"

"Apparently, there's new evidence."

"Evidence of what? It was an accident."

"I'm not sure." Ripley glances toward the door again and grins at someone coming in. "Hey! I heard you were a big hit."

Over my shoulder, I see a pot-bellied guy with a balding head and a ginger beard approach the bar. His royal-blue T-shirt says Salty's Sing-a-Grams. "I'm not sure about that. The owner didn't seem too happy."

"That's just her face."

"I don't know. When I launched into '99 Bottles of Beer on the Wall' and all her customers joined in, she left in kind of a huff."

Ripley laughs. "My fault, not yours. Can I get you a beer on the house?"

"Sure," he says. "Thanks."

Ripley pours the singer a beer and sets it down in front of him. "Thanks for your service today."

"No problem. I also yodel, if you'd like to send another one sometime."

"That's a fucking great idea. I'll be in touch." Picking up his towel, he begins drying glasses again.

"You sure there's no history between you and Yasmine?" I ask.

His grin grows wider. "I didn't say that."

Around nine on Wednesday night, I'm lying on my couch watching baseball, Merlin dozing on the floor next to me, when I get a text from Mila.

Mila: *Hi.*

That's it. Just a hello.

Everett: *Hey.*

Her move.

Mila: *I'm sorry.*

Everett: *About what?*

Mila: *The voicemail I left. I didn't mean what I said. Can I call you?*

Everett: *Sure.*

When my phone vibrates in my hand a moment later, I sit up to answer it. Try to sound casual, maybe a little bored. "Hello?"

"Hey. Sorry to call you so late. I just left the hospital."

The inclination to play games melts away at the sound of her voice. "That's okay. How's your mom?"

"Recovering. She can come home tomorrow. And I'm one hundred percent sure the entire unit will be elated to see her go."

I laugh, making Merlin pick up his head. "Yeah?"

"She has *not* been an easy patient. In her opinion, the doctors are all unreasonable, the nurses are either complete fools or sadists, and as for me, I will never understand how hard this has been for her."

None of that surprises me, but all I say is, "Sorry it's been rough."

"Anyway, I didn't call to talk about my mom. I called to apologize for the weird voice message I left you on Monday. I've been spiraling about it for two days."

I lean back. Get more comfortable. "Okay."

"I didn't mean what I said. Well, I meant the part about 'thank you for the sandwiches,' but not the part about 'it was good to see you and take care.'"

I can't resist teasing her a little. "It wasn't good to see me?"

"No, it was! But it came out so wrong—I didn't want you to think..." She pauses and exhales. "I was trying not to be *overzealous*."

"Why?"

"I don't know." Her voice grows smaller. "My mother said this thing that got in my head—she's *so* good at that—and it made me freak out that I was being too forward with you."

"What did she say?"

"That I come on too strong. She said men don't like it when women are overzealous and I should basically play hard to get."

"Um, did you tell your mother that you are currently playing *impossible* to get?"

She laughs. "I told her the other night we were just friends. But when she heard that you'd brought me food, she jumped to conclusions."

"Look, you don't have to worry about being overzealous with me. In case my behavior over the weekend did not make it clear, I am very zealous about you. So whatever amount of *zeal* you feel is cool with me."

More laughter, and the sound of it eases a tension in my chest I didn't realize was there. "Okay. How was your day?"

"I had a phone call with Tad Hart this afternoon."

"What happened?"

"He refused to accept the initial soil assessment results and wants to fund a second round of tests with a firm of his choosing." I imitate his blustery voice. "'You should always get a second opinion, son.' When I told him that wasn't possible and we had to move on to cleanup options, he hung up on me."

"Oh no. So what's next?"

"I'm not sure. Whether or not we build the community center, we *have* to clean up the site. But without their financial help, it won't happen. On top of that, I don't really want to alienate the Hart family."

"Hmm," she says. "That *is* a conundrum. I'll give it some thought, too."

We chat for another ten minutes or so, and then she says she should probably get some sleep. Tomorrow will be a busy day getting her mom home.

"Good luck with everything," I tell her. "And reach out if I can help."

"I will. Thank you."

"Night."

We hang up, and I sit there for a few minutes, looking at my bare walls and wondering what I might put there to impress someone like Mila, who knows shit about art. I reach over and scratch Merlin behind the ears. "What do you think?" I ask him. "Should I invite her over? Ask her opinion?"

Merlin's tail thumps the leather couch enthusiastically.

"Yeah. Maybe I will."

Although I think about her nearly nonstop over the next few days, I know Mila is busy with her mom, so I wait until Sunday afternoon to check in with her.

Everett: *Hey. How's everything going now that you're back at home?*

Around ten that night, I get a reply.

Mila: *34*

The number perplexes me.

Everett: *34 what?*

Mila: *Days until I can go back to NY.*

I laugh, wishing I could hear her voice.

Everett: *Can you talk? Is it okay to call you?*

Mila: *Yes.*

I tap her name in my phone, and she picks up quickly.

"Hi."

"Hey. Sorry about your week."

"It's okay. I just keep reminding myself that she's in pain." Her voice is strained and quiet, and I imagine her patience is stretched thin.

"Can you get out of the house at all?"

"Only for thirty minutes at a time. Next week should get a little better."

"Are you able to put your headphones on and draw or something?"

"I'm trying." She exhales. "But I have to be able to hear her call for help."

"Can I bring you anything? Food? Wine? Some organically grown cannabis? I know a guy."

She bursts out laughing, which makes me grin. More than anything, I wish she could come over right now. We'd stretch out on the couch under a blanket. Fuck around like teenagers in the dark.

"That's the first time I've laughed all week," she says. "Thank you. But no, I don't need anything."

"You promise you'll let me know if you do?"

"Yes. I was thinking about the problem you have with— Oh shoot. My mom is calling me. She must have to use the bathroom again."

"Go," I tell her, full of admiration and respect for the job she's doing. I'm not sure I'd be able to handle it. "We can catch up another time."

On Tuesday, I drop off a little care package for her. It's nothing fancy, just an apple pie my mom asked me to bring and some takeout from one of my favorite restaurants. I knock on her door a little after four in the afternoon.

When she answers, she's in socks, sweatpants, and a hoodie that says *Rooted in the Bronx*. Her hair is in sort of a nest on top of her head, and her face is free of makeup. The sight of her lips reminds me of kissing them, and I want so badly to do it again.

She looks surprised to see me. "Everett," she says, tucking a stray lock of hair behind her ear. "Hi."

"Hi." I hold up the brown paper bag. "I brought you some dinner. Swedish meatballs with cardamom bread from Iron Kettle."

She gasps. "You didn't have to do that!"

"There's an apple pie from my mom in there, too."

"Oh my gosh!" Her eyes mist over. "This is so sweet. I might cry."

"Don't cry. Just eat."

"Thank you." She takes the bag from me, still looking like she might burst into tears. "It's been a rough day, and I had no plan for dinner. I'm really grateful."

I smile and stick my hands in my pockets. "It's no big deal."

She glances over her shoulder. "My mom's resting. If you give me a second to put this in the kitchen, I can come out and chat for a minute."

"I don't want to keep you."

"No, please." Her eyes close. "I could use a break."

"I'll wait right here."

She comes back out a few minutes later, and we sit on her front porch with the door open so she'll be able to hear her mother call through the screen. Wrapping her arms around her legs, she lowers her chin to her knees. Instinctively, I go to put my arm around her, but then I pull it back.

"So, how are things going?" I ask.

"Well, I bought the detergent that gives her sensitive skin a rash. I fold clothes wrong *and* put them away in the incorrect drawers. I moved her reading glasses too far away on her nightstand for her to reach. The water I ran for her bath was freezing, so clearly I am trying to give her hypothermia. Oh, and she *hates* the walker the surgeon and PTs told her to use. It's monstrous of me to force it on her."

I shake my head. "You're a saint. I can't imagine having to do all that for my mother."

"You'd do it if it had to be done."

"I guess, but I wouldn't have your patience. I hope she appreciates you."

"I think deep down she does." Her tone is a little wistful. "She's said a few times that she's glad I'm here."

"Good."

"Guess what?" She straightens up. "I'm seeing Yasmine Friday night! We reconnected last week, and it's been so nice. I can't believe I waited so long to reach out."

"See? I was right." I elbow her side gently. "Now you should reach out to Gabi."

"Maybe." She pauses. "By the way, I meant to ask you—have

you seen those Landing Pad posts from the Diner Detectives about looking into the fire?"

"Ripley mentioned something about that the other night. But I haven't seen the posts."

"They claim to have new evidence."

I look down at her and shrink back slightly. "Seriously?"

"Yes." Her blue eyes are wide. "But what could it be? Anything material would have been found back then, or destroyed in the fire. You don't think…"

"What?"

"It's just… You don't think anyone else could have been there, right? It's the only thing they could have 'discovered' after all this time, but I know the front door was locked. And the back door locked automatically, didn't it?"

I think for a moment. "Yes. I always had to use my key to get in if that door wasn't propped."

"That's what I thought, too. Weird."

"Mila?" Her mom's voice floats out from inside.

"Coming, Mom!" Sighing, she rises to her feet. "Guess I have to go in. Thanks again for bringing dinner. I really appreciate it."

"Anytime." I stand too, facing her. "Let me know if you can escape for a cup of coffee or a drink sometime. I'll even let you park in my spot."

"Deal. And you let me know next time you're coming over. I'll at least brush my hair." She tries to cover her head. "I'm a mess right now."

"You're beautiful right now."

She blushes, her freckles swimming in a sea of pink. "Thanks."

I want to hug her so badly, but I don't.

Later that night, she texts me.

Mila: *Dinner was delicious. And the pie was so good! I forgot how good your mom's baking is. I wrote her a thank-you note—I'll drop it in the mail tomorrow.*

Then she sends me a screenshot of the photo of me at the lemonade stand with the little girls.

Mila: *This pic of you is so adorable. I can't stop looking at it.*

Everett: *The real thing can be yours. Toddlers not included.*

She hearts the message, leaving me to wonder.

Chapter Twenty

WELCOME TO THE LANDING PAD

Community Updates From The Hart's Landing Gazette (Online Edition)

POLICE BLOTTER: Several residents reported phallic graffiti chalked on their driveways on Monday morning. If you have information, please contact Detective Samuels at samuelsf@hldps.net.

EVENTS: Bakers participating in the Founder's Day Best Pie Contest are reminded that use of artificial flavoring will result in disqualification.

Comment from PieQueenJudy: ☝ We know who you are, cheaters.

GazetteMod: Please refer to our Code of Comment Conduct by clicking here.

Comment from PieQueenJudy: It's not a violation of the code to tell the truth.

[GazetteMod has closed this post to comments]

Community question (submitted by TeaLover55): Wednesday, the mayor was going on and on about Mila Ferguson's artistic talent at the town council meeting. Last night, he was spotted buying a dozen pink roses at Petals on Pine. Can anyone confirm that Mila got the flowers?

Comment by KnittingBiddy: I can! The mayor also dropped off a pie at the Ferguson house on Tuesday afternoon. He and Mila sat on the porch for several minutes, looking quite cozy.

Chapter Twenty-One

Mila

I have to laugh as I scroll through Friday morning's Landing Pad. Penises drawn in sidewalk chalk. Competitive pie baking. Obsessing over the mayor's personal life.

Hart's Landing at its best.

I suppose that last one should make me a little angry, since it involved a lot of eyes on me as well (and I suspect two of them belonged to Vera Pratt), but it's hard to feel anything but happy as I sip my coffee and admire the roses on my work table.

Everett brought them over last night as a thank you for the artwork I did for the Founder's Day poster. He knocked on the door around seven, and I invited him in, but he couldn't stay.

"I'm late for an emergency meeting of the Concerned Citizens Brigade," he said with a grimace.

"Oh my. The graffiti?"

"First a stoplight, and now this." Everett shook his head. "Hart's Landing is nothing but a den of vice."

I pat his broad chest. "If anyone can save us, you can."

"I'm going to try. Talk tomorrow?"

"Sure. Thanks again for the flowers. And good luck finding Dickelangelo."

He laughed and jogged to his truck while I stood in the doorway and watched him go, wishing for things I couldn't have.

After teaching my classes on Friday morning, I discover a new email in my inbox.

To: Mila@lavenderladybug.com
From: Harts_Landing_Bartok@gmail.com
Subject: Interview for Diner Detectives

Dear Ms. Ferguson,

I hope this email finds you well. My name is Daniel Bartok, and I'm the president of a true crime club in Hart's Landing called Diner Detectives. We enjoy taking a look at local mysteries and cold cases in our town and seeing if we can crack them!

As you know, the fire at Tart and Soul remains one of this town's most dramatic and mysterious events. Since this year marks the tenth anniversary, we thought it would be interesting to see if we can discover what actually happened that night. New evidence has come to light that we think you'll be interested in.

After all, it could clear your name!

Please let me know if there's a time we can talk.

Sincerely,
Daniel Bartok

I read over the email several times. Is this guy serious? What could possibly clear my name? I was the employee on the closing shift. I was responsible for ensuring all the equipment was off. I should have been more mindful of the flour dust when I swept.

I shouldn't have burned that letter.

I delete the email and close my laptop.

But it nags at me for the next few hours.

What if somehow there *was* evidence that I did my job right—that the fire wasn't my fault? I've spent ten years agonizing over my actions that night. Swimming in guilt. Drowning in shame. Do I owe it to myself to hear what Daniel has to say?

After lunch, I head out for a walk. When I reach the river, I sit cross-legged on the bank, pull out my phone, and call Everett.

He picks up fast. "Hey you."

I smile at the sound of his voice. "Hi."

"How's your day?"

"Pretty good. How was your meeting with the Concerned Citizens Brigade?"

"Unproductive. I mostly just listened to them fuss about the 'moral turpitude' of Hart's Landing and try to avoid saying the word 'dick.'"

Laughing, I pluck a blade of grass and play with it. "What did they say instead?"

"All kinds of things. Willy. Member. Ding-dong. Vera Pratt lowered her voice to a whisper and spelled P-E-N-I-S. I almost choked trying not to laugh."

"That sounds just like her." I lean onto one elbow and stretch out my legs. "So I want to ask you about something."

"Shoot."

I tell him about the email I got from Daniel Bartok. "My gut reaction was to trash the email and leave the past in the past. But… I can't stop thinking about it. What if there *is* something that could clear my name?"

"So meet with him. What's the worst that could happen?"

Going from wrongly accused to knowing for sure I'm guilty. "I don't know. I'll give it some thought."

"Looking forward to your night out tonight?"

"*Yes*. Getting out of my house for a few hours is going to feel so good." I watch a fishing boat coast down the river toward the lake. "What are you up to?"

"The usual. Hanging out with the guys at the pub. Practicing my throw."

"I'll be right next door at Novel Vine. Maybe we'll run into each other."

"If I'm lucky."

I smile. "You make me want to break all my rules, you know."

"Say the word, Freckles. I'll smash those rules to pieces for you."

My stomach flips. "I'll remember that."

We hang up, and I lie down on my back, staring up at the sky. I've got a tele-therapy session this afternoon. Should I tell my therapist about Everett? My mind wanders to my last session, when I told Hugo about my no-dating rule.

He wasn't thrilled.

"Avoidance doesn't build skills, Mila. If you want to learn healthy boundaries in a relationship, wouldn't it be better to practice *within the context of a relationship*? A quarterback doesn't improve his passing plays off the field without a receiver."

Hugo loves a sports metaphor.

"It's not forever," I argued. "Just for a year. And I'm already halfway through. I only have six more months to go."

He also disliked my arbitrary timeline. "So all you're doing is waiting out the clock? That's not building skills, either. Healing won't happen in isolation, Mila. Give it some thought."

I gave it some thought, and I concluded that the rule made sense. It was nice and clean. It was hard and fast. Wasn't that sort of like a boundary?

Now I realize how much easier it was to stick to that rule when Everett McKean wasn't offering to smash it.

You sure we can't see where this goes? Because I feel like we could have a lot of fun together, Freckles. No strings attached.

He makes it sound so easy.

But am I capable of that? I never met a string I didn't want to tie around my finger. In a double knot. I know "friends with benefits" situations work for other people, but would one work for me?

I'm just not sure.

Nowhere in my mother's house offers complete privacy. So, when it's time for my session, I go out to the driveway and sit in the car.

"Hey, Mila." Hugo greets me from behind his desk, the glare of his screen reflecting in his glasses. "How are things going?"

"Pretty good," I say. "My mom's surgery went well, and she's back home now. She's pretty miserable and cranky, but I expected that."

A slight smile. "And how are *you*?"

"Fine." My default answer for so many years, it comes out instinctively.

"And things between the two of you?"

"About the same. She hasn't changed." Immediately, I add, "It's hard because she needs me so much right now. She's dependent on me for everything, from getting dressed to using the bathroom to making meals."

"Remember that it's okay to say no to minor requests. If something is medically necessary, of course you should do it. But if there are non-medical tasks she's asking you to do, or if she's simply trying to monopolize your time so that you have none for yourself, those are good opportunities to practice 'no.'"

I nod slowly. "We've had some nice talks," I say. "She told me my father was an artist. I never knew that before." Characterizing that conversation as a "nice talk" is a stretch, but I don't want to be too negative.

"That's interesting." Hugo resettles in his chair. "How do you feel learning that?"

"At first, I was shocked. Then sort of fascinated, because it means my artistic talent has roots. I wanted to know more, but that's all she would tell me. I had to let it go. But it really bothers me that she never told me before."

"Can you say that to her?"

"I could, but I know what she'd say."

"What?"

"That it upsets her to talk about him. That she just wants to forget him. That he was a liar who abandoned us, so what difference would it make if he was Pablo Picasso?" I glance out the window and watch a pair of little brown house sparrows hop around on the grass. "And I guess she's right."

"Still, it wouldn't hurt to let her know that you're upset about the deception, as long as you don't expect her to take any accountability for hurting you," Hugo says firmly. "Because she won't."

"I know."

"And look at it this way. Now that you know about this connection to your heritage, it belongs to you. She's not part of it, and she can't take it away."

"That's true." I sit up a little taller. "I like that idea."

"Good." He pauses. "So what else is going on?"

I take a deep breath and tuck my hair behind my ear. "I went to dinner with someone. It was sort of a date."

"Oh?" Hugo's bushy salt-and-pepper eyebrows rise above his glasses. "Did you have a good time?"

"I had a great time. But now I'm scared."

"Of what?"

"Our connection feels…intense. I guess I'm afraid of repeating my usual patterns. Getting sucked in too fast."

"This is someone you just met?"

"No. It's someone I grew up with. The older brother of one of my childhood best friends."

"So it's someone you already know and trust."

"To a point. I mean, he *seems* trustworthy, but I haven't seen him in ten years. Yet I find myself telling him very personal things. It seems like it should be concerning behavior, doesn't it?" Part of me wants him to say yes. To tell me to put on the brakes.

"Not necessarily." He shrugs. "You have a spark. You find him easy to talk to. Those are good things."

"I *really* like him," I confess. "I can't stop thinking about him. But I made that no-dating rule for a reason."

"So maybe you just slow down a little instead of pushing him away completely. You don't have to swing for the fences every time you're at the plate. A single is good, too. Even a walk gets you on base."

I smile at the metaphor. I never played baseball, but I know exactly what he means.

I also know myself. And I have a feeling there will be no walking around the bases if Everett McKean is pitching.

I'll probably just charge the mound.

Chapter Twenty-Two

Mila

Just before seven that night, I hurry down the stairs from my room. "I'm heading out, Aunt Jackie." I grab my purse from the hook by the front door. "You're sure this is okay?"

My mother's younger sister smiles at me from the couch. She resembles my mom, although she's several inches shorter with a much rounder shape. "Of course! You deserve a night off—and how fun to reunite with an old friend."

I grin with excitement. "I can't wait."

She beams as she looks at my baggy jeans and cropped floral blouse with flutter sleeves. "You look adorable, by the way."

"Thank you."

"And I'm all set to sleep on the couch, so don't worry about what time you get home. Pull an all-nighter if you want."

I laugh. "There will be no all-nighter, but I'll try not to wake you when I come in. Call me if she needs anything, okay?"

"I will."

"She hates the walker, but encourage her to use it."

"I'm on it."

"The meds are all lined up on the kitchen counter with detailed notes."

"I saw."

"And the pajamas she likes are clean and folded on top of her dresser. She'll need help getting into them."

"Am I going to have to kick you out of the house? Go!" She waves me off, and I laugh, pulling the door shut behind me.

It was always strange to me how different my mother and her sister were, given how alike they looked. I used to love sleeping over at my cousin Lauren's house because my aunt would bake cookies with us or paint our nails or braid our hair. And she was so free with hugs and I-love-yous. I was envious.

Downtown, I find a parking spot in the public lot. As I walk toward the bar, I see the Founder's Day poster I designed in a shop window. I gasp in surprise and stop to admire it. Leaning closer, I notice that a little note has been added at the bottom. *Artwork by award-winning local botanical illustrator Mila Ferguson.*

My heart skips a beat. Everett remembered my award? Not only did Connor skip the ceremony, he didn't even ask me about it afterward. I'm flattered that Everett not only recalled that small piece of our conversation but put it on the poster. I keep walking, noticing the poster in nearly every window along Main Street. It puts an extra spring in my step.

I'm about to enter Novel Vine when a tall, broad-chested guy barrels out with a huge grin on his bearded face—it's Ripley. He steps to the side and holds the door open for me. "Hey, Mila."

"Hi, Ripley." I slip past him. "Thank you."

"My pleasure. Have a good night."

Inside, I look around, taking in the long, white marble bar on the right, the plush pink bar stools, the black-and-white honeycomb tiles on the floor. On the left, above pink velvet banquettes, the entire wall is lined with black bookshelves. Along the back wall are mirrored shelves, giving the illusion of more depth, and the front window houses a curved nook.

Not every seat is taken, but it's busy, with women in pairs or trios chatting softly over glasses of wine, the occasional burst of laughter ringing out over an Olivia Dean song. The vibe is elegantly cozy, feminine, and lush.

Spotting Yasmine behind the bar, I break into a smile, my throat growing tight. She looks almost exactly the same—short and bombshell-curvy, shoulder-length brown hair, heart-shaped face. As if she knows I'm there, she looks over at me right away. Her mouth falls open, and her shoulders twitch, as if she's sucked in her breath. Next thing I know, she's taken off running.

Careening around the end of the bar, she launches herself at me, flinging her arms around my neck. For a moment, we just stand there clinging to each other and crying softly. Emotions crash over me like a series of waves. Gratitude for her forgiveness. Longing for the past. Mourning the years and friends we've lost. Regret for my mistakes. Yearning to go back and be the girls we were before anything went wrong, but also hoping we can repair the damage and build a new friendship as the women we are now.

When we finally let go, our faces are a mess and we're both talking at once.

"Oh my God, it's good to see you."

"I am so sorry it's been so long."

"You haven't changed a bit!"

"Neither have you!"

"I was so scared I'd never hear from you again. I felt like that part of my life just vanished."

"I don't know why I didn't reach out sooner. Please forgive me."

"It's okay, it's okay." Her hands grasp mine, her moss-green eyes shining. "You're here now. That's what matters."

My eyes are drawn to the gold chain around her neck.

The ladybug charm dangling from it.

I gasp. "You still have it!"

"Of course I do." She touches the charm. "I hardly ever take it off. You don't wear yours anymore?"

A lump forms in my throat. "I lost it the night of the fire."

She nods in understanding.

I take a breath and look around, determined to stay in the present moment. "This place is so beautiful, Yasmine."

"Thank you." Her lips curve into a thousand-watt smile. "I'm really proud of it."

"How long have you been open?"

"Just over a year."

"And business is good? Everyone I talk to has great things to say about it!"

"It's pretty good." Yasmine tucks her hair behind her ear. "Summer is definitely the best time because of all the tourists, but this September is going fairly well. I'm a little worried about the winter—January nearly killed me this year—but I've got some ideas to keep people coming in. Although..." She glares at the wall Novel Vine shares with The Axe & Barrel. "A lot of people just want the same old pint of beer at The Axe on a Friday night."

I look at the wall too. Knowing Everett might be just on the other side of it makes my heart do jumping jacks.

Yasmine tugs my hand. "Come sit at the bar. Let me pour you a glass of wine, and you can tell me how it's going with your mom."

I slide onto one of the plush pink stools. "I'm dying for a glass of wine," I tell her, "but please don't make me talk about my mom."

She laughs. "Is it that bad?"

"She's just...my mom. You know how she is."

"I remember," she says. "So let's talk wine. We have several flights, and our daily specials are listed along with tasting notes on the chalkboard behind the— Oh my God." As she glances over her shoulder, her smile morphs into a scowl. "I'm gonna kill him."

I follow her line of sight and notice that the chalkboard notes have been edited to say things like, "Not as good as Bud Light" and "Pairs well with deez nuts." (That note is accompanied by an abstract little doodle of what I imagine is supposed to be a guy's junk, and I wonder if Dickelangelo hasn't just incriminated himself.) In contrast to the elegant script above, the comments are printed in sloppy, spiky capital letters—totally a dude's handwriting.

"Kill who?" I ask.

"Ripley Wilder, that's who!" Yasmine hurries over to the chalkboard, grabs a rag, and wipes furiously at the unauthorized notes. After having a few terse words with the other bartender, who holds up her hands like she didn't see anything, Yasmine returns to me.

"Everything okay?"

"Apparently, his mission in life is to ruin my vibe." She places a short food menu in front of me and frowns at the shared wall again. "I should have known better than to put Novel Vine next to his pub. It was the perfect location, but his pranks are driving me insane!"

"Clearly, he hasn't changed."

"Not a bit," Yasmine confirms. "If anything, he's *worse* than he was in high school."

"Think he could be the person drawing the dicks around town?"

"I heard about that." Yasmine's angry face relaxes a little. "I wouldn't put it past him, but I doubt it. He's pretty well known in the community, and most of his bullshit seems to be aimed at me. He still calls me 'Veep' because he knows how much it bugs me."

"He stole that election," I say loyally. "I'll never believe otherwise."

Yasmine laughs. "Me neither. But enough about him. What can I get you to drink?"

I sip wine and snack on a cheese and charcuterie board, stealing moments with Yasmine whenever she can chat with me. I learn that she veered from her plan to attend Northwestern University after a gap year and instead worked in restaurants while taking business classes at a nearby community college. She got interested in wine the summer she worked at a winery in northern Michigan called Cloverleigh Farms. The winemaker there encouraged her to get some education, so she saved up enough money to start training to become a Certified Sommelier.

"What did that involve?" I ask, spreading soft white cheese on a slice of toasted baguette.

"Classes in theory and tasting and service. Learning about the major wine regions of the world. Getting experience in vineyards, wineries, restaurants."

"So you worked in vineyards?"

She nods, expertly pulling a cork from a bottle. "In Michigan, Italy, and France."

"Wow!" I take a sip of my wine. "So how did you end up back here?"

She sighs as she pours two glasses of red. "There was a man."

"Uh-oh."

"We were supposed to open a wine bar together. It did not go well."

"What happened?"

"I invested a lot in him—money, time, work, feelings." She sets the bottle down and speaks quietly. "He took me for everything."

"Oh God, Yaz. I'm really sorry. Men can be such assholes."

"I was pretty lost afterward. Not to mention broke. I had to move in with my parents for a little while, start saving again. I was working as the sommelier at Wardwell House when this building became available. I decided I didn't need a partner and opened Novel Vine myself."

I lift my glass. "Here's to your fresh start."

She smiles, pours herself a small amount from the bottle of red, and touches her glass to mine. "To old friends and new beginnings."

Goose bumps prickle my arms. "To old friends and new beginnings." We both drink and set down our glasses. "Speaking of old friends and new beginnings," I say, "I heard the old foundry site where we used to meet up might be repurposed into a playground and community center."

Her eyes go wide. "Really? It's a mess now."

"It was kind of a mess back then, too," I say with a laugh. "We just didn't care."

"All we cared about was that no one could hear us talking shit about people. "

"Or see us drinking Boone's Farm right from the bottle." I pick up my glass of red. "This is much better."

She groans. "God, I hope so."

"It's funny that you were the only one of us who refused to drink that shitty wine. Your palate was refined even then."

"I think it was more that I was afraid my parents would find out.

I remember how much trouble my sister got in for drinking in high school."

I nod, remembering how unruly Yasmine's older sibling had been. How determined Yasmine was as a kid to be the opposite of Sara, even though we secretly envied how fearless and wild she seemed.

"What's your sister up to these days? Does she live in town?"

"God, no." Yasmine shakes her head. "She's out in California, living on some kind of commune. She swears she won't set foot in Hart's Landing again."

I laugh ruefully. "Pretty sure I said the same thing the day I left."

"Well, I'm glad you reconsidered." She refills my wineglass.

"Do you ever hear from Gabi or Rachel?" I ask.

"No. I've seen Gabi's mom and brother, and I know she lives in Detroit and occasionally visits, but she hasn't reached out to me or come into the bar. And I haven't heard anything about Rachel since she left for Yale."

"Me neither. My mom and I ran into Mrs. Hart at the grocery store a couple weeks ago. She said Rachel lives in Florida and works for the family business."

Yasmine pours a glass of white for another customer. "I saw Mrs. Hart around town a couple times this summer, too. I said hello once or twice, but she always seemed to be in a hurry. Either that or she doesn't want to talk to me."

"I kind of got the same impression. But it's hard to tell, because it's not like she was ever warm and fuzzy." I pop a dried fig into my mouth. "So I guess Rachel never went to law school?"

"Honestly, I have no clue. She was so upset after everything that happened, she wouldn't talk to anyone."

"I wonder if she ever gave that letter to Lydia's sister."

"I don't know that, either." Yasmine delivers two glasses of wine to a pair of women down the bar. When she returns, she says, "I've seen her, though—Alice, I mean."

My eyes go wide. "Really?"

"Yeah. She came in here over the summer with friends. And

then, another time, I saw her in the grocery store. She was wearing scrubs, and she looked…" A small smile curves Yasmine's lips. "She looked so much like Ladybug. I think it broke my heart a little."

"Did you say anything to her?"

Yasmine shakes her head. "Nothing more than social small talk. I didn't want to bring up anything painful. But God, the look of her. Same wild blond curls as Ladybug, same dimples. Same smile. And when I heard her laugh…" She shivers. "Eerily familiar. It's like I went back in time."

I smile sadly, recalling Ladybug's distinctive, uncontrollable giggle. "Speaking of going back in time, have you heard of a group in town called the Diner Detectives?"

"Yes," she says. "It's like a club for amateur sleuths. They like to revisit unsolved mysteries and see if they can succeed where detectives failed."

I pause for a sip of wine. "Their latest project is the fire at Tart and Soul."

Her eyes widen. "I didn't realize there was any mystery left to solve."

"I didn't either. But take a look at this." I pull up both the Landing Pad post and retrieve the email from Daniel Bartok out of the trash. "He claims there's 'new evidence.'"

"Oh my God! Are you going to meet with them?"

I shake my head. "I don't think so."

"Why not?" Her eyes are bright with excitement. "Whatever they have could clear your name once and for all. Wouldn't it be a relief after all these years to know that it wasn't your fault?"

"I guess," I hedge, chewing my bottom lip. "You really think I should do it?"

After a ticket prints at the computer behind her, Yasmine pours two flights of wine. "I would. Haven't we run from the past long enough?"

While she delivers the order, I mull over her words. Is she right? Have I run from the past long enough? I think about what Everett said too—what's the harm? The worst that could happen is that the evidence supports the accepted truth: that my carelessness caused the fire.

But what about the best-case scenario? What if, by some miracle, there is evidence to support the idea that something or someone else might have caused—or even contributed to—that explosion?

My friends are right, I decide, tossing back the rest of my wine. And whether it's the liquid courage or my determination to finally face the past, I put down my glass and pick up my phone.

To: Harts_Landing_Bartok@gmail.com
From: Mila@lavenderladybug.com
Re: Interview for Diner Detectives

Dear Daniel,

Thanks for your email. I'd like to meet and learn about the new evidence you've uncovered. Please let me know when you'd like to talk.

Sincerely,
Mila Ferguson

"I did it," I tell Yasmine when she returns. "I emailed the guy back and said I'd meet with him."

"Eeeeep!" Yasmine claps her hands. "This is so exciting! Can you imagine if what they have changes everything?"

I put a hand over my stomach, which feels like I'm cresting a steep drop on a rollercoaster. But it's a good feeling. A feeling of anticipation. Of hope. "I could use some change. And maybe some more wine."

"You got it." She pours me another glass. "So I want to ask you something, but you don't have to answer if you don't want to."

"Ask away."

"My mom heard you got married and divorced fairly quickly." It's not actually a question, but I hear the curiosity—and kind concern—in her tone.

I nod and take a swallow of wine. "True."

"I'm sorry."

"It's okay. I think the whole disaster was the kick in the ass I needed."

Yasmine looks interested. "How so?"

"I have to learn to love myself before I love someone else."

She taps her glass to mine again. "Amen."

"Which was why I'm not supposed to be dating right now. I'm taking some time to figure out who I am and what I want when I'm not trying to please someone else." Are my words slurring slightly? My lips are warm from the wine. Maybe a little numb.

"I think that's really smart."

"I think so too, but…" My thoughts wander to Everett's wide shoulders and brown eyes. His crooked grin and sun-kissed skin. His deep, sexy voice.

"But what?"

I take another long swallow. "There's this farmer."

Chapter Twenty-Three

Everett

When I see Mila walking toward me at the back of the pub late Friday night, I wonder if she's a figment of my imagination. Like maybe I've been thinking about her so hard that I conjured her up.

But she keeps coming toward me with a huge smile on her face, as if she's over the moon to see me. And while I'm glad to see her too, something feels off.

When she gets closer, I know what it is. She's drunk.

"Everett!" She waves both hands high over her head. "You're here!"

"I'm here."

"Me too, and I just did a shot of Fireball." She laughs and gestures toward the bar.

"Um, you did two shots of Fireball," says Yasmine, who's standing behind her. "And I'd just like to say that I voted against both of them." She shoots an evil stare at Ripley, who's also with them.

He holds up his hands. "In my defense, I didn't realize *someone* had been plying her with wine all night next door." He cants his head toward Yasmine with an accusatory glare.

Yasmine makes eye contact with me, mimes a steering motion and shakes her head. The message is clear.

I glance at Mila's lopsided smile, doing my best to keep my eyes off her bare midriff in that flirty top she's wearing. "How are you getting home?"

"That's a *good question*," she says, poking my chest. "But I'm not ready to go. Let's have another drink."

"I don't think that's a good idea. Did you drive here?"

She thinks for a moment. "Yes. In my mother's car."

"I'll take you home."

"To your place?" She seems excited about that, but it's easy enough to ignore temptation and be responsible when she's clearly inebriated.

"No, yours. But I'll drive."

"Oh." Her face falls and then lifts again. "Your truck? I've never done it in a truck before."

Sweet Jesus, how much alcohol has she had tonight? I inhale and exhale, gathering strength. "No, in your mom's car. Are you ready to go?"

"Yes." An emphatic nod. "But I think we'll have a lot more space to maneuver in your truck."

Praying for strength, I ask her to give me a minute, gently tucking her into the chair I just vacated. I hustle over to the throwing lane, where Hunter and I are mid-game. Ben is home with Vivian tonight. "Hey, listen," I tell Hunter. "I gotta take Mila home. Maybe someone can throw for me."

He cocks a brow. "I thought there was nothing going on."

"There isn't. She just drank too much, and I want to make sure she gets home safely."

"Um, you sure about that?" The next thing I know, Mila has wrapped her arms around me from behind, pressing her cheek against my shoulder blade.

"You're so big," she gushes. "And you've got so many nice, hard muscles. But you're cuddly, too. Like a big snuggle bear."

Hunter nearly chokes on his beer.

"I'll throw for you," Ripley says, his expression concerned. "You get her home safely."

"Thanks." I detach Mila's hands, which are locked around my waist, and turn around. "Let's go."

"Okay." She gazes up at me with bleary, adoring eyes.

"Bye, Snuggle Bear," Hunter calls.

Ignoring him, I take Mila by the shoulders and aim her toward the exit.

"I'll walk out with you," Yasmine says. "I told my bartender I'd only be gone for a few minutes." The three of us start walking toward the front of the pub.

"Wait!" Mila stops moving so suddenly that I bump into the back of her and have to catch her before she falls forward. "I have to go to the bathroom."

"It's over there," Yasmine says, pointing just beyond the bar. "Do you want me to go with you?"

"No." Mila gives her a smile and pats my chest. "I'll be right back. Don't go 'way."

I watch her walk unsteadily to the bathroom, glad when she makes it without tripping. "How much did she drink?"

Yasmine looks guilty. "I'm not entirely sure. I probably refilled her wine glass one too many times. But it was just so good to see her, and we were talking and reminiscing nonstop. I was about to call her an Uber when she suddenly decided she wanted to come over here and find you." She frowns in the direction of the bar. "Then Ripley offered her shots. It took her from tipsy to tanked real fast."

Mila returns a couple minutes later, and we make our way out of the pub. On the sidewalk, Yasmine opens her arms, and Mila flings herself into them. "Thank you for the wine, and for being so wonderful. I'm sorry I wasn't better at keeping in touch."

"That's okay, honey." Yasmine rubs her back. "We found each other again, right? And this time, we'll do better. Get some sleep, okay?"

"Okay." They let go of each other, and Yasmine gives me a smile. "Thanks, Everett. Good night."

"Night, Yasmine."

"She's so pretty," Mila murmurs dreamily, watching her friend slip inside the wine bar. "I remember in high school how I was so jealous of her curves. I had no boobs." She laughs, looking down at her chest. "Not that I have much going on there now. My butt is better."

Actually, her tits are great—on the smaller side, the perfect size to fit the palm of my hand. Or get my mouth on. And as far as that apple-cheeked ass, I want to sink my teeth into it.

But I will be good tonight.

I will be good tonight.

I will be good tonight.

"Where are you parked?" I ask.

"The public lot." She giggles. "Not in your spot this time."

We start down the block with her clinging to my arm like a koala to a tree branch. Along the way, she takes deep breaths and tilts her head back to look at the sky. "Stars tonight," she says. "They look like confetti. Like they're falling on me."

I chuckle. "Make a wish."

"Good idea." She closes her eyes, and immediately her sneaker snags the edge of an uneven sidewalk square.

I catch her before she goes down. "Keep your eyes open, okay?"

"But you have to close your eyes when you make a wish! And I really want this one to come true."

I don't ask.

A minute later, we reach the parking lot, and after some searching, she manages to lead me to her mom's car.

I hold out my hand. "Can I have your keys?"

"Sure." She hunts around in her purse for a minute, pulls them out, and lets them dangle from her fingers. "Found 'em."

I reach for them, but she snatches her hand away. "Wait!"

"What?"

She grins up at me and hiccups. "Can I see your tractor, Farmer McKean?"

"My tractor?"

"Yes. I want you to"—*hiccup*—"plow my fields."

I try not to laugh. "Can I just have the keys?"

"Are you saying you don't want to plow me?" With a hand on

each of my shoulders, she rises up on tiptoe and brings her lips close to mine. Temptingly close. Agonizingly close. I can practically taste the Fireball on her tongue.

But she's drunk, and I'm not that guy. "Not tonight."

"Why not?" *Hiccup.* "We won't even be breaking my rule because we're not going to date. We're just going to be bends with frenebits." Frowning, she tries again. "Friends with benefits. It's where you can have sex with a friend, but it doesn't mean anything. It's just for fun, like you said."

I manage to grab the keys out of her hand. "Friend, there will be no benefits while you're in this condition."

"But it will be good for me. Healing doesn't"—*hiccup*—"happen in isolation, Everett."

"Come on, Freckles," I say gruffly. "I'm taking you home." Taking her by the arm, I march her around to the passenger side while she resists like an obstinate toddler. After helping her in, I get behind the wheel. "Put your seat belt on, please."

She buckles herself in without saying anything and stares straight ahead, hands in her lap.

"Mila. Don't be mad."

She only hiccups in reply.

At her house, I ask where she wants the car.

"Driveway is good. But how're you gonna get back to town?" Her words are slurred.

"I'll walk."

She hangs her head. "Sorry."

"It's fine. It's not far." And I'm going to need the air to cool off anyway.

"Okay. Thanks for the ride." She exits the car abruptly, heading straight for the house. The front door is unlocked, and I watch her go inside. It doesn't occur to me until the door is already closed behind her that I still have her keys.

I send her a quick text.

Everett: *Hey. I forgot to give you your keys back. Should I leave them in the car? Or in the mailbox?*

I wait a few minutes, but she doesn't reply.

Everett: *If I don't hear from you tonight, I'll just drop them off to you early tomorrow.*

Another five minutes. No response.

She probably already crashed. I get out of the car, lock the doors, and stick the keys in my pocket. I'll bring them over to her in the morning, see how she's feeling.

It'll give me an excuse to see her again.

That night, I struggle to fall asleep. I lie there in bed, hands behind my head, staring into the darkness but seeing Mila's flirty smile. Her ass in those jeans. The bare skin below her blouse. I want to kiss her there. I want to kiss her everywhere.

Groaning, I slide my hand beneath the covers and fist my cock.

My conscience knows I did the right thing turning her down, but right now my body has the floor. I imagine her above me in the dark, her mouth on mine, the taste of whiskey on her lips. I can practically feel that long red hair trailing my chest as she shimmies her way down my legs. At the first stroke of her tongue across my crown, I suck in my breath. Her playful laugh floats up at me as she wraps her hands around my shaft and licks me like vanilla ice cream off her spoon.

Sucks me like caramel sauce off her finger.

Takes me to the back of her throat.

Fuck, fuck, fuck. She grips me tightly, working her hands up and down my length, the tension in my body climbing, the muscles in my legs going tight. With my eyes closed, I see her lips moving up and down my cock. I hear the soft, surprised little sounds she emits as I jerk my hips off the bed, fucking her hot, lush mouth. I feel the unbelievable heat and friction and suction driving me higher, harder, closer to the edge. My stomach muscles clench. Time stops. Hovers. Teases.

Two seconds later, I erupt with a long, drawn-out groan, lost in my fantasy's grand finale, during which Mila not only lets me come in her mouth but swallows every drop and licks her lips afterward.

Breathing hard, I fall back against my pillow. The release felt good, but it hasn't solved my problem. I don't want her any less.

After cleaning myself up, I climb back into bed and wonder which version of her I'll get tomorrow.

The one who wants me to respect her boundaries?

Or the one who wants me to plow her fields?

Chapter Twenty-Four

Mila

Saturday morning, I wake up to a killer headache, two texts from Everett, and the sinking feeling I've done something regrettable. Groaning, I fall back onto my pillow, which feels like a cinder block beneath my pounding skull.

My brain slowly pries open the lid on consciousness, like a zombie pushing aside the cement slab on her burial vault. But the realizations that come with the light make me want to crawl right back inside the dark safety of slumber.

Did I really call Everett *snuggle bear*? Ask him to plow my fields? Mansplain friends with benefits to him?

I'm afraid the answer is check, check, check.

Beatrix hops up on the bed and meows.

"It's bad, Bea. It's real bad." Discovering that I've slept in my jeans and blouse from last night, I undress, throw on some sweats, and follow the heavenly scent of coffee downstairs. In the living room, my mother and aunt are sitting on the couch sipping from steaming mugs.

My mother's eyes widen when she sees me. "Good Lord, Mila. You look like something the cat dragged in."

My aunt gives me a sympathetic smile. "Did you have fun?"

I nod. My brains rattle like marbles. "Yes. Too much fun."

"How did you get home?" my mother demands. "I hope you didn't drive."

"I didn't. Everett drove me."

My mother purses her lips. "So where's my car?"

"It's here. He drove me home and walked back downtown."

"That was nice of him," Aunt Jackie says with a smile.

"I thought it was a girls' night." My mother's tone is slightly accusatory.

"It was. But later, we went over to the pub, and some guys we knew were there."

"Well, I'd say I hope you didn't make a fool of yourself, but there's a picture on The Landing Pad that makes it clear I'm too late."

"Photo?" My God, could this actually get worse?

"Show her, Jackie."

My aunt scrolls on her phone and hands it to me. "I think it's cute."

Bracing myself, I look at the picture with one eye open, holding the phone slightly away from myself, as if a little extra distance might help.

Community photo: [Alt text: Mila Ferguson wraps her arms around Mayor McKean's waist from behind. She wears a goofy smile and her eyes are squeezed shut. The mayor looks back at Mila with a puzzled expression.]

Caption: Talk about sizzle! Mila and the mayor left together. Neither returned.

My hangover goes full nuclear as I examine Everett's face in the photo. Whoever described his expression as "puzzled" was being generous. I would say he's giving big FML vibes.

In short, it is not cute.

I hand the phone back to my aunt. "Well. That's embarrassing."

"Oh, what's the point of being young if you don't have a foolish night out every once in a while?" Aunt Jackie grins. "Coffee's on, if you'd like some."

"Thanks. I'm just going to take a quick shower first." I leave the living room and head for the bathroom, but the scent of dark roast lures me into the kitchen. As I'm pouring myself a cup, I hear my mother's voice.

"My God, she looks awful."

"Oh, leave her be. She had a good time."

I pause with the pot in the air. Clearly, they don't realize I can still hear them.

"She's been acting so strangely since her divorce."

"Poor thing." My aunt clucks her tongue. "Is she heartbroken?"

"Who knows? It's not like she tells me anything."

Because you'll use it against me, Mom.

"And after all that money spent on a wedding," my mother tuts.

My skin prickles with anger, tension stiffening my limbs.

"Didn't they pay for it themselves?"

"Well, yes, but I planned the whole thing. And do you think either one of them ever thanked me?"

At this point, my skeleton feels like it's been forged by Hart Iron Works.

Of course I thanked her. Countless times, even though she took over when I would have liked to make my own decisions. Even though she complained all night that everything was wrong. Even though she made my wedding about her from start to finish.

For fuck's sake, she wore white.

Don't be ridiculous, darling. It's eggshell.

She's still talking. "I mean, I didn't expect it from *him*—what can you expect from a man?—but you'd think my own daughter, my flesh and blood, would be more grateful."

"I'm sure she was."

"I don't know, Jackie. Something is wrong with that girl. I try and try with her, but she doesn't listen to me. I could have told her not to marry that playboy. You could see it in his eyes that he was a cheater. But my daughter has a weakness when it comes to men. She only goes for the ones who mistreat her—it's as if she enjoys it! And once she falls, she's done for. I don't know if she'll ever get it right."

Five minutes later, with the water running so hot it scalds my skin, I let the tears come.

Chapter Twenty-Five

Everett

I wake up to three messages from her.

Mila: *Hi. I'm really sorry I didn't see your texts last night. I came in the house, fell face down on my bed, and passed out.*

Mila: *We have an extra set of keys for the car, so don't worry about bringing them over. If you want to leave them at the register at the farm store, I can pick them up later.*

Mila: *I'm also sorry about the way I acted. I really need to stop humiliating myself around you.*

Still in bed, I prop myself up on one elbow and text her back.

Everett: *I don't know, I kinda like it.*

Everett: *At least there was no fire this time.*

Mila: *Only the towering inferno that was my dignity.*

Everett: *How's your head?*

Mila: *I would like to trade it for someone else's. Preferably someone who made better decisions last night.*

Everett: *Did you have fun with Yasmine?*

Mila: *Yes. That part of the night was lovely.*

Everett: *Good. I have some work to do this morning, but I can swing by your house this afternoon with your keys.*

Mila: *I really don't mind coming to get them. It'll give me an excuse to get out of the house for a few minutes. Just leave them at the store.*

Everett: *Let's compromise. Text me when you get here. I'll come and meet you.*

Mila: *You don't seem to understand that I'm trying to avoid seeing you.*

Everett: *I understand. But I guess if you want those keys back, you've got no choice.*

Mila: *This is mean.*

Everett: *I'll show you my tractor.*

Mila: *OMG*

Everett: *I might even give you a ride on it.*

Mila: *Please stop.*

Everett: *Just don't shoot any whiskey before you get here.*

Mila: *I'm never shooting whiskey again.*

I chuckle and type one final message.

Everett: *See you this afternoon, Fireball.*

Mila: *SWEET JESUS, WHAT HAVE I DONE?*

AXE GODS

Ripley Wilder: *Good morning, Snuggle Bear.*

Ben Hart: *The fuck?*

Hunter Gannon: *He's talking to Everett.*

Ben Hart: *Is there bromance in the air?*

Ripley Wilder: *No. I didn't stand a chance once that redhead came back to town. Now he's her Snuggle Bear and I'm just the substitute axe thrower.*

Ben Hart: *What the hell did I miss?*

Hunter Gannon: *The redhead got drunk, and the mayor got a new nickname.*

The Fucking Mayor: 🖕

I planned to spend the day doing equipment maintenance, but before I leave the cabin, I get an emergency text that we're short-staffed and wind up playing tour guide all day long. With Merlin at my side, I give tractor-pulled wagon rides, describe life on a cherry farm, and—my personal favorite—conduct cherry-pit-spitting contests with the kids. In between tour groups, I check my phone for messages from Mila, only to be disappointed each time.

I grab a snack in the general store, where my mother is at the register. "I got the nicest thank-you note from Mila Ferguson yesterday. Did I tell you?"

"No."

"*Handwritten*," she gushes. "And the notecard had little flowers drawn on the front of it. I bet she did it herself."

"She probably did."

Mom's smile is somehow angelic and devilish at the same time. "So sweet. Maybe I'll invite her for Sunday dinner tomorrow."

"Mom, stop."

"What, you can invite her to dinner, but I can't?"

I give her a look that says *You don't fool me one bit* and head back outside.

By four o'clock, I still haven't heard from her, so I decide to reach out. Maybe she can't get away from her house.

Everett: *Hey, just checking in. You still want to come by?*

Mila: *Yes. Sorry. My mother has been extra needy today. But I'll be there in twenty minutes!*

Everett: *No problem. I'll meet you by the big cherry in front of the general store.*

Since I smell like sweat and fertilizer, I run back to the cabin and take a quick shower. Afterward, I apologize to Merlin for leaving him behind, jump into my truck, and take the long, winding road up to the front of the farm.

As soon as I spot Mila sitting on the boulder-sized resin cherry showing off the farm's logo, my pulse quickens. She's wearing black yoga pants and a gray zip-up sweatshirt, and her red hair is loose and windblown. I park next to the store and walk over to her. "Hey."

"Hey." She slides off the big cherry and stands up.

I hold out the key fob. "As promised."

"Thank you." She takes it from me and tucks it into the pocket of her hoodie. Up close, her eyes appear pink and puffy. Is it from a hangover, or has she been crying?

"You okay?"

"I'm fine."

She isn't fine. Not even close. "Do you have to get back right away? Can you go for a walk?"

"I don't know," she says hesitantly. "I told my mom I wouldn't be gone long."

"No pressure. You just look like you could use some fresh air and sunshine. Maybe a friend."

She wavers, shifting her weight from one foot to the other. "That does sound nice. Let me call her real quick."

She taps her screen and puts the phone to her ear. "Hi, Mom. Would it be okay if I was gone another hour?"

She glances at me. "Just taking a walk at the farm, getting a little fresh air. But I don't have to. I can come right home."

She turns away. "Mom, you're not a bother. I can—"

She looks up at the sky and listens for a minute. "Okay. I won't be long. Thanks." Ending the call, she faces me again. "She said it's okay."

"Good. Let's go." As we start wandering down the road that meanders through the property from front to back, I try to think of something that will make her smile.

And damn if Ripley Wilder's advice doesn't pop into my head.

Chapter Twenty-Six

Mila

"Where are we going?" I ask Everett as we walk along the well-trod dirt road.

"It's a surprise." He gives me a sideways grin that sets butterflies loose in my stomach. Everything about him fills me with longing, from his mud-caked work boots to his worn-in jeans to the faded-gray Henley shirt that hugs his chest tightly enough to show off the bulging muscles underneath. His nose is slightly sunburned, and his hair is damp, like he just got out of the shower. He is rugged, masculine perfection.

I, on the other hand, am a wreck.

I made an effort to rehydrate, de-puff, and put some color back into my cheeks, but I am definitely not my best self. I slip my hands inside my sleeves and bunch up the cuffs inside my fists.

"You cold?" he asks.

"No. Just trying to pull a disappearing act."

"Why?"

I kick a small rock up the road. "Because I'm embarrassed about my behavior last night."

"I told you, I didn't mind." He nudges me with his elbow. "I thought it was funny."

"It wasn't funny, Everett. It was mortifying. For God's sake, I asked you to *plow my fields*."

He laughs. "You did. I was flattered. And also tempted."

"I can't imagine why." I catch up to my rock and kick it again.

"You know why." He pauses. "And I hope you know why I resisted that temptation."

"Because I was too sloppy drunk?"

"You were more adorable than sloppy, and it was nice to see you having fun. But consent is important, and I didn't think you were capable of giving it in that condition. You didn't sound like yourself."

"Yeah. Sorry about the mixed messages. My wires got a little crossed."

"It's okay." We come to a fork in the road, and he slips his hand inside my arm, pulling me to the left. "This way."

Forced to abandon my rock, I let him lead me.

"How's your mom doing?"

"Physically, she's improving. But she's driving me insane. I promised myself I wasn't going to let her get to me, but no matter how hard I try, she fucking *gets* to me."

"I'm sorry."

"No, *I'm* sorry." Exhaling sharply, I shake my head. "I feel like I'm always unloading my bullshit on you."

"I don't mind. Do you want to talk about it?"

"Not really," I say, unable to quell that conflicting urge to protect my mom. Or maybe it's myself I'm protecting. There's something shameful about the way I let her talk to me. I know it's wrong, but I can't seem to find the backbone to stand up to her.

I think about the conversation I overheard this morning. Those orchids in the basement. All the ways she makes me feel like I'm a disappointment to her. To myself.

Something is wrong with that girl.

My head hurts. The need to break down gathers in my chest like storm clouds, heavy and thick. I try everything to hold it in—box breathing, sensory grounding, counting backward from 100 by sevens—but I can't.

Stopping in the middle of the road, I start to cry.

Everett says nothing, but he turns me into his arms and lets me sob against his chest, his hand moving up and down on my back.

"God, I'm sorry." I use my sleeve to mop up my face. "I did not intend to fall apart in front of you."

"Hey." He puts two fingers under my chin and lifts my face. "You can fall apart in front of me whenever you need to. You never have to pretend to be somebody else, or act okay when you're not."

I meet his warm brown eyes and manage a smile. "Thanks."

"I mean it. I don't want the pretzel Mila. I want the real thing." He tilts his head like he's thinking hard. "Although Fireball Mila might be fun under the right circumstances."

I laugh, but it turns into a groan. "That's twice now I've tried and failed to put the moves on you."

"You know what they say. Third time's the charm."

My mouth twitches, and I turn away.

We continue walking, and I take deep breaths, savoring the earthy smell of the sunbaked dirt, dried grasses, and wildflowers. My artist's eye can't resist trying to imagine how I'd capture the leafy kaleidoscope of autumnal color. At this hour, the light is soft and golden, as if everything is dripping with honey. Neat rows of cherry trees stretch out over gently rolling hills, their fruit long gone except for a few remaining pieces that glimmer like rubies in the sun.

"God, it's beautiful here." I stop to admire the view. "I wish I could draw it."

"Why don't you?"

I laugh. "With what, a stick in the dirt?"

"Come back with your sketch pad sometime. You've got an open invitation." He takes my hand and squeezes it. "This way."

"I'm never leaving," I announce. "I hope you know that."

From somewhere close by, Everett laughs. I can't see exactly where he is because I'm lying on my back in the gambrel-roofed barn with my eyes closed, cuddling the baby goat draped across my chest. All around me, more of them jump and play and bleat. It smells like fresh hay and sun-warmed pine, and the wide double doors are open to the September breeze.

"What's this one's name?" I ask.

"I'm not sure. My mom tends to name them after sitcom characters, so that could be Johnny, Moira, David, Alexis, or any of the Golden Girls. She likes the really old classics, too, so it could be Mork or Mindy, Lucy or Ethel, or maybe even Arthur Fonzarelli."

I giggle. "Let's call him Fonzie."

Another goat walks over my legs, and uncomplicated joy flows through me. "You know, I had no idea playing with goats would make me so happy. What is it about them?"

"I don't know, but my cousin teaches goat yoga in here, and apparently, it's very popular."

"Is that why I smell essential oils?" I sniff again, catching hints of lavender and maybe eucalyptus.

"Probably."

Fonzie ambles off me, and I open my eyes, propping myself up on my elbows. Everett is sitting on the clean-swept cement floor a few feet away, leaning back on his hands, legs outstretched and crossed at the ankle. Several baby goats are hopping on and off his lap or over his calves. One puts two hooves on his chest, like she wants to slow dance.

I grin. "I think she likes you."

"Told you I was good with animals." He pets the goat on his lap, nuzzling it behind the ears.

"You're good with everybody." Watching him be sweet to a baby goat is doing things to my insides. "Especially me."

"I like you." He sends me a dark-eyed scowl. "Even if you did call me 'Snuggle Bear' in public."

My head falls back as I laugh. "I'm sorry. I think I was trying to communicate that your body is big and hard, but also warm and inviting, and I wanted to be close to it."

The goat moves off his lap, and he leans back on his hands again. "Do you still want to be close to it?"

Our eyes meet, and something electric passes between us. The air is still and hot. "Yes."

"So come here."

"What?" My heart jumps into my throat.

"You heard me."

I wait for him to smile, to tease me or make a joke, but he doesn't. Barely aware of making the decision to do it, I get on my hands and knees and crawl toward him. At his side, I hesitate, sitting back on my heels.

"Closer," he says.

Desire flows through my veins like molten lava as I climb onto his lap, straddling his hips. I unzip my sweatshirt and peel it off, revealing a tight white tank top, which I'm wearing without a bra—one of the few benefits of having smaller breasts. Everett's eyes immediately drop to my chest, thirstily drinking in the way my nipples poke through the thin, ribbed cotton.

"Is this good?" I ask.

"You tell me."

"Tell you what?"

"How close you want to be."

"Close enough to experience your rough edges."

That makes him laugh, but there's a growl beneath it. "Sweetheart, my rough edges would already have your back against that wall while I fucked you like an animal."

I gasp. "Really?"

"Really." He brings one hand to the back of my neck, gripping it hard. "You have no idea how rough I want to get with you."

"What's stopping you?"

He hesitates, stroking the hollow at the base of my throat with his thumb. "I promised myself I'd be careful."

I lean closer to him, putting my hands on his chest, my lips at his ear. "What if I don't want you to be careful?" I whisper as his cock thickens beneath me. "What if I *want* my back against that wall?"

"I'd worry you were doing it for me."

I freeze. "Why?"

"I guess because of everything you've told me. About how you like to please people. How you prioritize what others want and not what you want."

Anger burns under my skin. He's throwing my words back at me, treating me like I can't take care of myself, like I don't know what I want. It's embarrassing and patronizing, and it deflates my sexual confidence like a popped balloon.

I jump to my feet. "Then just forget it."

"Fuck." Everett stands up and adjusts the crotch of his jeans. "Mila. Don't be upset. I—"

"I can't help it! You said you liked me. You told me to be myself around you. You said the third time's the charm and invited me to sit on your lap, and I *crawled over to you* in this *goat barn,* and then you made me feel bad about it!"

Behind me, a goat bleats noisily.

"Exactly!" I shout in its direction.

Furious with Everett and with myself, I storm out of the barn.

Chapter Twenty-Seven

Everett

"Mila, wait!" I take off after her, stopping only to make sure the barn's double doors are secure so the goats don't escape.

How did I screw that up so completely?

One second, she was on my lap, driving me crazy with her tits in my face and her ass on my crotch and her voice saying dirty things in my ear, and the next, she was standing there yelling at me. I catch up with her before she reaches the road and grab her by the arm. "Hey!"

"Let me go!" she yells. "This is obviously not meant to happen."

"Mila, I just wanted to make sure you knew what you were asking for. I feel protective of you. I always have."

"Stop it!" She glares at me, the fire in her eyes matching the intensity of that red hair, which is burnished by the sun. "Don't you dare treat me like a child, or like you know what's best for me. I realize I'm the emotional equivalent of a junk drawer, but I'm not a baby, I'm not drunk, and believe it or not, I wasn't saying those things to please *you*, Everett. I said them for *me*! And I ended up humiliating myself again." She tries to shake off my grip. "Now let go of me!"

"No."

We stare each other down in what feels like a face-off, center ice.

Tightening my grip on her forearm, I drag her back toward the barn. But rather than go inside, I haul her around the back, where we'll be hidden by the trees. I pin her against the wall, my chest to her back. Instinctively, she braces her hands on the wood just above her shoulders.

"What are you doing?" she asks, fighting for breath. Her cheek is pressed against a plank of white pine.

"I'm showing you my rough edges." I wrap my left hand lightly around her throat and place my right on her stomach, over her tank. Her sweatshirt got dropped somewhere between the road and here. "Want me to stop?"

"I don't know. You're confusing me." She doesn't make a move to get away, but her breaths are short and shallow. I wonder if her heart is racing as fast as mine.

"I know. It's so fucking unfair." I stick my boot between her sneakers and kick her feet apart. My cock is fully hard, bulging against the zipper of my jeans. "The truth is, Mila, I want it both ways with you."

"Huh?"

I slide my hand down her stomach, between her legs, stroking her through the soft cotton of her yoga pants. "I want to be the good guy, the one you can trust not to take advantage of you, but also the guy who fucks you up against a wall. I want to respect you and ruin you at the same time." I speak low in her ear, my voice gritty with desire. "It's a problem."

"Or not," she whispers.

I take it as permission.

My hand slips down the front of her pants, inside her underwear, and I'm delighted to discover she's already wet. Dipping my fingertip inside her, I rub the silky warmth over her clit. Light and gentle. Sensual little circles. "I don't think you understand the things I want to do to you."

She writhes above my hand. "Tell me."

"I want to make you come right here, right now, just like this. I want you to make a mess all over my hand. I want to hear you moan. Curse. Say my name."

She struggles for words, either because what I said was too much or because my hand between her legs is causing her brain to short-circuit.

"Are you going to give me what I want, or should I put the brakes on again? It's up to you."

She squirms. "Someone might see."

"So tell me to stop." I rub her a little harder, a little faster.

"Oh God. Everett."

"Tell me you don't want this." I plunge my fingers inside her again, gratified by the way she rides my hand.

"It's been. So long. I can't– I can't," she pants, her words coming in raspy, broken fragments as her body grows tense.

Using the hand on her throat, I pull her back from the wall and hold her tightly against my body. Put my lips at her ear. "Say no, Mila. Say it now, or I'm going to make you come."

"I'm *so bad* at no," she whimpers.

"Then say yes."

"*Yes.*"

The word is like a match to kindling. "Listen to me." I move my fingers firmly over her soft, swollen clit. "You're going to do what I say. You're going to give me this thing you've never given anyone else. You're going to come exactly when I tell you to. Okay?"

Her only reply is a helpless moan.

"That's it, gorgeous. You're almost there." Taking my hand off her throat, I move it down her chest until it covers one breast. "Did you take that sweatshirt off just to tease me?" I play with her perky little nipple, pinching it through the thin material of her tank. "Did you know how badly I'd want to get my mouth on your tits?"

She arches her back, pushing her ass back against my erection, which strains against my jeans like it might bust the seams. I work my fingers harder and faster, feeling her grow more aroused with every second. I growl with frustration. "God, you're so wet. I'd give anything to fuck you right now. My cock is so hard it hurts."

"Do it. Fuck me."

A sinister laugh rumbles through my chest. "You're not giving the orders here, sweetheart. I am." Sensing that she's on the verge,

I keep the pressure and rhythm steady. "You're close. I feel it. Five seconds close."

"Yes." She gasps for air. Throws her hands around the back of my neck.

"Four."

"Oh God—Everett."

I take it up a notch. "Three."

"Fuck, fuck, fuck—" She rocks her hips frantically against my hand.

"Two."

"Yes— Yes—"

"One."

She cries out as the climax hits her, her legs buckling, her body bowing forward. I wrap an arm around her rib cage to keep her upright and feel the pulse of her orgasm against my soaked fingers. It's so hot, I nearly come in my pants.

She recovers, falling forward, palms and cheek flat on the barn wall. Her breathing is quick and heavy. "Oh my God. What just happened?"

I brace my left hand above hers on the wood and bury my face in her sweet-smelling hair. For a moment, I leave my other hand where it is, curved around her soft, swollen pussy. "You got what you asked for. Did you like it?"

"Yes. I just can't believe I did that *outside*. In broad daylight." She laughs weakly. "This is definitely the kinkiest thing I've ever done, and I once wore a sexy nun outfit for a guy who had a Catholic fetish. He made me stand him in the corner and spank him with a ruler. Tell him over and over again how he'd sinned."

"I sincerely hope this was a hotter experience for you."

"It was. No question."

I bite her shoulder lightly and remove my hand from her pants. "But do you still have the outfit?"

"No." Laughing, she turns to face me, putting her back against the wall. When she looks up, her face is flushed, her expression slightly curious. “So what now?”

I put my other hand against the wall, closing her in between my arms. “Now, my little fireball, I have to go clean up after the goats, because they probably made a mess on the yoga floor.”

Her smile turns coy as her hand reaches out to stroke me through my jeans. “But what about this?”

I allow myself to enjoy the pleasure of her touch for a moment, even though it shoots bolts of lust through me that won’t find any place to land just now. “That will have to wait for another day.”

“Another *day*?” Her eyebrows hike up toward her hairline. “That doesn’t seem fair.”

“I’m not concerned about justice, Mila. I just wanted to make you feel good.”

“You did. But I want to return the—”

I cut her off with a kiss. “This wasn’t a favor. This isn’t transactional. You don’t owe me anything, you don’t have to repay me, you don’t have to do anything except go to sleep tonight with a smile on your face. That’s all I want.”

Her lips fall open, and she blinks. Then she launches herself at me, throwing her arms around my neck. Laughing, I recover my balance and twine my arms around her back. Lift her off her feet and hold her close.

“You’re so good to me,” she says, her voice muffled in my neck.

“You make it easy.” I give her a squeeze and set her on her feet. “But I should probably let you go home.”

“What time is it?” She pats her hips, but her pants don’t have pockets. “I lost my phone. I think it’s in my hoodie.”

I take my phone from my back pocket. “It’s almost six.”

Her face blanches. “Shit. I’ve been gone for almost two hours. But I don’t want to leave yet.”

“Because you like the baby goats?” I tease.

“Because I like you.” Her hands move up my chest. “I want… things.”

“What kind of things?”

She puts a palm over my dick again and whispers in my ear. "I want to make you come. I want to know the sounds you make. I want the weight of you on my body. I want the taste of you in my mouth."

It takes all my strength not to throw her over my shoulder, carry her off to my cabin, and make her mine for the night.

After we retrieve her sweatshirt from the barn, Mila checks her phone and realizes she missed a call from her mom. As we hurry back to the parking lot, she calls her back, texts her, calls her again. No answer or reply.

I feel fucking terrible. "I'm sorry, Mila. I shouldn't have kept you here so long."

"I'm sure she's fine," Mila chirps with false confidence, picking up her already frantic walking pace. "She's probably just being passive-aggressive—letting me know she's not happy I was gone this afternoon."

Just as we reach her car, her ringtone sounds.

"It's my aunt." Mila accepts the call. "Hello?"

I wait while she listens, hoping everything's okay. But within seconds, her face drains of color, and I know something has gone very, very wrong.

Chapter Twenty-Eight

Mila

I drive straight to the hospital, blowing stop signs, cutting people off, failing to yield. I figure it will serve me right to be pulled over and issued a ticket.

"Your mom had a fall," my Aunt Jackie said. "I called the ambulance, and they took her to the ER. Meet me there."

At the hospital, I park crookedly and race inside. I spot my aunt sitting in the waiting room and rush over, dropping into the chair beside her. "Aunt Jackie," I pant, winded and nearly hysterical. "What happened?"

"I'm not exactly sure." My aunt looks tired and worried. "From what I can tell, she tried to make it from the couch to the bathroom without using the walker and fell. Somehow she managed to get back to her phone and call me."

"Oh, no." Guilt smothers me like an avalanche, and I bury my face in my hands. While I was cavorting with baby goats or moaning against the side of a barn with Everett's hand in my pants, my mother was lying on the floor, suffering alone. "How is she?"

"In a lot of pain. But her vital signs were okay, and they gave her some meds. They're doing X-rays now to see if she dislocated an implant or fractured anything. They'll likely keep her overnight."

My eyes fill. "I feel awful."

"It wasn't your fault." She rubs my back. "I hate to leave you, honey, but I promised Lauren I'd babysit this afternoon."

"It's okay. I'll keep you posted." I stand when she does and give her a hug. "Thanks for being here."

When she's gone, I pull out my phone. Several texts from Everett have come in.

Everett: *How is she?*

Everett: *I'm so sorry. It's my fault.*

Everett: *I shouldn't have asked you to stay.*

Mila: *Still waiting to hear. It's not your fault. She tried to get to the bathroom without her walker apparently.*

Everett: *I feel like a dick, keeping you away from home for selfish reasons.*

Mila: *I stayed because I wanted to.*

Everett: *Are you still at the hospital?*

Mila: *At the ER. She's getting X-rays.*

I also have a message from Yasmine.

Yasmine: *Hey! I just wanted to tell you how much fun I had last night. Thank you so much for coming into the bar and hanging out with me at work. Next time I'll take a night off! Hope your head is okay today! Coffee soon?*

Mila: *My head is a mess. I loved hanging out at your bar, and I'm sorry I lost my mind there at the end of the night. Next time, I'll skip the shots.*

Mila: *My mom had a fall today, so I'm at the ER with her right now, fingers crossed it's not serious. Coffee sounds good. I'll text you.*

Yasmine: *Oh no!! Keep me posted!*

I like her last reply and approach the desk to ask for an update.

"Let's see." The nurse checks her computer. "Looks like she's still waiting on an X-ray. They're backed up. Once those are done, the on-call orthopedic surgeon will look them over and examine her. Then they'll call you back. Maybe an hour?"

"Okay. Thanks."

Despondent, I return to my chair. While I slouch in my seat, I replay the episode with Everett in my mind like a movie, frame by frame. I close my eyes and feel the warm wood of the barn wall beneath my palms. Hear his gritty, country-road voice in my ear. Experience the sensation of being slowly tied into a knot, then unraveled all at once.

I berate myself all over again for enjoying the memory.

I'm slumped to one side, head propped on my knuckles, when a pair of familiar brown boots appears on the floor in front of me. My eyes travel up from the lug soles to the faded jeans to the gray Henley I cried into earlier today. Above it all is the face that sends my pulse skipping like a flat stone over the lake.

I straighten up. "Hi."

"Hey," Everett says softly. "How is she?"

"No word yet."

"And how are you?"

"Okay."

He holds out a white paper bag. "I brought you some dinner. I figured you hadn't eaten."

I stare at the bag, from which a savory scent is emanating. "You're always feeding me."

He nudges my sneaker with his boot. "You're always needing to be fed."

"Thanks, but I'm not hungry."

"No?"

"No." A cavernous groan chooses that moment to thunder through my empty belly. The woman three chairs down looks over at me.

"Here." He lowers himself into the chair my aunt vacated and hands me the bag. "Meat pasty from Sawbuck Tavern. I hope it's still warm."

"I can't eat." But my mouth is watering.

"Oh. Well, do you mind if I eat it? I already had dinner, but I love these things." He opens the bag and takes out the meat pie, which is wrapped in foil.

I gaze longingly at the flaky, golden crust. "Go ahead."

"God, can you smell that?" He brings the pasty to his face and inhales. "You sure you don't want just one bite? I mean, I feel like it might be a worse punishment to know what this tastes like and *then* deny yourself the pleasure."

"You're right." I reach for it. "I'll try it."

He laughs and offers me a napkin from the bag. "I'll find you something to drink."

By the time he returns with a bottle of water in his hand, I've polished off half the meat pie. "Jesus, this thing is good. What the hell do they put in it?"

"Probably a lot of butter and salt. I try not to think about it." He sits down, uncaps the water, and hands it to me. "Here. I feel like you need to stay hydrated today."

"Thank you." I finish the pasty and down half the bottle of water. That's when I notice there are a half dozen people watching us. "This town has a definite staring problem. As mayor, you might want to look into it."

"We've somehow become the hottest couple in Hart's Landing."

I cringe. "I take it you saw the photo on The Landing Pad?"

"I did."

"With my luck, there'll be an aerial photo of us against the barn wall tomorrow."

A half laugh, half groan resonates in his chest. "Let's hope not."

I get up to throw out the empty bag, and when I drop into my chair again, Everett puts his arm around me. It's such an easy, simple gesture of support, and yet it makes me want to cry. A partial sob squeaks from the back of my throat, and I try to cover it up with a cough.

Everett's voice is quiet. "Are you really okay?"

"This day is kicking my ass. The highs and lows are extreme."

His thumb caresses my shoulder. "I get it."

"I had *one job* to do here, and I failed. What if it's a sign?"

His thumb stops moving. "A sign?"

"That bad things happen when I put myself first."

"Mila. Look at me."

I do, and the depth of caring in his dark eyes is like a balm to my soul.

"Your mom did not fall because you messed around with me," he says. "Your mom fell because she didn't use her walker. That could have happened even if you were there. You could have been upstairs. Doing laundry in the basement. Making dinner in the kitchen."

"Okay, but you're talking to me like I'm a rational person when you know I'm hardwired to believe everything is my fault. I'm the daughter of a woman who turned guilt trips into an Olympic sport. I have a lifetime of gold medals."

"Baby, it's time to stop playing her games." His voice is low but forceful. "Don't let her do this to you anymore."

I swallow hard. Hugo once asked me why I was so afraid to stand up to my mom, and I couldn't answer him. But we both knew the reason.

I don't want to be abandoned, even by my narcissistic mother. She's still my *mother.* The only parent who stuck around.

If she can't love me, who could?

"It's just how she is," I say.

Everett's jaw is tight. "That doesn't make it right."

"It's also how *I* am. I wish it wasn't, but it is. The little kid in me still wants her approval."

Everett's mouth opens, but he closes it without speaking.

"You think I'm weak—a doormat—to let myself be treated this way." Of course, these are *my* thoughts, not his. But it's like I want to hear him say it, to confirm what I believe about myself. Like I know the cliff is straight ahead of me, but instead of hitting the brakes, I floor the gas pedal.

"Not at all. I just wish I could do something to make it better for you."

His calmness soothes me. "You're here. You're listening." I tip my head onto his shoulder. "It's enough."

His arm is warm and comforting around me. My eyes drift shut and stay that way until I hear my name.

"Mila Ferguson?"

Picking up my head from Everett's shoulder, I look over toward the desk and see a nurse standing there with a clipboard. I stand and raise a hand. "That's me."

She smiles. "You can come on back."

"Go on," Everett says, rising to his feet. "Call me later if you can."

"I'll try." I face him, wishing we didn't have to separate. "I might not be able to get out of the house much for the next week. I don't want to take the chance of leaving her alone again."

"That's okay."

"I'm sorry about—"

But he doesn't let me finish. He pulls me into his arms and holds me close, like he doesn't care who sees or what people will say. "No apologies, remember? I won't accept them."

"Okay." The word barely squeezes past the lump in my throat.

"Whenever you need a friend, you know where to find me. Or a benefit," he adds, his voice quiet and deep. "I'm here for that, too."

The nurse leads me back to a small exam room, where my mother lies on a wheeled bed with her eyes closed.

"Mom?" I approach and pick up her hand, which is cool to the touch. Her eyes don't open, and she doesn't say anything.

"She's probably drowsy from the meds," the nurse explains, checking her IV.

"Miss Ferguson?" says a voice from the doorway.

I turn to see a brown-skinned woman in a white coat, a long, black braid over one shoulder.

"Yes, that's me." I'm still wearing the sweatshirt that fell on the ground earlier, and I try to hide the dirty spots with my bag.

"I'm Dr. Anand." She flashes a smile and checks her tablet. "Your mother's condition is stable. The X-rays don't show any fractures, but they do show a dislocation of her right hip implant. The good news is that the implant itself appears intact, and the left is fine."

"What does that mean? Another surgery?"

"Maybe not. An orthopedic surgeon is going to try a closed reduction, which is a procedure to manipulate the implant back into place without opening up the incision. If that doesn't work, we'll have to revisit the possibility of another surgery."

"Okay." I wring my hands together and glance at my mom. "Is she in a lot of pain?"

"Yes," says Dr. Anand with disturbing frankness. "The fall was pretty bad. But she's more comfortable now than she was when she arrived."

"Will the procedure be done tonight or tomorrow?"

"Tonight. Besides the amount of pain your mother is in, prolonged dislocation increases the risk of avascular necrosis, or bone tissue death due to compromised blood supply."

I must look horrified, because the doctor pats my arm. "Don't worry. We'll get her all taken care of. Once she's sedated, the procedure will only take fifteen to thirty minutes, and then she'll be admitted. If the reduction goes well, she'll be released after twenty-four hours of observation."

"Okay. Thank you, Doctor."

"You're welcome. They'll be in to get her shortly." Dr. Anand and the nurse leave the room.

Tentatively, I move back to her side. "Mom?"

"Mm."

"Are you okay?"

"Do I look okay?"

Tears fill my eyes. "I'm so sorry. I shouldn't have left you alone so long."

"I told you to go, didn't I?" Her tone is devoid of emotion.

"Yes, but you needed my help and I wasn't there. Will you forgive me?"

"For goodness' sake, Mila. Don't be so dramatic."

Taken aback, I'm not sure what to say. She isn't going to guilt-trip me? Or is she saving it up for later, when she has more energy?

"I hope you at least had a good time."

"I did," I reply carefully, worried about giving her ammunition for a future battle. "I hadn't been to that farm in a long time. I'd like to go back and sketch there. But not until you're okay to be on your own."

"I'll be fine. I just twisted the wrong way."

"Well, from now on, you use the walker or you call me for help when you need to use the bathroom."

"I wasn't trying to get to the bathroom, I was trying to get to my bedroom closet. I was feeling nostalgic and wanted to look at my scrapbooks."

"Oh." My mother has gorgeous scrapbooks, full of programs, reviews, and photos she saved from her dancing days. When I was little, she used to bring them out and we'd pore over them together. She'd tell me stories about the other dancers, her partners, the costumes, the sets, the choreography. "I'd like to look at them, too," I say. "Maybe when you're back at home, I'll bring them out and we can look at them together?"

"That would be nice."

A nurse knocks on the open door. "Ms. Ferguson? We're ready for you."

She closes her eyes again. "Guess that's my cue. Wish me luck."

I pat her arm. "You'll do great, Mom."

She smiles as she's wheeled past me. "Thank you, darling. Now go home and take a shower. You smell like a barnyard."

Chapter Twenty-Nine

Everett

After leaving the hospital, I head home, take Merlin out one last time, and stretch out on the couch. I turn the TV on and attempt to watch a baseball game, but it's not long before I give up and turn it off. It's too hard to focus on balls and strikes when all I can think about is pinning Mila against the back of the barn.

My fingers inside her.

The way she moved.

The memory is enough to make me hard, but I resist the urge to get myself off. It doesn't feel right, knowing where she is and what she's going through. The guilt she's suffering.

It infuriates me, the way Eliza manipulates her. The way she has Mila convinced that everything is her fault. And my chest hurts every time I recall what Mila said about the little kid in her still trying to win over her mother. I wish I could convince her to stop.

People like her mother and my father don't change.

How many years did my mom spend making excuses for my dad? Trying to shield my sister and me from the worst of him? Believing things would get better if she just stayed with him, tried harder, kept her promise until death did them part? Her loyalty was nothing but a trap.

When Gabi and I were little, we'd hear our father yelling at our mom after we'd gone to bed. Hear our mom attempt to placate and defuse. Hear his alcohol-fueled rage and her tearful pleas to be quiet so the kids didn't wake up. Often, Gabi would sneak into my room and ask to sleep in my bed. Sometimes, we'd play games to drown out the noise.

One night when I was about twelve, the fight was louder than usual, and I heard something crash and shatter. I bolted out of bed, took off running down the hall, and burst into their bedroom.

My mother, wearing her nightgown, was kneeling next to the broken remains of a lamp. My father, disheveled but fully clothed, was standing across the room. “Go back to bed,” he ordered.

My hands clenched into fists. My heart was hammering inside my scrawny chest. I looked at my mother, who managed a teary-eyed smile. “It's fine, sweetheart. I just knocked over a lamp.”

Knocked over a lamp? There were two lamps in the room, one on each bedside table. The one on my mother's side was intact. The one on my father's side of the bed, next to where he was standing, was missing.

Above my mother's head was a mark on the wall.

“Go on back to bed, sweetie,” she said, her eyes pleading with me.

“You heard your mother.” My father's words were slurred.

After that, I slept with a baseball bat underneath my bed.

I must have dozed off, because I wake up when my phone vibrates. Groping around for it on the couch, I check the screen. *Mila calling.*

I sit up so fast I drop the phone in my lap and fumble to get it to my ear. “Hello?”

“Hey. I'm sorry to call so late.”

“Don't be.” I clear my throat. Run a hand through my hair. “How did everything go?”

“Fine. Turns out the fall dislocated an implant, but they were able to set it right.”

“That's good. Was she upset with you?”

“Hard to say. I kept trying to apologize, and she told me to quit being so dramatic.”

"That's good, I guess."

"She has to stay at least one night in the hospital, but she should be able to come home tomorrow night."

"Are you still there?"

"No, I came home to clean up and feed Beatrix. I offered to go back and stay the night with her, but she said not to bother. That one of us might as well get a good night's sleep."

Some real generosity? "That was nice of her."

"Yeah, I was glad. I didn't want to spend the night in her room."

"I don't blame you."

"I want to spend it in yours."

That's when I hear the knock.

My hair stands on end. From his crate in the corner of the living room, Merlin barks once, but it's more sleepy than ferocious. I rise to my feet as excitement balloons in my chest, keeping the phone at my ear as I walk to the door. When I pull it open, she's standing on my front porch wearing a giant fuzzy cardigan, flip-flops, and an uncertain expression.

"Hi," she says.

"Hi." We lower our phones at the same time. Then she shivers, because for fuck's sake, it's probably fifty degrees and her legs are bare.

"Christ. Get inside." I grab her arm and pull her into the cabin, kicking the door shut with my foot.

She drops her bag and clutches her sweater together at the chest. Her expression is that of someone looking at a carnival ride they really want to get on, but now that they've reached the head of the line, fear is kicking in. "I don't know what I'm doing here."

"I didn't ask."

"I was home alone in bed and starting to spiral about everything—like literally just coming apart at the seams, pieces of me scattering in every direction, and all I could think of was that I feel better around you. So I jumped in the car and drove here. In my pajamas." She sheds the big sweater, and my eyes about pop from my head.

Her barely-there navy shorts are edged with white lace. The matching top with skinny little straps is loose but cut low. Her nipples poke through the satin, begging me to kiss them.

My phone clatters to the floor. My dick springs to life.

I step forward, take her head in my hands, and crush my mouth to hers. Her lips are an open invitation, and my tongue sweeps between them. A want more powerful than any I've ever known courses through me.

She's *here*.

As if I need proof she's real, I run my hands all over her body, anywhere I can reach. Down her sides. Over her hips. Around her back. She flings her arms around my neck and presses her chest to mine. Sliding my palms down the curve of her spine, I grab that luscious ass and bite her lower lip. She moans softly, and my cock surges with need.

With a quick glance at my windows to make sure the shades are down, I slip my hands beneath her top. She sucks in her breath as I cover her breasts with my palms and tease her tight little nipples with my thumbs. When she raises her arms, I lift her top over her head. Blood thunders through my veins—in one direction—as my hungry eyes glide over her creamy vanilla curves, her rosebud nipples like cherries on top.

Bending down, I fasten my mouth to one pebbled tip. Her fingers slide into my hair as she arches and sighs. I switch to the other breast, flicking its stiff peak with my tongue, licking a circle around its crest, relishing the satin texture of her skin.

Reaching between her thighs, I discover two things. First, she isn't wearing panties underneath those fuck-hot little shorts. Second, she's already wet.

I have to get my mouth on her.

Capturing her at the waist, I throw her over my shoulder. She squeals and kicks her feet, losing one flip-flop by the couch and the other at the entrance to my bedroom.

At the foot of my bed, I lean forward, and she tumbles onto her back. It's dark in the room, but light slants in through the doorway, shining on her like a spotlight. My eyes drink in her sunset hair, her luminous skin, those midnight-blue eyes.

"My God, you're beautiful."

Her lips curve into a smile. "Thank you."

I inhale the scent of orange blossom. "And you smell fucking delicious."

She makes a come-hither motion with her hand. "Come closer, I'll give you a taste."

"A taste?" I laugh as I whip off my shirt. "Sweetheart, I'm going to fucking eat you alive."

"Like the big bad wolf?"

I hook my hands around the backs of her knees and yank her ass toward the edge of the bed. "He's got better manners."

Slipping my fingers inside the waistband of her shorts, I pull them down her legs and drop to my knees.

Run my rough, calloused hands up the insides of her soft, smooth thighs, pushing them apart.

Brush my thumb up the soft pink seam of her pussy.

Breathe in the honeyed scent of her, letting her feel it when I exhale.

And then, having reached the extent of my dining etiquette, I go at her like a starving lion.

I bury my face between her thighs, devouring her with a ravenous mouth, fucking her with my tongue. She writhes and moans above me, clutching the sheets, gasping for air. My cock throbs every time she says my name.

Which is often.

Especially once I slide my fingers inside her, plunging them deep enough to make my dick bulge with envy.

"Oh God, Everett," she whimpers. "You're so good at this."

Eventually, I stop gorging myself like she's my last meal and start paying attention. Because I don't just want to consume her; I want to *learn* her. What she needs, what she wants, what she's too shy to ask for. I'm determined to know her body like I know my own.

"Tell me what you like." I take my mouth off her only long enough to get the request out.

"Are you kidding? You want me to talk while you're— Fuck—" She squirms beneath me as I nibble and suck and play a little more gently than before. "While you're doing *that*?"

"Yes. For instance, do you like it slow?" I take my time now, swirling and circling and stroking her clit. "Or do you like it fast?" I flutter the tip of my tongue against the swollen pearl, quick as a hummingbird's wings.

"Yes," she manages, the word wrenching out between her teeth.

I laugh and give her more of both, going slow and soft until she moves her hips in a way that tells me she wants more, then sucking her into my mouth like a butterscotch candy, flicking her quick and hard.

Her sounds become desperate. She grabs a fistful of my hair. Finally, I sense the tension in her body reaching the breaking point, and I ease my fingers back inside her, curving them in search of the sweet spot. Within seconds, her cries grow more frantic and closer together. Then I feel it—the rhythmic pulse of her orgasm against my tongue, the squeeze of it around my fingers. Only when her body relaxes and her hand unclenches in my hair do I take my mouth off her.

But I haven't gotten enough. Not even close.

Chapter Thirty

Mila

There's light in the room, but I can't see.

There's probably enough oxygen, but I can't breathe.

And surely I have one or two brain cells left knocking around in my head, but I can't think.

Where am I? What just happened? Why does my body feel like I'm floating among the stars?

I mumble something unintelligible.

From the foot of the bed, a deep, gravelly laugh. "What was that?"

"I'm not sure," I admit, lifting myself onto my elbows.

He jumps to his feet and swipes his forearm across the lower half of his face. "I'm a messy eater."

My face burns, but my toes tingle. "I don't mind."

Lord have mercy, he's scorching hot. I haven't seen him shirtless since he was a teenager, and I thought he was muscular then, but adult Everett is something else. His shoulders are so wide, his arms so thick. He has pecs and deltoids and abs—*my God, the abs.*

He starts unbuttoning his jeans, and I scramble onto my knees. "Wait. Let me." I slip the button through the hole and lower the zipper. Grabbing his jeans at the hips, I pull them down enough for his erection to spring free.

He finishes kicking them off and stands before me again. I lick my lips. Stare like a fiend. Wrap my fingers around his hot, hard cock.

My God, the cock.

It's thick and long and solid, and I love the way his eyes close as I stroke it root to tip. The way his breath hitches when I caress the crown. The way he puts his hands in my hair as I kiss his chest.

His skin is warm beneath my lips, and he smells good—like

woodsy soap and sex. As I work my hand up and down his length, I think about that chest hovering over me as he pushes inside my body. My insides contract again, like an aftershock.

As I skim my mouth over his upper body, lust continues to gather force at my center like a hurricane. He has some hair on his chest, which was never a turn-on for me before, but which is suddenly the sexiest thing I've ever seen. He has the brawny, rough-hewn, sun-bronzed body of a grown *man*, and suddenly I realize that I've only been with immature, self-centered, twenty-something boys.

I brush my lips over one hard nipple. Lick it. Take it between my teeth and lightly bite. A low growl resonates in his chest as I kiss my way down the center of his body, over sculpted ridges and smooth valleys, his abdominal muscles flexing as he thrusts into my hand. Scooting back a little on the bed, I lean forward and take the tip of his cock in my mouth.

"Oh fuck." His fingers tighten in my hair.

With one hand wrapped around his shaft, I lick the velvety crown with long, decadent strokes. I circle it with sensual swirls. I slip it between my lips and suck. A bead of silky, salty liquid spreads over my tongue, and his cock grows thicker in my hand.

I take him deeper, sliding my lips past the head about an inch and then dragging them up again. He groans as I repeat the motion a few times, taking him in farther with every dip of my head until, finally, he hits the back of my throat.

Above me, Everett's breaths become more ragged. I peek up at him, and he's looking down at me like an angry god. "You're killing me," he says. A muscle in his jaw twitches.

I remove my mouth from him just enough to smile. "Good." Then I lower my head again, working my hand harder and faster while I do everything I can with my mouth to make his legs give out. He curses and growls, his fists clenched in my hair, his hips flexing in long, hard strokes. For a moment, I struggle to breathe.

"Fuck, I'm sorry." He pulls his hands out of my hair and backs off. "Told you I was an animal."

"You're not." I take a second, glancing up at him. A smile creeps onto my lips. "I don't want respect right now, Everett. I want ruin."

It's like I flipped a switch. Everett tosses me onto my back and kneels between my thighs, stroking his cock. "Should I get a condom?"

Breathless—*oh God, this is really going to happen*—I shake my head. "I have an IUD. I was tested after my marriage ended, and I haven't been with anyone since."

"I've gone longer than you have. I'm afraid I might go off like a rocket." He centers himself, teasing me with the tip. "But I have to get inside you."

I hold my breath as he eases inside me, inch by hot, hard inch. He's big. He's thick. He's long. And just when I think I can't take more, he goes deeper. I gasp, and he checks in.

"Yes?"

I nod, remembering to breathe. When he reaches my limits, he lowers his lips to mine and kisses me the way he did on the bridge, the kind of kiss I feel within muscle and bone, along every vein, inside each beat of my heart. Our tastes mingle on our tongues.

He begins to move with long, unhurried strokes. Once my body adjusts to the size and strength of him, I melt into the way he fills me. The warmth of his skin. The muscles in his back, moving beneath my hands.

The slow, sensuous undulations of his body over mine make me feel like I'm being slowly coiled. I feel it low in my belly. In my arms and legs, which are wrapped around him. Deep within my core. I make noises I've never heard myself make—loud, sensual, guttural moans that come from a place beyond abandon.

Surely no two people have ever fit together so exquisitely.

"It feels so good," I whisper. "Like your cock was made for me."

"Mila." Everett holds still, bottomed out inside me. "If you want this to last, you can't say things like that."

"But I mean it." I rock my hips beneath him. "Don't stop."

He groans and begins to move again, harder and faster this time, his hips driving with deep, powerful thrusts. I bring my knees up to take him deeper.

"I want to give you what you need." His voice burns with urgency. "I want to take care of you. I want it all."

As need overwhelms me, I moan into his neck, which is damp with sweat and smells fucking delectable. I suck it. I lick it. I nip it with my teeth. My hands slide down over his muscular ass and grab it hard, pulling him into me, my body begging for more. He circles his hips, grinding against my clit until every nerve ending in my body is sparking, the current too much for my system to bear.

He's with me. Panting, I rake my nails down his back. Dig my heels into the backs of his thighs.

He moves his hands beneath my ass and tilts my hips. The more intense angle is like pouring gasoline on a fire. I'm right at the precipice, that agonizing space between the viselike grip of contraction and the delirious pleasure of release.

A growl rips from his throat, followed by a series of ragged breaths that punctuate every thrust. Everett buries himself deep inside me and his cock begins to throb, which sends me over the edge. I rock my hips beneath him as the waves crash through me and over me and pull me out into deeper waters. I can't breathe, but I don't care.

Let me drown, I think, my body contracting around his as his body releases into mine. *Let me drown.*

When he collapses on me, I feel his heart banging through his chest, knocking against my ribs. I imagine my heart hearing the sound. Wanting to open up. Wanting to tear down the flimsy walls I've built. Wanting to obliterate anything that would keep us apart.

This friends-with-benefits thing is bullshit, says a voice in my head. *You're going to fall in love with him. In fact, you're halfway there.*

Everett picks up his head. "What?"

"I didn't say anything."

"Your body just tensed up. And your breathing got fast again. Are you okay?"

"I'm fine." My God, how can he read me so well? "Maybe just need a little air. And some water?"

"Of course. Sorry." He lifts himself off me and rolls away. "I'll be right back."

I watch him walk out of the bedroom—his gorgeous, naked ass drawing my eye like a magnet—and hear kitchen noises a minute later. While he's gone, I talk myself out of a meltdown.

You're fine. This is just post-climax emotional overload. You can handle this. You're not being bulldozed. You're not turning yourself into emotional cookie dough. You're not pretending. Just enjoy this, okay?

This is the problem with trying to hear my own voice. There isn't just one Mila inside my head. There are two—one of them is a scared kid, and one of them is a (mostly) mature adult. To stave off the panic, I ground myself in the present using my senses.

Five things I can see… Light coming through the doorway. A pillow that fell to the floor. A wooden dresser, its top drawer ajar. A jacket hanging on a hook. Shades pulled on the window.

Four things I can feel… The softness of frequently-washed sheets. Cool air on my warm skin. My hair spilling over my shoulders. Tenderness between my legs.

Three things I can hear… Ice plunking into a glass. Water running. Footsteps.

Two things I can smell… Fabric softener. Sex.

One thing I can taste… Everett's kiss.

Everett appears in the bedroom doorway, a tall glass of ice water in his hand. My heart's still racing, but the voices in my head are fading.

He hands me the glass. "Here you go."

"Thank you." I take a few cool sips, concentrating on the way the icy water feels sliding down my throat.

He climbs back into bed and leans back against the pillows. "So, what time do you have to be at the hospital tomorrow?"

"I should get there by ten. And I'll need to go home and change first, since I can't really show up at the hospital looking like I did on your doorstep."

"Right." His expression is concerned, like he's pondering a

complicated math problem. "And how many hours of sleep do you need?"

I laugh. "I don't know. At least a few."

"Okay, so it's midnight now, and you have to be at the hospital by ten, which means you'll want to be home by nine—"

"Better make it eight. I need to get some things done before I go."

"So that means you'll need to leave here by like seven forty-five, which gives me a little less than eight more hours with you."

He exhales, shaking his head like he's a general telling his troops their chances of winning this battle are slim. "Factoring in a few hours for you to sleep, and the requisite recovery time I'll need between rounds, it looks like we can only have sex like…three more times before you leave. That's not enough."

He appears so crestfallen that I burst out laughing. "Everett, I'm not going back to Brooklyn until the middle of October."

"That's still a finite amount of time, during which I'll have to share you with other people and things. But since keeping you hostage here and supplying you with endless orgasms isn't an option, I'll take what I can get."

After one more sip of water, I set the glass on the bedside table and nestle along his warm, honed body. He pulls the sheets to our waists, and I lay my head on his chest. If anything has ever felt this good, I can't name it. It's even better than playing with baby goats.

"I have an idea for you," I tell him, playing with the hair on his chest.

"Mmm. I've got ideas for you, too." He slides a hand over my ass.

"My idea is about your problem with Tad Hart and the foundry site. I've been pondering it."

He exhales. "Did you have to put Tad Hart in my head right now?"

"Just let me tell you what I was thinking."

"Can I tell you what *I'm* thinking? It involves you leaving lots of claw marks on my back. Possibly some reverse cowgirl. And a number between sixty-eight and seventy, but don't ask me to tell you what it is."

"I won't."

"Okay, fine, it's sixty-nine."

I pick up my head and look at him. "Can I get this out, please?"

He sweeps a fingertip across my cheek and over the bridge of my nose. "I was also thinking about connecting these freckles with the tip of my—"

"*Everett.*"

"Sorry." He kisses my nose. "I'm a despicable, filthy beast, and I'm obsessed with you. But please tell me what you're thinking."

My heart stutters wildly at his admission—*I'm obsessed with you*—and warmth floods my face. It takes me a few seconds to recover. "Um. Okay, so at dinner, you were telling me about how cleaning up the contamination will be a long, expensive process."

"Yes."

"I might be able to help."

"I'm listening." He shifts in the bed and buries his face in my neck, kissing my throat.

"How are you going to listen and do that at the same time?"

"I'm excellent at multitasking." He brushes the depression at the base of my throat with his tongue, sending a shiver up my spine. "Go on."

I try to stay focused. "Right out of college, I worked for an educational publishing company, illustrating science textbooks and journals. One of the things I worked on was a research project on hyperaccumulators."

"Your brain is so fucking hot." He kisses his way across my collarbone, his hand stealing between my thighs.

I laugh. "You're not even listening!"

"I am. I am." His mouth moves lower, his tongue flirting with my nipple until it stiffens into a peak and practically hums with arousal. "Hyper-kazoom-ulators. Sexy. Go on."

I try my best, I really do.

"*Hyperaccumulators.* They're plants that naturally pull contaminants from the ground and store them in their tissues. When harvested and properly disposed of, they gradually clean the soil."

"God, you're turning me on." He takes the tingling tip into his mouth and sucks.

"Everett, I'm trying to teach you something." I swear I put my hands in his hair with the intention of lifting his head off me, but all I do is hold him to my chest. Arch my back. Open my legs.

His fingers slip inside me, gliding in and out with an easy motion of his wrist. "And I appreciate it. You're without a doubt the sexiest science teacher I've ever had, even hotter than Mrs. Shelton in middle school."

I picture the thirty-something English teacher with the tortoiseshell glasses and long auburn hair. "You had a crush on Mrs. Shelton?"

"I've got a thing for redheads, sue me." He rolls onto his back, taking me with him. "But would it be possible to postpone the conclusion of this lesson until such time as I'm better able to pay attention?"

Bracing my hands on his chest, I sit up and straddle him. His erection is trapped between us, thick and hard. My heart hammers wildly as I look down at him, and I grow dizzy with disbelief.

How is it possible I'm in *Everett McKean's* bed right now? How can I be the girl he's looking at with fire in his eyes? How is that my waist he's gripping, my knees bracketing his hips, my finger tracing the lines on his stomach?

I begin to move above him, sliding along his hard length, warm and wet.

He speaks in a hushed, reverent tone. "I still can't believe you showed up at my door tonight. This better not be a dream."

I smile. "Not a dream."

"I don't know if I believe you."

I lift myself off him, position the tip of his cock at my center, and lower myself down until my ass rests on his groin. "Is that real enough for you?"

He shakes his head. "Still feels like a dream."

Smiling seductively, I bring my hands to my breasts and roll my hips in a slow circle. I play with my nipples. I watch his eyes grow glassy and his chest begin to heave. "How about now?"

He sits up, bringing his lips close to mine. "You know what? I give up. This will never feel real."

I want to agree, but my words are obliterated by his kiss. My thoughts are next to go, decimated by the way he grabs my ass and moves me against his gyrating hips. The angle has the tip of his cock tapping that hot button inside me, the one that makes my body clench and quiver. Then I can't see, my vision overtaken by stars.

All I can smell is his skin.

All I can taste is his tongue.

All I can feel is the sweet, hot friction where our bodies are joined, where pleasure pulses between us like a drum.

I get very little sleep that night.

Chapter Thirty-One

Everett

I wake up holding her.

The scent of her perfume and sex all around me. My face buried in her soft, coppery hair. My chest against her back.

At some point last night, she stole the covers, which are mostly bunched up in her arms, but I don't care.

This feels too good.

A quick glance at the digital clock on my bedside table tells me it's just after seven. Around four in the morning, when we'd finally exhausted ourselves, we set an alarm for seven-thirty. So, for a moment, I simply lie still, listening to the sound of Mila's breathing, enjoying her warm skin against mine and the rhythmic rise and fall of her chest.

Everything about her is sexy. Those never-ending legs. The satin skin. That gorgeous mouth. Her taste, her touch, her hands on my body. The way she moves. She's so fucking flexible and limber. And the sounds she makes when I get inside her? The words she whispers in my ear? *Harder. More. Right there. I want ruin.*

My cock stirs under the sheets, tapping at her ass like a salesman at the door. I don't even move, but inside a minute, I'm fully hard. I suspect she's awake when her breathing quickens, then I know it for sure when she reaches behind her hip. Takes my cock in her hand. Strokes me with a firm grasp.

Licking my fingers, I reach between her thighs, careful not to be too rough after everything I put her body through last night. She sighs softly, her back arching. When she's dripping, I pull one of her legs over my hip and enter her from behind.

I use my hand to make sure she comes first, and only when her moans subside and her body goes limp do I begin to thrust inside her. With every deep, hard stroke, she emits a sharp cry—different from the sounds of pleasure she made last night. Instinctively, I know she's too sore for me to finish.

Pulling out, I roll her onto her stomach and straddle her thighs. I slide my dick between them and rub the length of it along her slick, wet pussy while she moans into my pillow. When I'm close, I fist my cock with one hand while filling the other with one luscious round cheek. I don't last long. A few hard pulls and I'm making a sticky wet mess on her ass. Watching my cum drip onto her skin is so filthy hot, I never want it to end. Grunting like a beast, I keep stroking my dick until every last drop is gone.

When it's over, I brace a hand on either side of her and hang my head. "Sorry," I say, out of breath. "Did I hurt you?"

"No. I'm just a little tender this morning."

"I could tell." I drop a kiss between her shoulder blades. "I'll be right back. Don't move."

In the bathroom, I grab a clean hand towel and run the faucet until the water warms. After wetting the towel, I wring it out and hurry back into the bedroom just in time to hear the alarm going off. I hit the snooze button. "Good morning."

She giggles, turning to look at me. One side of her cheek is resting on a pillow, which she's hugging to her chest—I'm never washing that pillowcase again. Her face is flushed, her lips are puffy, and her hair is a mess. "Good morning," she says softly.

She's the most beautiful thing I've ever seen.

I clean her up with slow, gentle strokes. "Is the towel too hot?" I ask, concerned about the red patches it's leaving.

"No, it feels good. I just have the most sensitive skin on the planet, so all you have to do is look at me and it will leave a mark."

"I did more than look last night." That's when I notice other blemishes on her body. A bruise on her hip. A scratch on her shoulder. An abrasion—from my scruffy jaw?—on the back of her thigh.

"Yes, you did. I enjoyed every minute of it." Another giggle, this one full of mischief. "And don't worry, the marks will fade."

I hope they don't.

I catch myself before I say it out loud, afraid the sentiment will sound too possessive. Too harsh. Maybe even too kinky. I don't want her to think I enjoy inflicting pain on her. I don't need to *own* her. And I certainly don't want to hurt her.

It's not really about the marks, I realize, watching her get out of my bed, resisting the urge to toss her right back into it. It's whatever this is with us—*that's* what I don't want to fade. This time together. This connection.

This feeling.

Fifteen minutes later, we say goodbye at my door. I have nothing on but a pair of jeans. Mila has on the little blue pajama shorts she arrived in and a green John Deere hoodie of mine she discovered hanging on the back of the bathroom door. She asked if she could wear it home, which made me stupid happy. It's gigantic on her, hanging down below the hem of her tiny shorts.

But seeing it on her makes me want to throw her over my shoulder all over again.

Merlin, ecstatic to make a new friend, is trying his best to jump up and lick her face. I drag him off her, even though I understand the instinct. Mila laughs, leaning down to show him some love.

"What a cutie," she says as he slobbers all over her—again, an urge I fully comprehend. "Is he always this way with strangers?"

"Pretty much. Merlin is *not* a guard dog. If an intruder gets in, it will be me protecting him." I watch as he lies down on the floor and looks up at her adoringly, hoping for a belly rub.

Laughing, she gets down and obliges. "Well, you're good at it. Isn't he, Merlin?" A moment later, she gets to her feet. "I should go."

"I hope your mom is doing better. Will you let me know?"

"Of course." A hesitation. "I'm not sure when I'll be able to—"

I shake my head. "Don't worry about it. I'm just glad you came over. Even if you did hog the covers all night."

She laughs, covering her face with her hands. "I am a total cover hog. But I get so cold!"

"I will gladly volunteer to keep you warm whenever body heat is needed."

Dropping her hands, she looks around, as if noticing our surroundings for the first time. "Wow, you weren't kidding about the walls in here. Your taste in interior design is…stark."

I pinch her side. "So fix it for me, Freckles."

"Be nice, or I won't help you with your phytoremediation."

"My what? Oh, is this what you were talking about last night?"

"Yes, and I bet you can't tell me a single thing about it because you were *not listening*." She gives me her best angry teacher face, but it's still fucking adorable.

"Yeah, I barely passed Mrs. Shelton's class either. Will you explain it to me again when you're not naked?"

"Will you stop calling me Freckles?"

I pretend to think it over. "Only if you move in with me."

She laughs. "We spent one night together, Everett. That seems like a drastic step two."

"Wait 'til you hear step three."

She scoops up the fuzzy sweater she arrived in last night, which is still lying on the floor where she dropped it. "I better get out of here before I get pregnant."

"That's step five. Don't skip ahead."

Another laugh bubbles from her. "You're unhinged."

"I know." I catch her one last time around the waist and put my lips at her ear. "But you do something to me."

I spend the day doing the equipment maintenance I didn't get around to yesterday, but my work pace is slow. Not because I'm tired—I feel oddly energized today, even after only a few hours of sleep—but because I'm so distracted by thoughts of Mila. I purposely didn't shower this morning, and I can still smell her on my skin. Sometimes, I just stop what I'm doing, sniff my arm, and lose ten minutes recalling her hair on my pillow, her leg over my shoulder, her hands fisted in damp, twisted sheets.

I can't remember the last time I felt so consumed by someone.

Around noon, I text her.

Everett: *You really need to stop taking up so much time in my head. It's rude. I'm trying to work.*

She laughs at the message and replies.

Mila: *SAME. I'm sitting here in this hospital room at my mother's bedside thinking the dirtiest thoughts. She's asked me twice what I'm smiling about.*

Everett: *What was your answer?*

Mila: *The mayor's dick.*

I'm chuckling at her response when she messages again.

Mila: *I said I was just happy her fall wasn't more serious and that the adjustment was successful.*

Everett: *Good girl.*

Mila: *Are you trying to turn me on?*

Everett: *I wasn't, but I can if you'd like me to.*

Mila: *Better not. She just asked me who I'm texting that's making me blush.*

Everett: *Then I'll save it for another time.*

Mila: *I should get off my phone. The look of disapproval I'm getting is growing more intense.*

Everett: *Okay. Hang in there. I'm thinking about you.*

Mila: *XOXOXO*

After lunch, the sky clouds over, and by three o'clock, raindrops begin to fall. Deciding to call it a day a little early, I head home, grab a shower, and sit on the couch with my laptop on the coffee table in front of me. I want to do a little research on that soil cleanup method Mila told me about.

Of course, I didn't pay enough attention to even remember what it's called—phyto-something? I'm forced to Google "plants that eat contaminants."

Aha—phytoremediation.

As rain drums on the cabin's roof, I begin to read.

What it is. How it works. How long it will take.

The cost. The risks involved. How it might affect the community.

The environmental benefits. What the site might look like during the process and once it's complete. Examples of plants and trees that could be used.

A plan begins to take shape in my head, and I can't wait to talk to Mila about it.

I wish I knew when I'd see her again.

The rain doesn't let up, so I put Merlin and my toolbox in the truck and head over to my mom's to fix a few things I've been meaning to get to.

My mom is out, and the house is shadowy and silent. The kitchen smells sweet, like maybe she baked waffles or cinnamon rolls for breakfast. The aroma elicits memories of weekend mornings when I was a kid, before things got bad. On weekend mornings, my dad would wake me up early to go fishing. When we got home, the kitchen would smell like this, and there would be breakfast waiting for us on the table.

But there are other memories in this kitchen, too.

I stare at a crooked cupboard door and remember how mad my dad used to get if Gabi or I accidentally slammed them. His head was always pounding on Sunday mornings, his temper foul.

Goddammit, don't bang those doors!

We weren't doing it on purpose. The cabinetry was old—no soft-close hinges like modern kitchens have. All it took was a less-than-gentle push, and they'd slam loudly and bounce right back open again.

One summer morning, when I was sixteen and Gabi was fourteen, she was baking muffins, opening and closing cabinets to grab what she needed. Slumped at the table, nursing his hangover with a beer, Dad had already yelled at her several times about the noise. I was pouring a glass of orange juice and inwardly pleading with Gabi to be more careful. I could see his rage building. Sense it buzzing in the thick, hot air.

Sure enough, she closed a cupboard door too hard for his aching skull, and he banged his thick fists on the table and pushed himself up. "Goddammit, girl. I warned you."

I put myself in front of my sister. "Don't," I said as he lurched in her direction. "She didn't do it. I did."

"I saw her."

"You saw wrong."

Gabi started to cry. She knew what came next.

"Go upstairs," I said over my shoulder.

She scooted out from behind me just as our father threw a right hook at my face, catching my jaw.

He tried to throw a second punch, but this time I was able to move out of the way. He fell forward onto the counter, knocking Gabi's bowl full of muffin batter and a carton of eggs to the ground. Bouncing backward, he toppled onto the floor.

Our mother appeared in the kitchen doorway, a stricken look on her face. She hurried to his side and helped him up. Leading him out of the room, she looked at me over her shoulder, her eyes full of tears.

I shook my head and motioned for her to go. Later, she'd come to my bedroom and cry, begging my forgiveness for not doing more. But what could she do? She wasn't going to leave him. She thought her duty was to stay by his side.

When she left, I cradled my sore jaw. Moved it from side to side.

My sister was trembling in the corner. "I'm sorry," she whispered, tears streaming down her face. "I'm so sorry. It was my fault. I hate that he punishes you for things I do."

"It's okay. He's got shitty aim."

Choking out a laugh, she ran at me and threw her arms around my neck. "Why don't you hit him back?" she asked, her voice muffled against my chest.

"I don't want to hurt him," I said. "I just want to protect you."

I'm fixing the hinges on a cabinet door when my phone vibrates on the counter. I glance at the screen and see a text from Mila.

Mila: *Hey, I have a little time and I'd love to see you.*

My pulse kicks up. I set down my screwdriver and reply.

Everett: *Want to meet me in town? Grab some dinner?*

Mila: *Actually, I was wondering if you'd like to come over. I have a lot of groceries here, and I could make us something.*

Everett: *You do not have to cook for me. You're already taking care of your mom.*

Mila: *I enjoy cooking. Especially for someone who will appreciate it.*

Everett: *In that case, what time is dinner? And what can I bring?*

Mila: *You can come over now. Bring your appetite.*

Everett: *You know what you're asking for, right?*

Mila: 🔥

Chapter Thirty-Two

Mila

His knock sends me sprinting to the door, barefoot and breathless. When I open it, his smile makes my stomach flip like an Olympic diver. When he steps inside and kisses me, the pounding of the rain echoes the ferocious thrum of my heart.

"Sorry, I'm soaked." He releases me from a damp hug. "It's still coming down."

"I know. I'm not looking forward to getting my mother into the house later. I hope it stops before then."

"You look pretty." His eyes roam over my flouncy pink miniskirt with the strawberry print and my soft ivory crewneck. "I like that skirt."

"Thank you." I shut the front door while he removes his wet boots. He looks good, too, and my skin warms thinking about his body beneath the jeans and light-blue plaid flannel. It gives me a thrill to realize I know what he looks like naked. I know what he *feels* like naked. I know what it's like to have all that sinew and muscle moving above me in the dark. It's better than a secret.

"I brought you something." Everett hands me a bag with two bottles of wine in it. "I wasn't sure if you like red or white, so I got one of each. And I know nothing about wine, so the guy at the store chose them. They have screw caps, which seemed weird to me, but he says they're good."

I laugh. "I like both red and white, and he's right, screw caps are fine. Come on in, and we'll open one up."

He follows me into the kitchen. "What did you— Jesus, it smells good in here."

Smiling, I lift the lid on my skillet. "Thanks. It's burst tomato and summer squash pasta. The tomatoes are from my mom's garden."

He inhales deeply. "I'm drooling."

"Good." I add the burrata on top of the cooked bucatini, which is tossed with red tomatoes, slices of yellow and green squash, sautéed garlic, and olive oil.

As the cheese begins to melt, Everett comes up behind me and wraps his arms around my waist. Buries his face in my neck. "I'm so glad you texted. I've been thinking about you nonstop."

I smile as pure joy radiates throughout my body. This is what I hoped married life would be like. Cozy Sunday night dinners just the two of us. Cooking together. Drinking wine. Sharing something more important than meal prep and conversation. Something that makes me feel warm and safe. Something exactly like what I feel now, with Everett's chest pressing against my back, my body tucked in his embrace.

It's a little disconcerting.

Turning off the heat beneath the pan, I tap his arm. "I need to tear the basil."

He lets go of me. "Would you like a glass of wine?"

"Sure. Glasses are in the cupboard there."

"Which one?"

"Hmm. Let's do the white."

"Guess what I did this afternoon?" he asks as he pulls two glasses down.

"What?"

"I educated myself on phytoremediation."

Impressed, I stop pulling basil leaves off their stems and look over at him. "Did you really?"

"Yes. I think you might be on to something." He unscrews the cap from the bottle and pours. "But I have some more questions for you."

"I might not know the answers," I say, resuming my task. "I was only the illustrator on that project, not the actual scientist."

"My questions are more about what the area could look like while the cleanup's happening." He sets a glass of white down next to my cutting board and leans back against the counter. "Have you ever been to one of those sites?"

"Yes." I quickly tear through the leaves, then pick up my wine for a sip. "And they can be beautiful, peaceful spaces. There's something really lovely about them. They represent transformation—a place where something damaged becomes healed."

He nods, looking at me thoughtfully. My body temperature rises beneath his gaze. "I need you," he says.

"Huh?" I accidentally dump all the herbs in a pile on top of the pasta instead of sprinkling them.

"To help me sell this idea to the Harts. They don't want a public conversation about contamination cleanup. But the way you just described it was so beautiful. I'm afraid I won't be able to do it justice like you can."

"Oh." He's talking about business. Of course he is.

"Would you be willing to meet with the Harts and say what you just said to me? Convince them we can spin this into something positive?"

"It *is* something positive. I suppose I could try." I take two wide, shallow bowls down from the cupboard, flattered he asked for my help. "When are you thinking?"

"The sooner the better."

"Okay. Let me see how it goes with my mom once she's home. In the meantime, you really need a scientist. You should reach out to the environmental science department at the nearest university and see if they can recommend a consultant for you."

"That's a great idea. I'll do that tomorrow." He takes my face in his hands and drops a kiss on my lips that I feel from head to heels. "Thank you."

My cheeks grow hot. "I'm happy to help. That place is special to me. I love the idea of making it into a safe space for kids to play."

"We'll do it. Together."

I'm rinsing dishes and loading the dishwasher when Everett comes into the kitchen and sets his empty bowl on the counter. I pick it up and stare into it. The bottom's so clean I can see my reflection. I look at him incredulously. "Did you lick this?"

"I may have." He ropes his arms around me and puts his lips at my ear. "When something is that delicious, I don't let a drop go to waste."

Desire oozes through me, syrupy and warm. He begins to kiss my neck, starting just behind my ear and working his way down. His right hand sneaks between my legs, bunching up my skirt. One finger teases my clit through my panties. "I want my tongue right here."

"Everett." His touch fills my mind with the color red.

"You going to serve dessert or do I have to serve myself?"

Something between a laugh and a groan escapes me. "I have to go back to the hospital soon."

"I will be *so* quick," he says, turning me around. After a kiss that steals my breath and whatever is left of my responsible adult brain cells, he drops to his knees on the kitchen floor. Reaches beneath my skirt. Pulls down my panties and tosses them aside.

Then his head disappears beneath the strawberry print, his hands gripping my thighs. His tongue paints a line up the seam of my pussy with one long, slow stroke.

I lean back against the counter, my head falling to one side. Sheets of rain blur the kitchen window, and I can barely make out the Pratts' house on the other side of the driveway. But I see light and movement, as if someone is cooking a meal or washing the dishes. It strikes me as absurd that regular people are just going about their Sunday evening as if everything's normal, everything's fine, the world is not about to explode.

Meanwhile, Everett's face is buried between my legs, his lips and tongue relentless in their pursuit. He's aggressive, demanding, ravenous. He hooks one of my legs over his shoulder. I grasp the counter behind me to keep my balance, crying out as the spasms threaten to bring me to the floor.

"Upstairs," I pant, the orgasm still rippling through me. "Now."

He looks up, his mouth wet. "I thought you had to—"

"Now," I repeat, grabbing him by the arm and hauling him to his feet.

I drag him out of the kitchen, through the living room, up the stairs. When we reach my bedroom, we tear off each other's clothes with impatient hands. Skirt. Sweater. Bra. Belt. Flannel. Jeans and underwear at once. By the time Everett reaches behind his neck to wrench off his white T-shirt, I'm already backing up toward my twin-sized bed.

Unlike last night, when we took our time, exploring every inch of each other's skin, wringing pleasure out of every hour, kiss by caress by sigh, tonight is a race for the finish. In less than thirty seconds, he's kneeling on the mattress with my legs over his shoulders, driving his cock into me with quick, hard, thrusts. I'm still tender from last night, but it's the good kind of sore—the raw ache left over after your body has been pushed beyond what you think it can bear.

Pain and pleasure course through my body side by side until Everett pitches forward and changes the angle, moving against me in a way that gives pleasure the lead. I put my hands on his ass and pull him into me, lifting my hips in tandem with his. My second orgasm builds in a different spot than the first, deeper and more intense. My world is reduced to a singular point where desire spools like a ribbon until suddenly it unfurls in glorious, shimmering waves.

Everett's climax strikes like lightning, thundering through his body as he throbs inside me.

He falls onto my chest, hot and sticky and panting, but he obviously recalls the way I struggled for air when he did that last night, because he flips onto his back, pulling me on top.

For a moment, we're silent, our hearts beating hard against each other's, my wilted body splayed across his. The rain provides a steady hum on the roof above us, and the sky has turned from ash to charcoal. The room is warm and cozy, my body has never been treated so well, and there is absolutely nothing to be sad about.

But of course, I start to cry.

"Hey." Everett strokes my hair. "Are you okay?"

"I'm fine," I say. "This week has been a lot, and I think I'm just, like, emotionally overwhelmed. My feelings are confused about who's doing what. I swear to God I'm happy right now."

Laughing a little, he holds me close. "This week *has* been a lot for you."

I take a few slow, deep breaths and focus on Everett's fingers making little spirals along my spine, as if he's circling each vertebra. Within a minute or so, the tears stop. "God," I say, pressing my forehead right beneath his collarbone. "I think I got snot on you. This is so embarrassing."

"I don't know. I feel like you've done worse."

"That's not funny."

His chest rumbles with laughter. "Sorry. Look, I told you before, you can fall apart in front of me when you need to. I can take it."

I sniff. "Okay."

"You know what I can't take? How small this bed is. I don't even fit in it. It ends at my ankles."

I smile, kiss his chest, and rest my cheek on it. "It did not affect your performance."

His arms tighten around me. "Good."

While I clean myself up and get dressed, Everett finishes tidying the kitchen to save me some time. We say goodbye at the front door with a lingering kiss, even though I'm late.

"Thanks for dinner," he says.

"You're welcome. Thanks for not running scared when I do weird things like cry when I'm happy."

"You couldn't scare me off if you tried."

I chew my bottom lip. "I don't know about that."

"Listen. You stole my parking spot, you made my manly truck smell like orange blossoms, and—worst of all—last Monday, you cost me the top spot on the leaderboard at The Axe & Barrel."

"How did I do that?"

"It was that voicemail you left me. It threw me off my game. But I'm still here. Want to know why?"

My heart is playing hopscotch in my chest, one beat here, two there, a skipped beat in between. "Why?"

"Because I like you. I really, *really* like you." He slings an arm around my waist, pulling me close. "But you ever cost me the top spot again, Freckles, we're going to have a talk."

I'm late getting back to the hospital and rush in with an apology on my lips. But it turns out that my mother developed a low fever that afternoon and her doctors are a little worried. Her temperature came down to normal after a dose of Tylenol, but she won't be released tonight.

She's quiet and listless, but I sit in her room watching TV with her until she dozes off. When I'm confident she won't wake up again tonight, I check the time on my phone—almost nine. Should I text Everett? See if he's still up?

No, says a warning voice in my head, the one that always reminds me to wear sunscreen and a bike helmet and wait for the crosswalk signal to turn white before stepping off the curb. *Spending two nights in a row together is not friends-with-benefits behavior. It's desperate. It's needy. It's "I know what I said, but I have to be with you." It's beyond overzealous.*

Sighing, I decide the voice is right. My body longs for him like it's already addicted to his touch, but my brain overrides the system.

Reluctantly, I put my phone back in my bag and watch another couple of episodes of *Friends*. But I keep glancing down at it. Does he want me to reach out? Does he miss me like I miss him? Am I being obsessive?

Yes. Stop it.

I sit on my hands to prevent myself from texting him. I figure if I wait long enough, it will be too late to message him. He's a farmer. He wakes with the sun. He needs his sleep. And how much sex does one woman need anyway? I'm already so sore that even Charmin Extra Soft feels like sandpaper. I have bruises. Scratches. Bite marks.

But I like them.

My leg jitters all the way through "The One Where Monica and Richard Are Just Friends." I'm going out of my mind. I want him. I need him.

I should definitely not see him tonight.

Just after ten, I sneak out of my mom's room and slip down the hall. *Don't do it. Leave your phone in your bag. It would be rude to text him at this hour.*

As soon as the elevator doors close, I take my phone from my bag. There are multiple messages from him.

Nine o'clock:

Everett: *I can't stop thinking about you.*

At nine-thirty:

Everett: *Your taste is still on my tongue. What kind of magic is that?*

Five minutes ago:

Everett: *I'm still awake. Text me if you see this tonight.*

Everett: *This is me being overzealous.*

My fingers are typing before my willpower can stop them.

Mila: *Hey. Turns out my mom has to stay another night.*

Everett: *Is she okay?*

Mila: *Yes, she just had a low-grade fever. But they want to make sure there's no infection.*

Everett: *Where are you now?*

Mila: *Just leaving the hospital.*

Everett: *Come over.*

Mila: *But it's so late.*

Everett: *Come over.*

Mila: *I have to teach in the morning.*

Everett: *Come over.*

Twenty minutes later, I'm on his porch. This time, he knew I was coming and must have watched for my headlights in the dark, because he pulls the door open before I can knock.

The moment it closes behind me, we kiss with a passion that feels like a fever. I jump up, wrapping my legs around his waist and taking his face in my hands. He puts my back against the door and leans into me, his hands gripping my thighs, his tongue lashing into my mouth.

I've never experienced desire like this before. My chest is full of exploding stars that shoot throughout my body, to my head, to my stomach, to the ends of my fingers and toes. Yearning for him swells at my core, a hunger that demands to be satisfied. A thirst that must be quenched.

"This thing with us," he says, his words hot on my lips. "What is it?"

"I don't know," I whisper. "But I'm scared."

He tips his forehead to mine. "Everything will be okay, I promise."

"You don't know that. No one can know that."

"Then let's just enjoy the moment." His mouth moves down my neck. "We have the whole night together. We don't even have to think about tomorrow."

"But the thing about tomorrow…" I shiver as his tongue dips into the groove at the base of my throat. "Is that it always shows up."

Chapter Thirty-Three

Everett

Monday morning, we're awakened by loud knocking on the cabin door.

Mila bolts upright, clutching the covers to her bare chest. "Oh my God. What time is it?"

Groggy, I open one eye and look at the clock. "Just after eight."

"Shoot. I have to go. I have to teach class at ten." She scrambles off the bed and starts hunting around for her clothes. Whoever is at the door pounds a few more times.

Cursing, I roll out of bed and tug on some sweatpants. Mila darts into the bathroom in her underwear, her bra dangling from one hand and her sweater balled up in the other. "I can't find my skirt," she whispers.

"We'll find it. Let me deal with whoever's here." On my way to the door, I run my fingers through my hair, which I'm sure is a mess. I figure this has to be a delivery guy getting an early start on his route today, or maybe Carlos, my operations manager, has a problem that couldn't wait. Either way, I'm aggravated that my time with Mila has been cut short. I pull open the door.

And come face-to-face with my sister.

"Rise and shine, brother." Like me, she has brown eyes and an athletic build, but her hair is straight and blond. This morning, it's pulled back into her usual ponytail. She's wearing sweatpants, a tank top, and running shoes.

I blink at her. "Hey. What are you doing here?"

"It's good to see you, too." She crosses the threshold and gives me a quick hug. "I texted you last night that I was driving up. I got in late."

"I was, uh, busy last night. I didn't look at my phone."

My sister eyeballs me critically. "Those dark circles under your eyes are brutal. You should try my rose-hip and carrot-seed eye serum."

"No, thanks." Like my mom, my sister is always concocting skincare products from weird ingredients. They're convinced Big Pharma is putting toxins into everything you can buy at the store. I glance over my shoulder at the bathroom door while Gabi turns her attention to my dog.

"Hi, Merlin!" She kneels down to greet him. "How's my favorite therapy school dropout?" Merlin lets out a happy *ruff* and tries to jump up and hug her.

The bathroom door opens a crack, and I see Mila's panicked face. She tries to mouth something at me I can't understand, but when Gabi straightens up, she disappears behind the door.

"I thought maybe I'd catch you before you left. See if you wanted to go for a run and talk about this thing with Mom. Last night, she—" Gabi breaks off mid-sentence. Merlin has brought her something in his mouth.

Something pink and ruffled with strawberries on it.

He drops it at her feet and wags his tail, proud of his accomplishment. My sister bends down, picks it up, and holds it out. "This is a new look for you."

"It's, uh, not mine."

Her eyebrows rise. "Someone left her skirt here?"

"Um… Yes?"

She cocks her head. "Yes, question mark?"

Fuck me. I have no idea if I should make some shit up or be honest. Gabi and I don't usually keep secrets from each other, but I also want to protect Mila.

My sister gasps. "If someone didn't *leave it*, does that mean the someone is still here?"

I glance toward my bedroom. My early-morning, fuck-fuddled brain cannot think of a way out of this mess.

"Whose skirt is this, Everett?" Grinning, she shakes it in my face.

That's when the bathroom door opens. Mila comes out, wearing her sweater from last night, her underwear peeking out below. "It's mine," she says tentatively. "Hi, Gabi."

Gabi's jaw drops. The skirt falls to the floor. She looks at me, then at Mila, then turns and runs out of the cabin.

"Oh God." Mila looks at me with tears in her eyes. "I'm so sorry. I shouldn't have come out."

"No, no, it's okay." I scoop her skirt off the ground and hand it to her. "I should have told her we were…in touch."

"She still blames me for the fire," Mila says, staring at the skirt clenched in her fists. "For what happened to your dad that night."

"Baby. Stop." I put my hands on her shoulders. "You were not responsible for my dad's heart attack that night."

"But it was the fire that caused it! That's the only explanation! That's why she wouldn't even speak to me afterward."

"Mila, there were other things happening. Things you know nothing about."

But it's like she doesn't even hear me. "This is why I haven't been able to bring myself to reach out to her. This is what I was afraid of."

"I'll talk to her."

"No, don't!" Mila looks up at me, panic in her face. "Please. Look, let's just—just slow down a little. This is a lot."

"What do you mean, slow down?"

"I mean, the last couple days have been really intense. I think it would be a good idea just to sort of…pause. Take a breath." She hurriedly puts on her skirt. "Don't you?"

No. Fuck no.

But I'm not going to push her. "If that's what you want."

"I just think it's best. I need to get my mom home from the hospital, and you have things you need to focus on, and I think some time to just process everything would be good."

"Okay," I say stiffly.

We don't kiss goodbye.

After Mila has gone, I throw some clothes on, put Merlin on the leash, and head over to the house. As I approach, I spot my sister sitting on one of the rocking chairs on the back porch. Her thighs are tucked against her chest, and she's got her arms wrapped around her legs. Her eyes look puffy and her nose is red, as if she's been crying.

I hate it when my sister cries. It stirs up bad memories.

I mount the steps slowly, put Merlin in the house, and drop into the chair next to Gabi's. For a minute or so, there's just silence between us.

She speaks first. "I'm sorry."

"I'm sorry, too."

"What for?"

"I should have told you."

"It's none of my business." She rests her chin on her knees. "Although seeing her come out of your bathroom with no pants on *was* a pretty big shock."

"I wasn't expecting company," I say dryly.

She's silent for a moment. "How long has it been going on?"

"That's an interesting question." I lean back in the chair and set it in motion.

Gabi picks up her head and stares at me. "Have you been in touch with her all these years?"

"No, no. I never talked to her after the fire. I just thought about her from time to time. Then I saw her downtown a couple weeks ago, and it stirred up some old things."

"Did she move back here?"

"No. Her mom had surgery, and she's here for a month or so to help her recover."

"Oh." Gabi goes silent again, lowering her chin.

"What the hell happened with you guys?"

At first, more silence. Then, slowly, "It was a combination of things."

"Like what?"

"Things we did. The way we reacted. We were only eighteen, you know? Feelings were so big."

"Feelings about *what*?"

She takes a deep breath. "We had this pact. The four of us."

She doesn't need to tell me who "the four of us" are. Gabi, Mila, Yasmine, and Rachel were inseparable from before I can remember. And, of course, there was Lydia. "What kind of pact?"

She shifted in her chair. "We'd promised Lydia that on her birthday in August, we'd do something that involved facing a huge fear. The idea was to live one night like it was our last. In honor of her."

"Okay," I say, still unclear on how everything connects.

"Her birthday was August tenth. The night of the fire."

"Oh shit." Events of that night come back to me piece by piece.

What happened at the bakery.

What happened at home later that night.

The rumors flying through town the next day.

"Each of us had a different task to complete." A pause. "I mean, you know what I did."

I hear the sorrow in her voice, and that gut instinct to protect her kicks in. "You were right to do it."

"Sometimes it doesn't feel that way when I remember what happened afterward."

"You did the right thing, Gabi." My voice is firm. She might have doubts about her actions that night, but I don't.

"I don't know, Everett." She wipes tears from beneath her eyes. "The price was really high. And I wasn't the only one who had to pay it."

"Nothing that happened was your fault. If anything, it was mine."

She sniffs. "Either way, my life imploded that night, and I did not handle it well. Dad was in the hospital. Mom was a wreck. You had to deal with the police. We knew we'd lose the bakery. We thought we might lose the farm. Suddenly everything was scary and uncertain, and I took it out on my friends."

"It's been ten years. Have you ever thought about reaching out to them? Making amends?"

"Of course I have." Fresh tears slip down her cheeks. "Every New Year's, it's my resolution. To patch up those friendships. To own up to what I did wrong and beg forgiveness. But it means digging up some dark shit that I've kept buried all these years. It means revisiting the worst night of my life."

She lifts the bottom of her tank top to her face and wipes her eyes. "So somehow every year, I make excuses to avoid it. But I hate myself for being so weak."

"I'll tell you the same thing I told Mila—it's not too late. There's no statute of limitations on reconnecting with old friends."

"I know." She goes silent, and, for a moment, the only sound comes from the sparrows and chickadees in the trees behind the house. "I'll reach out to her. It's time."

"You know, it kind of surprises me that you didn't reckon with all this before. You're so into health and wellness and 'alignment'. It's your entire career."

"I'm into *other people's* health and wellness and alignment," she clarifies. "And it's my career for a reason—I focus outward, while my clients focus inward."

We're both silent for a moment.

Then she says, "I quit my job."

A sharp turn of my head. "You did? Why?"

"I don't want to work in corporate anymore. No more overpriced hotel spas and soulless franchises. That's not how you make people feel better." She shakes her head. "I want to do my own thing."

"Like cuddle counseling?"

She reaches over and pokes me. "It was cuddle *therapy*, not cuddle counseling. And don't knock it—I helped a lot of people *and* earned money to pay off my grad school loans."

"Doesn't matter. Getting paid to hug people is weird, and I will *always* knock it. It's my job as a brother."

She sticks her tongue out at me.

"So what will you do now?"

"I'm still figuring that out. But I gave my two weeks. In the meantime, I thought I'd move back here. Live with Mom. Help at the farm." Her voice gets quiet. "It's not like I don't owe you."

"Does that mean you'll judge the pie contest at Founder's Day?"

"Oh, *hell* no."

I poke her. "Brat."

She pokes me right back. "Bully."

I smile at the old nicknames. "Mom will be glad to have you back. And I'd be grateful for the help around here."

"Then that's what I'll do." She rises to her feet. "Want some coffee?"

"Yes, please."

"Be right back." She goes into the house and returns a couple minutes later with two steaming mugs. After handing one to me, she sits in the rocker again. "So, tell me what's going on with Mila. She always had the biggest crush on you, as baffling as that is."

"I'm not sure what's going on. We've spent some time together over the last couple weeks, and it's been good. But she just asked to take a step back."

"She did?"

"She says she needs to catch her breath."

"That's my fault," Gabi says. "I just shocked the hell out of her, and Mila always was a little skittish. I can talk to her."

"It's not just that. She went through a lot with her ex-husband, and she's only been divorced about six months. She told me up front that she didn't really want to start anything."

"I didn't even realize she got married." Gabi sounds sad. "We always promised each other we'd be each other's bridesmaids." She sips her coffee. "I wonder if Mila had a big wedding."

"No clue. All I know is that her mother was critical of all her choices."

Gabi makes a noise from the back of her throat. "Her mother was a real piece of work."

"Still is."

"And Mila never knew her dad. That has to mess with you."

"Yeah."

"Man." Gabi sighs." Are we all just destined to spend our lives working through the shit our parents handed us?"

I take a sip of my coffee. "Probably."

My mom opens the screen door and steps out onto the porch. "Anybody want pancakes?"

My sister and I both raise our hands.

"They'll be ready in a few." She looks at Gabi. "He tell you about Mila?"

"Mom." I glare at her.

"He did," says Gabi.

"Did you notice the way he talks about her?"

I stand up. "Okay."

"What? I'm just saying." My mother shrugs before returning to the kitchen.

"She's right, you know." Gabi rises to her feet. "There's definitely a way."

"There's no *way*," I say, annoyed.

She's laughing now. "Oh, there is totally a way."

I roll my eyes and open the screen door, giving her a light boot in the ass as she enters the house. But after the tears, it's good to see her smiling.

And there *might* be a way I talk about Mila.

More importantly, there's a way I feel about her.

I'm just not sure what to do about it.

Chapter Thirty-Four

WELCOME TO THE LANDING PAD

Community Updates From The Hart's Landing Gazette (Online Edition)

PSA: The Curb Appeal Society reported several violations over the weekend. Please be advised:

⇨ Fourth of July decor must be removed by August 1st.

⇨ Garden hoses should be wound neatly, not thrown in a pile.

⇨ Boats and Jet Skis may not remain parked in driveways for more than three days.

Comment by ANONYMOUS AXE GOD: Do we have a policy on garden gnomes?

Comment by CASBetsy: Thank you for asking. Gnomes and other fanciful ornamentation should not exceed twelve inches in height.

Comment by ANONYMOUS AXE GOD: What about flamingoes? Can I flock on my lawn?

Comment by CASBetsy: Another wonderful question! We ask that residents adhere to native bird species when selecting avian-themed lawn ornamentation.

Comment by ANONYMOUS AXE GOD: Thank flock.

GazetteMod: @ANONYMOUS AXE GOD Please refer to our Code of Comment Conduct by clicking here.

Comment by ANONYMOUS AXE GOD: @GazetteMod go flock yourself.

[GazetteMod has closed comments on this post.]

Police blotter: Residents reported more explicit drawings chalked on the riverside path. Persons with information about the identity of the perpetrator(s) should contact Detective Samuels at samuelsf@hldps.net.

EVENTS: All are welcome to join the Diner Detectives next Tuesday morning at 10 a.m. at Ernie's Diner. Prodigal resident and arson suspect Mila Ferguson has agreed to be interviewed.

Chapter Thirty-Five

Mila

After leaving Everett's cabin, I race home, cover my messed-up hair with a baseball cap, and teach my classes on autopilot.

When I'm done, I take a quick shower and head over to the hospital, where my mother is scheduled for release around one in the afternoon. After bringing her home, I spend the rest of the day trying to take care of her without letting on that I'm a total wreck.

We order dinner in, but I can't eat. We watch her favorite reality TV shows, but I can't concentrate. I make up a bed on the couch to be closer in case she calls for me, but I can't sleep.

I check my phone relentlessly, even throughout the night, but there's never a message from Everett.

What did you expect? You told him to slow down. You told him you needed a break. He's not going to push you. That's not him.

I hear Hugo's voice: *Avoidance doesn't build skills, Mila.*

By the time the sun comes up Tuesday morning, I know I've made a mistake. I pick up my phone and shoot Everett a message.

Mila: *Hey. Sorry about the way I acted yesterday. Let me know when you can talk.*

Everett: *You're up early.*

Mila: *I'm not sure I was ever down.*

Everett: *I didn't sleep that well, either.*

Mila: *I can't leave the house for too long today, but do you think we could grab coffee this afternoon? I'd like to talk.*

Everett: *Sure. You let me know what time. I'm flexible.*

Relieved, I heart the message and lie back again.

Later that morning, I get an email from Daniel Bartok.

Dear Ms. Ferguson,

I'm thrilled that you're up for a chat! How about Thursday? I could meet you at the diner any time after 5:00.

Let me know if that works for you!

Sincerely,
Daniel Bartok

Oh, right.

With all the excitement (and sex) over the weekend, I sort of forgot I agreed to meet with him. But I've made up my mind to go through with it, so I reply that I'll meet him at 5:30 Thursday evening. I explain that I can't stay long, but I'm eager to hear what his club has uncovered about that night. I give him my phone number and tell him to text me where he's sitting once he arrives.

After lunch, I help my mother with her exercises, which tire her out. "I'm going to lie down," she says, working her way slowly toward her bedroom with the walker.

I glance at the time—it's just after two. "Okay with you if I run out for a bit?"

"Where?" she asks.

For some reason, I don't want her to know the truth. "I just need to run a few errands. I'd like to check out that new art supply store. I could use a few new brushes. I won't be long."

"That's fine," she says, disappearing around the corner.

Mila: *I'm free! Can you get away?*

Everett: *Yes. Riverfront Roast in about 20?*

Mila: *Perfect.*

After giving my hair a quick brush, I put on a little mascara and lip balm and dash out of the house.

Everett is waiting for me out on the sidewalk in front of the coffee shop. My heart beats faster as I approach him. "Hi," I say.

"Hi." He looks like he's not sure if he should hug me or not. His hands are jammed in his pockets.

I open my arms to embrace him. His chest is warm and solid against mine. "Thanks for meeting me last minute."

"No problem."

Inside, it smells like strong coffee and pumpkin spice. I order a latte with whipped cream and cinnamon; Everett gets a decaf dark roast. We find seats across from each other at a tiny booth for two in the back.

I dip my tongue in my whipped cream. "Mmm. Tastes like pumpkin pie. Fall is definitely here."

Everett takes a sip of his decaf.

"I used to love fall as a kid—the colors, the smell, even going back to school. It always felt like getting a fresh start. Like, *this year will be different*." I laugh. "Somehow, I imagined the coming of autumn would magically transform me into a new person. Someone confident and popular. Someone Everett McKean might actually notice."

His smile seeps into my bones, melting them like butter. "I noticed you."

"Eventually," I say, a flush creeping up my neck. "So how's Gabi?"

"She's fine. We talked after you left. I'm pretty sure she's going to reach out to you this week."

"I'd like that."

"She feels bad for the way she reacted, and she apologized for running out. She was just shocked."

"I get it. I panicked too." I play with my napkin, folding it accordion-style. "Not just about Gabi, but about us."

He sips his coffee. "Why?"

I take a deep breath. "I started to worry that my skis were out from under me, you know? I think I needed a little time to make sure that I wasn't attempting a slope too steep for me to handle. I don't want to be one of those people who wipes out and their equipment is scattered all across the mountain."

Everett's lips twitch. "Yard sale."

I return his grin. "Yard sale."

"It's okay," he says, the tension in his shoulders loosening. "I don't want to push you into something you're not ready for. But I hope you know that I'm nothing like your ex. I'm never going to hurt you like that."

"I know you're nothing like him. Rationally, I know." I take a breath. "But *I'm* like *me*. And sometimes my rational brain takes a break and my insecurity takes the wheel and I freak out a little."

He leans forward, elbows on the table. "What can I do to help?"

"Just promise you'll always be honest with me. That I'll always know where I stand with you."

"That's easy."

"Thanks." I lift my drink to my lips and slurp up some whipped cream, let it melt on my tongue. "So what brought Gabi to town?"

"Actually, she's moving back to Hart's Landing."

I set my cup down with a thump. "She is?"

"Yes. But she's here right now to help our mom find a treatment for her fibromyalgia that doesn't involve habit-forming pain meds. Mom won't take them." He hesitates. "Our dad got addicted to opioids before he died."

"That's hard. Your poor mom."

"By the way, I forgot to tell you that she loved the card you sent her."

I smile. "I'm glad."

"Did you draw something on the front?"

"Yes. An apple blossom, since she sent an apple pie."

He gives me a mock scowl, eyes narrowed. "You've never drawn anything for me."

"Give me your napkin." I dig in my purse for a pen.

"Mila, I was kidding. You don't have to draw anything for me. I already took my clothes off for you."

Laughing, I grab his napkin and slide it toward me, then begin sketching. "Hush. Artist at work."

"What is it?" He cranes his neck to get a better look, but I hide what I'm doing with my latte.

"Something that reminds me of you."

"A sturdy oak tree with a massive trunk?"

I giggle. "No."

"Some kind of giant mushroom with a thick, hard stem?"

"Nope."

"I got it—a very firm, very *large* eggplant."

"None of the above." I finish up the rudimentary sketch and slide the napkin toward him. "Now guess."

He stares at it. "Cherry blossoms."

"Yes!"

"Holy shit. I can't get over how easily you just drew this. You're amazing."

Heat flushes my cheeks, and I pick up my latte. "It's just a scribble."

He stares at it for another minute before setting it aside. "I had a conversation with Dr. Kevin Yang from the environmental science department at MSU this morning."

"Oh yeah? What did he say?"

"I'm in luck. Turns out phytoremediation is a particular interest for him because of water contamination in the Great Lakes Basin. Did you know that the Great Lakes supply more than ninety percent of the country's surface fresh water?"

"I did not," I say, laughing at his professorial tone. "But that's very interesting."

"And the freshwater supply is at risk due to pollution from

landfills, brownfields, and other industrial bullshit. Dr. Yang told me he's overseen the installation of several phytobuffer networks as part of ecological restoration, and he said he'd be glad to take a look at the foundry site and give me some advice."

"Oh, Everett, that's perfect. It makes me so happy to think about that place being reimagined in a positive way."

"He also suggested establishing a mini research center where students—and even the public—could study the process of phytoremediation and learn more about environmentally friendly cleanup. I might be able to get some additional funding that way. A federal grant."

"I love that idea! When's he coming up here?"

"In two weeks. The Wednesday after Founder's Day. In the meantime, he asked me to send him all the test results so he can look them over."

"Fingers crossed this is the answer." I hold up both hands to show him.

He smiles. "I have a good feeling."

All too soon, he walks me to my car and kisses me by the driver's side door.

"I wish I didn't have to go," I tell him. "Maybe I can escape again tomorrow."

"I'd like that."

"Oh, I forgot to tell you—I changed my mind about meeting with that Diner Detective guy. We're going to talk on Thursday."

Everett's eyebrows rise. "Oh yeah? Why the change of heart?"

"Yasmine said something on Friday night about running from the past, and I realized that's part of my problem. I run away from things that scare me, especially when they involve any kind of confrontation. I'm trying to get better at that."

"I support this." He slips both hands into my hair, cradling my face. "I support you." Then he kisses me again.

A long, slow kiss that tastes like coffee and cinnamon and a new beginning.

The following afternoon, I'm working in my back-bedroom studio when my mother calls to me from the living room.

"Mila? There's someone pulling up to the house! Did you invite friends over? I'm not dressed for company!"

"Maybe it's a delivery," I call back.

"The person is coming up the front walk, and they're not carrying a package!"

The doorbell rings.

Exhaling, I set down my colored pencil and go to the living room.

"I don't want anyone to see me," my mother hisses from the couch, clutching her robe around her. "I never got dressed today."

"Relax, I won't invite anyone in."

I pull open the front door and gasp.

It's Gabi.

Chapter Thirty-Six

Mila

She's wearing jeans and a slouchy beige sweater that falls off one shoulder. Her blond hair is in a nest on top of her head, and her expression is somber. In her hand is a big plastic bag full of cookies. "Hi."

"Hi." My heart pounds like a sprinter's feet on the track.

"Can we talk?"

"Of course. I'll come outside." Over my shoulder, I say, "Mom, it's Gabi. I'll be just outside." I step out onto the porch, pulling the door shut behind me.

We stand face to face. Gabi isn't as tall as Everett, but she's got a few inches on me. She's also wearing thick-soled brown boots, and I'm barefoot. I have to look up to meet her eyes, which are so much like her brother's that I feel it like a punch in the gut.

But her face is just *hers*, and seeing her this close again puts a lump in my throat. A thousand memories engulf me, and I want to hug her, but I don't know if I'm supposed to. Is she my old friend? Or is she a stranger?

"I made you some cookies," she says, handing me the bag. "I still stress-bake."

I take it from her, my taste buds perking up at the sight of the golden-brown snickerdoodles. "You always did make the best cookies."

We look at each other for a moment, an awkward silence hanging like a curtain between us. How did we come to this?

And then she moves, closing the distance between us and throwing her arms around me. I hug her back, and for a moment, the two of us just hold each other and cry softly. She smells like she used to—like cinnamon and sugar and vanilla—and the scent rolls time backward.

"Mila, I'm so sorry."

"Me too."

"No, you have to let me get this out. I've been holding onto this for way too long." She releases me and wipes her eyes. "Nothing that happened that night was your fault. I'm sorry everyone made you feel that way—it was wrong."

"But I wasn't careful enough closing up, so maybe it *was* my fault."

"No." She shakes her head. "That fire was an *accident.* It wasn't your fault my father hadn't renewed the insurance policy. It wasn't your fault the company denied the claim. It wasn't your fault we had to sell." Another deep breath. "Other things went down that night—really horrible things—that had nothing to do with you. Things I never talked about. Instead of turning to my friends for support like I should have, I shut everyone out."

A chill ripples through me, and I hug the cookies close to my chest.

"At the time, I thought I had good reason for acting the way I did. Later, I saw things more clearly, but it felt too late to make it right. And I was so ashamed." Another sob breaks loose from her chest. "Even talking about that night is hard."

"Then we don't have to."

"But can you forgive me?"

"Of course I can," I choke out, throwing my arms around her again. "I ran away and shut everyone out, too. Believe me, I understand."

"You guys were the best friends I ever had," Gabi says. "And I've missed you so much."

Reluctantly, I let her go. "I hear you're moving back. We should get together as soon as possible—you, me, and Yasmine."

"I'd love that." She takes a deep breath. "I'm actually heading over to her bar right from here. I don't want to waste any more time.

We've been apart long enough."

Next to us, the front door opens. My mom appears in fresh clothing, her hair neatly brushed, her makeup done. "Gabi! My goodness, it *is* you!"

"Hi, Ms. Ferguson." Gabi does her best to pull herself together and smile. "How are you feeling?"

My mother emits a heavy sigh. "Oh, I have good days and bad. Would you like to come in? Mila, why are you making her stand on the porch?"

"Thank you, but I can't today," says Gabi. "I'm taking my mother to see some fitness places. She'd like to do some strength training."

"That's so important at our age. When I'm all recovered from my surgery, I'll be starting up a fitness and flexibility class for women. Tell Patricia she should join us!"

"I'll do that." She smiles at my mom and then me. "Let's get together when I get back. I'll ask Everett for your number."

"Perfect." I blush, remembering the way she caught us in his cabin on Monday.

With my mom hovering, she can't say much more, but she does take my hand and give it a squeeze. "I'm happy for you."

"Thank you." I hold up the bag. "And thank you for the cookies."

"You're welcome. I'm going to take some to Yasmine, too. I need to tell her I'm back and, well… It felt like old times baking for you guys again."

We exchange one last smile before she turns and heads down the walk.

That night, I sleep better than I have in months. It feels like everything is falling into place—like the scattered pieces of my life are coming together. Maybe not in exactly the same way they did before, but in a new way that makes me feel almost whole again.

I wonder if it can last.

The following night, I enter the diner at five-thirty.

The place is full of memories.

As teenagers, we liked Ernie's because it was cheap, open late, and the booths were the perfect size to fit five of us. It was our favorite hangout after late-night study sessions and high school dances, or when the Michigan winters made sitting outside at the foundry impossible.

As soon as I push open the glass door, I'm greeted by the familiar smell of fresh coffee and fried food. The walls are cluttered with artifacts that tell the story of the town's history: black-and-white photographs, framed newspaper clippings, company store ledger pages, vintage menus. Daniel has texted me that he's sitting in a booth near the squat-bellied cast-iron stove, and the worn wood floors creak under my feet as I make my way back.

I pause for a second by the burgundy vinyl booth we'd always claimed was "ours."

This is the booth where we hung on Lydia's every word when she told us what it was like to kiss a boy. Where I mastered the cherry stem trick with my tongue. Where we celebrated Gabi's state championships. Where we brainstormed campaign strategies for Yasmine and tried to talk Rachel into dumping her unfaithful boyfriend.

It's where we all cried when we learned the cancer was back.

"Mila! Over here!"

I look in the direction of the cast-iron stove and see a guy waving at me. Clean-shaven and fair-skinned, he's medium height and maybe in his mid-thirties, wearing glasses, a plaid button-down shirt, and khaki pants. His dark hair is receding slightly. I walk toward him. "Daniel?"

"Dan is good." He holds out his hand, and I shake it. "Nice to meet you."

"You too."

"Please sit down." He gestures to the empty booth, and I slide in across from him. "Are you hungry? Would you like something to eat or drink?"

"No, thank you. I have to go home and make dinner for my mom, so I can't stay long."

The server comes by, and Dan orders the meatloaf and an iced tea. When we're alone again, he reaches into the pocket of a jacket next to him on the bench. "I'm sure you're anxious to know about the new evidence."

"Very," I admit.

"I won't keep you in suspense." He places his closed fists on the table. In each of them appears to be a small plastic baggie. "These items were found by a bystander in the alley behind the bakery the night of the fire. We have reason to believe they belong to someone who was there for a short time after the bakery closed, but who left right before the explosion. Strange, isn't it?"

"I don't know. Because I don't know what's in your hands."

He turns one fist over and opens it up. "Exhibit A. The ponytail holder."

I take one look at it and roll my eyes. I can't help it. "That's mine."

"Are you sure?"

"Yes. One hundred percent. I used that kind of holder to put my hair up every single day for ballet class."

Dan looks a little deflated. "Well, what about this?" He turns his second hand over and uncurls his fingers slowly. "Exhibit B."

I squint at the bag. Then I gasp. "My necklace."

"This is yours, too?"

"Yes." My eyes are filling with tears. "It's my ladybug charm necklace. I lost it that night."

"Oh." The disappointment in his voice is evident.

Heart racing, I pluck the bag with the necklace from his hand and reach inside it. The clasp is broken, so I hold it up by both ends of the chain. The ladybug dangles in the center. My throat is so tight that my voice comes out squeaky. "I never thought I'd see this again. Can I have it back? I can give you proof it's mine if you'd like. I have a bunch of photos of me wearing it."

"That's okay. You can take it." He looks so dejected that I feel bad.

"I'm sorry the evidence didn't turn out to be more exciting," I say.

"Me too." He sighs. "I'm trying to start a true crime podcast. This was going to be my first case."

I smile sympathetically. "I was actually hoping you *did* have something to clear my name."

He lifts his chin, like he won't accept defeat. "I still believe there's more to the story."

"I don't think so, Dan," I say gently. "Investigators were positive it was a flour dust explosion that originated at the back of the kitchen. An oven or burner must have been left on, and I missed it. I confessed to being distracted that night. But the only other person there was Everett McKean."

"There's a witness who says otherwise," he blurts.

"A witness to what?"

"I'm not at liberty to say." Dan looks frustrated but resolute. "I'm trying to convince that witness to come forward."

"I don't understand. Didn't the police interview everyone who was there that night?"

"Not this person. They were gone by the time police arrived." He hesitates. "It's the same person who found the items in the alley."

"Oh."

"Would you be willing to talk to this person? That might be enough to bring them—and their story—into the public eye."

"I don't know, Dan. At some point, shouldn't we just leave the past in the past and move forward?"

Dan shakes his head. "Impossible."

"What do you mean?"

"The past is always with us. The people we've known, the places we've been, the experiences we've had. All of it shapes our present reality and therefore influences the future. And it's always possible to discover new things about the past, isn't it? Memory can tell a story that skips a page, and it's only later you learn it was there all along." He stops. "And then the present is reshaped once more."

His words remind me of learning that my father was an artist. It did feel like discovering I'd skipped a page in a book. Knowing doesn't necessarily change the ending to my story, but it fills in a gap.

Maybe Dan is right. Maybe the past still matters. Maybe there are still things to be learned.

"Let me know if the witness is willing to meet with me," I say, scooting to the end of the booth and getting to my feet. "At the very least, I'd like to thank them for returning my necklace."

"Okay."

I tuck the chain and charm back into the baggie so I don't lose it. I can't believe how lucky I feel to have it back after all these years. "It was nice meeting you, Dan. Good luck."

Chapter Thirty-Seven

Everett

Everett: *Hey, let me know how it goes with budget Sherlock. I'm thinking about you.*

I send the text around four in the afternoon, but I don't hear from Mila until around nine, when she FaceTimes me. Seeing her freckles on the screen makes my chest feel tight. Or maybe it's her eyes. Or her hair.

"Hey, you."

She smiles. "Hi. Sorry I didn't answer your text sooner. It was a lot to type, and I figured I'd get my mom taken care of and call."

"That's okay." I lie back on my couch. "So, how did it go?"

To my surprise, her face lights up. "Good. He had two items to show me that someone found in the alley right before the fire started. Both of them turned out to be mine."

"What were they?"

"One was a necklace I lost that night, and it's really special to me. I'm so happy to have it back."

"Seriously?"

"Yes. It's a ladybug charm on a gold chain. We got the charms after Lydia died, and I never took mine off. I was devastated when I realized it was missing."

"Oh, yeah. I think I remember those bug necklaces. Gabi had one too, right?"

"Right. I wonder if she still has hers. I should ask her."

"So what was the other thing he had?"

"A ponytail holder."

"Seriously? That's it?"

"That's it. And it was definitely mine."

"So much for the mysterious new evidence."

"Maybe not," she says, her eyes widening, her tone full of intrigue. "Dan claims there's a witness who saw someone leaving the bakery after it was closed but before the fire started."

"It was probably me. Remember? I left to go move the truck."

"Right." She sighs. "Anyway, I think the guy was thoroughly disappointed in me. He was hoping to have enough juicy details to make a true crime podcast."

"What about the witness? Are they willing to come forward?"

"Dan's going to find out." Her eyes sparkle. "Maybe there's still time for a plot twist."

"Embarrassing music you'd never admit to liking out loud," Mila says the next night. We're on FaceTime again, even though it's after midnight and we keep saying we should hang up and get some sleep. "Go."

"I believe I've already confessed to a substantial yacht rock playlist," I tell her, stretched out in my bed now. "But I am not ashamed of it. You?"

"I know the words to every single song in any Disney princess movie ever made. You never want to watch *Beauty and the Beast* with me. I am insufferable."

"I never want to watch a Disney princess movie ever, so we're good." Though truthfully, I'd watch anything Mila wanted to if it meant she'd curl up with me under a blanket. I'm craving the orange-blossom scent of her. "What other kinds of movies do you like?"

"Nineties rom-coms starring Julia Roberts are my favorites, hands down," she says. "*Pretty Woman*, *Notting Hill*, *My Best Friend's Wedding*… I could watch them all on a loop every day. She was always my favorite because she had red hair like me."

"Can't say I've seen any of those."

"What?" Her outrage jumps off the screen, and she bolts upright so fast that she scares her cat out of the frame. "We need to remedy that as quickly as possible. What are *your* favorite movies?"

"I like a good heist flick. Or a crime thriller. Scorsese."

"Which Scorsese do you like best?"

"Hmm. Maybe *Goodfellas*."

"Never seen it."

"Come on," I scoff, "it's a classic!"

"Our first movie marathon will be very eclectic. But you should know that I cry at everything."

"Why doesn't this surprise me?"

She looks thoughtful. "Can I ask you a question?"

"Shoot."

"What did you think of me back then?"

"Back when? I've known you for like twenty years."

"Okay, not when I was a *kid*, but like… When I was a teenager. That last summer… When I kissed you."

"I liked you."

She waits for me to go on. "That's it?"

I laugh. "What else is there?"

"Did you think I was cute?"

"Definitely. But you were my little sister's friend and it didn't feel right to do anything about it. I told myself you were off-limits."

"You asked me to go to the beach with you that night."

"Did I?"

She squawks in disbelief. "You don't remember?"

I laugh. "It's been ten years, Freckles. What happened before the fire is a little hazy in my mind."

"Well, I remember everything. It was really hot that night, and you said we should go swimming."

"Ballsy of me."

"Not as ballsy as what I did."

"That's true."

Her face scrunches up like she's in pain. "God, I was so awkward."

"Nah. I was into you. And if my world hadn't exploded that night along with the bakery, you would have known it long before now."

"Really?"

"Really."

"I still feel so bad about—about everything."

"Don't look back," I tell her. "What's past is past."

She exhales, her eyes closing for a second. "Sometimes, it doesn't feel that way at all."

I don't see Mila in person for the rest of the week.

We were supposed to meet up for lunch on Friday, but her mother developed a migraine and asked her to stay home.

On Saturday, she recovered but requested that Mila take her to do some outlet shopping two hours away. Mila and I made plans to meet for a late supper together, but when they returned, the long ride in the car had given her mother such a bad ache in her hips that she was unable to stand and cook dinner. Could Mila please take pity on her and stay in to make the meal?

"I'm sorry," she says later that night on another video call. "I'm dying to see you."

"You don't owe me an apology," I tell her. What I *want* to say is that her mother is going to keep doing this until Mila refuses to let herself be manipulated.

But I keep my mouth shut.

Sunday afternoon, I'm at my mom's house fixing a leak in the kitchen sink when Mila sends me a text.

Mila: *FREEDOM! I escaped the house and I probably have an hour.*

Everett: *Cabin?*

Mila: *I'll be there in 15.*

I slip my phone into my back pocket and test the faucet one more time. "I gotta run an errand. Can Merlin stay here?"

"Yes, but I thought you were staying for dinner." Her tone is aggrieved. "I just took the pork chops out of the pan."

"I'll come back." I'm already halfway out the door.

Racing out to my truck, I jump behind the wheel, execute a reckless three-point turn, and tear down the dirt road toward the cabin.

I arrive first and wait for her outside, leaning against the back of my truck. It's wild the way my heart jumps at the sight of her stepping out of her mom's car wearing my enormous John Deere hoodie, her hair in that messy knot on the top of her head.

She runs right for me and lassos my neck with her arms and my hips with her legs. Our lips crash together, and I realize too late that I haven't showered today and probably smell like some combination of manure, gasoline, and fried pork chops.

Eventually, she slides back onto her feet. "I missed you," she says, out of breath. "Is that dumb? It's only been four days."

"Not at all. I missed you too. So much that I went running out of my mother's house to spend an hour with you when she just put dinner on the table."

She laughs. "You chose seeing me over eating a meal?"

"To be clear, I expect to have both at once." I pull her inside.

As soon as I enter my mom's kitchen again, I get the third degree. "What was that all about?" she asks the moment the door shuts behind me.

"What?" I pretend I don't know what she means and head to the sink to wash my hands. Her suspicious stare feels like needles on my back.

"You running out of here like the place was on fire."

"That's a little dramatic." My glance falls on a section of countertop my father replaced ten years ago with a laminate that doesn't exactly match the original, giving it an unintentional two-toned look. "I think it's time we fixed these counters."

"Don't try to change the subject. Where did you go?"

Merlin's head is going back and forth between us like he's enthralled with a tennis match.

I grab a plate from the cabinet and fill it with pork chops and mashed potatoes at the stove. "The hardware store."

"For what?"

"For what?" I repeat.

"Yes, what did you run out of here to get at the hardware store?" She leans to one side, looking around me toward the door. "I didn't see you come in with a bag or anything."

"I didn't buy anything."

"You raced out of here at a hundred miles per hour to go to the hardware store, but you didn't buy anything while you were there?"

"That's right." I dig into my food, already cueing up a compliment I hope will end this third degree. "Mmm," I say around a mouthful, "so good."

Mom rests her elbows on the table, arms folded. "Nice try. You look a little sweaty. Was it hot in the hardware store?"

Instead of answering, I get up to pour myself a glass of milk. Which I don't even like.

"And your fly is down."

I quickly zip myself up and return to the table.

"Are you going to tell me or not?" My mother is losing patience with me.

"Tell you what?"

"If something is happening between you and Mila Ferguson!"

"I told you, we're just—"

"I know what you told me. What I don't know is if you're lying to *me* or to yourself."

"I'm not lying to anybody!"

"So have you been seeing her?"

"You could say that."

"How much longer is she in town?"

"A month."

"Oh." Sounding satisfied, she relaxes in her chair again. "That's plenty of time."

I cock a brow at her. "Plenty of time for what?"

"A haircut, for one." She waves her fork in my direction. "You're looking a little shaggy."

Chapter Thirty-Eight

Mila

"You're in a good mood today," my mother remarks in a suspicious tone. It's Wednesday afternoon, and she's drinking coffee and watching me water her plants. "What's that about?"

I decide to be honest. "I'm seeing Everett later."

"Oh." Her expression grows sullen. "You're abandoning me to run around with your boyfriend?"

"He's not my boyfriend, and I'm not abandoning you."

"I thought you said you and Everett weren't dating."

"It's casual," I say, although my feelings for him are about as casual as a sequined ball gown. "I volunteered to help him with Founder's Day this weekend."

"I wasn't born yesterday, Mila." She sniffs. "I hope you're at least being careful."

"About what?"

"About everything." She takes a sip of tea. "Given your tendency to get carried away, you should protect yourself."

My gut instinct is to get defensive, but then I recall a technique Hugo told me about called the gray rock method, which involves giving only neutral, unemotional responses. Nothing she can use to provoke an emotional reaction. "All good," I say, my tone casual.

"You can't depend on a man to be responsible."

"Mm." I go to the kitchen to refill the pitcher.

She falls silent, probably annoyed that I didn't give her anything to work with. A sense of triumph has me smiling at the sink, even while it grates my nerves that she can't let me enjoy myself away from her.

"So what are you going to do when you leave town?" my mother asks when I return to the room.

"We haven't talked about it."

"Well, you'd better. There's nothing worse than thinking you're on the same page as someone and discovering you were wrong all along. And you have a tendency to be wrong about these things."

Pressing my lips together, I refuse to give her the satisfaction of an argument. When I'm done watering the plants, I grab the dust mop and run it around the living room's wood floor.

My mother continues to observe me. "What time are you leaving tonight?"

"Around six."

"And where are you going?"

"Not sure."

"Well, how long will you be gone?"

"I don't know."

More silence.

"What about dinner?"

"Leftovers are in the fridge."

"Are you having dinner out?"

"Maybe."

"What are you wearing?"

"I haven't decided."

She huffs, frustrated that I'm not dancing to her little tune. "You're not being very forthcoming, Mila. It's not helpful at all, and frankly, it's *rude*."

Saying nothing, I leave the room and take the dust mop back to the basement, where it hangs from a peg at the bottom of the stairs. While I'm down there, I switch the laundry from the washer to the dryer and take a moment to celebrate this victory—this wall that I managed to put up between her words and my feelings.

That's when I spot the orchid drawings in the cardboard box, and an idea takes shape in my head.

When I pull up at the cabin, it's just after six. The sun hangs low on the horizon, bathing everything with warm, red-gold light. I jump out of the car just as Everett comes out the front door, and we meet halfway between the car and house.

The way we rush toward each other, you'd think we've been separated by war, uncertain we'd ever meet again. In reality, it's only been three days since we had the cabin quickie.

I laugh as he scoops me up and swings me around, my feet in the air. When he sets me down, our mouths come together, and I feel his kiss ricochet through me, bouncing off every molecule in my body.

When we take a second to catch our breath, he buries his face in my neck. "God, you smell good. I missed you."

"I missed you too."

Eventually, he pulls his upper body back, keeping his arms locked around my waist and his hips pressed to mine. His brown eyes tour every part of my face. "You're so fucking beautiful."

"Thank you." Warmth expands in my chest as I look up at him, and for a moment it's like my heart can't contain all the things I'm asking it to hold—joy, gratitude, awe, trust, hope. I lace my fingers at the back of his neck. "You got a haircut."

"My mom gave me shit about my shaggy hair over the weekend."

I laugh and ruffle it with my fingers the way I used to dream about doing. All around us, sunrays slant through the gaps between the trees, dust motes dancing in the glow. I feel as weightless as those particles, as radiant as the shimmering light. Has any moment of my life ever been this perfect?

Not far from us is a certain sycamore. Over his shoulder, I see its branches swaying against the sky. "I cannot *believe* I tried to climb that tree."

Everett pivots and squints as he looks toward the top. "You guys got pretty high up."

"Yeah. Even Gabi panicked, and we started yelling for help."

"It was pure luck I was nearby. I remember I came running just in time to see Gabi jump to the ground, and I was terrified she'd broken an ankle or something. But she was fine."

"And I was still hanging there, convinced I was going to die."

"I remember standing beneath you, telling you to let go, and you wouldn't. You just kept saying you were afraid to fall."

"And you kept saying you were right there, and you wouldn't let me get hurt. So I let go."

He turns to face me. "You let go? I thought you lost your grip."

"No. I let go. You were so sure you could catch me."

"Want to know the truth?" He gives me his lopsided smile. "I wasn't sure at all. But then suddenly you were flying toward me, and somehow I managed to get my arms around you. I must have timed it just right."

"My feet never hit the ground," I confirm.

He moves to my side and wraps an arm around my shoulders, then starts walking me toward the porch. As we go, he drops a kiss on my temple. "I was just glad you weren't hurt."

"Then you made us promise two things. First, that we'd never tell any adults about it."

"I didn't want Gabi to get in trouble."

"And second, that we'd never do it again."

"I didn't want you to fall if I wasn't there to catch you."

"Everett." The autumn breeze whispers over my skin. "Would you still catch me?"

He holds me tightly and puts his lips at my ear. "Every fucking time."

We're almost inside when I remember the large brown paper bag in my car. I jog back for it, then follow Everett into the cabin.

"I hope that's not dinner," Everett says, shutting the door behind me. "I got pizza for us."

"It's not dinner." Once he slips off his boots, I instruct him to shut his eyes.

He does as he's told. "Are you taking your clothes off?"

"Not yet." Pulling the framed orchids from their wrappings, I prop them up on the kitchen counter against the backsplash. Merlin wanders over to say hello, and I give him some attention.

"Can I open?"

"No. Just wait." I take him by the arm, leading him to the counter. "Okay. Now."

He opens his eyes and stares at the drawings. Leans closer. "Holy shit. Are these yours?"

"I drew them, yes. But they're yours now."

He glances at me. "Are you serious?"

"Yes. Do you like them?"

"They're beautiful, Mila. I love them." He admires the orchids again, and I feel proud of the delicate veins on the leaves, the shades of purple in the petals, from lavender to plum, the graceful curve of the stems. Even the spidery roots have their own beauty. He shakes his head. "My walls are not worthy." Then he pulls me into his arms and kisses the top of my head. "Thank you."

"You're welcome." I rest my cheek on his chest. "Full disclosure, I took these from my mom's house. I drew them for her last Christmas, had them framed and everything. Then I found them in a box in the basement the weekend I got home."

"I'm sorry." His arms tighten around me, like he wants to shield me from the hurt.

"I hope you don't mind that they're sort of a second-hand gift."

"I don't mind at all." He kisses my temple. My cheek. My chin. My neck.

"Do you want to hang them up?"

"Can we do that later?" His hands trace the curves of my ass. "I've got another activity in mind. One that involves fucking you with my tongue. Probably my hand. And definitely my cock." He puts his mouth at my ear. "I want you like a fiend."

I rub my palm over the bulge in his jeans. "Show me."

"I told Hugo about you." I lick some tomato sauce off my finger. We're sitting on the bed with the pizza box between us. I have on the T-shirt Everett stripped off as we stumbled into his room, and he's wearing only his navy boxer briefs.

"Who's Hugo again?" Everett finishes his first slice and picks up a second.

"My therapist."

"Oh." His expression is a mix of pleasure and surprise. "What did he say?"

"He was glad actually. Hugo wasn't in favor of the no-dating rule because he says avoiding relationships isn't the same as learning to navigate one in a healthy way." After one last bite, I put my crust in the box.

He glances down. "You don't eat the crust?"

"Never."

He picks up the crust and bites into it. "See, this is why it could work out for us."

I laugh and wipe my hands on a napkin. "Because I don't like pizza crust and you do?"

"Not just that. You cook, I do dishes. You draw the art, I hang it up. You get cold at night, I like providing the body heat that keeps you warm."

"Hmm. That does make us sound very compatible. But it's not quite enough." I lean back on my hands. "Butter on movie popcorn?"

He shakes his head. "Just salt."

"Which end do you peel a banana from?"

"Um, the end with the stem. Don't you?"

"No. Not since I learned that monkeys peel from the other end because it's easier. You literally just pinch and open."

"Interesting."

"Okay, we're one for two. Now for the big one." I swing my legs over the side of the bed and walk out of the room.

"Where are you going?"

"I have to check something in your bathroom."

"What?"

I flip on the light and open the top right drawer of his vanity. Lying there is a tube of Colgate. Smiling, I swipe it and return to the bedroom. "You passed the test," I say, holding it up. "The tube is properly squeezed from the bottom, not the middle. And the cap was on."

He laughs. "If it wasn't, were you going to go home?"

"No. The sex is too good." I toss my hair over my shoulder and strike a flirty pose. "Plus, I look cute in your clothes."

"Fuck yes, you do." His eyes darken with hunger again, but not for food. "Did you get enough to eat?"

"Yes."

He closes up the pizza box and takes it to the kitchen while I replace his toothpaste in the bathroom. We meet in the bedroom, where he lifts his shirt over my head, sweeps me off my feet, and tosses me onto his bed. Ditching his underwear, he climbs on top of me, and I wrap my legs around him.

"I'm sorry I don't have more time." I slide my hands along his thick-muscled biceps. "I wish I could stay all night."

He lowers his head so that I can feel his lips brushing against mine when he speaks. "Baby, it still wouldn't be enough."

After round two, I lie snuggled up along his side with my head on his chest, an arm and a leg tossed over him. The lamp gives his bronzed skin a golden glow. "I don't want to leave," I say lazily.

"I'm not kicking you out."

"But I should go soon."

His arms tighten around me. "Maybe I won't let you go. Maybe I'll keep you here forever. 'I'm sorry, Eliza, I have no idea what happened to your daughter. You'll have to find someone else to boss around.'"

I laugh. "That wouldn't be any fun for her. It's only me she wants to control."

"I don't know how you stand it." He rubs my back. "I wish she appreciated you."

"Sometimes she does." My voice sounds weak.

"When? I have only ever heard her say nice things to you once—about your dancing. And right afterward, she called you a disappointment because you didn't get into Juilliard. I'll never forget it."

The usual list of excuses I always make for her is on the tip of my tongue. But when I open my mouth, what comes out is something else entirely.

"Actually, I did get in."

His hand stops moving on my back. "What?"

"Juilliard. I wasn't rejected. I got in."

"But—"

"I lied. When I got the acceptance letter, I replied that I was quitting dance and going to another school. Then I told my mother I hadn't been accepted."

"Why?"

My heart is pounding so hard. "Because I knew she'd make me go."

"You were that afraid of her?"

"I was afraid of being forced to live a life I didn't want. So I lied." A sob catches in my throat. "But I felt horrible about it. I still do."

"Oh, baby." He strokes my back again. "You didn't owe her that acceptance. It was your life. Your decision."

"Still. It was dishonest. It was me running away from something hard instead of facing it."

"Hey. Look at me."

I pick up my head and look into his eyes. He frames my face with one hand.

"You have nothing to be ashamed of. You did what you had to do to lead the life you wanted. I think it was brave."

"But I didn't have the guts to stand up to her."

"Mila. You were a *kid*. You stood up for yourself the only way you could." He caresses my cheek with his thumb. "She raised you to feel like her love was conditional. Something to be won. It's not surprising you were afraid to tell her a truth she wouldn't like."

"You don't think I'm a bad person for lying to her?"

"Not at all. I wish you'd stand up for yourself more often."

"Direct confrontation is not my style."

"It's mine," he grumbles. "Can I fight for you?"

His protectiveness warms me all over. "No. I appreciate the offer, but you cannot meet my bully at the flagpole."

He exhales. "Sorry. I'm not trying to make this about me. It just tears me up inside, the way she treats you. And when I see something wrong, I want to fix it."

"You can't fix this, Everett. Only I can fix me."

"Hey." He lifts my chin and levels his eyes with mine. "There is nothing broken about you—nothing that needs to be fixed. I just can't stand the thought of someone hurting you. That's all."

Putting my head on his chest again, I soak in the heat of his body and the comfort of his embrace. I want to tell him everything.

"Everett."

"Hm."

"I burned the acceptance letter that night. At the bakery."

A pause. "You did?"

"Yes." My voice trembles. "I lit the corner of it on fire from a burner on the stove and let it burn in the sink. And I *swear to God* I made sure that burner was off."

"Shhh." He tightens his arms around me. "I believe you."

"You do?"

"Yes. And I think I would have noticed if a burner was on. I would have smelled the gas or seen the flame."

"For ten years, I've been carrying that around with me. I never told anyone—I was too afraid of getting in even more trouble. It made me feel so alone."

"You're not alone anymore." He kisses the top of my head. "And you're not the only one who has secrets from that night."

"What do you mean?"

He doesn't answer right away.

"You can tell me. I won't judge."

"It's pretty dark," he says quietly.

"That's okay." I want to know everything about him. The dark and the light.

He takes a couple of breaths while he thinks it through, his chest rising and falling beneath my cheek. When he speaks, his voice is solemn. "The night of the fire, my father didn't have a heart attack. He fell down the stairs. And it was my fault."

I gasp. "What happened?"

"He was drunk and furious. Out of his mind. He'd already taken a swing at me, but I was worried he was going after Gabi."

I pick up my head. "Your father hit you?"

"Sometimes. If he was drunk enough. Or angry enough."

"My God. I had no idea." My blood ices over with fear. Was this my fault too? "Wait a minute. Was he angry about the fire? Is that why he hit you?"

"He was angry about a lot of things in his life. That night, he was furious with Gabi. But he never hit her—he'd hit me in front of her, because he knew how much it hurt her."

"Oh, Everett." A deep chasm opens in my chest, sympathy and sorrow rushing in.

"I was trying to de-escalate the situation, but he just wouldn't give up the fight." He pauses. "I had a baseball bat in my hand. He came at me, and I moved out of the way. He lost his balance, stumbled toward the staircase, and fell backward." Everett's voice breaks.

"It wasn't your fault," I tell him. "You did what you had to do. You were keeping the people you love safe."

"He needed surgery after the fall. That's when he got hooked on the pain pills. He never really recovered."

My heart—my entire body—aches for him. And for Gabi, too, who was suffering in silence all that time. She never told us about her dad.

"Publicly, we went with the story about the heart attack causing the fall. It was just easier."

I brush the back of my knuckles over Everett's cheek. "I'm so sorry. I knew your dad was a drinker, but I never knew things were violent at home."

"We didn't talk about it. It was embarrassing."

My eyes fill as I recall what Gabi said last week.

There were other things that went wrong that night—really horrible things—which had absolutely nothing to do with you. Things I've never talked about.

Now it makes more sense. And even though it hurts to think she felt like she couldn't come to her friends with the whole truth, I'm glad she had her brother. I wish I had family who loved and protected each other the way they did, in good times and bad.

"You and Gabi are so lucky to have each other. "

He kisses my fingertips. "You have me too."

Everything around us blurs and fades. In this moment, I'm overwhelmed with longing for him that rises from the deep and quickly rushes over my head. Powerless against it, I lower my cheek to his chest again and tuck my arms around him, holding on as if he's a life preserver in choppy waters. My eyes close, and his heartbeat anchors me.

I've been gone for hours. Much longer than I said I'd be. The responsible adult in me, the one who jumped on a plane two days after my mother called, knows I should get up, get dressed, go home.

But the part of me that loves being touched, held, and cherished, begs me to stay.

In his arms, I am wanted. I am forgiven. I am understood.

Everett and I don't get out of bed until after nine p.m. Once I'm dressed, I check my phone and discover I missed a series of texts from my mother. They started almost the minute I walked out of the house.

Mom: *The schedule you left for my evening meds doesn't seem right.*
Mom: *I got all the way to the kitchen with my walker, but you put my favorite mug on the highest shelf. I can't even reach it without my back spasming.*
Mom: *I'm out of the sensitive skin body wash I need. Can you please pick some up and bring it home in time for my bath at 8:00?*
Mom: *Where are you? I thought you said you wouldn't be late. It's almost 9:00!*
Mom: *Can you please call me?*

Everett notices my troubled expression. "What's wrong?"

"My mother. She's been messaging me all night for petty things. She just wants to interrupt my time with you."

Everett's face remains impassive. "I'm sorry."

"Don't be. I'm not." I sigh as I lean down to tie my sneakers. "But I better get home. Can you send me a photo of the orchids on the wall after you get them up?"

"Of course. Thanks again for giving them to me. You're sure your mother won't miss them?"

"Unfortunately, I'm positive."

When I straighten up, he tugs me into his arms. "This is a better home for them. They'll be appreciated here."

"Yes. They will."

My mother is sitting on the couch in her pajamas and robe when I get home. She has a book on her lap, which she sets aside when I come in.

"Where have you been?" she demands, pushing her reading glasses to the top of her head.

"I was with Everett." I shut the door behind me.

"I texted you several times tonight. I needed you."

I refuse to let her force me into delivering a phony apology. "I didn't see the texts until after nine."

Her lips purse. "What did you do all night that kept you so busy?"

"Not much."

She pouts, unable to do anything with that gray rock. "Well, it's very late, and I'm exhausted now that I waited up for you."

I say nothing as I take off my sneakers.

"Would you mind helping me to bed now?"

I do, then say good night and leave the room, turning the light off on my way out.

Fifteen minutes later, I'm settling on the couch for the night when a text from Everett comes in.

Everett: *Did you make it home okay?*

Mila: *Yes. I just put the toddler to bed.*

Everett: *Was she mad you were late?*

Mila: *Of course. And she'll probably punish me for a few days.*

Everett: *You don't have to take it. You didn't do anything wrong.*

Mila: *I'll be okay. I had the best time with you tonight. It was worth it.*

The next thing I get is a photo of the orchids hanging in his living room.

Mila: *They look so good!!!*

Everett: *I love looking at them. Thank you for trusting me with them. With everything.*

My screen grows a little blurry, and my throat feels tight.

Mila: *I do trust you.*

He hearts the message.

Everett: *Good night, Freckles.*

Mila: *Night.*

Setting my phone aside, I close my eyes and imagine his warm body curled around mine in the dark. I wonder how often he and Bella spent the night together and feel a sharp pang of jealousy.

Eighteen days until I go back to New York.

For the first time, I wish I didn't have to leave Hart's Landing quite so soon.

Chapter Thirty-Nine

Everett

The day before the Founder's Day celebration is a nightmare.

The rented tents and portable restrooms don't arrive on time, the stage for the main musical acts collapses during setup, and some teenage assholes vandalize the commemorative Founder's Day banner, which now reads **FART'S LANDING: 150 YEARS STRONG!**

Fuckers.

By the time I get home, I'm cranky, hungry, sweaty, and exhausted. I check my fridge—empty, of course. I'm muttering a foul string of curse words when someone knocks at the door.

When I open it to find Mila standing there with a takeout bag, all the bullshit I dealt with that day melts away. I pull her inside and fold her into my arms. Even Merlin is happy, nudging her legs with his head and then dropping onto his back, waiting for a belly rub.

"God, I'm glad to see you," I tell her. This day has been a disaster."

She holds up the bag. "Will meat pasties from Sawbuck Tavern make it better?"

"You're an angel sent right from heaven."

"You should see the underwear I have on."

I groan. "You're making me choose between sex and sustenance?"

"You can have both. Eat first."

"Can you stay?" I ask, afraid she'll say no because her mother needs dinner, a pain pill, a fucking kidney.

She smiles at me. "I've got a couple hours."

While I scarf down meat pasties standing at the kitchen counter, she tells me about the email she got from Dan Bartok this afternoon.

"Apparently, that eyewitness is willing to talk to me."

"Are you going to do it?"

She shrugs. "I don't know. I don't think there's much point—like you said, it was probably you this person saw leaving the bakery that night—but part of me is curious, you know?"

"So meet with him."

"I might."

I shove the last bite in my mouth and head for the bathroom before I'm even done chewing. "Give me five minutes. I just need to shower the sweat off."

"Take your time," she calls. "Merlin and I are going to get better acquainted."

I clean up, put on fresh clothes, take three seconds to apply some deodorant, and throw some product in my hair. When I come out of the bathroom, I find her sitting on the floor in front of the couch giving Merlin a belly rub. "Be careful. He's not going to let you leave."

She smiles up at me. "He's a sweetheart."

"Merlin. Go lie down."

My dog looks over his shoulder at me with an expression that can only be described as *fuck you, pal*, and stays right where he is. "Come on, dude. Give me a break."

He doesn't move.

Exhaling, I go to the cabinet and grab a treat, which I place in his crate. Food does the trick—like father, like pup—and once Merlin is safely contained, I sit on the couch and tug Mila onto my lap. "Come here. I just want to look at you."

She loops her arms around my neck, tousling the hair at the back of my head. "Liar."

Our mouths come together, and despite what I just said, my hand wanders beneath her shirt. The moment I touch her bare skin, I know I won't stop there. With an easy flick of my fingers, I unhook her bra and take her breast in my hand, teasing her nipple with my thumb. Tipping her backward, I lay her down on the couch and lift her shirt, fastening my mouth to one taut peak and taking the other between my fingers. My gentlemanly behavior continues its steady decline, and I kiss a path down her belly, undo her jeans, and pull them off.

Pushing her thighs apart, I bury my face between her legs. In less time than it takes to drive from the front of the farm to the back, her hands are in my hair and she's coming against my tongue.

It makes me so fucking hot that I knew her so well, that I can get her off so quickly. My cock is like a cannon barrel, hard and thick and ready to explode. I sit up, shove my pants to my knees, and yank her on top of me. Her body is loose like a rag doll's. Both of us moan as she sinks down on my cock. She's wet and warm and deliciously snug.

When she rests on my lap, she pauses for a moment, her eyes closed, her face impossibly beautiful. Her cheeks are flushed, her hair tousled, her freckles like tiny little stars across her nose. She opens her eyes and locks them with mine. They're devastatingly blue.

For a moment, I can't breathe. My chest is radiating with an energy that my heart feels too flimsy to contain. It's coursing throughout my entire body, zipping along my veins, every nerve ending on fire.

It occurs to me that I might be in love with her.

It's not like any feeling I've ever experienced before. With Bella, love was a gradual descent, something light and buoyant. A feather falling through the air.

With Mila, it's a spiraling, head-over-heels plummet through space. I'm powerless against it—not that I'm putting up a fight. I *want* to love her. I want to take care of her. I want to make her happy. I've spent years telling everyone I'm too busy to date, and now all I want to do is introduce her to people and say the words, "This is my girlfriend, Mila".

Can I convince her she's safe with me? To give us a chance?

As she begins to move above me, I fight the urge to come too soon. When it's over, she'll have to leave, and I'll have to miss her.

But I'm only human, and in no time at all, my body surrenders to the moment, to the friction, to the invincible need to fuck her and fill her and feel her come. She clutches me hard as her climax hits, crying out as her fingers dig into my shoulders. Afterward, she rests her forehead against mine. Our chests rise and fall quickly.

After a minute, she says, "I'll be right back."

While she's in the bathroom, I pull up my jeans and ponder my revelation.

I'm in love with her.

I can't say exactly when it happened, but it could have been any of a dozen moments. When she tied that knot in the cherry stem with her tongue. When she let me kiss her on the bridge. When she asked me to plow her fields. When she showed up on my doorstep in her pajamas. When she cooked dinner for me. When she came running at me wearing my sweatshirt. When she gifted me those orchids. When we confessed our deepest secrets to each other in the dark and I felt all the acceptance I ever could have hoped for.

There are so many moments etched on my mind. Engraved in my heart.

I want more. I want a lifetime of them.

When she comes out, I pull her onto my lap again, knees on either side of me. "What am I going to do with you?"

She plays with the collar of my flannel. "Right now, you have to let me go, or I'll probably get grounded."

"I don't mean right now."

"What do you mean?"

"I mean, I already don't get enough of you, and you're right here in Hart's Landing. What happens when you go back to Brooklyn in a couple weeks?"

She plays with a button on my shirt. "I've been trying not to think about it."

"I love being with you. I wish we didn't have a sell-by date."

"I love being with you, too. But it's only been a month.

Everything is still new and shiny." Her eyes meet mine, and they're full of trepidation. "Don't you worry that could change?"

"It doesn't feel like it could."

"But that's the trick, isn't it?"

I brush her hair back from her face. "You're scared."

"Of course I'm scared." Her laughter is self-conscious. "I don't trust this feeling, Everett. I don't know how to fully relax and enjoy it. I don't know how to stop worrying that none of this is real, that if you knew the real me, you wouldn't want her."

"Hey. Are you pretending with me right now?"

"No."

"Have you been pretending with me at all since you've been home?"

"No." A smile flutters past her lips. "You've definitely seen the full mess of me."

"And I'm still here."

She swallows. "You're still here."

I tip my forehead to hers. "I'm not going anywhere. That's all I'm saying."

Later that night, I escape to the pub for a beer. But I take so much shit from my friends, I almost wish I hadn't.

"Hey, look who showed up," Ripley says as I approach their table near the throwing lanes. "And he's spit-shined and spiffy!"

Ben leans over and sniffs me. "Is that something other than fertilizer I smell on you? Could it be cologne?"

"I'm getting haircut and grooming products, too," Hunter adds, eyeing me suspiciously. "Is this about the girl?"

I try to play it cool. "What, a guy can't get a haircut?"

"Sure, a guy can get a haircut. But he can't get a new shirt at the same time and expect his friends not to mess with him." Ripley grins. "So, is it a *thing* now, Snuggle Bear?"

Tipping up my beer, I roll my eyes. "It might be a thing. But don't fucking call me that ever again."

"I knew the baby goats would work." Ripley looks smug.

"It was the line about the tulips, right?" Hunter elbows me.

"So is she staying for good?" Ben asks. "Does this mean you have to buy matching towels and alphabetize your spice rack?"

"No. We're just seeing how it goes."

Hunter parks himself on a stool across the high-top from me. "Does she know how bossy you are?"

"She was forewarned."

"Does she know about your shitty yacht rock playlist?"

"She is aware."

"Does she enjoy the smell of manure?"

"She's non-judgmental."

"Does she know you own overalls?"

"I don't wear them that often."

"So you're, like, really into her," Hunter says, the concept completely foreign to him.

"Yeah. I am." I take another pull on my beer.

"Did she agree to judge the pie contest or something?" Ripley asks.

I laugh. "I wish."

"Wait, wait." Ben holds out his arms, like he needs to pause the world. "So is this official? You're, like, not single?"

I don't even hesitate. "I wouldn't call myself single right now."

"But being single is so great," Ripley argues. "You can do what you want. You don't have to answer to anybody."

"I *am* doing what I want. And you know what?" Mila's face fills my mind. Her body. Her scent. Her voice. Her kiss goodbye earlier this evening. The way I miss her already. "I'll answer to her. I will gladly fucking answer to her."

Chapter Forty

Mila

Hart's Landing is gifted with a gorgeous autumn afternoon for its Founder's Day celebration.

I'm ridiculously excited, just like I used to be on this day as a kid. There were contests and junk food and games and a parade. The end of the day was marked by a massive fireworks display, and afterward everyone danced to live music under the stars.

I asked my mother if she'd like to attend any of the festivities, but she said no. She won't admit it, but she doesn't want anyone to see her with her walker, and she isn't getting around well enough without it yet.

Secretly, I'm pleased I won't have to babysit her all day.

Since the crowd will be huge and parking will be difficult, I decide to ride my old bike downtown. After locking it up, I locate the volunteer tent and report for duty.

The woman in charge of volunteers has her back to me when I approach, and when she turns around, I'm surprised to see it's my high school art teacher. "Hi, Mrs. Frye. It's Mila Ferguson."

"Mila!" She smiles, deep grooves bracketing her mouth. Other than a few more lines on her face, she looks much the same as she did ten years ago, with medium brown skin and black corkscrew curls threaded with silver. A colorful scarf around her neck. Beaded jewelry she made herself. "It's so good to see you!"

We shake hands over the table and catch up for a few minutes. When she hears about my career, she clasps her hands at her chest. "A botanical illustrator—that's so cool! I wonder if you'd be up for coming into one of my drawing and painting classes, maybe talking to the students?"

"Sure, I'd love to. I'm here for two more weeks." I ignore the way my heart aches at the thought of leaving in such a short time.

We exchange contact information, and she says she'll be in touch. After checking her list, she assigns me to raffle-ticket sales and directs me to a booth over by the food and beverage trucks. For the next few hours, I greet familiar and unfamiliar faces, peddle 50/50 tickets, and answer questions about my mother's recovery.

Around four, I finally hear from Everett.

Everett: *Hey! Where are you?*

Mila: *Selling raffle tickets by the food trucks.*

Everett: *I'm just finishing up at this pie nonsense. Be there soon, unless a fight breaks out. Judy Gillis is giving Vera Pratt a very beady eye.*

A few minutes later, I spot Everett walking toward my booth. My replacement has just shown up, so I vacate the chair for her, swing my bag over my shoulder, and head in Everett's direction.

My stomach flutters madly as I get closer to him. I love the way he catches my eye and communicates without words that he's happy to see me. When we reach each other, he kisses my lips in full view of everyone around. "So, who won Best Pie, Judy or Vera?"

"Neither. The ribbon went to a seventeen-year-old girl from Hart's Landing High who has her own baking channel on YouTube with fifty thousand followers. Judy and Vera are now claiming age discrimination."

I laugh. "Of course they are."

As we walk down Main Street, people smile and say hello, but there's a degree of curiosity in all their faces. I find I don't mind their stares—in fact, I like that people see us together, see me as his. I like being here with him by my side.

I love being with you.

I wish we didn't have a sell-by date.

I'm not going anywhere, Mila. That's all I'm saying.

But what is he *thinking*? What kind of future does he see for us?

Does he want me to move back to Hart's Landing?

The idea turns my bones to jelly.

I don't want to say goodbye. But I also don't want to derail my life and end up heartbroken in Hart's Landing with my mother watching from a front row seat. Telling me I was a fool. Pointing out all my mistakes, my weaknesses, my wishful thinking.

Everett said he wasn't going anywhere. But for how long?

I hate that fear is the overbearing emotion, stomping on anything that's trying to sprout—hope, security, happiness. I don't want to feel like a child again, afraid to go after the life I want. It's the only life I have.

And tomorrow is never guaranteed.

"You're quiet." Everett glances down at me. "Everything okay?"

I smile. "Yes. Just taking it all in."

At the end of Main Street, we turn toward Riverfront Park. Under the gazebo, actors costumed in historical garb are performing a scene about the town's founding, and on the lawn beyond it, kids are competing in all kinds of footraces—sack, three-legged, egg-and-spoon.

Everett stops walking. "I better not walk any farther. I don't want Judy or Vera to see me."

I laugh. "That's okay. I promised Yasmine I'd be at her wine-tasting event, and it starts in ten minutes."

We turn around and start walking back. "I'm grabbing a beer with the guys, then I have to announce the first band of the evening on the main stage," Everett says. "Can we hook up after that? Maybe around seven?"

"Yes."

He kisses my cheek. "I'll find you."

We part ways, and I'm walking toward Novel Vine when someone calls my name. Shading my eyes with one hand, I see Daniel Bartok walking toward me. "Hi, Dan."

"Hey." He's grinning widely. "Good news. The witness is willing to talk to you. Are you still up for a chat?"

I shrug. “I suppose. But I don’t think anything will come of it.”

“Just hear him out. That’s all I ask.”

“It’s a him?”

“Yes. But that’s all I’ll say for now. Can you meet us early next week? Maybe Monday at five?”

“I think so. Diner again?”

“Sure. See you then.”

Five minutes later, I’m sitting at the bar at Novel Vine when Everett, Ripley, Hunter, and a handsome older guy I assume is Dr. Ben Hart all come through the glass door.

The energy in the room immediately shifts. Conversation halts.

Behind the bar, Yasmine’s smile morphs into a scowl. She and her staff have just poured the first wine of the tasting, and her event is about to get started. “What are you guys doing in here? The beer tent is up the street.”

“Maybe we don’t want beer,” Ripley says. “Maybe we heard about your little tasting party and we want to be supportive.”

“Sorry,” Everett murmurs as he presses up behind me. “I mentioned it, and he took off like a rocket.”

Yasmine’s eyes narrow. “You don’t want to support me, Ripley Wilder. You just want to harass me.”

“That seems very unfair after I convinced all my friends here to come to your bar instead of going to the beer tent.” Ripley gestures to the guys.

“Well, as you can see, there are no empty seats.” Yasmine’s hand sweeps through the air. It’s true—every spot at the bar is taken, and all the tables are full.

Ripley looks at the bar full of women, many of whom have turned their attention to the group of hot guys who just injected the feminine vibe with testosterone. “Can’t we just stand here with

Mila? Look, she even has two glasses."

"That's because we're tasting two wines," Yasmine says through her teeth.

"We can make room." My generosity earns me a dirty look from Yasmine. But Everett is tight against my back with an arm around my waist, and I don't want him to take it away. On either side of me, women make room so Ben and Hunter can access the bar too. Everett makes the introductions.

"Mila, this is Ben Hart."

The doctor smiles and gives me his hand. His hair is graying slightly at the temples, but he's got mesmerizing blue eyes that must have women all over town inventing medical emergencies. "Nice to finally meet you," he says.

"You too," I reply, wondering what he meant by *finally.* Has Everett been talking about me?

"And you remember Hunter."

I turn to my left and smile. "Sure. Good to see you again."

"You too," he says with a nod. He's got the same angular beauty he had in high school, but he's definitely packed on some muscles since then. They're on full display in a tight shirt that says HLFD on the front in block letters. Like Ripley, his arms are decorated with ink.

"Do you guys even like wine?" Yasmine eyes the men with suspicion.

"Who doesn't like wine, am I right?" Ripley queries, opening his arms and glancing around. A chorus of female voices assures him that everyone here does indeed like wine.

"I do," Everett answers.

"Me too," says Ben.

"It's okay," says Hunter, glancing longingly in the direction of the beer tent.

"Fine." Relenting, Yasmine brings out a few more glasses. "You can stay, but you have to behave."

Ripley touches his chest. "I'm just here to learn about wine, Veep."

She looks up at him with her chin lowered, her stare murderous. "Strike one."

Ripley grins. "Are you interested in balls, too?"

Ignoring him, Yasmine raises her voice and speaks to everyone in the bar. "Today we're tasting two wines, a warm climate and a cool climate pinot noir. It's a versatile grape that grows well in both environments, and the effects of terroir are distinct in the wines."

"Terroir. Got it," Ripley says, like he's committing it to memory.

Yasmine continues to pretend he's not there, but it's hard since he's the biggest guy in the place, inked and bearded to the max, and he's standing right in the center of the bar, directly in front of her. "This first wine is from Alsace, which is a cool climate region. I had the opportunity to work at a winery there while I was studying for my sommelier exams."

"She's so fancy," Ripley whispers, except somehow it's loud.

"This wine has a fruit-forward profile with floral notes, subtle spice, and mineral undertones. Give it a taste and see if you can pick out any particular fruits or flavors."

Everyone picks up their glass and takes a sip.

"I taste cherry," Everett says, inhaling with his nose in the glass. "And I smell them."

I sniff the wine and taste again. "Maybe raspberry?"

Yasmine nods happily. "You're right. This wine definitely has both."

"Hmm." Ripley swirls his wine and tosses half of it back. "I'm getting strong notes of overpriced grape juice with undertones of pretension."

The women surrounding him giggle, and Yasmine shoots him a dagger of a glance as she continues to talk about the wine.

"Shit," Everett whispers in my ear. "I probably shouldn't have let him come here. What's with them? Did they date or something?"

"No. They've just always been like this. Senior year, they both ran for Class President, and Ripley won," I tell him, keeping my voice low. "It drove Yasmine crazy because she'd been on student council for years. She was super-organized, always had a plan, never missed a deadline, had great ideas, and really cared. Ripley was just popular. And he promised everyone he'd invite them over to his house for a giant pool party if they voted for him."

"And she won Vice President?" Everett guesses. "That's why he calls her Veep?"

I nod. "Exactly."

We watch as Ripley slams the remaining wine in his glass like it's a shot of whiskey and plunks the glass down. "I'm ready for the next one. Could I get a more generous pour?"

Again, the women within earshot laugh flirtatiously.

Everett shakes his head, but he also chuckles.

"Jesus, he's an asshole," says Ben.

Yasmine is talking about the second wine now. "This is a warm climate pinot noir from the Paso Robles region of California's Central Coast. It has a fuller body and a richer mouthfeel."

"Mouthfeel?" Ripley repeats dubiously. "Is that really a word?"

Yasmine doesn't look his way but holds up two fingers in his direction. "It has lower acidity, softer tannins, and a smoother texture. The flavor profile includes darker fruits and spices."

"I taste chocolate," Hunter says. "Is that dumb?"

"Not at all." Yasmine offers him a smile. "You're spot-on, actually. "

Hunter thumps Ripley on the arm. "Did you hear that? I was spot-on."

"Hmmm." Ripley holds his glass up to the light like he's examining its color and then sips. "This pinot definitely has a robust character of trying too hard to impress you and wishing it was a pilsner instead."

Everyone laughs, and the color in Yasmine's face approaches the shade of wine in our glasses. "Three," she says. "You're out."

Laughing, Ripley finishes his wine and puts some cash on the bar. "Don't be so serious. When you're done here, come over to the pub and have a beer on me."

"I don't want anything on you, Ripley."

"I'll get him out of here," Everett says, giving my waist a squeeze. "Text me later."

"I will." I lift my face, and he kisses my cheek before shepherding Ripley and the guys out.

As soon as they're gone, Yasmine wipes her brow. "Thank God. Tell Everett I'm grateful."

"I will."

Her eyes catch on the charm at my throat, and she gasps. "You're wearing the necklace! I thought you said you lost it!"

"Oh my God, did I forget to tell you?" As the bar fills with chatter, I catch up Yasmine on my meeting with Dan. "So my name wasn't cleared, but I did get my ladybug back."

"I love that." Yasmine pulls hers to the outside of her shirt. "I wonder if Gabi still has hers."

"We'll have to ask her. Can you believe she's moving back?"

"I know! It feels… I don't know, like kismet somehow. You coming back to take care of your mom, Gabi moving back for good. Who knows?" Yasmine's green eyes sparkle like emeralds. "Any minute now, Rachel might pull up in that old BMW she inherited from her brothers. Remember that thing?"

I burst out laughing. "Yes! It always smelled like sweaty lacrosse equipment and Ralph Lauren cologne."

"And Ladybug would drench the seats in that body spray she loved—what was it called?"

"Sweet Pea Seduction," I say, remembering the way we used to tease her about it.

Our laughter fades. Yasmine's expression goes soft, and I know we're both thinking about Lydia. I don't know what path my life would have taken if things had been different.

If Lydia hadn't been sick.

If we'd never made the pact.

If That Night had never happened.

But something deep inside me is *sure* I would always have

ended up here, in this moment. I'm not saying I wouldn't change how I got here—because God knows I'd do almost anything to have Lydia standing beside me and Yasmine right now—but getting to the present feels…inevitable.

"Now all we have to do is convince you to move back," Yasmine says, and it's a question as much as a statement.

I laugh. "You know what? A month ago I would have said it was out of the question."

"But today?"

I glance at the door Everett just went through. "Today feels different."

Yasmine and I meet up with the guys to watch the fireworks. When they're over, everyone makes their way to the bandstand. As we're walking toward the music, Hunter falls into step beside me.

"Hey, Mila. I wanted to ask you about something. I mean, about someone."

"Sure."

"Are you still friends with Rachel Hart?"

I glance at him in surprise. "No, we lost touch. I wish I was."

"Oh. I thought maybe you knew where she ended up after high school. She tutored me in math senior year."

"I remember her talking about it," I say.

He laughs. "She tell you what a shit math student I was?"

"Not at all."

"Anyway, I was just curious about her. She was cool."

"She was." It surprises me that Hunter describes her that way. Rachel was a lot of things—smart, kind, responsible, classy, ambitious… But cool? To a guy like Hunter Gannon? It strikes me as odd, for some reason. What could they possibly have had in common?

"Well, if you ever talk to her, tell her I said hi."

"I will."

"I always felt bad about that night," he adds. "But I never got to talk to her."

He walks away before I can ask him what he means. Before I can call him back, we reach the bandstand, where a group of local musicians is playing everything from golden oldies to country to classic rock. Ripley motions toward the bar set up on one side of the dance floor. Everett squeezes my arm. "Be right back. Want anything?"

"No, thanks."

As soon as they're gone, I grab Yasmine's hand. "Hey. Hunter Gannon just asked me about Rachel."

Her eyes widen. "What about her?"

"Just like, 'Are you still friends with her? Where is she now?' That kind of thing. He said he was just curious. Because he thought she was cool."

"*Cool*?"

"I know. That's what I thought."

"I remember she tutored him. Maybe she was just really patient."

"But then he said something else."

"What?"

"He said, 'I always felt bad about that night, but I never got to talk to her.'"

Yasmine's jaw falls open. "Like *That Night*?"

"It has to be. That's the night she banged up her dad's old car." Part of me wonders if anything *didn't* go wrong the night the bakery burned down. "But why would *he* feel bad about it? How did he even know about it?"

She shakes her head. "I have no idea."

"I really want to find her," I say.

"Me too." Yasmine tugs on her bottom lip.

"Do you think Ben Hart knows anything?" I ask, watching as

the guys make their way back to us. "Everett says he's some kind of distant cousin."

"Dr. HartThrob you mean?"

I laugh. "Is that what they call him?"

"Yes. I hear a lot of chatter about Dr. HartThrob at the bar."

"What's the scoop?"

"Divorced, one daughter, ex-wife is remarried and lives about twenty minutes away."

That's all we have time for before the Axe Gods descend upon us.

"Veep! Let's dance," Ripley says, trying to take Yasmine's hand.

She snatches it back. "Not in a million years."

Half an hour later, I'm still wondering about Rachel and how I might find her. I'm also thinking about Gabi moving back and Yasmine being here already. Something is calling me home, too, and it feels strong tonight. I look around, imagining a life here.

Ben Hart is talking to a group of young girls, and I assume one of them is his daughter. Ripley is showing off his two-step moves with a pretty blonde on his arm, and Yasmine is pretending not to watch. Hunter is chatting with another guy who's also wearing an HLFD shirt. Everett stands behind me, his arms wrapped around my waist. The song ends, and the band begins the familiar opening strains of "Something" by the Beatles.

"Want to dance?" Everett asks in my ear. "This one is more my speed."

"Sure." Placing my hand in his, I follow him onto the dance floor. He pulls me close, and we begin to sway to the music.

"I feel nervous dancing with you," he says.

"Why?" I tilt my head back and look up at him.

"You're so good. What if I don't have any rhythm?"

"You have nothing to worry about. Your rhythm is perfect, although I already knew this about you."

He smiles and promptly steps on my toes. "Oh shit. Sorry!"

"It's okay." I press my cheek to his chest and think of all the summers I dreamed of dancing with him like this, on this very night, on this very dance floor, under these very stars.

It was worth the wait.

Chapter Forty-One

Mila

The day after Founder's Day, my mother asks me if I'll get her scrapbooks down from her closet shelf.

"Sure," I say. "Can I look at them with you?"

"Of course." She looks pleased.

I practically float into her bedroom. I've been on a cloud all day today, remembering the things Everett said Friday, how it felt to dance with him last night, the possessive way he likes to stand behind me with an arm around my waist.

It feels right. All of it.

My mom's closet is neatly organized, and I have no trouble spotting the storage bin on the top shelf labeled ELIZA MISC. But it's heavy, and there's a box on top of it, so I run to the basement and grab a small stepladder.

Once I'm up on the ladder, I can easily slide the box on the top to the side and pull the storage bin down. As I slide it over the edge of the shelf, something else comes with it and hits the floor. I carefully step down the ladder and set the bin down, pausing to sneeze at the dust I disturbed. When I turn around, I discover a plain manila folder on the rug in front of the closet.

I pick it up with the intention of sticking it back on the shelf when something slides out—a drawing. When I glance down at it, I suck in my breath.

It's me.

I reach down and pick it up, holding it by one corner. Within a few seconds of studying it, I realize my mistake.

It isn't me. It's my mom.

She's about my age in the pencil sketch, maybe even younger.

The artist drew her head, neck, and one bare shoulder. The other is covered by a cascade of hair. I look closer, marveling at each finely drawn eyelash. The lightness in her eyes. The shading beneath her jaw and cheekbones. Most astonishing to me is the expression on her face. I'm not sure I've ever seen it before. It's vulnerable and alluring at the same time. She's exquisitely beautiful. I have the sense that whoever drew this loved her face. Loved her.

It's not signed.

Heart pounding, I open the folder, hoping to find more artwork, but it's empty.

More than anything, I want to show her what I found and ask her about it. Did she remember posing for him? Did he draw her often? Does she still think about him?

But what's the use? She won't answer my questions honestly. She might even be offended I asked. Ask me why I insist on making her talk about painful pieces of her past. Twist things around so I end up apologizing for wanting to know my own story.

"Mila, what's taking you so long?"

"Coming!" I tuck the sketch into the folder and slip it back onto the shelf, resigned to being kept in the dark.

But then I change my mind.

I don't want to run from these conversations anymore. Maybe she won't give me any answers, but I can at least find the strength to ask the questions.

I grab the folder and place it on top of the scrapbooks in the bin. Then I carry it out to the living room where she's sitting on the couch.

"I found something," I tell her.

"What?"

Setting the bin down, I pick up the folder and hand it to her. "This."

She opens it up. Inhales sharply. For a fraction of a second, I see pain flicker across her face. Then her expression goes steely again. "Where did you get this?"

"It fell out of your closet when I pulled down the bin." I lower myself onto the couch. "It's beautiful. Can you tell me about it?"

"There's nothing to tell." She tosses it onto the coffee table. "I don't even know why I kept it."

"Obviously, it meant something to you." I pause. "Did he draw it? My father?"

"He must have." She reaches into the bin and pulls out a scrapbook. Opens it up to a page in the middle and points to two photos of herself in Swan Lake—one as Odette, the virtuous white swan, and one as the temptress black swan, Odile. She taps the page. "This was a role you were born to dance. Well, it's two roles, of course."

"I'd like to know more about him."

"You had the technique but also the dramatic expression. You could have mastered those fragile, boneless arms of the dying swan."

"Mom."

"Of course, the role is famously demanding. It required almost superhuman stamina. Maybe you wouldn't have had the strength."

I press my lips together. "Can you please answer my question?"

She turns a page. "Aurora in *Sleeping Beauty.* That's a role you'd have been suited for, too." A long sigh as she brushes her hand over the page. "But my dreams for you have turned to dust."

"*Mom.*" Grabbing the book off her lap, I drop it back in the bin and stand up. "Stop avoiding this. I want to talk about him."

"Well, I don't." She folds her arms over her chest and scowls up at me. "And I won't. He made his choice."

"You'd rather sit there and make me feel bad about the life *I've* chosen?" I touch my chest.

"I'm not trying to make you feel bad, Mila. I'm just saying I had *hopes* for you."

The hurt nearly chokes me. "God, Mom. Do you know how bad that makes me feel?"

"How do you think *I* feel?" She gestures toward the mantel behind me. "Every day, I look at that crown, and I feel sad thinking about what might have been."

Outrage crashes through my veins. I turn around, snatch the tiara off the shelf and march toward the front door.

"Where are you going with that?" she demands. "It's mine."

"Actually, it's mine. And I'm taking it out of here so you never have to look at it and feel sad again. You're fucking welcome."

I walk fast, fueled by fury. I don't even know where I'm going.

At the corner, I turn left and realize my feet have led me to the park where I walked with Everett the day after our first date.

I plunk myself on the bench we sat on, the tiara beside me, and pull out my phone.

Mila: *I need you.*

Everett: *Where are you?*

Mila: *The park. Our bench.*

Everett: *I'll be there in 15 minutes.*

It's a little chillier today, and I left the house in a tank top. I wrap my arms around myself and try not to shiver. A little less than fifteen minutes later, Everett enters the park and jogs over to the bench.

"Hey." Right away, he notices I'm cold and whips off his sweatshirt. "Here, put this on." He holds it out for me, and I slip my arms in, pulling it over my head.

"Thanks." It smells like him, and I inhale deeply, letting the scent fill my head.

He sits down next to me and picks up the tiara. "What's going on, babe?"

"I had a fight with my mom."

He gathers me close to his side. "Talk to me."

I tell him about finding the drawing. About trying to ask my mother about it and being ignored and then insulted. "So I took the thing she cared about and left."

He kisses my head. "I'm proud of you."

"You don't think I acted like a child throwing a tantrum?"

"Not one bit." He turns the tiara this way and that. Its rhinestones catch the light. "Damn, this thing is heavy."

"I know. It hurts to wear."

"What are you going to do with it?"

"I don't know." Out of the corner of my eye, I spy a garbage receptacle. "Trash it?"

The idea of putting one of my mother's most prized possessions in the garbage fills me with equal parts glee and dread. In so many ways, this tiara represents the version of me Mom loved best. Part of me will always crave her approval, her love. But if I put the tiara in the trash, would I be throwing away any chance of capturing that approval and love ever again?

And... Do I care?

"If that's what you want to do, I'd understand. But there won't be any getting it back."

"True." I think for a minute, letting myself bask in the handful of good memories I hold in the most secret corners of my heart. The day we painted my dresser. The Christmas morning we made hot cocoa from scratch. The warm, unbridled embrace she wrapped me in when I won my first scholarship at YAGP. "I guess I don't really want to destroy it. I just wanted her to know that it hurts my feelings when she acts like I peaked at sixteen."

When she dismisses my artwork as doodles.

When she tells me I can't trust my heart.

When she makes it impossible to know if I am loved.

The quiet stretches over us like a blanket. Everett is in no rush to fill it, leaving me space to feel all my feelings—the sad ones and the ugly ones in equal measure. Eventually, he says, "So maybe just keep it for a while. You can give it back later, *if* you want."

"Okay." The thought makes me feel better.

"I talked to Gabi this afternoon," he says, as he casually slides the tiara onto the bench behind him and turns his body to block it from my view—subtly giving me the chance to stop seeing, talking, and thinking about it. *This man.* "She conned me into helping her move next weekend."

"What a good brother." I snuggle closer into his side, wrapping my arms around his waist. "Thanks for coming to be with me. I know you're busy and lots of people depend on you."

"Anytime, Freckles. I told you before. I'm here for you when you need me. Doesn't matter the time or place or reason."

"Will you come to the diner with me tomorrow to meet the mysterious eyewitness?"

"Of course I will."

"Thanks." I close my eyes and wonder if this is what it feels like.

Unconditional love.

The next night, Everett picks me up just before five. As soon as I see his car pull into the driveway, I hurry out the front door, eager to escape the tension in the house.

"Hey." Everett leans over and kisses me once I'm buckled in. "How's it going?"

"Okay. She's still giving me the silent treatment."

"I'm not surprised."

"I don't know what else she wants from me. I apologized for what I said."

"I don't even think you owed her an apology."

I hold up my hands. "I know, but I have to live with her. At least for two more weeks. I've learned that sometimes it's just easier to say the thing she wants to hear."

"If you say so." Everett backs out of the driveway and heads for town.

"She asked me where the tiara was." I glance into the back seat of the truck, where the bejeweled monstrosity rests on the leather. "I told her it's in a time-out."

Everett chuckles. "Was she mad?"

"What do you think?"

We park in the mayor's spot and walk to the diner. Everett takes my hand as we amble down the block. "All set for tomorrow at the foundry? Dr. Yang says he'll be there at eleven."

"Yes. I'm excited to hear what he has to say."

"I'm excited to meet this mysterious eyewitness." He opens the diner door for me. "Who do you think it could be?"

"I have no idea," I say as we make our way toward the back. "Someone who likes trash-picking in the alley, I guess. I keep trying to—"

I stop walking. Grab his arm. "Oh, my God. It's Stevie."

Chapter Forty-Two

Everett

"Stevie?" I follow her line of sight to a booth at the back of the diner, where two guys are sitting side by side. When they see us coming, they slide out and stand up. "Who's Stevie?"

"Stevie MacDougal. He's the tall one with the reddish ponytail. I used to babysit him, and he had a huge crush on me."

"That explains why he'd pick up things in the alley he thought belonged to you."

"He used to come to the bakery all the time when I was working. He was short and scrawny and wore glasses with lenses an inch thick."

She tugs my sleeve. "And he was there that night! I gave him a free cherry lemonade. He was like, twelve at the time."

"Well, come on." I take her hand again, and we keep walking. "Let's see what he knows."

After a brief round of introductions, Mila and I slide into the booth across from Dan and Stevie, who still looks at Mila with a rapt expression that reminds me of the way Merlin looks at bacon.

"So what's this all about, Stevie?" Mila asks kindly.

"Uh." Stevie scratches the side of his neck. "I was kind of… there that night."

"I remember." She smiles. "I gave you a lemonade."

"Right." Stevie beams at the memory. "And then I left because you had to close up, but I didn't really go home. I rode my bike around for a while, and then I sort of loitered in the back alley because you always left out the back door when you closed up."

Man. This kid had it bad.

"Because it locked automatically," Mila says. "The front had to be locked with a key, which I didn't have."

"I saw the truck from the farm arrive and park in the alley," he says.

I raise a hand. "That was me."

"And I saw you unloading the truck and bringing things in. Then the truck left, and I thought Mila was alone." He pauses. Scratches his neck again, which I notice is kind of red. "It was dark by then, and I was worried about her leaving so late by herself."

I picture a scrawny twelve-year old with Coke-bottle glasses standing guard at the back door of the bakery and try not to smile.

"You were taking a while, so I rode my bike down the alley to the end of the block and practiced some wheelies. When I turned around, I saw someone coming out the back door."

"Who?" Mila asks.

"I couldn't tell."

"You didn't see the person go in? Only coming out?"

"Right." He hesitates. Scratches again. "But see, my glasses had gotten smudged, so I took them off to clean them real quick. By the time I got them on again, the person was gone."

"Gone where?" I asked.

Stevie shrugs. "I didn't see the direction they went."

"Are you sure you saw anyone at all?" I ask Stevie. "You said it was dark by then. You were down the alley. And you didn't have your glasses on. Maybe it was just a shadow."

Stevie considers this, then shakes his head. "I saw someone."

"Was it a man or a woman?" Mila asks.

"I think it was a woman. I thought I saw long hair." He looks despondent. "But I can't say what color, because it was dark."

"A guy can have long hair," I point out, gesturing to Stevie's ponytail.

Stevie looks even more glum. "Anyway, as soon as I got my glasses on again, I rode as fast as I could down to the bakery to look around. That's when I found the necklace and the hair tie. I kept them, thinking they were Mila's, and I planned to give them back. But I had to get home or I was going to get in trouble—I was already late. I got about two blocks away when I heard the explosion."

Mila clutches her chest. "Thank God you weren't still in the alley! You might have been hurt!"

Stevie looks pleased that Mila is grateful for his safety. "I didn't say anything to anyone about where I'd been or what I'd taken."

"Why not?" I ask.

He looks embarrassed. "I was afraid they'd take the things away from me. I wanted to return them to Mila myself. But I never got the chance. So I just hung on to them."

Dan speaks up. "When the club decided to take a fresh look at the fire, Stevie reached out to me. He told me the story of what he'd seen, and I was obviously intrigued."

"Dan convinced me to come forward in case anything I saw could clear your name," says Stevie. "I'd never thought about it like that."

Dan shrugs. "At the time, I thought maybe he was wrong about the items being yours."

"They were definitely mine." Mila looks at Stevie. "And as nice as it might have been to rehabilitate my reputation as an accidental arsonist in this town, I was happy to get that necklace back. I'm glad you saved it all these years. So thank you."

His cheeks redden. "You're welcome. I'm sorry I can't recall more."

"That's okay."

"But what about the person he saw?" Dan persists. "Don't you think that could be something worth pursuing?"

"Pursuing how?" Mila wonders.

"We could see if any of the other businesses on the block had cameras in the alley," says Stevie.

"Even if they did, how likely is it they'd still have footage from a decade ago?" I ask.

"I could post about it," Dan suggests. "I could just ask the person to come forward. They obviously know who they are. I could hint that we're asking around about camera footage. Maybe that would spook them into coming forward."

"Would I get in trouble?" Stevie asks, scratching his neck again. "I don't want the police to come after me because I didn't come forward back then. I've been so nervous about that, I gave myself hives."

"I don't want Stevie to get in any trouble either," Mila says. "If what you discover will mean any consequences for him, you can't go public with his name."

"Deal. So do I have your permission to post about it?" Dan asks eagerly. "If someone comes forward, I'll definitely have enough material for my podcast. I won't need to use Stevie's name. He can stay anonymous."

Mila looks at me, and I shrug.

"Okay, why not?" she says. "Go ahead and post."

Chapter Forty-Three

WELCOME TO THE LANDING PAD

Community Updates From The Hart's Landing Gazette (Online Edition)

PSA: Members of the Sweet Harts Baking Club are circulating a petition to ensure that future winners of the Founder's Day Best Pie Contest are registered members in good standing with the SHBC. A second petition requiring contestants to have at least twenty years of regular baking experience will be voted on at the next meeting.

POLICE BLOTTER: Door camera footage captured the town's vigilante graffiti artists in action. Click here to view (offensive drawing has been blurred). While police are as yet unable to identify the culprit, residents are encouraged to come forward with information.

Community question submitted by TeaLover55: We've all seen Mila and the mayor. My question is, what happens when she leaves town again?

GazetteMod: Please ensure Community questions represent legitimate inquiries. Thank you!

Comment by ANONYMOUS AXE GOD: Here's a legitimate inquiry, @GazetteMod. Why are you such a buzzkill?

[GazetteMod has closed comments on this post.]

EVENTS: A special meeting of the Diner Detectives will commence this Friday at 10 a.m. on the village green. From club president Daniel Bartok: "Our intrepid sleuthing has uncovered evidence that there was a third person at Tart and Soul the night of the fire. WAS THIS YOU? If so, please come forward! Rest assured, you can remain completely anonymous if you prefer. We are simply looking to piece together the events of that night."

Chapter Forty-Four

Mila

Tuesday morning, my mother sits on the couch with her prune face on. It's an expression I've grown accustomed to since the tiara theft. "When will you be back?" she asks.

"I'm not sure." Shrugging into my denim jacket, I go over to the window and look out. The sky is the color of an elephant, and heavy clouds are rolling in fast. Hopefully the rain will hold off until after our meeting with Dr. Yang at the foundry site.

"Well, I have an appointment at one-thirty, so you'll have to be back in time to drive me."

I turn to stare at her. "What appointment?"

"With Dr. Hart. My PCP."

"When did you make it?" I check my phone. "It's not on the calendar."

"Early this morning. I haven't had a chance to add it to the calendar." She picks at a thread in her sweater. "But I need it. I have an awful rash."

"What rash? Where?"

"My arms." She arches a brow. "Do you think I'm making it up?"

"Show me the rash, Mom."

She purses her lips. "This is very disrespectful, Mila. I don't know what's come over you the last week or so. First the tiara and now this."

"I'm just asking to see the rash."

Her eyes are full of indignation, but she pushes up her sleeves, and sure enough, there's a rash on both of her inner arms. "There. I hope you're satisfied." She scratches at the raised red marks.

My shoulders slump, and I close my eyes. Guilt pokes holes in my anger, letting all the fight out. "Sorry. I'll be back at one to take you."

When I arrive at the foundry site, Everett and a black-haired, light-brown-skinned man I assume is Kevin Yang are standing on the cracked pavement of the old parking lot. Behind them is a massive vacant lot where the imposing foundry once stood. Adjacent to that is a two-story red-brick office building with arched windows, decorative brickwork around the glass, and an entrance with "Hart Iron Works, Est. 1893 " carved into the limestone above the door.

I grab my backpack and get out of the car. It hasn't started raining yet, but the wind has picked up, and my hair blows around my face.

As I approach, Everett is giving Dr. Yang a little history. "Twenty years ago, Hart Iron Works built a modern foundry in a different location, and the original was torn down. The administration building was spared demolition, and several uses have been proposed and discarded. The family would like to donate it to the town for a community center, but as we've discussed, there are issues with that." He turns and sees me, his eyes lighting up. "Hey."

"Hi." I want to throw my arms around him, but I keep my cool in the presence of the professor.

"Dr. Yang, this is Mila Ferguson," Everett says. "She's a botanical illustrator and grew up here. It was her idea to explore phytoremediation as a possible solution to the contamination problem."

Dr. Yang extends his hand and a smile. "It's Kevin. Very nice to meet you."

I give him a smile. "Thanks for letting me tag along today."

"Of course." He glances at the lot, then down at the tablet he holds. "I've reviewed the test results. It's quite the project you've got here, but I think phytoremediation *is* a viable cleanup solution. What's your budget?"

As they discuss numbers, I move closer to the lot, stepping around a fallen warning sign and some rusty metal scraps. Holding my windblown hair off my face, I scan the area. The Hart mansion can be seen high on the hill to the east, and the land slopes gently toward the lake to the west. The foundry site itself is scattered with gravel, bare patches of dirt, and fractured concrete slabs, with weeds growing up through the cracks. The faint outline of the foundry's footprint is still visible, and the perimeter is lined with an ugly, rusted chain-link fence.

But it's full of memories. Secrets. Laughter.

I can hear it on the wind, an echo from the past. And I can picture five bikes parked along the perimeter before there was a fence. Five girls sitting in a circle on a concrete slab. Five teenagers passing around a bottle of cheap wine.

What's most amazing to me are the birch saplings and vegetation that have grown up through cracks in the dirt. Stubborn things, determined to grow, despite their surroundings. Something about it strikes me right in the heart.

I think about that final time the four of us met here. Four friends with good intentions, trying to keep a promise. Unaware they were about to lose each other.

Fragments of memory come to me like pieces of a mosaic, reassembling to form the whole. My late arrival. Gabi's homemade cookies. Rachel's tearstained face. Yasmine's clipboard. Being told that my assignment was to kiss Everett McKean.

It makes me smile, but I'm also choked up. I want to turn back time. I want to warn those girls not to let go of each other, not to let hard things tear them apart. *I know you've been through a lot*, I would tell them, *but you need to lean into each other, not shut each other out.*

I touch the ladybug charm at my neck. There's some detail escaping me—some missing piece of the mosaic—but I can't think what it is.

When I hear my name, I look over my shoulder and see Everett and Dr. Yang to my left along the fence. Everett puts a hand on my shoulder. "What do you think? Can you see a garden there?"

"Absolutely. I already want to draw that plant over there with the yellow flowers." I point to it.

"That's wild mustard," says Dr. Yang. "Part of a species that are good hyperaccumulators—they can tolerate higher levels of certain metals than other plants."

"Did someone plant it?" I ask, surprised.

"No, it's a weed. But it tells us that nature has been working on this problem already, at a very slow pace. We can accelerate that."

"What do you recommend as a plan of action?" Everett asks.

Dr. Yang opens his tablet. "Based on the results you shared with me and the particular contaminants you're working with, I'd suggest Indian mustard and sunflowers for the first two seasons—they grow quickly and begin extracting metals immediately. Then pennycress and ferns for more targeted chromium extraction. Eventually, willows and poplars along the perimeter for deeper soil remediation. Every season would look different."

Everett nods. "How long would it take?"

"For complete remediation, five to seven years," the professor answers. "But you'd see progress within the first year. And the costs would be spread out over time instead of being one massive bill like you'd see for dig and haul cleanup."

I exchange a look with Everett—that's good news.

"And would the *building* be usable while the plants are doing their thing?" Everett asks.

"Yes. Since the remaining structure is on a concrete slab," Dr. Yang says, pointing at the old office building, "it's safe to use while remediation is going on outside. You could conceivably allow it to function as a community center as quickly as you could repurpose it." He frowns and pulls his cell phone from his pocket. "Excuse me, I have to take a call."

Dr. Yang walks away with his phone to his ear while I envision a field of sunflowers growing tall and strong, faces to the sky. I imagine kids wandering through paths of plants, learning about the important job they're doing, maybe drawing what they see. I even picture myself instructing them, showing them how to capture light, color, texture. Demonstrating how basic shapes become complex forms in nature.

A circle becomes an apple. A cup becomes a tulip. A cylinder becomes a branch.

What is now an ugly toxic problem for Hart Iron Works can transform into a beautiful symbol of the Hart family's continuing commitment to the town and a legacy of Everett's leadership.

I see those four girls again, this time surrounded by sunflowers, ladybugs flying from bloom to bloom. "I can see it, Everett. It's going to be so pretty."

"Let's hope Tad and Tiffany Hart think so."

Facing him, I place a hand on his chest. "They will. We'll convince them together. When I get home later, I'll draw something you can show the Harts—a vision of what it could be, complete with a sign that says 'The Hart Healing Gardens' or something. Rich people love to put their name on things."

"Mila, you don't have to do that."

"I want to," I insist, pulling back to look up at him. "I want to be part of this."

"You already are. And your time is—"

I put a finger over his lips. "Let *me* worry about my time. This is important, Everett. It's not just about the Harts. It's about the health of this community, the generations of kids who will come here and learn. It's about the greater good in Hart's Landing. A lot of people think I burned something down here. Can you please let me help to build something up?"

A smile cracks his serious facade, and he shakes his head, removing my finger from his mouth. "How am I supposed to say no to that?"

"You can't." Rising onto my toes, I smile. "I win."

In the end, Dr. Yang lingers so long that Everett and I only have about fifteen minutes together. After watching the professor drive away, we climb into his truck and exchange a despondent look. Fat raindrops pelt the windshield.

"I wish I had more time," I say. "My mother scheduled a doctor's appointment for one-thirty. She has some kind of rash on her arms, and I was a big jerk about it."

"You were?"

"Yes. I thought she was making it up, so I demanded to see the rash. And it's true—her arms are all broken out." I poke myself in the chest. "I'm the asshole."

"You're not. She's been gaslighting you your entire life. No one would blame you for doubting her. But maybe I can take your mind off it." He brings my hand to his lips. Kisses each of my knuckles. The inside of my wrist. My palm. When he looks up at me, I lean toward him and our mouths come together. His other hand slides into my hair and grips the back of my head. Our tongues speak wordlessly about other places on our bodies they'd like to be.

The rain falls harder, coming down in thick torrents that coat the truck's windows, obscuring us from the outside world. I move my hand to his thigh and run my palm up to his crotch. His cock is already swelling, and I rub it slowly through the denim. A low, agitated sound rumbles from deep in his throat. Moving a little closer to him, I unbuckle his belt. Pull it through the loop. Slip the button of his jeans through the hole. Inch the zipper down. His erection springs free, and I fist it, working my hand up and down his hot, hard flesh.

"Mila." He's breathing hard. "You don't have time."

"Stop micromanaging my schedule." I give him a playful smile before lowering my head to his lap.

He groans as I swirl my tongue around the crown, then suck the tip. "Then again, this might be over inside a minute."

When I pick up my head to laugh, he lifts his hips just enough to shimmy his jeans down his legs. The sight of his muscular thighs, his gorgeous cock, and the sculpted V on his lower abdomen make my insides quiver and my underwear feel hot and sticky. Immediately, I lean forward and take him in deep, sliding my wet mouth all the way down his shaft until I feel him tap the back of my throat. He growls, his hands moving into my hair, gathering it in his fists so it's out of the way.

I work my hand and mouth together, alternating long, slow strokes with tight, hard pulls. Outside, the downpour grows more intense, battering the truck with a relentless roar. Inside, the sound of Everett's breathing is jagged and quick, and his hips begin to lift as he thrusts up into my mouth. I struggle for air, but when I taste him, I only want more. The sounds I make are greedy. Messy. Indecent.

I sense him nearing the edge.

"Fuck. Mila." His words are a warning.

I don't stop. His hands tighten in my hair, his guttural moans drowning out the rain. He falls silent for a second, like he's holding his breath, before exhaling in ragged bursts. He comes at the back of my throat, but I feel the pulse of his climax throughout my entire body, and I don't stop until he lets go of my hair.

Easing him from my lips, I swallow the salty warmth of him and pick up my head. Wipe my mouth with the back of my hand.

He stares at me in utter disbelief. "It's a crime that I came and you didn't."

"You could try taking that up with my mother, but I doubt she'd see it your way."

"I'll make it up to you next time we see each other."

"Hey." I wag a finger at him. "This wasn't a favor. This isn't transactional."

Laughing, he zips, buttons, and buckles up. Then he pulls me toward him, hauling me across his lap so I'm wedged between his chest and the steering wheel. The interior of the truck feels warm and cozy.

"You're not really going to be gone in two weeks, are you?" He plays with my hair. "Because I want more than this with you, Mila. More than just stealing time when we get the chance. I want movie nights and Sunday dinner at my mom's house and lazy winter mornings where we just stay in bed because we feel like it. I want to give you the cherries from my old-fashioneds and watch you knot the stems with your tongue. I want to step on your toes every Founder's Day on the dance floor. I want to kiss you hello and goodbye and good morning and good night and sometimes, just fucking because. I want a thousand little everyday things."

My hopes rise like bread dough. "That sounds beautiful."

"Then come back to Hart's Landing for good," he urges. "I know I'm asking you to upend your life to be with me after you told me you didn't want to be in a relationship. It's not fair. *I'm* the asshole."

I laugh. "You're not. It's just a really huge decision."

"What's holding you back? Is it about work? Is it about your mom? Are you worried about us? Talk to me."

"I don't think work would be too much of an issue. I can design from anywhere. I *would* have to let the college know I wasn't returning after first semester, but I think they could replace me." At the thought of my mother, I grimace. "My mom is definitely a deterrent, no way around it. But it feels wrong to let my inability to maintain healthy boundaries with her get in the way of what we could have."

"You've come a long way. Look how you stood up to her the other day."

"That did feel good," I admit.

"How are you feeling about us?" he asks quietly, his brown eyes warm as melted chocolate. "Do you have doubts? Because I don't."

"You don't?"

"No." He cradles my face with his hands and brushes my lips with his thumb. "I'm in love with you, Mila. Every part of you, every version of you, every minute of the day."

My heart drums as loudly as the rain on the roof. Chills blanket my arms.

"I'm not saying that to put pressure on you. I'm just used to running right at a thing when I'm scared of it. And right now I'm scared of watching you walk out of my life again and always wondering if I could have worked harder to keep you close."

My eyes fill. "You mean that? What you said?"

"Yes. For the first time, I can see forever with someone, and it's you."

"I love you too," I tell him, and it feels deeper, more real, more honest than it's ever felt before. "And maybe we've both wondered enough."

I'm sitting next to my mom in the waiting room of the Hart Primary Care Clinic when the door opens and her name is called. I look up from my phone and gasp.

It's like seeing a ghost.

The blond curls. The dimples. Even the timbre of her voice.

Within seconds, I realize it must be Alice Sweeney, not Lydia. When she sees me, the smile widens. "Mila, right?"

It takes me a moment to find my voice. "Yes."

At this point, my mother has reached her. She's getting around with a cane now, which she hates only marginally less than the walker.

Alice smiles at her. "How are you, Ms. Ferguson?"

"Oh, I'm fine. Got my handy-dandy cane. All I'm missing are

the top hat and tails, right?"

Alice laughs, and I nearly fall out of my seat. She sounds so much like Lydia. She looks at me once more. "Would you like to come back?"

"No need." My mom answers for me. "She can just wait here."

The door shuts behind them.

I reach for my phone. This calls for a group chat.

Mila: *You guys, I'm at the Hart Clinic, and I just saw Alice Sweeney! She's a nurse here!!*

Yasmine: *OMG! Did you talk to her?*

Mila: *I said hello, but nothing more. I'm dying to know about the letter, but I don't feel like I can ask her.*

Gabi: *OMG THE LETTER! I forgot all about that.*

Yasmine: *Probably not cool to ask about it right away. We need to find Rachel.*

Mila: *We do.*

Gabi: *Count me in! How are you guys? Seeing your names pop up in my texts just now made me so happy.*

Yasmine: *Me too! I'm good. Ripley Wilder is still the bane of my existence, but I'm trying to find inner peace. God knows outer peace is impossible with him next door.*

Mila: *I'm good too. My mom is…still my mom, but I'm helping Everett with a project at the old foundry site that's really amazing.*

Gabi: *I can't wait to get back to HL and be with you guys again.*

Yasmine: *When's the move?*

Gabi: *This weekend. Sorry to steal E from you for a couple days, Mila!*

Mila: *Worth it.*

When we get home from the clinic, I retreat into my studio and close the door behind me. Thankfully, my mother takes the hint and allows me time to work, which I spend sketching ideas for the healing gardens. I work right up until my alarm goes off at 4:57 p.m., which reminds me that I have a five o'clock session with Hugo.

My mother is in the kitchen making a cup of tea when she sees me heading out the side door with my phone in my hand.

"Where are you going now?" she asks.

I turn to face her. "I just have to make a call."

"You can't make it in the house?"

"It's an appointment with my therapist. I do them on Zoom."

Her eyebrows rise. "I didn't know you were seeing a therapist. For what?"

"For my mental health."

"Do you talk about me?"

"I talk about a lot of people in my life," I say carefully.

"What do you say about me?"

"Mom, that's not really—"

"You know, you can talk to me about personal things, too."

I check my screen. It's 4:59.

"After all, no one loves you more than I do. And I *know* you better than anyone. Spending money for a stranger to tell you things about yourself doesn't really make sense, does it?"

"I have to go or I'll be late for my appointment." I'm out the door before she can delay me any longer. Fuming, I race through the rain, jump in the car, and get on the call. "Sorry I'm late."

Hugo can tell right away that something's wrong. "What's going on?"

"She tells me she loves me, but she makes me feel like shit. This cannot be love." I'm shaking with anger, furious that I let her ruin my good mood. I was so happy with Everett just hours ago.

"Okay," Hugo says calmly. "Let's talk about it."

"Love should not feel like a weapon that's used against you. Literally, every time she says she loves me, I brace for the bombshell that I know is going to follow. It's like she can't say it without also reminding me that I'm not worthy of it because of all the ways I'm a disappointment or a failure. She makes it sound like she's doing me a favor by loving me. Like it's tiresome and hard, but it's her job." I shake out my hands, which have balled up with tension.

"So what would the opposite be? What would it feel like to be loved?"

Like it feels when I'm with Everett.

"To be loved would be…to feel accepted." The words come out slower as I sink into the way I feel around Everett. "To feel appreciated, even though I know I'm not perfect. To have my feelings validated, whatever they are. For example, when my mother hurts my feelings and I tell her so, if she would just *take ownership* of that instead of twisting it around and making it my fault for being too sensitive. Somehow, I always end up apologizing." Slamming my eyes shut, I shake my head. "I'm sick of it. I hate myself for it."

"Give yourself some grace, Mila."

"But I let her treat me that way." I drop my forehead onto the tips of my fingers. "Why do I do that?"

"Because you don't think you deserve better from her," Hugo says quietly. "And that misbelief has created a cycle wherein you continuously try to earn love and approval. You cling to the hope that someday you'll receive the validation you've always craved."

My throat constricts. "But I won't."

He shakes his head. "Not from her, you won't. She's not capable, Mila, and that's not in your control. But let's back up a moment to something that *is* in your control. What does self-love look like to you? What does it mean?"

I give myself time to think. "I've been thinking it means protecting myself from potential emotional harm, but maybe that's not it. Maybe that's just avoidance, like you've said."

"Okay."

"Maybe self-love means forgiving myself for being imperfect. Not apologizing for everything. Accepting that I am lovable. That someone could actually love me for me."

"I like that definition."

"But how do you get there?" I ask desperately. "How do you get to the place where you know you deserve love, *and* you can accept it, even though it's a risk?"

My therapist smiles. "That's the work."

Chapter Forty-Five

Everett

On Thursday afternoon, Mila texts that she has a surprise for me.

Everett: *What is it?*

Mila: *Can I come over and show you?*

Everett: *Only if you're prepared to stay the night.*

Mila: *Hahaha. I can stay a little while, but not the whole night.*

Everett: *Then don't wear anything cute.*

Mila: *So not the strawberry skirt?*

Everett: *NOT THE STRAWBERRY SKIRT*

When I see the beautifully detailed rendering of Mila's vision for the healing gardens, my jaw drops. "Holy shit. It's beautiful, Mila."

"You like it?" Her smile is full of pride. "It's obviously just a rough sketch, but I think it will get the point across."

"A rough sketch? Are you fucking kidding me? I can't believe you drew this in just two days. Did your mother take a vacation or something? Did you move into the garage?"

She laughs. "I put some serious boundaries around my working hours."

"Good."

"And, honestly, she hasn't been talking to me much."

"She's punishing you for standing up for yourself," I tell her. Then I frown. "Sorry. Not my place to say so."

"No, it's okay. You're right. She doesn't like it that I don't just let her walk all over me anymore." Mila places the drawing back inside the portfolio she used to transport it. "Any word from the Harts?"

"Yes. Tad's assistant just got back to me today. We're meeting on Tuesday, which is perfect because the town council meeting is Wednesday. I'd love to be able to present this plan with their backing."

"Do you want to bring the art?"

I put my arms around her. "I want to bring the artist."

She smiles, her arms coming around my neck. "You do?"

"Yes. Please come with me. This is our project, not just mine."

Color explodes in her cheeks. "Really?"

"Really. I want your name on it, too. It's about time Hart's Landing remembers you for something other than that fire."

She kisses me. "I love you, Everett McKean."

"I love you too. This town is really a nice place to live, you know. Charming streets, friendly people, beautiful views, lots of history. You should consider making it your home." I begin walking backward toward my bedroom. "Have I mentioned I'm the mayor?"

"Okay, I'm getting out of bed for real this time." But she doesn't even make it to the edge of the mattress before I grab her arm and pull her back on top of me.

"No." I flip her over, pinning her down. "I never get enough of you."

"You're not playing fair."

"It's my rough edges." I bite her shoulder. "And you're the one who wore that skirt."

Eventually, I let her up and watch from the mattress as she scoops up her clothes and gets dressed. She's fixing her hair in the mirror over my dresser when she notices something on the top.

She picks it up and turns around. "You saved this?"

"What is it?"

"It's that silly scribble I did of the cherry blossoms on the coffee shop napkin."

"It's a memento," I correct.

She laughs. "It's just a doodle."

"But it's *your* doodle." I get out of bed, take the napkin from her, and place it back on the dresser as if it's made of blown glass. "So I'm keeping it."

She folds her arms over her chest and leans back against the dresser. "Stop it."

"Stop what?" I ask, tugging on a pair of sweatpants.

"Being so good to me. How am I supposed to make a rational decision about moving back here when you do things like this?" She gestures at the napkin.

I laugh as I pull a T-shirt over my head. "Maybe I don't want you to make a rational decision. Maybe I just want you to follow your heart."

"My heart has a *terrible* sense of direction," she informs me. "It makes wrong turns. It ignores warning signs. It's easily lost."

"But it's *your* heart." I tip up her chin so she has to meet my eyes. "So I'm keeping it."

Just before six, Merlin and I walk her out to the car. "I'm leaving pretty early tomorrow for Detroit."

"Oh that's right! Gabi's move is this weekend." She grins, jingling the keys in her hand. "When will you get back?"

"Probably late Saturday night."

"Are you taking Merlin?"

"Nah. He'll stay with my mom." I smile as she scratches him behind the ears and his tail wags with joy. "What are you up to this weekend?"

"Tomorrow afternoon, I'm visiting Mrs. Frye's advanced art class at the high school. I might meet Yasmine for a drink tomorrow night. Other than that, just work. I want to add a little more detail to the healing gardens poster and then maybe get it matted. What time is the meeting with the Harts on Tuesday?"

"Three p.m. at their house."

"Ooh. I've never been to the Hart mansion."

"I was there once. It's old and dusty. But it does have art on the walls."

She tilts her head. "Are they art collectors?"

I rack my brain, trying to remember what Mrs. Hart rambled on about while leading me down the hall to Tad's office. "I think Tiffany might be into paintings?"

"Hmm. That could be useful to us. I'll see what I can find out." She puts a hand on my cheek and kisses me. "Have fun with Gabi. Say hi for me."

"I will. I love you."

That smile. I'll never get tired of it. "I love you too."

I arrive at Gabi's apartment around noon on Friday, and we spend the entire day packing up her place and bickering. We argue over whose playlist to listen to, who learned to ride a bike without training wheels first, which one of us would be more likely to win a survivalist reality show, who's better at cornhole, and what toppings to order on the pizza for dinner.

(For the record, I am the superior cornhole player.)

But we manage to get the kitchen and living room pretty much done, although she has a ridiculous amount of shit. Around seven, we sit down at the kitchen table with pizza, paper plates, and a couple of beers.

"So, how's it going with Mila?" Gabi asks.

"Good."

"You're still hanging out?"

"Yeah. As much as we can."

"When does she go back to New York?"

"End of the month." I tip up my beer. "But actually, I'm hoping she'll move back."

Gabi looks surprised. "Wow. I didn't realize it was that serious."

"It's getting there. But don't tell Mom I said that. She'll overreact and start planning a wedding." I finish off the crust of my first slice, and it makes me miss Mila.

Gabi is quiet for a minute, then asks, "How has Mom's pain level been this week?"

"About the same. She's struggling to get around, especially up and down those stairs."

"When I was home, she kept mentioning her friend Theresa's place at the new condo complex. Apparently it has a fitness center?"

"She's mentioned that to me, too."

"Can you get a membership without living there?"

"No idea." I wipe my hands on a napkin and pick up my phone. "But I bet I can find out if I post a question on the Landing Pad."

Gabi takes a bite of her pizza. "What's that?"

"It's the *Gazette's* online community message board. It's supposed to help residents find out what's going on around town, see safety alerts, buy and sell things. But mostly it's gossip and shit-talking."

She laughs. "Let me see." Taking my phone, she scrolls down the page. She bursts out laughing. "Someone's drawing dicks on driveways?"

"Yeah."

She turns the phone sideways and studies the art. "Interesting." The scrolling continues while she takes another bite. "What on earth are Diner Detectives?"

"It's some kind of true crime club in Hart's Landing, and they're looking into the bakery fire. They claim to have new evidence that might clear Mila's name."

Gabi stops chewing. "Huh?"

"They reached out to Mila and said they believe a third person might've been there that night."

"What makes them think that?"

"Well, first they thought they had some kind of evidence that someone else was there—stuff some kid found in the alley before the fire started that night." I finish my second slice and contemplate a third. "But it all belonged to Mila."

"Do they think a third person *started* the fire?"

"Not necessarily. They just think there's more to the story. Apparently, the kid also saw someone leaving the bakery through the back door that night, after Mila closed up but before the initial explosion."

"Does he know who it was?"

"No. Didn't get a good enough look."

"Why does it even matter at this point? It's not like anyone was hurt. The worst that happened was that we had to sell."

"*Mila* was hurt," I point out. "Maybe not physically, but her reputation suffered. And she feels a lot of guilt about the fire. To this day, people still say she's responsible."

Gabi's eyes widen. "They do?"

"Oh yeah. She hates it."

Gabi sets her half-eaten slice on her plate. "That sucks. I feel bad."

"The lead *detective*"—I put the word in air quotes—"thinks proving someone else was there that night could clear her name. He's trying to create buzz for a podcast. He posted asking for the third person to come forward."

"Huh." Gabi gets up from the table and dumps her paper plate in the trash.

"You're done eating already?"

"Yeah. I wasn't that hungry."

"An hour ago, you said you were starving."

"I'm dramatic, okay? I just want to get this done and go to bed." She heads into the living room and starts loading books into boxes.

That night, I crash on Gabi's couch. I send Mila a quick text to say good night, but she doesn't answer right away, and I figure she's out with Yasmine. Exhausted, I set my phone aside and close my eyes. I drift off in minutes.

"Everett."

I hear my name whispered through the fog of heavy sleep. "Hm?"

"Everett." It's Gabi's voice. She touches my shoulder.

Propping myself up on my elbows, I blink at her in the dark. "Are you okay? What time is it?"

"It's just after two." She sits on the couch at my feet. "I need to talk to you."

Chapter Forty-Six

Mila

Friday afternoon, I spend an hour in the art room at the high school speaking to Mrs. Frye's advanced students about botanical illustration and choosing art as a career path.

There are about two dozen kids in the room, mostly seniors, and even though I worried they might be bored with the topic, they're quiet and pay close attention. Afterward, Mrs. Frye asks if I'd like to see some of the students' work.

"I'd love to," I say.

She asks the kids to take out their most recent projects. "They're adding to their collections from last year," she explains, "getting ready to showcase their best pieces in the Autumn Arts Fair later this month."

"Fantastic." Sipping from my water bottle, I move from table to table, praising the delicate brushstrokes in a watercolor, the perspective in a landscape, the shading in a charcoal portrait. "These are really good. Lots of talent here."

I turn down the next row, and an abstract painting catches my eye. "Oh, I love this."

"Thanks." The artist, a pale boy with a bleached-blond buzz cut wearing an oversized sweatshirt, doesn't meet my eye.

"This is Felix," Mrs. Frye says. "I keep trying to get him to display his work at the art fair, but he won't."

The kid shrugs.

"You should," I tell him. "This is very impressive."

I stand still for a moment, studying the canvas. Something about it pulls me in. The way the colors seem to vibrate. There's a sense of movement—of expansion—beneath the brushstrokes. The sweeping curves and spirals. It's chaotic, yet I can find organic shapes within the depths.

One shape in particular catches my eye.

It's hidden inside the composition, but it's unmistakable.

And I realize who this kid is.

Dickelangelo.

I glance sharply at the artist, but he's still looking down. "Can I see some of your other work?" I ask.

"Show her your folio," Mrs. Frye urges.

I can tell the kid doesn't really want to do it, but he reaches into his backpack and pulls out a binder. Setting it on the table, he pushes it toward me, and I thumb through the plastic-covered pages, more convinced than ever that Felix is behind the phallic graffiti in Hart's Landing. His work is eye-catching and clever, and he's done a good job hiding the phallic imagery within each composition, but I can see it.

"Amazing. But you don't like displaying your work?" I ask him, knowing full well he's displayed it for all to see on driveways and public paths.

He mumbles something I don't catch, and the bell rings. He looks up at Mrs. Frye, and I notice his startling hazel eyes. "Can I go?"

"Of course." She smiles at him. "Have a good weekend."

Felix shoves his folio back into his backpack, swings it onto his shoulder, and carefully moves his painting to an easel at the back of the room. Then he puts headphones on and files out with the rest of the class.

Mrs. Frye sighs. "He doesn't have support for his art at home. Money is tight, and his family has told him there's no money for college. He's expected to get a job."

"Why doesn't he like doing the art fairs?"

"I think he just figures there's no point." She looks toward the door. "He tries to pretend he doesn't care, but I think he does."

"Couldn't a counselor help him or something?"

Mrs. Frye shrugs. "He's not terribly involved at school. I think art is the only class he doesn't regularly skip. His freshman year, he got into quite a bit of trouble for pulling the fire alarm, and his reputation with teachers never really recovered."

A twinge of sympathy pinches my heart. "Got it."

"Well, thanks for coming today. How much longer are you in town?"

"About ten days," I tell her, my gut clenching at the thought of being separated from Everett, even temporarily.

"Well, if you have time next week to speak to my beginner classes, I know they'd love it as well."

"Sure. I'd like that." We say goodbye, and I head out.

But Felix stays on my mind.

Is there anything I can do to help him? Would he even accept my help? Do I tell Everett I suspect he's the artist behind the driveway dicks? I don't really have any proof beyond my intuition and my eye.

So, later that afternoon, when I catch sight of him bagging groceries at the Hart's Landing Food Mart, I make my way over. "Felix?"

He looks my way for a second but doesn't stop what he's doing. "Yeah?"

"I wondered if we could talk for a minute."

"I'm working."

"I don't mind. We can talk right here."

He places eggs, butter, and a box of cake mix in a bag. Says nothing.

I shift my grocery bag to one hip. "I know it's you."

A quick glance that barely meets my eyes. "Huh?"

"The graffiti," I say quietly. "I know it's you."

"I don't know what you're talking about." His tone and the set of his jaw grow defensive. But he looks around to make sure no one's listening to us.

"Can we go outside for a minute?"

He frowns. "Hey, Penny, can I take my break?"

The woman at the cash register nods. "Sure. Five minutes."

I follow him out of the store onto the sidewalk. When he turns to face me, his expression is blank, but his leg jitters. "Your style is really distinct, Felix. Your work has confidence and flow, and so much personality. With more maturity and experience, it's only going to get better."

He stays silent, but I can tell he likes the compliments.

"Look, I can appreciate wanting to push boundaries, and I'm not here to get you in trouble. But you have to stop with the graffiti."

"You still don't know it was me."

"Yeah, I do. I saw the hidden...*shapes* in your folio drawings. Very clever. I bet Mrs. Frye never noticed a thing."

That brings a smug half-smile. "Nope."

"She told me your family isn't supportive of your art."

The smile disappears. He glances at the parking lot.

"Mine wasn't either. But it's what I wanted to do, so I found a way to do it."

"We're different."

"Sure. But I want to help you."

He meets my eyes. "Why?"

"Because you've got so much potential. Because you need it. And because I know what it's like to be judged in this town for *one* bad decision you made when you were young."

"Oh yeah, I heard about that. You set the fire at the bakery, right?"

I frown at him. "I didn't *set* it, okay? But yes, it happened on my watch."

"Right."

"Anyway," I say, shifting my grocery bag higher on my hip, "I won't give your name to the police if you promise me you'll stop scandalizing the old ladies of Hart's Landing and start using your art as a force for good."

"Like how?"

I've thought about this. "If all goes well, a community center and garden is going to be built on the old foundry site. Kids will come there for art classes and experiences."

He's already shaking his head. "Can't afford them."

"Actually, I was thinking you could help out there. Assist the instructor. Show kids how to capture what they see in the garden on paper."

His leg stops jittering. "Seriously?"

"Yes. And then if there are classes offered at your level, I'd see to it that you're on scholarship. You could take them for free. At the very least, you'd have studio space to work in."

He can't quite hide a smile. "That would be cool."

"So, do we have a deal? No more Dickelangelo, at least in public?"

"Okay."

"Good. I'll reach out to you when the community center is up and running."

He glances into the store. "I should get back to work."

"Go ahead."

He heads for the Food Mart's automatic door, getting close enough for it to open before he turns around. "Hey, Fire Lady? Thanks."

"You can call me Mila, actually. And you're welcome."

He nods. "Thanks, Mila."

"You're welcome, Felix. See you around." As I make my way to my mom's car, I think about the community center. About the new beginning it will give to a place that means so much to me. About all the kids who will learn to love making art there. About the good it will do for the environment, for the town, for Everett's legacy.

I want to see it come to life. I want to be part of it. I want to stand beside Everett while Tad and Tiffany Hart cut the ribbon and take credit for everything.

And I want my own new beginning.

Even if it's right back where I started.

Chapter Forty-Seven

Everett

"What's up?"

Gabi covers her face with her hands and rocks back and forth in the dark.

"Did you have a nightmare or something?"

"No. I haven't been able to sleep at all."

"Why not?"

She takes a deep breath. "I was there that night. At the bakery. I'm the other person that kid saw."

"What?"

"And I might have left an oven on."

"*What?*" I bolt upright. "Gabi, what the fuck? Are you serious right now?"

"Yes." She starts to cry. "It could be my fault, all of it. The fire, the damage, having to sell, Mila shouldering the blame. I'm a horrible fucking person. I hate myself for it. I've always hated myself for it." Her sobs are uncontrollable now.

"Wait a minute. Slow down." I run a hand through my hair. "Start from the beginning. Why were you there that night?"

"To bake. I'd just had a massive fight with Dad, during which he told me I was a stupid fucking idiot who'd never go anywhere or do anything with my life. Mom tried to defend me a little bit, but he shattered a beer bottle against the wall and told her to shut up, so she did. You know how she was back then."

"Yes." I can imagine this scene playing out perfectly, even though I wasn't there. The bloodshot eyes. The screaming. The sound of the bottle hitting the wall.

"I stormed out of the house and drove around, crying and

miserable. I just wanted a quiet place away from the house to stress-bake," she sobs. "So I ran home and got a key for the bakery."

"But we were there," I say, still trying to wrap my head around what she's telling me. "Mila and I were there. I didn't see you."

"All the lights were out. And I didn't see your truck or her car in the back. I thought you'd gone."

"All the lights *were* out," I say, remembering the darkness in the bakery that night before Mila kissed me. "And I'd moved the truck. Mila had biked to work."

"I let myself in the back door. When I pulled the key out of my pocket, my necklace must have fallen out. The clasp had broken earlier in the day, and I'd tucked it in there. The ponytail holder, too—I'd borrowed it from Mila that morning."

"Jesus." I rub a hand over my face.

"I was only there for like three minutes. Just long enough to turn on the oven. Then I heard you laugh. I realized you guys must still be up front, probably messing around in the dark, and I took off, being careful not to let the door slam so you wouldn't hear it. I didn't want to break the spell." She cries even harder. "I thought I turned the oven off. But maybe I didn't. Maybe I didn't."

"Why didn't you ever say anything?"

"Because," she weeps. "That night was so awful. I didn't even know about the fire until later, when I got home. I'd gone to the beach and sat there by myself, way down past where everyone hangs out. I didn't want to talk to anyone. And then when I did get home, well… Things got out of control fast."

I close my eyes. Clench my jaw. Some of this is my fault too.

"Mila shouldered all the blame," I say quietly.

"I know." A fresh torrent of sobs breaks loose. "I know she did, but I was afraid if I admitted what I knew, Dad would take it out on you. He always hit you when it was me who did something wrong."

Feelings fight for dominance inside me. I'm shocked at what I'm hearing. I'm furious with Gabi for not speaking up back then. I'm terrified of what will happen when Mila finds out.

But I cannot listen to my sister cry without trying to comfort her. It's obvious she's in agony over this. I scoot closer to her and hang an arm around her shuddering shoulders. Her body judders with heaving breaths. "Come on. It'll be okay."

"I felt so guilty, I couldn't face her. That's why I cut her off. That's why I cut everyone off. I couldn't be around my friends because I knew they'd see through me. I couldn't bear it."

I grimace. "For ten years?"

"I know!" she wails. "I *know*. Like I told you before, I wanted to reach out so many times. I swore to myself every year that I would do it, but I was too chickenshit. I made excuses. I would say, 'well, no one was hurt,' or 'no one got in trouble,' or 'it doesn't really matter now, anyway.'"

"It would have mattered to Mila," I say grimly.

"I know. You're right, I know." She buries her face in her hands, and I can't help turning her into my chest. She spends several minutes blubbering on my shoulder, getting tears and snot all over my shirt.

When she's finally calmer, I go to the bathroom and look for tissues. Unable to find any, I bring her a roll of toilet paper.

"Thanks," she says, ripping off a section to blow her nose. "I wanted to tell you so many times. I really did. But then I thought it would just be a burden. And you'd already done so much for me."

"I'd do it all again," I tell her. "But you should have been honest with me."

"I know, and I'm so sorry."

"And you have to be honest with Mila, too."

"I will," she says solemnly. "I swear to God I will. But I just got her back. Don't make me do it right away."

"Gabi."

"I promise you, Everett. I promise on my *life*, I will tell her. I just need a little time."

"How much time?"

"A couple weeks?"

My stomach lurches. "She'll be gone by then! And you can't expect me to be with her and keep this a secret. That's not fair." I recall the day in the coffee shop when she asked me to always be honest with her, and I promised I would be.

"I didn't realize how serious you guys were until tonight, or I would have come clean sooner! Please, Everett." She clasps her hands under her chin. "One week. I am begging you. I'll deal with Mom. I'll volunteer anywhere you need people. I'll even judge the pie contest next year."

"Damn right you will." I sit down again. Hang my head in my hands. "How am I supposed to keep this from her? It feels like lying. And she doesn't deserve it."

"It's not lying."

"She trusts me, Gabi. We have something really good. Really honest."

"I'm happy for you. You guys deserve each other. And you're going to be together—this will only be a blip."

"You'd better be right." I lean against the back of the couch. "Because she's the one. I don't want to lose her."

"You won't." Gabi puts a hand on my arm. "I promise."

I hardly sleep that night, and I'm a wreck in the morning. I guzzle extremely large cups of coffee while we finish packing and load the truck. Gabi and I don't say much to each other, and we don't ride home together—I drive the truck, and she drives my pickup. She sold her car last week.

I text Mila before we leave, saying that we're heading home. She hearts the message and tells me she misses me and to drive safely.

I feel guilty already.

We arrive in Hart's Landing around nine on Saturday night. Ripley's working, and Ben has Vivian, but Hunter shows up when

I put out the call for help unloading the truck. We get everything into the house in about two hours, then my mom feeds us all a late supper of chili and cornbread.

A hundred times, I take my phone out to text Mila and ask her to come over, but I never go through with it. I'm dying to see her, but I can't face her. Not yet. I'm afraid she'll take one look at my face and know I'm keeping something from her.

When he leaves, Hunter thanks my mom for the food.

"Of course! You should come for Sunday dinner tomorrow," my mom says. "I'm making a pot roast, and there's always plenty."

"That sounds great, but I have to work tomorrow."

"Next time, then."

Hunter nods and gives us a wave. "See you."

"Night, Hunter. Thanks for the help," I call, tipping my chair back on two legs.

"Why don't you invite Mila for Sunday dinner?" Mom suggests. "I've hardly seen her for more than two seconds."

"I could." I must not sound too enthusiastic about it, because my mom gives me a puzzled look.

"Are things okay between you two?"

"They're fine," I say, letting the chair legs hit the ground. I take my bowl over to the sink. "I'll ask her."

I collect Merlin and head back to the cabin. Too wiped out to even shower, I fall into bed and send Mila a text.

Everett: *Hey.*

Mila: *Hey! How did the move go?*

Everett: *I'm glad it's done.*

Mila: *Aww. You're such a good brother.*

Everett: *My mom wants to invite you for Sunday dinner.*

There's a slight pause before she replies.

Mila: *That's nice of her. Do you want me to come?*

Great. Now she thinks I'm a dick for putting it that way.

Everett: *Of course I do.*

Mila: *Then I'll come. What time?*

Everett: *5:00 is usually when we eat.*

Mila: *Should I come to the cabin a little earlier? Or should I go right to the house?*

Everett: *You can come to the cabin earlier.*

Another pause.

Mila: *Okay. I'll see you around 4?*

Everett: *Sounds good.*

I set my phone down and close my eyes. My head hurts. I'm fucking exhausted. Angry. Dreading this week. A moment later, my phone buzzes again.

Mila: *Everything okay?*

Everett: *Yeah, sorry. I'm just tired.*

Mila: *You had a busy couple days. Get some sleep. I love you.*

Worn out, I crash before texting her back.

Sunday morning, I realize my mistake.

Everett: *Sorry! I fell asleep. I love you too.*

She hearts the message.

Mila: *That's okay. I'll see you this afternoon.*

Dragging myself out of bed, I pull on some clothes and pray I can get through the week without disappointing any of the people who are counting on me.

That afternoon, she comes to the cabin before dinner. The minute I open the door, I scoop her up and lift her right off the ground, crushing my mouth to hers. If I'm kissing her, I can't meet her eyes. I don't have to lie. I won't say shit I shouldn't.

"I missed you too," she says with a laugh when I set her down. She lets me pull her right back to the bedroom, and we spend the next half-hour making up for a couple of days apart. The only words we exchange are the one-syllable kind.

Afterward, as we put ourselves back together, I ask how her weekend was.

"You'll never guess what I did on Friday." She's bubbling with excitement. "I've been dying to tell you about it."

"What?"

Tugging up her jeans, she sends me a satisfied grin. "I solved a problem for you."

"Which problem?"

She tosses her hair. "I discovered the identity of Dickelangelo."

"No way!" I sit down on the bed and pull on my socks. "Who is it?"

As we get dressed, she tells me about this kid named Felix, how talented he is, how she spotted the dicks hidden in his artwork. "I had a hunch it was him. And then he confessed. Can I borrow your hairbrush?"

"Sure." Next to her at the mirror, I run my hands through my hair. "So he agreed to stop doing it? Just like that?"

"Yes. He's not a bad kid—he's just frustrated." She pulls my brush through her hair with long strokes. "His parents don't have the money for college, and they don't support his art. He refuses to participate in the school art fairs, probably because he's all 'fuck the system,' so he just wanted to show off what he can do. Cause a fuss. Disrupt." She shakes her hair, and it cascades down her back.

God, I could watch her do this every single morning.

"The dicks were definitely a disruption," I say.

"He promised me he'll use his talent for good from now on." She turns to face me. "Assuming all goes well Tuesday and the community center is a go, I'd love to get him a job there helping with art classes."

"If all goes well Tuesday, you can have anything you want." I drop a kiss on her freckled nose.

She grins, and it feels like a stab to the heart.

We walk hand in hand to my mom's house, and the moment Mila walks in, my mom and Gabi pounce on her. My mother asks about Eliza and the recovery, Mila's art, and what she thinks of all the changes in Hart's Landing. Gabi wants to hear all about living in New York City, the different jobs Mila's had since college, how she started her own design studio.

I sit back, happy to eat, observe, and be silent.

But I'll be glad when the week is up.

"Well?" Mila sits back on my couch. "What do you think?"

It's Monday night, and for the last two hours, we've been working on our approach for tomorrow's meeting at the Hart mansion.

"I think it's brilliant, and it's going to work." I pull her across my lap, catching her within my arms. "I don't know how to thank you for all the time and effort you're putting into this."

"Don't you?" she teases, one brow raised.

I bury my face in her neck, because every time I look into her eyes, my stomach hurts. "Can you stay a while?"

"How long is a while?"

I kiss my way down to her shoulder. "Fifty years?"

"That's all you want?"

"You know what I want."

"And what if I said yes?"

I pause, my lips on her collarbone. "Are you serious?"

"I've been thinking about it, and I think it's the right choice for me." She takes a breath. "I'll move back to Hart's Landing."

I pick up my head so I can meet her eyes. "I didn't pressure you into it, did I?"

"No. I made the decision on my own, and I made it for me. I want to be brave enough to take a chance on happiness."

"You have no idea how much that means to me."

"It won't be right away," she cautions. "I have to go back to Brooklyn for the rest of the semester—and give Jess time to find a new roommate—but I should be able to move by the end of January."

"Take all the time you need."

"I'll need to find a place to live and work that is *not* my mother's house."

"I'll help you."

She inhales slowly. "And I have to tell her. She's going to have an *opinion*."

"Not your problem, babe." Rising to my feet, I carry her to the bedroom, toss her onto the bed, and stretch out above her. "I'm going to do everything I can to make you happy here."

"I believe you," she says, wrapping her arms and legs around me. "I trust you."

Her words wrench my heart.

Chapter Forty-Eight

Everett

"Let me be clear." Tad Hart leans back in a leather chair. It creaks under his weight. "Neither Hart Iron Works nor the Hart family will be held responsible for standards that didn't exist fifty years ago."

Mila and I are seated across from the Harts in their library, a dark, wood-paneled room with high ceilings and bookshelves stretching up every wall. The carpets and curtains are faded from the sun, and it's dusty as fuck. I've sneezed like five times already.

"That's not what this is about," I reply, fighting off yet another tickle in my nose. "This is about moving forward, not looking back."

Beside me, Mila slides forward so she's balanced at the edge of her seat. "And doing it in a way that will shine a positive light on the Hart name." Her eyes slide to mine, and I give her a nod. She's up first.

"Mrs. Hart." Mila addresses the woman in the chair next to her husband. "May I show you something?"

It was Mila's idea to appeal to Tiffany directly. She did a little research over the weekend—because she's fucking brilliant—and discovered that Mrs. Hart majored in art history with a specialization in Postimpressionism. I had no idea what that meant or how it would be useful, but Mila said to trust her.

Which I do. Completely.

And knowing that she trusts me feels like a knife in my gut every time I think about what I know and she doesn't. As if she can sense my nerves, she sends me a reassuring smile as she reaches into her portfolio. Carefully, she removes the matted illustration, placing it on the coffee table between us, facing the Harts.

"Oh, how lovely." Tiffany leans forward, her fingers steepled over her chest.

It's more than lovely. It's a gorgeously detailed sketch of what Mila imagines the foundry site can become. I thought her early drawing was good, but that was a seedling compared to this tree in full bloom. It's lush and colorful and vibrant. Tiffany is awed.

Tad remains ramrod straight, looking at the drawing as if it's a giant turd on the table. "What is it?"

"It's the foundry site, dear," says Tiffany.

Tad harrumphs. "Doesn't look like the foundry site to me."

"It's what the site could become," Mila clarifies. "Not a toxic embarrassment or a legal liability, but a symbol of progress and redemption. A place of healing."

The old linebacker's face retains its granite expression, but he's been negotiating deals since before I was born and knows better than to give anything away. I see the flicker of interest in his eyes as Mila elaborates on her drawing.

"Sunflowers are natural metal extractors and begin working very quickly. They're also a symbol of warmth and abundance. The way they always have their faces to the sun suggests steadfastness and loyalty. And because they can grow so tall and strong, they're symbols of resilience. It's no wonder Van Gogh painted them so often."

"Oh, I just love those paintings!" Tiffany gushes. "Van Gogh once said, 'The sunflower is mine.' They had special meaning for him."

Mila smiles at her. "They'll have special meaning to Hart's Landing, too. There'll be walking paths through different gardens, and students will be able to learn about the remediation process and plants with superpowers. I was even thinking it could be a place where students learn to draw and illustrate the cleanup cycle." She tucks a strand of copper hair behind her ear.

My heart. She's so fucking beautiful.

"Mila is a well-known botanical illustrator," I say, my chest so full it could burst. "She drew this after seeing the site to show us what it could be."

"You drew this?" Tiffany Hart's eyes widen, her voice rising to a high pitch. "My goodness! It's exquisite!"

Mila blushes. "Thank you."

"And what's that sign say?" Tad points a thick finger at the drawing.

Tiffany peers closer. "Hart Family Healing Gardens," she reads, clasping her hands beneath her chin. "Oh, isn't that beautiful?"

"Is this real science?" Tad asks, his skepticism obvious in his furrowed brows. "Or is it New Age, hippie-dippy pseudoscience?"

"It's very real, and very forward-thinking," I tell him. "Dr. Yang from MSU has signed off on the entire phytoremediation plan. The university is prepared to partner on this project."

"What's that mean?"

This is my part—the nuts and bolts, dollars and cents. I wipe my sweaty hands on my pants and sit up taller. "The structure we're proposing creates a limited partnership where the Hart family contributes the initial funding for remediation but transfers the property to the Hart's Landing Community Foundation. The foundation would then collaborate with the university for the actual work."

"Potentially insulating the family from direct liability," Tad muses, rubbing a hand over his jaw.

"Exactly."

Mila speaks up. "Mr. Hart, I grew up hearing stories about how your family built this town, how Hart Iron Works provided jobs for so many—and took care of their families. I just took my mom to the Hart Primary Care Clinic. There's a Hart Animal Rescue, too, which demonstrates care for all living things. That legacy is real and important." She gestures to her illustration. "This will show care for the environment in a way that acknowledges the past but builds something better for the future."

I watch Tad's face, imagining the calculations happening behind his eyes. He isn't convinced yet. He might like the story about his caring family legacy, but he doesn't make emotional decisions.

I have one more card to play. "The alternative is less appealing for everyone—no community center, no healing gardens. The EPA has already contacted the town expressing interest in the site. If they designate it for Superfund cleanup, we would lose control of the narrative entirely."

Tiffany places her hand on her husband's arm. "Tad, imagine the gala we could host for the opening. Perhaps I could even commission a sculpture for the entrance. We could invite the Kennedys!"

The corner of Mila's mouth twitches.

"And the cost?" Tad asks.

"Significantly less than traditional remediation," I say. "Dr. Yang estimates around three hundred thousand for the initial phase, with maintenance costs of roughly seventy-five thousand annually over five years."

Tiffany is nodding, already convinced. She probably has a designer purse collection that costs more than that. Tad is the harder sell, but I'm confident he'll recognize that this solution offers a path forward that protects both his family's finances and their reputation. He's a blowhard, but he's not a fool.

Finally, he nods. "Okay. You have our cooperation. But we'll need to see more detailed plans. Cost breakdowns, timelines, the structure of the foundation, the exact legal protections."

"You'll have them as soon as I can get them done. This project is currently my top priority." I exchange a triumphant look with Mila. "Mr. and Mrs. Hart, would it be okay with you if we submit the proposed plan for approval at tomorrow night's town council meeting? If it goes through, you could schedule that press release."

"Fine." Tad stands up, indicating that our meeting is over.

"I'll walk you out," says his wife.

At the front door, we shake hands and promise to be in touch.

"Mrs. Hart, I wonder if I could ask you one more thing," Mila says.

"Certainly." Tiffany smiles and checks her watch.

"I've lost touch with Rachel, your niece. Do you happen to have contact information for her?"

"Oh." Tiffany Hart looks puzzled, although her forehead doesn't wrinkle. "I'd have to see. Her mother might know, but we don't see Catriona too often, not since George died."

"Well, if you happen to come across a phone number or even an address, I'd be grateful. I'd like to reach out."

"I'll let you know."

As soon as the massive front door is shut behind us, Mila and I throw our arms around each other.

"You were perfect," I tell her. "This is all because of you."

Mila laughs. "It was a team effort. You knew just how to seal the deal with old Tad."

"He's easy. He might not care about the environment or the aesthetics, but he definitely cares about the numbers and his family name." We start down the tree-lined drive toward the truck. "And the drawing was… I don't even have the right words."

"Better than Van Gogh?"

"Still a hack."

We reach my truck, and I open the passenger door for her.

"What do you think?" She smiles up at me. "Should we go have dinner somewhere to celebrate the win?"

"Actually, I have to meet my mom and sister at home. We're taking her over to that new condo complex on the water to see about a fitness membership." I'm a total dick for being glad I don't have to face Mila across a table.

"Okay. Maybe we can FaceTime later?"

FaceTime isn't much easier. "I've got my axe-throwing league."

"Will you be late?"

"I'm not sure."

"Oh." Her face falls. She chews her bottom lip. "Everett, is everything okay?"

"Everything is great," I lie. "We just crushed our goal."

"I don't mean with the project. I mean with you. With us." She looks me directly in the eye. "Is there anything you need to tell me?"

I swallow hard, cursing my sister. "No. Everything is fine with us. I'm just– I'm just tired."

The attempt she makes at a smile is nearly enough to make me break down and confess. "Okay. But you'd tell me if there was something wrong, right?"

I start to say yes, but the word catches in my throat–it feels too much like a lie.

Instead of answering, I kiss her. And hate myself for it.

I corner my sister while my mom chats with a woman at the fitness center.

"You have to tell her," I say forcefully. "I feel so fucking bad every time we're together. I'm losing my mind."

"I will," she vows. "I just haven't seen her, and it's not something I want to do over text. I'm having lunch with her on Thursday, and I swear to God I'll tell her then."

"You better. Because I can't keep this up."

I get home from the pub by eleven and FaceTime Mila, but I'm tense and quiet on the call.

She tries a joke. "Did you end up in second place on the leaderboard or something?"

I want to laugh. To smile and tease her back. To celebrate what we did today. But I can't. I feel like I'm pretending the entire time, and I hate it. Now I know exactly how she must have felt when she had to twist herself into a pretzel to keep someone else happy. "No," I say. "I'm just tired."

The excuse is old and weak, and she knows it. After an awkward silence, she says, "Well, I guess I'll let you get some sleep."

"Okay," I say, even though I haven't slept right since Friday night.

"I love you," she tells me softly.

"Love you too," I say.

When we hang up, I rub my face with my hands.

If it were anyone other than Gabi who'd asked me to keep something from Mila, I would have said *hell no*. This is torture.

My sister gets two more days.

Thursday morning, I head over to my mom's to scavenge some breakfast—and run into my sister doing yoga on the back porch. At least, I assume that's what she's doing. Her hands and feet are on a mat and her butt is up in the air, her arms and legs straight. My hamstrings scream just looking at her.

"Morning," I say, climbing the steps.

"Morning," she returns, without coming out of her pose.

Inside the house, there's coffee in the pot and a plate of blueberry muffins on the counter. Sticking a muffin in my mouth, I pour some water for Merlin and reach for a banana from the fruit bowl. I'm about to peel it from the stem when I remember what Mila said about monkeys. Curious, I flip it over and try peeling it from the other end. It easily splits and comes apart, revealing the fruit beneath. "What do you know," I say, laughing a little. "She was right." I break it into pieces for Merlin, and he eagerly digs into his snack.

After pouring myself a cup of coffee, I steal another muffin off the plate and head outside.

My sister is now belly-down on the mat, but her chest is pressed up.

"Where's Mom?" I ask, dropping into a rocker.

"She had an early doctor's appointment." Gabi shifts into a different pose, her butt resting on her heels, her arms outstretched, palms on the mat.

"Did she fill out the application for the fitness membership at the waterfront complex yet?"

"No," she says, her voice muffled by the mat. "I actually don't think Mom wants a membership."

"Why not? She keeps bringing that place up."

"I know." Gabi picks up her face. "I think she wants to *live* there."

"*Live* there? Like, buy a condo?"

"Yes. A place without stairs or so many rooms to keep clean." She lowers her head again. "Can she afford it?"

"I don't know. Maybe. I'd have to talk to Sam." Sam is the financial manager who helped me straighten out the mess our dad left when he died. "We're still paying off some of those shitty loans Dad took out."

"That's what I figured." She comes out of her pose and sits cross-legged on the mat. Reaches for her water bottle and takes a sip. "Plus, who's going to live in this monster?"

"Um, I just moved you in. Don't even tell me you're leaving. My back still hurts from getting your dresser up the stairs."

"I moved in *temporarily*, mostly to help Mom. Or at least keep her company. If she leaves, there's no reason for me to stay. I don't need all this house. It was always supposed to go to you."

I shake my head. "I don't need all this house either."

"Maybe you should have some kids."

"Maybe *you* should have some kids."

She sighs and leans back on her hands. "Poor Mom. She wants grandchildren so badly."

"You don't ever want kids?"

Gabi shrugs. "I guess I'd never say never. I just have more things I want to do first."

"Yeah." I take another swallow from the mug.

"What about you?"

"I don't know. I've always felt like it was something really far off. But lately, I've been thinking more about it."

"Because you're thirty, old man?"

"That might be part of it," I say, flipping her off. "But there are other reasons."

"Does one of them have blue eyes and red hair and a name that starts with M and rhymes with tequila?"

"Maybe." I poke her leg with my boot. "Which is why I hate hiding something from her. You're telling her today, right?"

"Yes." She holds up three fingers. "Scout's honor."

I sip my coffee. "She's going to move back."

"Is she really?" Gabi's face lights up. "That's huge."

"I know. I'm not taking it lightly." I lean back in the rocker, setting it in motion. Looking out over the yard, I try to imagine myself as a father. Doing summertime things. Playing catch on the lawn. Filling a little plastic pool with water. Letting them squirt me with the hose.

Teaching a little brown-eyed boy how to identify the calls of birds. Bait a hook. Prune a cherry tree.

A little blue-eyed girl how to ride a bike. Tie her shoes. Swing a bat.

I think about collecting autumn leaves and ironing them between sheets of wax paper. About cozy winter nights—pillow forts, popcorn, movies, cuddling under the blankets. Bedtime stories. Christmas mornings. Footie pajamas. Hot cocoa.

Mila by my side. In my arms. Safe and warm.

The paint might be peeling, the windows might rattle, and the hallway is definitely still tilted, but it's ours. And it's nice, this life.

It's so fucking nice.

Chapter Forty-Nine

WELCOME TO THE LANDING PAD

Community Updates From The Hart's Landing Gazette (Online Edition)

PSA: At last night's town council meeting, Mayor McKean presented a proposal to transform the old Hart Iron Works site into a community center and healing gardens, funded by the Hart family. He introduced audience member Mila Ferguson as the artist behind the beautiful poster on display, and when the audience gave her a round of applause, she blew him a kiss. The proposal was unanimously approved, and the mayor celebrated by embracing the artist and swinging her into the air as all looked on in wonder.

GazetteMod: To review our posting categories, including what qualifies as a Public Service Announcement, please click here.

Comment by ANONYMOUS AXE GOD: Hey @GazetteMod, I've got a PSA for you: Don't be such a party pooper. Then again, what else is new?

GazetteMod: @ANONYMOUS AXE GOD One more personal attack and I'm banning you permanently, RIPLEY.

Comment by ANONYMOUS AXE GOD: This isn't Ripley, but he sounds like a really cool guy.

GazetteMod: @ANONYMOUS AXE GOD I can see your IP address on the back end. Stop being such a menace.

Comment by ANONYMOUS AXE GOD: @GazetteMod, if you wanted to look at my back end, you only had to ask. 🍑👀

GazetteMod: User ANONYMOUS AXE GOD has been banned pending Code of Comment Conduct review.

Comment by ANONYMOUS69: Nice try.

[GazetteMod has closed this post to comments]

Chapter Fifty

Mila

Something is off.

I've felt it ever since Everett returned from moving Gabi. I can't put my finger on what it is exactly, but he's different somehow. Quieter. Broodier. He doesn't laugh as easily. He doesn't talk as much. He seems tired and withdrawn. He doesn't tease me like he used to. Sometimes, I feel like he's reluctant to meet my eyes.

My brain jumps to conclusions. I must have done something. I must have scared him off. Or maybe he just changed his mind about me.

Maybe he's realized I'm a lot. Maybe the emotional meltdowns have worn down his patience. Maybe, the more he thinks about it, the more he realizes I'm not what he wants. He's regretting telling me he loves me. He doesn't want me to move back.

He's pulling away.

I know the signs.

As soon as I have the thought, I tell myself to stop being paranoid. Everett is nothing like any of the men I've dated before, and he's certainly not like the one I married. And it's not like he's ghosting me. He still returns my texts and FaceTimes me at night. He still kisses me like he means it, holds me close after sex, and tells me he loves me.

And he promised to always be honest with me. To never leave me in the dark, wondering where I stand.

He's worried about lots of things—his mom, his sister, the farm, the town—and I can't always expect to be his top priority. That's not how a healthy relationship works.

At least, I don't think it is. I've never been in one, so I don't know for sure.

But I do know that I've been ambushed by heartbreak before, and by Thursday afternoon, I'm a bit of a wreck. I'm leaving Monday. I haven't told my mother or the department head about moving back to Hart's Landing yet. I haven't mentioned it to Jess.

Am I protecting myself? Hedging my bets?

I lie awake in bed every night, going over and over conversations we've had. Replaying our time together. Obsessing over what I might have done or said that triggered this change in him.

And I just don't know.

I'm grateful for the lunch I have planned with Gabi at the diner this afternoon. As a surprise for her, I invited Yasmine to come along. The three of us keep talking about getting together but haven't made it work yet. It'll be like old times.

Just the distraction I need.

Yasmine and Gabi are already in our booth when I arrive.

"Sorry I'm late," I say, sliding in next to Gabi like I've done a thousand times before. "My mother always finds something that needs to be done right when I'm trying to leave the house."

"That's okay." Yasmine smiles across the table at us.

"Surprise!" I say to Gabi, gesturing at Yasmine. "I thought it would be fun for all three of us to have lunch."

"Great idea." Gabi smiles, but she seems on edge. She's been silent in the group chat lately, too.

For a moment, I wonder if something is wrong with Mrs. McKean, and they're keeping it under wraps. Could that be what has Everett so tense? But why wouldn't he open up to me about it?

No. Whatever is going on with him has to do with me. I'm sure of it.

The server appears with menus, and we laugh about how a lot of things have changed in Hart's Landing but the food at this diner isn't one of them. We order milkshakes, burgers and fries, and reminisce about old times.

Eventually, even Gabi seems to relax. "Remember when we laughed so hard our milkshakes came out of our noses?"

Yasmine points a fry at her. "Was that the night you wore those crazy high heels and tripped coming back from the bathroom?"

"No, it was the night Ladybug ripped her pants climbing over the fence."

"Oh right!" I laugh, reminding myself to stay in the moment with my friends and stop spiraling about Everett. "Why were we climbing a fence again?"

"They'd finally fenced off the old foundry site. We were outraged."

"That's right," I say. "Speaking of which, the site is going to be cleaned up and turned into a green space."

"I heard about that!" Gabi says. "They're going to make the old offices into a community center or something?"

"Yes. Town council approved it last night."

"Are you helping with the project?" Yasmine asks me.

"Sort of." I shrug. "Everett thought I'd be good at helping to convince the Harts to fund it."

"Um, Everett thinks you're good at everything," Gabi says wryly.

Heat flushes my face, and I look down at my menu.

"So give us the scoop." Yasmine's eyes glow brightly. "How's it going with you two?"

"Good, I think," I say, tucking my hair behind my ears. "In fact, I'm— I'm probably going to move back here."

Yasmine squeals and claps her hands. "Yay! I was hoping!"

"Wait, why only 'probably'?" asks Gabi, her face concerned. "Everett told me this morning you'd decided to move back for sure."

"Yeah, I guess I'm just nervous to commit to it out loud." I laugh nervously. "It's such a major thing, to move in order to be with someone. And I don't have the best track record where relationships are concerned. My perception can be really distorted. So while there's a part of me that says this thing with Everett is the real deal and I don't have to worry, there's another part of me that says I don't know shit about what's real, because I've been wrong about it every time. And making this move could be a giant mistake."

"You're not wrong," says Gabi, putting a hand on my arm. "Everett is crazy about you. Trust me."

"Thanks. Things have felt a little off this week, so I appreciate that." I shrug. "Maybe it's just me overthinking."

Gabi opens her mouth like she might say more, but Yasmine jumps in with a question. "So, Gabs, what are you going to do now that you're home?"

"I need to figure that out." Gabi picks up her water. "I'm not sure yet."

"God, it's so good to be with you guys." Yasmine puts a hand over her heart. "I was so scared we'd never be friends again."

I smile across the table at her. "I was, too. But maybe the lost time will help us appreciate each other more."

"I know we keep saying this, but we *need* to find Rachel. Get *all* of us back together again. I think Ladybug would love that." Yasmine touches the charm dangling beneath her throat. "Gabi, do you still have your necklace?"

"Huh?" Gabi stares at Yasmine. For a second, she looks pale.

"The ladybug charms we all wore." I touch mine too. "Do you still have yours?"

"No," she says, setting her glass down. "I lost it."

Her hand is shaking.

After lunch, I check my phone again but Everett hasn't called or texted. My last message to him—*Want to grab dinner later?*—hangs there like an ugly shower curtain. I wish I could unsend it.

Back at home, I find the house empty, which means my aunt must have taken my mom out for lunch or some shopping. It's a relief. I don't have the emotional capacity to deal with her right now.

I decide to stress-clean my bedroom. I start with Beatrix's litter box. Throw my sheets in the laundry. Haul the vacuum and a box of cleaning supplies up the stairs. Dust the furniture. Wipe the mirror over my dresser. Wash the windows.

I open my closet door and thumb through the hangers, reorganizing everything by color. I pair up my shoes and set them in a neat row. Dropping to my knees, I take a rag damp with glass cleaner and rub the mirror, careful to avoid the phantom graffiti left by my friends so many years ago.

Gabi's volleyball number. Rachel's toxic boyfriend. Yasmine's campaign against Ripley.

Ladybug's existence.

Choked up, I press my fingers to her name. Close my eyes and drop my chin. Tears prickle behind my eyelids, and I try to blink them away.

That's when I see it.

Wedged against the doorjamb at the very edge of the carpet. Something gold.

Fishing it out with my thumb and forefinger, I lift up a delicate chain. Leaning forward, I feel around until my fingertips find the missing piece.

The ladybug charm.

Confused, I slip the charm back on the chain and cup it in the palm of my right hand. Stare at it. Then I glance in the mirror. I'm wearing the ladybug necklace Stevie found in the alley. The one with the repaired clasp. The one I thought was mine.

But this one in my hand… It *has* to be mine. It must have come off while I was getting dressed for work That Night, and I was so worked up about having to kiss Everett that I didn't notice.

So whose necklace am I wearing?

Rachel's charm was on a bracelet. Yasmine still has hers. And Gabi—

I lost it.

Air leaves my lungs in a sickening rush. The room spins. Sweat breaks out on the back of my neck.

I think it was a woman. I thought I saw long hair.

Clambering to my feet, I shove the necklace in my pocket, race down the stairs, and run out of the house.

I knock on the front door of the McKean house, the sound of my knuckles on the wood drowned out by the drumming of my pulse in my head.

There has to be an explanation. Gabi could have lost her necklace behind the bakery another time, right?

But I saw it on her that morning at the foundry site. I remember it specifically, because she'd just put her hair up, and—

The ponytail holder.

Gabi borrowed my ponytail holder after I took out my bun. She made a comment about it being one of the fancy ones.

My stomach churns.

The door opens, and Mrs. McKean smiles at me, then opens her arms. "Mila! What a nice surprise!"

"Hi, Mrs. McKean." I'm swept into her embrace. It's soft and warm and welcoming. It's the kind of hug that says she's genuinely glad to see me.

The kind of hug I've never gotten from my own mother.

My throat clenches up, and I will myself not to cry. I'm a mess already.

"Are you looking for Everett or Gabi? Everett is out in the orchard somewhere, so I can't help you there, but Gabi is upstairs."

"I'm looking for Gabi, actually."

She steps aside and gestures toward the stairs. "Go on up," she says with a laugh. "I'm sure you remember the way."

"I do, thank you."

My legs tremble as I head up the stairs, which list toward the wall and creak beneath my feet. At the top of the steps, I walk straight down the hall toward the back of the house. Gabi's old room is to the left and Everett's is on the right, both overlooking the yard.

There has to be an explanation.

I raise my fist and knock.

"Come in!"

Turning the old-fashioned brass doorknob, I push the door open. Across the room, Gabi is putting away laundry. I dig the necklace from my pocket.

"Hey," she says. "I'm glad you're here. There's something I want to—"

"I found this." I hold up my hand, the chain with the charm on it dangling from my fingers. "It was at the edge of the carpet in my bedroom. It has to be mine."

Gabi's cheeks lose their flush.

"But if it is," I go on, tapping the ladybug at my throat. "Then this one, which was found in the alley behind the bakery the night of the fire, can't be mine."

"I—" Gabi swallows, her eyes full of panic.

"Is it yours?"

She nods.

"So were you— Were you *there* that night?"

She nods again.

My arm falls. "I don't understand."

"I was going to tell you," she says, rushing toward me. "In fact, I wanted to tell you today at lunch, but then Yasmine was there, and it didn't feel right and I—" She stops right in front of me and covers her mouth with her hands. "Oh God, Mila. I'm so sorry."

"I don't understand," I repeat, taking a step back. "When? Why?"

"I'd gotten into a huge fight with my parents—you know, after what I had to tell them. My father said horrible things to me, my mother was too scared to stand up to him, and I left the house." Her hands flutter nervously as she speaks. "When I'm stressed, I bake. You know that. I just wanted a kitchen."

"So you came to the bakery? But you knew I was there."

"Yes and no." Tears spill from her eyes, but she doesn't wipe them from her cheeks. "I knew you'd been there, but when I drove by, the place was dark. I thought you guys were gone."

"So you came in?"

"Yes. I'd taken my mother's key, and I let myself in the back door. When I pulled it from my pocket, the necklace must have fallen out. The clasp had broken earlier in the day, and I'd shoved it in there so I wouldn't lose it. Anyway, a few minutes after I got there, I heard my brother's laugh. I realized you guys were up front in the dark and I took off. I couldn't have been there more than five minutes, tops."

It clicks. "Long enough to turn the oven on to preheat?"

She nods miserably. "Yes. But I swear to God, I turned it off. At least, I thought I did… But maybe I didn't." Sobs break from her chest, and she wraps her arms around herself. "Maybe the fire was my fault."

I shake my head. "Why didn't you say something? All these years, you let me think I was solely responsible for that fire. You let this entire *town* think that. Do you know what that was like for me?"

"I'm sorry," she cries. "I can't tell you how sorry I am now. But at the time, I thought I was doing what was right."

"For who?" I demand. "Yourself?"

"No, for Everett." She takes a step toward me. "You don't know how our dad was. He used to hit Everett when I did something wrong. He didn't want to hit his daughter, but he didn't mind hitting his son. I thought if he knew the fire was my fault, he'd take it out on my brother." She shakes her head. "I couldn't let Everett take another punch for me."

My heart sinks like an anchor to the ocean floor. Everett being abused. Gabi forced to watch. Their mother powerless to help.

Part of me wants to apologize for being angry. To take Gabi in my arms and tell her I understand. To reassume the blame for something that wasn't my fault after all, put the guilt on like a heavy old coat.

But I don't.

"You still should have told me," I say, my voice shaking. "I've carried so much guilt and shame about that fire. To know that maybe it wasn't my fault would have alleviated a lot of pain."

"I'm sorry," she says, her tears quiet but intense. "I didn't know it was that bad for you."

"Because we never spoke again!" I'm trying to keep my voice down because I know Mrs. McKean is home, but it's hard. "I thought you hated me!"

"I didn't. I hated myself. And I couldn't face you—any of you!" She closes the gap between us and takes one of my hands. "Mila, please forgive me. I regret what I did that night with every ounce of my soul. And I'm so sorry it took me this long to come clean."

"But you didn't come clean!" I pulled my hand to my chest. "I had to come to you and ask for the truth. If you had just done it yourself, this might feel different!"

"I wanted to do it myself. Honest, I did." She wipes her eyes with the cuffs of her sweatshirt. "But I felt like I just got you back, and I asked Everett to give me a week."

I freeze. "What do you mean, you asked Everett to give you a week?"

Gabi's face goes green.

"Do you mean that Everett knew about this and—and didn't tell me?"

"Only since last weekend," she says in a rush.

"My God." Dizzy, I grab onto the door for support. "He said he loved me."

"He does!"

"No." I shake my head. "If he loved me, he would have told me."

"I begged him not to. It's my—"

I'm already out of the room. Pounding down the steps. Flying out the front door.

He knew, I repeat as I get in the car. Start the engine with numb fingers. Drive home on autopilot. *He knew. He knew. He knew.*

And he didn't tell me. After promising to be honest with me, he didn't tell me.

I think of all the chances he had. Sunday afternoon before dinner. Monday night at his house. Tuesday after we saw the Harts. Wednesday after the meeting. Thursday.

We've seen each other every day. We've talked. We've texted. We've gotten naked and had sex.

He looked me right in the eye and kept silent about something he *knew* was important to me.

The last six weeks replay in my mind.

The things we've done. The words we've said. The plans we've made.

For a frightening moment, I wonder if I've invented it all. Filled in blank pages with a story that wasn't real. Deluded myself with the intensity of our connection yet again.

You seem to fall in love very quickly.

A weakness when it comes to men.

There's nothing worse than thinking you're on the same page as someone and discovering you were wrong all along.

What if my mother's right? What if I'm just weak and oblivious? What if I'll always be alone?

Chapter Fifty-One

Everett

I hear my name being called across the field. When I look up, I see my sister running toward me at full speed.

What the hell?

I straighten up and start jogging in her direction. "What is it? Is Mom okay?"

"Mom's fine." She bends at the waist, hands propped on her knees.

"Look at the all-state athlete now." I smirk at her heavy breathing. But when she picks up her head and looks at me, her expression wipes the smile off my lips. Her skin is red and blotchy, her eyes bloodshot. Tears have left tracks down her cheeks.

"I'm sorry," she says.

An alarm goes off in my head. "For what?"

"Mila knows."

Every muscle in my body tenses. "Knows what?"

"That I was there the night of the fire. That I might have left the oven on."

"You mean you told her?"

Gabi shakes her head. "She found out before I had a chance."

"Fuck!" I point a finger at my sister's chest. "You were supposed to tell her today! You told me you were going to do it at lunch!"

"I was!" New tears trace the paths of the old. "But Yasmine was there, and it just didn't feel right."

"So how did she find out?"

The story about the necklace tumbles out between sobs and ragged breaths. "And then I accidentally let it slip that you knew."

"Fuck, Gabi. Fuck!" I lace my fingers and hook them behind my neck, tipping my face to the sky. I want to yell at my sister some more, but it makes me feel like my old man.

And I *never* want to be like him.

I take a few deep breaths, trying to slow the adrenaline coursing through me and calm my racing heart. “Okay. Was she upset?”

“Yes.” Gabi nods tearfully. “Very.”

“Tell me what she said.”

She shakes her head. “I don’t want to.”

“You have to!”

Gabi drops her face into her hands. “She said if you loved her, you’d have told her.”

“Fuck!” I pace back and forth, trying to make a plan.

“Everett, I’m sorry. This is all my fault, and I’m going to find a way to make it up to you—and to Mila.”

“You’ve done enough,” I say.

Then I take off running.

Chapter Fifty-Two

Mila

I go straight upstairs to my bedroom when I get home, wanting nothing more than to crash on my bed, pull the covers over my head, and let myself fall apart in a blanket fort.

But the sheets are in the laundry.

"Fuck it." Kicking off my shoes, I dive beneath the comforter anyway, wrapping it around me until the world is just a sea of pale blue. Then I curl up in a fluffy ball and cry into my bare pillow.

I'm not sure how much time goes by before I hear my mother calling me. "Mila?"

"What?"

"Everett is here."

Shit!

"I don't feel good!" I yell from my cocoon. It's not even a lie. "Tell him I'm not coming down!"

"Mila?"

Fuck. It's Everett's voice at the bottom of the stairs.

Still wrapped in the comforter, I shuffle to the top of the steps. The sight of him, in his jeans and plaid flannel, his brown boots and navy baseball cap, makes my knees weak. Even the smudge of dirt on his nose is hot.

But I can't give in.

"Go away," I say. "I don't want to talk to you right now."

"Mila, please come down." He puts a boot on the first step. "Or I'll come up."

"No!"

"Can't we talk about this?"

"What is there to talk about? You broke your promise to me."

"I'm sorry. If you'd let me explain—"

"I'm not interested in your explanation. It's obvious that we have different ideas about what this relationship is."

"Mila, we don't. Can you *please* come down?"

"What's going on?" My mother's voice butts in.

I roll my eyes and start down the stairs, still wrapped in my blanket cocoon. "Nothing, Mom. Everett, let's go outside."

Relief smooths the space between Everett's eyebrows when I reach the first floor. He opens the front door for me. Reluctantly, I leave my comforter at the bottom of the steps and follow him out.

"I can explain," he says when the door is closed behind us.

"Explain what? Why you hid something you knew would matter to me? Why you shut down and left me wondering what I'd done wrong? How you could look me in the eye and *lie* when I asked you if there was something you needed to tell me, because it was obvious to me you were pulling away?"

"I'm not pulling away, Mila. I love you." He steps toward me and holds my upper arms. His brown eyes are dark and sincere. "You have to believe me."

Everything inside me turns warm and liquid. My legs nearly give out. My heart splits wide open. *He does love me.*

The old me would melt at his feet or throw my arms around him or otherwise surrender the fight. Because that's the win, right? Love is what I always wanted.

But in this moment, I realize there's more to it.

And I love *myself* enough not to give in so fast.

"I thought I was losing it, Everett!" The dam breaks, and words pour out. Miraculously, I keep the tears pressing to follow at bay. "This whole week, I've been off balance. Wondering if what I saw was real. Doubting myself at every turn. Today felt like an ambush. And I get to be mad about it!" Never in my life have I raised my voice to someone like this. It's terrifying and liberating at the same time.

"Give me your mad," he says quietly. "I deserve it."

"You should have told me," I insist.

"I know. But Gabi made me promise to give her time to do it herself. I told her she should have come clean back then, but she thought she had good reason to stay silent."

I shake my head. "I understand why Gabi acted the way she did. She was eighteen and terrified. She thought she was protecting you. She panicked. But you're not a kid, Everett! And you made me a promise."

"Fuck. Fuck, I'm sorry," he says, closing his eyes for a second. "But sometimes family does things to protect each other, even when they don't agree with the decision. Gabi and I have been protecting each other for a long time. It's a hard habit to break, even once the danger has passed."

I wrap my arms around myself. "I wouldn't know. I've never had family like that."

He takes my face in his hands. "You do now."

"Mila?" My mother pokes her head outside. "What's all the yelling about? Should I call the police?"

"No, Mom. Go inside. I'll be there in a minute."

When she shuts the door again, I take a breath. "You should go. I need to think."

He searches my eyes. "Tell me I didn't fuck this up."

My throat tightens, and I take his wrists and push his hands down. "It's not just you. Maybe this was too much, too soon. Maybe I'm not ready for it."

"Don't say that."

The door cracks again. "Mila, are you coming in or not?"

"Please," I beg him. "Just go. I'm overwhelmed. If you love me like you say you do, give me space to breathe. That's what I need right now."

He wrestles with it before relenting. "Okay."

"Thank you." And though it almost breaks my heart to do it, I turn away from him and enter the house.

My mother stays by the window, arms crossed over her chest,

face pinched. "He's gone."

I nod, a sob catching in my throat.

"Don't say I didn't warn you," she says cruelly.

"Warn me?" I stand up a little taller.

"About men! They can't be trusted, not a single one of them." She points her finger toward the street. "I ought to call the police. Have him arrested for harassment!"

"Mom, he wasn't harassing me. He was trying to apologize."

She sniffs. "Don't believe a word he says. He waltzed into your life when you were heartbroken over your divorce and took advantage of you."

"No, he didn't." I fist my hands in my hair. "Stop saying negative things about him. And about me."

"Oh, so now I'm the villain?" She shrinks back, hand on her chest. "It wasn't *me* who made you cry."

"Not today, it wasn't."

Her eyes narrow. "If there's something you want to say to me, Mila, out with it. You've been acting like a sulky teenager for weeks now."

I swallow hard. Take a breath. This is it—the confrontation I've been too scared to have my entire life. "I don't think you love me, Mom. I never have."

She scoffs. "Don't be ridiculous. I'm your mother. Of course I love you."

"The only time I've ever pleased you was when I was dancing. And even then, you pressured me so much to be perfect."

Her open mouth makes it clear she believes *she* is the injured party. "I was hard on you because you were *good*, Mila. I wanted you to have the career I had! The career I gave—"

"Yes, I know—the career you gave up for me. I've known it all my life, Mom. I cut my teeth on the story of your magnificent sacrifice. And for a long time, I told myself that meant you loved me. But it didn't."

"I don't know what you're talking about," she huffs. "Once

again, you're my daughter. Of course I love you." Coming from her lips, the sentiment is sharper than a razor.

"But you blamed me for ruining your life—and I believed I did. I worked so hard to make it up to you, as if that was ever really possible. Tiptoeing around your moods. Doing every little thing you asked. Running when you called. But nothing was ever enough. *I* was never enough."

"This is all very dramatic, Mila."

I shake my head. "I know now that I'll never get what I'm looking for out of you. So I need to stop looking for it."

"What are you looking for?" she explodes, throwing her dancer's arms in the air. "Proof I love you? How about all these albums? All those photos on the mantel? That tiara I kept all these years, until you stole it from me?"

"Where are the orchids, Mom?"

"What orchids?"

"The ones I drew for you. I gave them to you for Christmas. Where are they?"

"I don't know." She looks around the room, like maybe she hung them on the wall and forgot. "They must be somewhere. Oh, I know! They're at the frame shop. I wanted to change out the dark wood for gold."

I shake my head. "They're not at the frame shop. They're at Everett's. I gave them to him."

She gasps. "You gave him *my* orchids?"

"You didn't want them."

"But they were *mine*. You had no right to just give them away! You could have at least asked."

"You'd have said no, Mom! But it was obvious you didn't care about them. They weren't really *yours*," I say, mimicking her inflection. "They were a piece of me that I gave to you. And I found them gathering dust in a box in the basement."

"I was going to hang them! I just forgot they were down there. Is that what all this fuss is about? Some silly flowers?"

It's almost laughable, her cluelessness. "It's not about any one thing, Mom. It's about how I've lived my entire life believing that something is wrong with me. That I'm too flawed to be loved. That I'm to blame for your unfulfilled life."

She sidesteps my point. A nimble pas de chat. "You're mad about your father, is that it? You want to punish me for keeping him a secret?"

This time, I do laugh. A choked gurgle escapes as another truth hits me. "No. It's not. I used to be desperate to know about him, but now I realize it doesn't matter—it wasn't really *him* I wanted. It was the connection. It was the relationship. It was someone on my side no matter what."

She looks at me as if I'm speaking nonsense. "I don't know what you want from me, Mila. I suppose I never have."

"It wasn't complicated, Mom! I wanted you to love me unconditionally!" Tears flow down my cheeks. "Instead, you made me feel like love was something I had to earn, and I fell short time after time."

Another eye roll, accompanied by a heavy sigh. "Oh, now we're back here again. It's *my* fault you didn't tell me you wanted to quit dance. It's *my* fault I couldn't read your mind. Somehow you probably think it's *my* fault you didn't get accepted to Juilliard, after I dedicated my entire existence to making sure you had superior training."

I look her right in the eye. "I did get accepted."

My mother goes still as a stone. Her voice is a whisper. "What?"

"I did get accepted. But I hid the letter and lied to you about it."

"You…" She leans forward and puts a hand on her throat. "You got in?"

"Yes." A sense of triumph invades my bloodstream like a drug. "So there you go. I didn't botch the audition. In fact, I fucking nailed it. My training *was* superior. Congratulations."

"I don't believe this." She clutches her chest. "You lied to *me*, and *you're* mad about it?"

"Yep."

She folds her arms again. Narrows her eyes. "This is all because of him, you know. Our relationship was just fine before you started hanging around with Everett McKean."

"No, Mom. That's the thing. It wasn't." I see now that any further discussion will be useless. She'll just keep me on this merry-go-round, trying to blame me or Everett or anyone but herself. My mother is never going to be happy, and that isn't my fault or my problem. So I do the only thing I can to protect myself.

I turn around and walk away.

Halfway up the stairs, dragging my comforter behind me, I hear her bedroom door slam.

I curl up on my mattress again, but I don't cry this time. Not because I don't feel sad, because I do—mostly for the little girl I was. The one always seeking approval and affection she was never going to get. The one who deserved better than she got.

But that girl is grown now, and in her place is a woman who stood up for herself today. Who didn't pretend to be fine when she wasn't. Who used her voice to speak her truth.

I'm proud of myself. I wish Hugo had been here to see it.

And Everett.

Everett.

My chest aches when I think about the fight we had tonight. Pieces of our conversation drift through my mind.

I love you. You have to believe me.

I want to. I want to believe that what I have with Everett is the real thing. That he loves me truly. Wholly. Deeply. I want to believe I'm worthy of that love. I want to accept it. Cherish it. Return it. Let it grow and surround me.

The weeks we've spent together replay in my head like a movie montage. I've been happier and more myself with Everett than I've ever been with anyone. If it wasn't for him and the way he loves me, I never would have had the strength to confront my mother tonight.

I know we belong together.

Tell me I didn't fuck this up.

I can't tell him that. Because he did fuck this up, and I'm upset.

The space in the center of my chest clenches, either to hold the pieces of my broken heart together or to shield the most vulnerable part of me from taking another hit. My whole life, Mom has made it clear that love and lies go hand in hand—that to have one means accepting the other. Call out the lie, lose the love. I learned that lesson young, and I've never forgotten it. I've never been *allowed* to forget it.

But it isn't like I can't appreciate Everett's reasons for not telling me the truth. His lie wasn't to hurt me—it was to protect Gabi. They lived through something I can't imagine, and even if they're thriving now, their history has left its scars. Everett will always be ultra-protective of his sister. They're close. They have each other's backs.

Sometimes family does things to protect each other, even when they don't agree with the decision.

I understand that. And I love how much he values family. I love Gabi, too, so much that I don't blame her for what she did or didn't do. I understand she was young and scared. And while I wish she would have been honest with me sooner, I don't have it in my heart to hold it against her—not when my heart is already holding so much.

None of us is perfect. We all make mistakes.

But family forgives. Family shows up. Family has your back no matter what.

I've never had family like that.

You do now.

Did he know how much those three little words meant to me? How I've longed my entire life for that?

Of course he does.

I shut my eyes and imagine myself cutting the ropes that tether me to the fear and shame of my past. To the idea that I'm not lovable. That I'm somehow incomplete because I have no idea who my father was. That I need to win my mother's approval and never will. That

I alone was responsible for the fire. I let myself feel the full hurt of every lie I've ever believed about myself, and then one by one, I let them sink to the bottom of a deep lake in my mind. It all stays in the muck like cinder blocks, while I float to the surface, unburdened and free.

I see myself moving back to Hart's Landing, but not as the same girl I was when I left. I see myself building a life here—a beautiful life.

I have a career I'm passionate about.

I have good friends.

I have peace with myself and who I am.

I have Everett.

I have a family—one I chose, and one I'll protect.

I have *love.*

My heart takes flight in my chest.

In the morning, I wake up early. After pulling on jeans and Everett's John Deere sweatshirt, I start down the stairs, hoping to get out the door without talking to my mother.

No such luck.

"Mila?" she calls from the living room.

Caught, I curse silently and plod the rest of the way down the stairs. She's seated on the couch with a cup of coffee. "Yes?"

She takes a sip. "Where are you going so early?"

"Out."

One eyebrow lifts. "Are we going to discuss last night?"

"I've said everything I need to for now."

"My feelings are very hurt, Mila."

"I'm sorry." I mean it. I don't want to hurt her.

"I suppose you're running to him now? To tell him what a terrible mother I am?"

"Actually, I don't plan on talking about you at all."

"Just remember, no one will ever love you the way I do."

"God, Mom. You know what?" With my hand on the door handle, I look over my shoulder at her. "I really fucking hope not."

For once, *I* make the dramatic exit.

As soon as I step out onto the porch, I freeze.

Everett's truck is parked on the street, exactly where it was yesterday, and I can see him behind the wheel. I'm totally confused. Has he been there the whole time? Didn't my mom say he left after I came inside?

I move slowly down the front walk and approach the truck on the passenger side. He's reclined in the driver's seat, arms folded across his chest. Hair a mess. Eyes closed.

Sound asleep.

A smile tugs at my lips. When I knock on the window, he jumps. Disoriented for a moment, he blinks a few times. Rolls his neck. Then he sees me. Our eyes lock through the glass, and my heart stops.

I try the handle—locked. He clicks the button, and I open the door, sliding into the passenger seat. Without a word, I throw my arms around him, and he pulls me hard against his chest. Kisses the side of my head.

"I'm so sorry," he says, his voice hoarse. "Can you forgive me?"

"Of course I forgive you. But wait." I pull back. "Have you been out here all night?"

"Yeah." He runs a hand through his hair, which only makes it stick up more. "I did leave, at first. Because I wanted to give you space to breathe, like you asked for. I went home and cleaned up. But then I came back. Because I want to show you that I'm here for you. That even though I fucked up, I won't *give* up."

He takes my hand. "I love you. And whatever it takes, I want to be with you."

I smile. "I love you too."

"Thank God." He weaves our fingers together. "Are we okay?"

"We're okay. And I'll make things okay with Gabi, too. We all need a little grace."

"I hate that I let you down." He kisses my fingers. "I won't let it happen again."

"I don't think you should promise me that, Everett. We're not perfect. We're going to get angry and hurt and take things the wrong way and say shit we don't mean. But we'll work through it."

"Yes. We will."

"And, honestly, I think I needed the chance to stand up for myself. I'm grateful you gave it to me. It gave me the courage to confront my mother after you left."

His jaw drops. "Did you? How did it go?"

I shrug. "No surprises. She is who she is. But I'm not who I was—not entirely—and that made the difference. So thank you for helping me believe in myself."

He hugs me to him again. "I'm so fucking proud of you."

"I'm proud of me, too."

"Where were you headed just now?"

"To find you and tell you I spent the entire night dreaming of our future in Hart's Landing."

"Yeah?" Releasing me, he sits back and gives me a smile that could melt a glacier. "You know I'm not rich."

"Doesn't matter."

"I'm a farmer who drives a beat-up truck, doesn't own a suit, and can't really tell the difference between a Van Gogh and a Dickelangelo."

I laugh. "Don't care."

"Someday I'll inherit a house, but every year something else will go wrong with it."

I grin. "Listen, I'm just happy you caught up. I've been waiting a decade for you to love me back."

He laughs. "Now it makes sense, the way I always wondered."

"And the way I never forgot. It's like your soul recognizes its missing piece, even if your brain needs more time to understand."

He kisses my hand again. "You've always been my missing piece, Freckles."

My heart is too full to answer.

We hit the diner for breakfast, and we're just finishing up when Everett looks at his phone. His brow furrows as he taps the screen.

"What is it?" I ask.

"A text from Gabi."

"Is something wrong?"

"Hang on." He scans the text on his screen. "Oh shit."

Chapter Fifty-Three

WELCOME TO THE LANDING PAD

Community Updates From The Hart's Landing Gazette (Online Edition)

EVENT: The Diner Detectives will hold a press conference TODAY at 9 a.m. at Town Hall. From club president Daniel Bartok: "Citizens interested in the truth about the Tart and Soul fire won't want to miss this."

Chapter Fifty-Four

Everett

"What's going on?" Mila asks.

I read my sister's text again in disbelief. "Apparently, there's some kind of press conference at Town Hall."

"Press conference? For what?"

"Apparently Gabi plans to confess publicly that she's to blame for the fire."

"*What?* When?"

"Nine o'clock."

"What time is it now?"

"Eight fifty-five." Our eyes meet.

"Let's go."

I throw enough cash on the table to cover our meal, follow Mila out of the diner, and together, we run down the block.

"Why is she doing this?" Mila asks, our feet pounding the pavement.

"To make it up to us, I think."

There's a huge crowd in front of Town Tall, but evidently the doors are locked. The moment they open, the mob pushes inside. Somehow, Mila and I get separated in the chaos, and I spend a few minutes searching for her in the entryway as everyone rushes past me.

I frown as someone jostles me with an elbow. Don't these people have jobs?

I call Mila's name and scan every face I see, but she's nowhere to be found. Eventually, I give up and follow the crowd inside.

The place is noisy and full—every seat taken. I haven't seen a crowd this big in here since my very first Coffee with the Mayor, when it seemed like everyone just wanted to get a look at me. Now Daniel Bartok stands on the stage at the far end of the room, preparing to speak at the lectern. I take up a position in the back.

Someone tugs my sleeve. "Mayor McKean! Isn't this exciting? It looks like the whole town is here!"

Vera Pratt's eyes might actually be twinkling.

"Have you seen Mila anywhere?" I ask her.

"No, I haven't. But I doubt she'd want to miss this." She laughs. "I wonder if this will make her look *more* guilty or less..." She's a little too excited about all this. Shouldn't someone her age have a sweet hobby, like mah-jongg or crocheting hats for newborn babies? The gleam in Vera's eyes tells me she's elevated gossip to a mercenary sport.

Before I can contemplate how terrifying that is, Dan taps the mic. "Can I have your attention, please? Folks, can I have your attention?" It takes a few more tries, but the audience eventually settles. "My name is Dan Bartok, and I'm the president of the Hart's Landing Diner Detectives."

"What's the new evidence?" someone shouts from the crowd.

"I'll get to that in a second. First, I'd like to thank you all for coming, and to express my gratitude as well for the many tips we've received over the last several weeks regarding what really happened the night of the fire at Tart and Soul."

"Was someone else there?" a woman calls out.

"As you know, investigators concluded that the fire was 'consistent with combustible material ignition,' presumably a flour dust explosion. Burn patterns revealed the kitchen as the point of origin, but beyond that, not much could be determined." Dan pauses to take a sip of water.

"Justice for Mila!" a man bellows.

I look in the direction of the sound. Who could that be?

"At the time," Dan goes on, looking more excited by the minute, "blame fell on teenage employee Mila Ferguson, since she was on the closing shift. It was her responsibility to ensure that all safety precautions were taken, including not kicking up too much flour dust during the nightly cleanup, and double-checking that all sources of heat were turned off.

"Now, the story goes that Mila was distracted that night by a flirtation with Everett McKean, and it was that distraction that indirectly caused the fire. However…" Dan pauses dramatically and looks around. "There's more to the story."

The crowd murmurs, everyone shifting impatiently in their seats.

"The Diner Detectives have learned that a third person snuck into the back of the bakery that night while Mila and Everett were up front. This person has confessed not only to being there undetected, but also to turning on an oven she forgot to turn off."

A collective gasp rises in the room.

"Essentially, this person is prepared to accept the blame for the fire. And that person is… Gabi McKean."

The noise level in the room suddenly ratchets up. Everyone is talking at once as Gabi rises from a chair in front, ascends the steps to the stage, and walks to the microphone.

"Is it true?" someone yells. "Was the fire your fault?"

"Yes, it's true," Gabi says, holding her chin high. "Mila Ferguson is not responsible for the fire at Tart and Soul."

"Yes, I am!"

My eyes widen in shock as I see Mila race up the center aisle and make a very impressive leap onto the stage. She stands beside Gabi and leans forward to speak into the mic. "I used the stove after closing time. I forgot to turn it off. I'm to blame."

"No, you're not!" Before I can stop my legs, they're carrying me toward the front of the room. I hop up onto the stage and take my place next to Mila. "I was…smoking in the back room. I was careless."

"What? You don't even smoke," Gabi says. "You've *never* smoked."

"I did that night," I lie.

"Everett, what are you doing?" Mila hisses.

"The same thing you're doing—what family does."

She grabs my hand and squeezes it.

"Actually, it was me!" Someone in the back shoots to his feet.

Stunned, I watch Stevie MacDougal make his way to the side aisle and run toward the stage. We scoot over to make room. By the time he takes his place at the mic, the crowd is on its feet, too.

"I was…" Frantically, he searches for an idea. "Playing with matches! Yes, I was a kid playing with matches. I went into the bakery that night to get a cherry lemonade from Mila, and then I hid in the back and played with matches." He wipes sweat from his brow and steps back into line with us.

Mila and Gabi each put an arm around him, and he looks like he just won a million dollars. By this time, poor Dan Bartok is so confused he has no idea what to say. He stumbles to the mic. "Anyone else want to claim responsibility for the fire?"

"What the hell? I will." Ripley comes trotting up the center aisle and jumps up on stage. A flabbergasted Dan moves aside, and Ripley grins at his audience. He pokes his chest with a thumb. "That's right. It was me."

"You!" It's a female voice I could swear belongs to Yasmine Khoury. "How did you start the fire?"

"I'm a walking, talking smoke show, sweetheart," he says cockily. After enjoying the laughter he gets, he backs up and stands beside Gabi.

We form a line now, all five of us. Arms around shoulders. We are family, friends, neighbors. Willing to stand up for each other. Willing to protect each other.

I move forward to speak into the microphone. "If I could speak again, just for a moment."

The audience settles so I can be heard.

“Like all of you, I came here hoping to learn something about the fire. But I think what I’ve learned today is something about Hart’s Landing. Sure, there are rumors and gossip. Yes, there are matchmakers and meddlers.” Laughter drifts from the crowd. “But when it comes down to it, we’re there for each other when it counts. We’re family.” I glance at Mila. “And nothing means more than that.”

Chapter Fifty-Five
Mila

LATE JANUARY

Everett's truck is there at the curb when I come out of the airport doors, dragging one large suitcase and carrying a smaller bag and a cat crate. I shiver at the icy blast of wind that smacks me in the face.

He jumps out and rushes toward me, catching me in his arms for a warm hug. "Hey, you."

"Hi." My heart thumps with excitement at seeing him again, and my eyes fill with tears, the way they always do. The separations have only gotten harder over the last couple months, every goodbye and each reunion more emotional than the one before. But this time is different.

This time, I'm staying.

When I open the rear door on the passenger side, Merlin greets me with an excited thump of his tail against the seat. I scratch his ears before placing Beatrix's crate next to him. "You two play nice back here," I tell them before hopping in the front. Everett takes my hand as he pulls away from the curb.

When I left last October, we promised each other we'd never let more than a couple of weeks go by without a visit, and we've stayed true to those words. Twice, I flew back to Hart's Landing, and twice, Everett came out to New York.

Once was in December. We stayed in the city, Christmas-shopped along snow-dusted avenues, admired the tree at Rockefeller Center, and had insanely hot hotel-room sex. The second time, earlier this month, he came to Brooklyn, and I introduced him to Jess. While he was in the bathroom, she grabbed me in a hug and congratulated me on finally finding a guy who deserved me.

My mother was a different story.

We're on speaking terms, although they're tepid on my part and cool on hers. Hugo and I have talked a lot about the best way to handle mending fences, which he says I only have to do if I want to. Just because she's my mother doesn't mean I owe her endless chances to stop making me miserable. And just because we're going to live in the same town doesn't mean I have to involve her in my life.

Over the last few months, when I've visited Hart's Landing, I've always let her know I was available for coffee or lunch, but I never stayed with her. At first, she was so furious that she refused to see me. But eventually, she gave in and treated me to silence over lattes or salads. Sometimes, she tried to provoke me with derisive comments, but my skin is too thick now for her barbs to penetrate. I can't say she never got to me, but it was rare.

As expected, she has *opinions* about my permanent move back to Hart's Landing. She thinks it's rash and unwise, and she foresees only disappointment ahead. When she realized I didn't even plan to stay with her while I looked for a place of my own, she set her fork down with a clank. "Are you *never* coming home again? What have I done to deserve this?"

"I'm making a new home," I told her. "And if you want to be part of my life, you'll support me."

She went silent, but I supposed it was better than a fight.

"Did all my boxes arrive?" I ask as Everett merges onto the highway.

"Yes."

"Sorry it's so much stuff. I promise to get it out of the cabin as soon as I find a place." On my last few visits, we looked for an apartment but didn't find anything just right. I've also looked at condos and small homes, but they're still beyond my budget at this point. The cabin is cozy, and Everett said I was welcome to live there, but there really isn't enough space for two people on a permanent basis, not to mention a cat and a dog. And there's no extra space for me to set up an office.

Tomorrow, I'll resume the search.

"No rush." Everett puts a hand on my leg, and I love the reassuring weight of it. Love the wide, calloused palm and the strong, dexterous fingers.

Half an hour later, we turn into McKean Cherries, which looks magical blanketed under a foot of snow. My artist's eye drinks up the late morning sun glittering across pristine expanses of white that ripple like waves across the lake. The buildings are closed up tight for the winter, giant icicles hanging from the eaves. Color is provided by evergreen trees, their branches heavy with snow, and by the occasional red cardinal or blue jay braving the cold to hunt for food.

"This place is so beautiful, even in winter." I wish I had time this afternoon to draw the way the snow clings to gnarled black branches against the periwinkle sky, the pop of a red barn in the distance. Maybe I can make time. After all, I won't be able to unpack much of anything at the cabin.

Distracted by the question of which colored pencils I'd use to capture the tones in the snow, I don't even notice when Everett pulls into the driveway of the main house instead of continuing around back toward the cabin. When he turns off the truck's engine, I'm confused.

"Did some of my boxes end up here?"

"They're all here." Something a little mischievous is hiding in his smile. He reaches into the back seat for Beatrix's carrier. Merlin jumps out too. "Let's go in."

"They're all here?" I jump out of the truck and follow him up the shoveled path to the front door. "Why?"

Without answering, he turns the key in the lock and pushes the door open. Merlin bounds into the house, but Everett steps aside and gestures for me to enter first. "After you."

Tentative without knowing why, I walk into the front hall. It's completely silent and smells like furniture polish, old wood, and this morning's coffee. A few seconds later, I hear Merlin slurping water in the kitchen. Everett closes the door behind us and sets the carrier down. Then he wraps his arms around me from behind. "Welcome home, baby."

I spin around to face him, my arms dangling limp at my sides. "Home?"

"If you want it to be."

"With your mom and Gabi?" I glance right and left, wondering where they are.

"Two days ago, we moved my mother into the new condo complex down by the water. She wanted single-floor living, and this place was too big for her to keep up. She's been hinting about it for months now."

"Where's Gabi?"

"We moved her into the cabin."

My head is spinning. My heart is galloping. I put my hands on Everett's shoulders and meet his eyes. "Wait a minute. What's happening?"

"I'm asking you to live with me. Here." His arms tighten around my waist. "I don't want to be without you, Mila. Every night you're not asleep beside me feels wrong. Every morning when I wake up, I want yours to be the first face I see. If being in love long-distance taught me anything, it's that I never want to waste a single moment being apart when we could be together."

"Everett." My voice is as fragile as tissue paper. "Are you sure?"

By contrast, his voice is solid as rock. "I've never been so sure of anything in my life." His eyes light up. "Come upstairs. I want to show you something."

He takes my hand and leads me up the steps, each one groaning as we make our way to the second story. Tugging me gently down the hall, he pushes open the door to his former bedroom. It creaks as it swings wide.

I gasp, my hands flying to my cheeks. Inside the room are my boxes, pushed along the back wall. But what has my stomach quivering and tears springing to my eyes is the drawing table set up near the east-facing window. Light streams in through the glass, illuminating the table's surface, which holds many of the supplies I'd sent ahead. My drawing lamp and pencils. Hot-pressed watercolor paper and a magnifier. A ruler and paint brushes.

"I wasn't sure what actually goes on the table," he says hesitantly. "And I wasn't certain which window you'd like either, east- or south-facing, but the table has wheels so you can move it around."

"Oh, Everett." I turn and fling my arms around him. "It's perfect. I don't know what to say."

His arms come around me. "Say you'll stay."

I can barely get the words out. "Of course I will. This is better than my wildest dreams."

"I want to make every single one of them come true."

"You are. You have." I pull back and look up at him, uncertain my body can contain the happiness filling me up. It pulses inside my heart and races through my veins and swims through my head. "You will."

He kisses me, and it's sweet and romantic. It's hopes and dreams and promises. Every inch of my skin tingles, and I know without a doubt that this house will contain my life's most beautiful memories.

But it's not long before the time apart catches up to us. Everett's hands wander beneath my sweater. My palm slides down the front of his jeans. He unhooks my bra with an easy flick of his fingers. I moan against his lips as his cock swells against denim. The kiss is different now. It's heat and greed. Hunger and demand.

Our clothes form a pile around us on the floor, and we sink down on top of them, too impatient to leave the room. And when he moves inside me, I don't care about the hardness of the oak floor beneath my back or the bruise I'll probably have on my tailbone or the fact that I didn't get my leggings all the way off and they're still bunched around one shin.

All that matters is that I'm here. I'm his. I'm home.

We finish quickly, our bodies anxious to share that familiar pulse after weeks apart. After catching his breath, Everett braces his hands above my shoulders and looks down at me. "I love you. Maybe it took us ten years to get here, but I plan to make up for lost time by putting you first every chance I get, every way I can, for the rest of my life. I know I'm not perfect and I'm going to make mistakes, but I will never, not for a single moment, take you for granted."

I thread my fingers into his hair. "I love you too. You're the best man I know, Everett McKean. It doesn't matter that we got a slow start—what matters is that we're here now." I smile with my whole heart. "And we're here forever."

Epilogue

Lydia

"Want to go for a walk by the river?" Everett asks, slipping his hand into Mila's.

Finally. I've been waiting *months* for this.

It's a warm late summer night, and they just had dinner on the back patio of Sawbuck Tavern.

Mila smiles, one of those sweet ones she reserves only for him. "Sure."

They stroll along Main Street, which is less crowded now that the high season—not to mention cherry season—is over. In July and August, Everett worked from before sunup to long after sundown. Now that it's September, life is easier. They have more time together.

Mila has never been happier.

Lavender Ladybug is thriving. The fall collection she designed for Ivy & Stone is wildly popular, and they've already asked her for another collaboration. She loves her role as Art Director of the new Hart's Landing Community Center, and every Tuesday, she teaches a botanical illustration class.

Recently, she hired a new assistant.

"How's it going with Felix?" Everett asks as they amble toward the river.

"Great, actually. He's surprisingly good with kids, and he's so talented."

"Good."

"Tiffany Hart was in class again this week," she says. "She's a regular now."

"Does she have any talent?"

Mila shakes her head. "None whatsoever. But she's very dedicated, and you should hear her going on about the healing gardens to anyone who will listen. You'd think it was her idea, not yours."

"Actually, it was yours," he tells her, taking her arm as they cross the street toward the bank of the White Pine River. "And I'll be eternally grateful. Did she ever get you that phone number you wanted?"

I listen carefully here.

"She did, but when I texted it, someone replied that I must have the wrong number."

"Weird."

"I might reach out to Rachel's mom. Oh, by the way, I saw *your* mom today," she tells him as they walk in the opposite direction of the river's flow. "She was working at the store and popped over to the house to say hi. She looks great! And you know what she told me?"

"What?"

"She's been taking my mother's morning stretch class at the dance studio twice a week."

"That's good." They reach the bridge. "Want to walk across?"

"Sure. It's like our first date all over again."

"It wasn't a date," he says, nudging her side. "Remember?"

"That's right. I had a rule in place."

"Not for long. You gave me permission to kiss you pretty quickly, as I recall." He lets go of her hand to put an arm around her waist.

"I was weak."

He chuckles. "I was nervous. You said *one kiss*, and I felt like everything was riding on it."

"Babe, I was done for the moment your lips touched mine."

They reach the center of the bridge and stop to look out. The sun looks like a gold coin in an orange and lavender sky. The river appears almost copper as it flows toward the deep-blue lake.

Mila sighs. "It's so beautiful."

"Yes." Everett is looking at her.

"I'm talking about the sunset, Everett."

"What sunset?"

Laughing, she turns to face him. Taps his chest. "You're hopeless."

"I remember I asked you that night if you'd ever thrown a stone into the water. You said yes, but you didn't say whose name was on it."

She rolls her eyes. "You *know* it was yours. I did it on my way to work the night of the fire. I thought it might bring me good luck."

"Maybe it did." His broad shoulders rise. "Look at us now."

"That's true," she says with a nod. "Are we the proof it's not just a Hart's Landing legend?"

"Maybe." He reaches into his pocket. "But we better not leave anything to chance."

She giggles. "Did you bring a stone with my name on it?"

"No." He drops to one knee. "But I did bring a rock."

Now we're talking.

Mila has gone still, her mouth open.

In Everett's fingers is a diamond solitaire glinting in the last few rays of daylight. "Mila Ferguson, one year ago tonight, we stood on this bridge."

Mila's hands fly to her cheeks. She hadn't realized the date.

"Since that time, you've taught me about loyalty, patience, and forgiveness. You've shown me that a heart can love deeper and stronger and more fiercely than I thought possible."

"You've taught me, too," she says softly.

"I used to struggle to imagine myself settling down—I just couldn't see it. I never met anyone who made me want to give up my independence. But now I can see a life with you so clearly. Not just the big, important things like marriage and family, but the small, everyday things, too. I will always eat your pizza crusts, hand you tissues during movies, and squeeze the toothpaste tube from the bottom."

Mila laughs through her tears. I wish I could give Everett a high five. He seems to understand something I've only really learned since getting to this side of life: whether the moment is bitter or sweet, laughter makes it better.

"Above all, you've shown me that what's meant to be will always find a way. And Mila, you and I are meant to be." He slips the ring on her finger. "Will you marry me?"

"Yes," she squeaks. "Yes." It's all she can manage before dissolving to pieces. She drops to her knees and buries her face in his shoulder. He lets her cry for a minute, stroking her hair and her back.

Eventually he brings them both to their feet. "Wow. This is a lot of tears. Even for you."

She chuckles and steps back to look at the ring on her finger. "Oh, Everett, it's beautiful! Look at the filigree on the band!"

"I thought you might like that," he says, sounding proud of himself. "I picked it out myself at the jeweler's in town, but if you don't like it, they said I could bring it back and exchange it."

Ahem. It was me who nudged him in the direction of that ring.

I have my ways.

"I love it." Mila tucks her left hand against her chest, covering it with her right. "Just *try* to pry it off me."

He laughs. "I'm happy to let it stay on your finger."

Mila places her palms on either side of his face. "I love you. You're the first and only man I have ever trusted with my whole heart."

"I'll be that man forever."

I sigh, and a breeze whispers over their skin.

Their lips meet in a kiss as soft as a cloud. As warm as the September sun. As deep as the river rushing beneath the bridge.

Mila was right.

Tomorrow does have a way of showing up, and it doesn't always go as planned. Tomorrows can be messy. Painful. Hard.

But what I hoped my friends would learn from their promise to me is that the best tomorrows come when you live today out loud.

When you love with your whole heart. When you show up in the world exactly the way you're meant to.

Then every tomorrow becomes a gift.

Mila and Everett understand this now.

"Ready to go?" he asks.

"Yes." She admires her ring again. He can't stop looking at her face, his adoration plain to see.

Neither of them notices the ladybug flitting above them.

A few seconds later, the happy couple takes their leave, as do I.

My work here is done.

For now.

Acknowledgments

Thank you to Liz Pelletier for believing in me, and to Rebecca Heyman for making this book (and this writer) so much better. We're just getting started! I'm grateful to my agent, Rebecca Friedman, for ten years of being in my corner. Thank you Kristie and Melissa Gaston for everything you do. Thanks to Catherine Glavin and Sierra Sisler for reading an early version of this book and giving me the confidence to go deeper. I'm truly grateful to author friends who cheered me on during the many months I worked on this book, especially Corinne Michaels. A big thank-you to my Entangled author liaison, Heather Riccio; Victoria Chew and her team for publicity; Melanie Smith and her team in marketing; Hilary Shelby for copyedits; and Elizabeth Turner Stokes for the swoon-worthy cover. To my mom and dad, thank you for instilling in me a love of books. To my readers (Harlots Forever), thank you for being so patient. Finally, to Paul, Phoebe, and Violet: your love and support mean more to me than you know.

Doubling the Trees Behind Every Book You Buy.

Because books should leave the world better than they found it—not just in hearts and minds, but in forests and futures.

Through our Read More, Breathe Easier initiative, we're helping reforest the planet, restore ecosystems, and rethink what sustainable publishing can be.

Track the impact of your read at: